W9-CTY-403

Praise for

THE WORLD BEFORE US

One of Amazon.ca's Top Ten Canadian Books of 2014

"A richly layered narrative harmonizing the past and present, dissolving the boundaries of time frames and showing the possible connections between people and places and objects. . . . *The World Before Us* is a well-constructed and thoughtful novel on serious subjects. The historical detail never overwhelms; instead it brings alive the past and shows the seamlessness of past and present, especially the human need for contact, which transcends time and place." —*The Vancouver Sun*

"A haunting tale of loss and reconciliation. . . . The novel's three timelines are deftly woven together, illustrating the ways life takes on meaning even through objects and places. Hunter refers to history as 'a shifting trickster' and uses that premise to hook readers, as they . . . embark on a quest for meaning and truth in the face of tragedy." —*Chatelaine*

"An ambitious new novel about the vitality of objects and history's knack for bleeding into the present. Intricate in both expression and construction, and dense in thematic implication, *The World Before Us* cleverly innovates while tipping a nod to classic Gothic tropes: dynastic rivalries, crumbling country houses, madhouses and vanished girls. Hunter is less tempted by spooky thrills than the chance to explore ways in which human affection resonates across time." —*National Post*

"*The World Before Us* is a powerful balancing act. . . . It moves confidently line-by-line, drawing us in. It is a novel of considerable beauty, threaded with violence and pain, a melancholic book with moments of grace and joy. It is a thought-provoking novel, haunting and haunted, rooted in the power of history and of the individuals within it, and outside it. . . . It is the sort of novel which forces you to look at the world—the people around you, the objects they hold dear—in a different light." —*The Globe and Mail*

"The novel's characters are deeply imagined and multi-layered, and brought to life through potent scenes and fresh images. . . . The startling narrative point of view deepens the story, and even adds odd flashes of humour. Hunter . . . is a versatile writer, and with *The World Before Us*, she has created her most ambitious and original work, one that demands the deep, concentrated focus of its readers." —*Quill & Quire*

"Once in a rare while a novel comes along to remind us of what great fiction can do: creating a world so sublimely felt that, for the hours we spend reading, we are lifted out of our own lives, and when we return we find ourselves immeasurably altered and enriched. *The World Before Us* by Aislinn Hunter is such a novel. It is a brilliant work of humanity and imagination, artful and breathtakingly beautiful, and it will continue to haunt long after you have finished reading." —Helen Humphreys

THE WORLD BEFORE US

AISLINN HUNTER

ANCHOR CANADA

ISBN 978-0-385-68066-0

This book is a work of fiction, although in some places actual events or
historical persons inspired the author. Fiction, whether used in constructing a
character's actions or a museum's contents, is a form of borrowing from both
the lived and the imagined worlds—although even the author cannot always
say what comes from one and what is born in the other.

Cover design: Anna Kochman
Cover images: (woman) Emily Nathan/Gallery Stock;
(landscape) Hilxia Szabo/Gallery Stock; (pattern) Carpet Museum Archive,
Kidderminster, UK © The Carpet Museum Trust/Bridgeman Images
Text images: (leaves) Shutterstock.com, (all others) Clipart.com
Text design: Kelly Hill
Printed and bound in the USA

Published in Canada by Anchor Canada,
a division of Random House of Canada Limited
a Penguin Random House Company

www.penguinrandomhouse.ca

10 9 8 7 6 5 4 3 2

Penguin
Random House
ANCHOR CANADA

For Robert Cowtan, Esq.

'The number of lives that enter our own is incalculable.'

— JOHN BERGER

'Our dead are never dead to us, until we have forgotten them.'

— GEORGE ELIOT

'It awes me when I think of it, that there was a time when you and I were not . . . But now there can never come a time when you and I shall not be.'

— ANNA ROBERTSON BROWN

'I can only say, *there* we have been:
but I cannot say where.
And I cannot say, how long,
for that is to place it in time.'

— T.S. ELIOT

How many ways to begin?

Near infinite.

Don't ask us what we think, none of us agree on anything. Start with the woods, says one. Start with the sky, says another, with the birds falling out of it, their bodies sent like arrows to the earth. No, begin with the great lawns and the peacocks and the sound the males' tail feathers make in their unfolding. Start with a kiss, with the teacup and its curl of painted ivy. Start with the afternoon the sky ripped open and a month's worth of rain poured through the gap—the whole city lifting trouser and skirt hems.

Start with Jane, says one, it's where we always begin—crowded around her bed watching the clock blink toward morning. Start with Jane because our stories are tied to hers and everything depends on what she does with them. But it is early, only four a.m., and Jane is sleeping, the curtains billowing out from the window, the moon tucked behind the clouds.

So start with the door she is dreaming about—its slant and chance opening. Yes, the door: what slips through, what goes missing.

PART I

1 The Whitmore Hospital for Convalescent Lunatics sat along a carriage track most people travelled only once. Imagine late summer: sunlight splayed over the rutted road and the copper peaks of the buildings, its warmth nested in the crowns of the trees and sinking into the bright-green lawn of the viewing mound. Because the inclement weather of the past month had finally ceased, the Matron was organizing a picnic. The patients, lined up inside the galleries, pressed their faces to the windows and watched as she marched past the fountain in

a trim black dress, two attendants with wicker baskets walking smartly behind her. The inmates Leeson and Herschel were in the gallery of the men's ward nearest the door. The girl was inside the women's gallery, at the front of the shuffling crowd, her attention on the attendant who was unfurling a cut of cloth over by the rose bushes, how the sheet lolled briefly on a pocket of air before being snapped into place on the asylum grounds.

It was the 2nd of August 1877. We know this because Jane has read accounts of the day and we have stood over her shoulder and read alongside her. One hundred and six souls were in residence that summer, most in the main wards, twenty or so in refractory care. We know that two of the attendants were off work with fever and that the Superintendent was in the city applying for a permit to extend the farmyard so as to better accommodate the new litter of pigs. A litter that Sir Thom, the hospital tabby, was attempting to avoid by slinking along the stone wall at the edge of the property.

Herschel studied the cat from his place near the window—a spot of ginger against the press of the woods, the animal flicking his tail when he came upon a cleft in the wall, which he then leapt into. A wisp of fresh air, of drying earth and dilly grass, slipped into the corridor just then through a gap between the door and its frame—a gap that Herschel noticed and tested with a nudge of his foot.

What happened next set everything in motion: Herschel opened the old matchboard door—opened it as if he were allowed, as if he were back home on his farm in P– on an ordinary morning, lifting his own door latch and unceremoniously starting out. The big man in full stride as the other inmates watched him turn onto the path that led to the gatehouse, his grey painting smock giving his form a ghostly shapelessness, his legs bare and hairy down to his boots.

The attendants on duty did not notice Herschel. Two of them had gone back inside to fetch hampers from the kitchen and the third, a lanky blond, was lingering near the door to the laundry flirting with the sisters who worked there. The Matron was alone on the grounds, kneeling by the fountain, smoothing out the large staff blanket and setting out the silver. When she finished she sat up, and Herschel, registering her broad back and the whorl of her red hair, veered away, moving steadily toward the wrought-iron gates. By the time he was pottering toward the woods and the collapsed section of the stone wall, she was folding the table napkins.

A flurry of cheers went up in the men's gallery when he made it to the stone wall. The other patients watched as the farmer lifted one leg and then the other over the rubble at the base of the cleft. For a split second Herschel seemed to waver there and then *whoosh*, he was gone, his whole frame swallowed by the trees.

Leeson blinked, trying to make sense of what he'd seen, worried that a hole or pit had been dug at the edge of the woods and that Herschel had lumbered into it. He pressed his hand against the glass, unsure of what to do, though he felt he ought to do something. From behind him came the sound of scuffling feet; he could hear Wick begin to titter. Feigning indifference, he studied the slot between the door and its support, the bare patch of stone floor that, minutes ago, had held conference with his friend. He hesitated a second, then dropped his hand onto the door handle. This agitated the men in the ward corridor further. Greevy, his grey hair wild, came forward to waggle a finger in front of Leeson's face, and with that gesture the newest inmate, Hopper, started on the window, his forehead *bump, bump, bump-*ing against the glass—a rhythm that inspired the musician to clap his hands, which in turn roused the poet.

'A Brisk Composition in Honour of the Occasion!' the poet shouted, and Hopper stopped. The commotion subsided. 'Unchain me!' the poet began, his voice filling the length of the gallery. 'Unchain me, unchain me, lest the hour's dark horses come.'

Slowly, so as not to set the group off again, Leeson inched the door open. A slat of sunlight fell onto the floor at his feet, brighter and more concentrated than what filtered through the quarrelled windows. He stared at it as if it were an accident, wondered if perhaps it had spilled out of a box, one that he had been entrusted with, one bearing a gift not intended for him. He waited to be called out and chastised, but nothing happened and no one came, and thinking only of Herschel, who might himself be in peril, Leeson stepped across the mat of honeyed light and scuttled out the door.

By the time he neared the fountain he was moving at a decent pace—just ahead of him were the Matron, the gatehouse and the belt of trees that Herschel had slipped into. Wisely, he gave the Matron a wide berth, treading as lightly as he could over the grass. Just as he moved past her, she straightened her back and turned toward the ward windows, a bowl of boiled eggs in her hand. Two dozen faces stared out at her, pale as dinner plates. Amused, she *tsk-tsk*ed under her breath and set the bowl back in the place she'd just moved it from.

Where Noble, the hall porter, had gone off to remains a matter of debate. He was still on poor terms with the Superintendent for falling asleep on watch and for glomming about near the windows while the female patients were jarring preserves in the kitchen. The asylum logbook for the 2nd of August states only that the event occurred around noon and that Noble saw nothing. The patients, once they were let out for lunch, did not raise the alarm, although a few of them, Hopper in particular, refused to settle down on a blanket, which prevented the head count from being taken for some time.

The girl, according to Leeson's later statements to Dr. Thorpe, caught up with him and Herschel in a clearing in the woods—the three of them tromping wordlessly along a muddy path and besting a modest hill before they came upon a narrow carriage track that led to town.

These are the woods of Jane's dream and we are sometimes the figures who pass through them. We watch the dream unfold the way Jane watches a film, as if it were something we might try to press a finger against, try to pause, as if that would allow us to rest beside a nearby elm, to point down different pathways. The thing about Jane is that even though she often dreams about these woods, she gets only some of it right. This is the problem with imagination: it is prone to filling in gaps, takes what it knows from one set of experiences and sinks them into another to create some semblance of truth, bridge time.

In fact Jane has been to that part of the country only twice, once when she was fifteen and William Eliot drove her up from London, and again when she was twenty-five and writing her MA dissertation on archival practices in rural nineteenth-century asylums. This is useful but it is not enough. When Jane imagines the north she thinks of the country freshness of the air—of honeysuckle and meadow grass—and of driving down the paved lane that led to the Whitmore, which was by then a shell of its former selves—asylum, hospital, school—empty and boarded up for decades. She doesn't think of legs not used to walking long distances or shoes that slip, bedbug bites, paths that dissipate into thistle or bodies scoured raw from the morning bath. She doesn't think of what it means to walk out of a door and know that you have changed the course of your life.

The door is the part of the story some of us like best. It was dull on the outside from years of weather; it was the colour of weak tea. You could run your fingers along the brace and over the stiles and not meet a splinter. It had a cast-iron lock with a small mouth meant to swallow a skeleton key. Lean close and sometimes there was the sound of the wind chattering in its teeth. And it was usually reliable: kept people and things in their proper places, made a *clop-clonk* sound when the mechanism was released all those times Noble unlocked it.

You might wonder what a door knows of time. About as much as we do. We know doors are meant to be passive: people come and go, move through them, think nothing of the crossing, come out sòmewhere expected. It is different for us; for us time is knotted. A door can open in the flare of the imagination and a century can reel across the threshold. One minute we might be with Jane in her London flat, appliances humming in the kitchen, and the next we could be back in those woods, couch grass whisking our legs.

Yes, we know there are Wheres and Whens but we have lost much of the distinction. We do not always know 'after' from 'before,' or either of those from 'now.' We do not know our own names, or the cities or towns we came from, the cottages or houses we called home. For us there is waiting and there is sleeping and there is the dull sense that we are doing both— sleepwalking down a long hall, waking in unexpected rooms.

This is why we need Jane. Her world is fixed, measurable: she turns on her laptop and there's a date in stern black type in the top right-hand corner of the screen; the pears she buys at the market, once composed in their bowl, convey the passage of time by the dwindling of their number and the mottling of their skin. We know that Herschel opened the Whitmore hospital door that afternoon in Yorkshire because Jane read that he did in Leeson's asylum casebook. We know from her copy of Dr. Thorpe's report to the Commissioners that Herschel's outdoor privileges had, a fortnight before, been revoked. We also know that there had been a month of rain—that the fountain was clogged with a thatch of green leaves shaken loose in a storm, that there were twenty small plots of earth waiting to be turned into gardens. And we know those woods. We know that on the 2nd of August, they carried the smell of wet must and the bright tang of decay. We know this because some of us were there.

According to Leeson's statement it took an hour of steady walking along the carriage track to reach the first junction. While he and Herschel and the girl stood to consider directions, a brougham with horses travelling at a good clip came up the road. It slowed and passed directly in front of Herschel, and hints of the city—leather and polish, a waft of snuff—cut through the mineral scent of the woods. The lone gentleman passenger tilted his top hat with the nub of his walking stick and glanced out the window, surveying the trio briefly before he tapped for the driver to hurry on.

Herschel watched the carriage depart and scratched his thigh, which was prickly from wading through some kind of nettle. He'd abandoned his trousers earlier that day on the way out of painting class because he'd dropped his brush on them and found the dash of crimson above the knee troubling. No trousers, he'd decided, was better than stained trousers, because trousers once stained would always be so even when the mark was gone. All he'd have to do was steer clear of the attendants, and he'd be at liberty to dress as sparingly as he pleased.

When the brougham was out of sight, Herschel turned to Leeson in the hope that his companion would decide on a direction and lead the way. But Leeson just stood there and stared into the distance, his dark trousers as spotless as his white-collared shirt and loose jacket, though his toe-capped shoes were muddy, as were the girl's flat-heeled boots and the hem of her brown dress. She'd come out, Herschel suddenly realized, without a shawl, and so was standing in a slip of sun, crossing her arms and rubbing them to keep warm.

Wordlessly they decided on a path that angled east, Herschel spotting the back end of a hare flashing through the woods and following it. Their pace was slow and all three were quiet, though Herschel *caw*ed a few times at the sheep mulching along a ridge of heather, something he was prone to do, having once, in better times, conducted a study of local birdcall.

The girl, all of eighteen, was especially quiet, though she did say thank you in a soft voice when Leeson extended his hand to guide her over a fallen oak. He would maintain later on that he didn't remember much of her, would only offer that she was given, throughout the afternoon, to biting her bottom lip and staring at her feet when there was cause to stop and assess a choice in direction. Leeson was caught up in his own concerns as he trod along: his knees past achy, his lungs on fire, though in the back of his mind, in the part filled with motherly advice and wifely admonishments to get outdoors, he was certain the pure air must be doing him some good. And he felt a kind of clarity, the near-joy of being unencumbered, of swinging one's arms and breathing deeply. Words he'd once used in his life as a solicitor started to come back to him: *consign, evince, bequeath.* He raised his eyes to the stitch of sky between the trees and the word *provision* sprang to mind; he opened his palms, flexed his fingers and the word *collation* formed in his head; he tightened his fingers into fists, thought, *Extremis.*

Blinking into the leafy canopy Leeson tried to sort out what each word denoted. In a copse fragrant with meadowsweet he remembered what it meant to bequeath something: personal property, business stock, land. He conjured the countenances of old clients: the pug-face of a blacksmith willing his smithy to his nephew, signing the document Leeson had drawn up for him with such trepidation that his signature seemed to slip reluctantly out of the nib of his pen. There was also the widow from L– who had fifty acres, a woman so pale her veins gave her temples a blue hue. Words that had sometimes mired themselves in Leeson's thinking, that had sat on his lunch plate like clumps of unrecognizable meat, suddenly attached themselves to lived circumstances. He thought, *intestate*, *codicil*, and saw an office in a dimly lit loft, a pocket watch that said it was early morning, then a drawer made of redwood that, when opened, revealed a thin stack of cream-coloured paper he'd cut into sheets himself. On the desktop there was a neat arrangement of stamps and wax, a taper on a brass holder. Just as he was about to inspect the post, his wife Emily appeared on the stairs to his office in her grey day dress, small pink flowers that seemed almost real stitched along her sleeve. Her smile was not as effortless as he would have liked, and there were dark circles under her eyes even though the baby had been born a month before and the doctor said Emily was fully recovered. Her pace was slow, one hand gripping the banister as she pulled herself closer. A fear rose in him, as he stood at his desk to greet her, that she was dragging a shackle behind her, that she would reach the top stair and the lead weight of the chain would snatch her backwards, send her plummeting to the landing. He sensed it even then—some yoke, some umbilicus pulling her away from him. Emily lifting her chin when she reached the top step, a tendril of blonde hair dampened against her forehead as she stepped toward him, opened her arms and said, 'Good afternoon, Charles.'

Leeson let out a *whoop* that rounded out into the woods

so joyfully he almost didn't believe it had come from him. He glanced up at Herschel's broad back and stooped shoulders, then back at the rosy face of the girl. It didn't matter that they ignored him; his mind was racing, so much so that he failed to notice they'd come to a worn path bordered by pollarded oaks. He looked at the oak closest to him and it wavered, became one of the trees that bracketed the park in his city, the park where he'd sometimes gone for midday walks, watched the brown backs of the ducks shining as they waddled out of the pond.

Up ahead Herschel trudged on, his boot heels clomping down with every step, mud from the last ravine they'd crossed spackled across the backs of his legs. Leeson wanted to call out to him but didn't, wanted to ask if the farmer could see the same apparition that he was seeing: a bench in a clearing, a high gate with curled finials and a woman with a parasol walking through it.

An hour or more passed and the trees overhead became fuller, knit themselves into rafters, growing as dark and sooty as a ceiling. Leeson's stomach grumbled and instinctively he reached a hand toward his pocket watch to check the time, only to discover that he was wearing a plain shirt and no waistcoat. The sky had become so dusky it was difficult to keep to the path, to squint past the trunks of the trees for the dining room table, blue-medallion wallpaper and brass lamps he expected to appear in the thicket. His right foot struck a root, sending him onto his hands and knees. It was only then, as he found his feet and brushed himself off, that he recalled he was in the country, near the Whitmore Hospital for Convalescent Lunatics, and remembered how he came to be there.

—

By the time Herschel stumbled out of the grove and happened upon the estate house, the sky had gone the blue-black of a rook—a bird that he preferred over jackdaws or magpies, not just for its shag feathers, but for the *kaarg* call it made when roosting at dusk, a throatier, more satisfying sound than the *pruc-pruc* of the raven. On the walk so far he had counted eleven different birdcalls, though in some cases he had not seen the bird, which he knew Dr. Thorpe would say left open the possibility that, like certain human voices, those birdsongs might be constructed—be things one *wants* to hear. But the country house, Herschel decided, was *not* imagined. From the end of its great lawn he could make out the protrusion of an arcaded portico and two storeys of darkened windows that flanked off in either direction. The house sat mutely save for one slit-eye casting lamplight between its heavy curtains and tufts of smoke drifting out of the chimneys. Instinctively Herschel ran through a list of the kinds of nests one might find up there, bird names flitting through his head like a host of sparrows. He was fond of roofs, had been known to set his body down on ledges, window peaks or near chimney stacks—good spots to rest after hours of flapping along.

When Leeson and the girl caught up to him, they too took in the house hunkered in the distance. From the edge of the lawn it appeared as if some large and ornate stone had been dropped from the sky into an impossibly manicured setting. The scent of burning wood in the air lent itself to the idea of warmth, a place to sit down, something to drink—tea perhaps, or a cup of water.

Leeson turned to Herschel and swung out his arm as if clearing the way of obstructions, and the farmer's round face filled with delight, though he didn't move. In the end it was Leeson who rapped the lion's-head door knocker against its plate, adjusting his cuffs while he listened over the *chirr* of crickets for the sound of footsteps. A minute later the door opened and a young footman with a centre part and a thin moustache appeared; he cleared his throat and moved his neck from side to side as if just settling into his collar.

'May I help you, sir?'

Leeson recognized the man's enunciation; it was the kind developed through practice. In better days he had heard the same forced diction from a variety of servants employed in the houses he visited for work. 'Yes, you may,' he replied. He brought his heels together in an effort to stand taller. 'Is the Master of the estate at home?'

The footman furrowed his brow and peered over Leeson's shoulder at the others. 'Might I ask who is calling?'

'Indeed.' Leeson smiled back at his companions, fighting the urge to explain Herschel's lack of trousers or to flatten his own hair where the grey bits always stuck out from the brown. He turned again to the footman. Behind him he could make out a columned entry hall, a modest candle chandelier, a thick Turkish rug and a mahogany table set against the back wall holding five or six leather-bound volumes stacked on their sides. He caught a glimpse of a large mounted bear, its open maw and the spread of its brown claws, before he shifted his gaze back to the books. There was a time in his life when he'd spent whole days poring over tomes such as these, some of them half the size of his desk, all of them embossed and bound in similarly dyed leathers.

'Sir?'

Leeson sighed. It wouldn't serve any purpose to be a pro-bate solicitor here, but the footman expected something. He glanced over the footman's shoulder again, wishing a glass of claret might appear to relieve him of his thirst. 'Please say that Mr. Charles Leeson is calling.'

'Mr. Leeson, is it?'

'Yes, and company—' He gestured vaguely behind him.

'And might I tell Master Farrington your business?'

'You may. I am here regarding a bequest.'

The footman furrowed his brow again, an expression that had annoyed Leeson the first time.

'Yes, a *bequest*,' Leeson repeated, savouring the shape of the word in his mouth, 'of books. I regret I do not have my card.' He patted down the front of his shirt as if it might sprout a pocket.

'Books?' the footman repeated somewhat dubiously.

'Yes. I am here in my capacity as—' and here he paused, considered a variety of overtures, and then said '—the Assistant Librarian of the British Museum,' hastening to add, lest the footman turn them away, 'London.'

In the end they stayed only briefly. George Farrington allowed his visitors to rest in the small parlour while he sent the maid for refreshments. Herschel plopped himself down on the horse-hair sofa, which meant that Leeson had to take the wingback that was situated farther away from the fire. The room was full of the sound of ticking clocks: a pillared carriage clock on the mantle, an ornate brass skeleton model with an ebony face on the tallest of the bookshelves and an old mahogany long-case on the opposite wall wedged between a stuffed grouse and a mounted fox. Two of the clocks were out of sync, so that every second had two beats, the confidently announced tick of the larger clock's brass hand followed by a faint echo from the bookshelf. Farrington did not seem to notice. His hospitality extended to a series of questions: Which way had they come to Inglewood? Were they expected elsewhere? And, less pointedly, what particular flora or fauna might they have noted on the way? These questions were followed by a brief declamation on the state of the surrounding countryside, after which the maid intervened with tea. It arrived on a gleaming silver platter that she set down on a table with claw feet carved so realistically that Leeson believed they were gripping the rug. George Farrington's mother, Prudence, joined them shortly thereafter, though she stopped upon entering the room, a strained expression on her long face as if she had suddenly come into contact with music she didn't care for. It was only when George greeted her with a warm 'Mother' that her beauty became apparent: the thin petals of her mouth relaxing into a pleasing fullness, her chin lifting to reveal the elegant length of her neck. She extended her hands and moved toward her son and the pleated hemline of her mauve dinner dress shushed over the carpets behind her. Leeson bowed deeply as she approached, but Herschel remained seated, his head cocked to study the intricately fastened brown nest of her hair.

Once Mrs. Farrington had settled in a high-backed chair near a corner of the room, Leeson returned to the task of explaining his charge—which he did rather unconvincingly between bites of oatcake. It was only upon reaching for his second oatcake— glancing around to mentally divide the number of cakes by the number of those in the room—that he noticed the girl who'd come with them was missing. He craned his neck toward the entryway, trying to recollect if she'd followed them in through the door.

'Of course I am quite familiar with the museum library,' George Farrington was asserting. 'Two of my own books reside there—one botanical, the other verse. Though I am,' he confessed, prodding the dwindling fire with a poker, 'serious about one art and a dabbler in the other.'

Leeson glanced at Herschel, who had become wholly distracted, first by the rash on his thigh and then by the half-dozen or so watercolour landscapes that hung in gold frames on the wall behind him. The farmer swivelled and rose on the sofa to get a better look, his smock lifting slightly as he did so.

'Those were painted by my uncle Reginald,' Farrington said, a hint of reprimand in his voice.

Herschel turned and sat back down, unsure of what exactly he'd done. He looked to Leeson, but Leeson was studying Farrington. The solicitor recognized his host now. It was the defect around his mouth that gave him away: an arced scar that tracked through one side of his dark-brown moustache and down onto his bare chin. *A climbing accident*, Leeson remembered the Superintendent saying, leaning sideways toward the Matron at the Whitmore. *Burma, I believe.* And Leeson, who had been standing nearby, had stepped forward to see whom they were discussing, and there was a gentleman—Farrington—in a top hat and bright blue waistcoat coming down the reception line at the Whitmore Ball, his boutonnière an exotic yellow bud with orange tips quite unlike any Leeson had ever seen.

It stood to reason, then, that if this was the celebrated botanist from the ball—and Leeson was fairly certain it was—he and Herschel were currently some ten or eleven miles from the Whitmore in the country house of the Farringtons, to whom much of the land they had traversed belonged.

Leeson stifled a yawn, realizing with a start that his host was speaking to him, saying something about the landscape the watercolours had been painted in. Obligingly he stood up to inspect the paintings, all the while wondering where the girl had gone off to, and whether or not some sort of sustenance beyond the oatcakes he'd already consumed might arrive. It did. His gaze had only just fallen into a rippled blue lake and the droopy willow that tickled it when the Farringtons' maid re-entered the room. She curtseyed quickly, keeping her chin down while her eyes darted to further survey the guests. Wordlessly she handed a cloth sack to Mrs. Farrington, who with one hand whisked the maid back through the door and into the hall. So it was that a mere quarter-hour after they had entered the house, they were sent on their way again, Mrs. Farrington ensuring they had the sack of ham and butter sandwiches in hand.

It was near midnight when Herschel climbed back over the stone wall, and he and Leeson trudged across the lawn and into their beds. The main building was dark save for a row of candles placed along one of the gallery's ledges.

The following morning a letter arrived at the Whitmore, delivered to the hospital clerk by a scrawny young man on a dun pony. It read:

> *Mr. George Farrington presents his compliments to the*
> *Governor of Whitmore Hospital for Convalescent Lunatics,*
> *and requests him to be so kind as to take precautions that*
> *his patients should not pay visits at Inglewood, as two did*
> *yesterday (one describing himself as an assistant librarian of*
> *the British Museum).*
>
> *Mr. Farrington is very glad if they in any way enjoy'd*
> *themselves here, and hopes they did not suffer from their*
> *long walk.*

George Farrington did not mention the girl in his note. And we know from the asylum casebook that in Leeson's interview with the Superintendent the next morning, he said he hadn't seen her after the walk up to Farrington's door, though he did comment on her absence and on the changing weather and on Herschel's discovery of a roe deer bedded down in a whorl of grass. Numerous times in his description of events Leeson used words like *intestate* and *disinherit*; he also talked of returning to work in law. He said, 'You cannot disinherit a ham, nor can you disinherit roast beef pie.'

Dr. Thorpe wrote *appears to be suffering from delusions* twice in the transcript margins, and five times wrote *tangent* . . . before the description of 'Activities Occurring on 2 August 1877' was returned to and set down.

The hospital logbook that Jane first examined when she was writing her dissertation detailed almost nothing of the inmates' escape. It noted that on the 2nd of August the laundry had been collected at eight, that the new hen had not lain. In hasty black ink underneath that someone had written *Patients C. Leeson, H. Morley and girl N– missing*, and then, in another hand, there was an added note: *Patient Hopper restrained at 2 p.m.* Finally, scribbled in handwriting so tight and angular Jane had to read it with a magnifying glass: *Mstrs H. Morley and C. Leeson returned.* On the 3rd of August the first entry states: *Letter from G. Farrington received.* This was followed by the domestics of the institution: a list of objects needing mending, a detailed order of supplies and foodstuff requisitioned from Morrington, a change in staff schedules.

No further mention of N– was to be found.

2 Jane wakes to the whooping sound of the corner grocer's store alarm. The grocer recently hired a new shop assistant and the alarm has gone off at six a.m. three days in a row. Jane knows that if she sticks her head out the window the shop assistant will be on his mobile phone shouting in Punjabi and waving one hand toward the security gate. It usually takes five to ten minutes for the alarm to stop, so Jane presses her pillow over her face to muffle the sound, the metallic tang of last night's sleeping pill still on her tongue.

It comes back to her then—the dream about the woods and the Whitmore, the dream about the girl she only knows as 'N.' Jane is glad to be thinking about her again, but there's guilt in the thought too. For the last six weeks, she's been too busy with work at the Chester Museum to spend any time on the Whitmore; all the research she'd been doing was stuffed reluctantly into a box and shoved under her bed. What Jane wonders, tracing her way around the edges of the dream, is how N got out of the hospital—not the act, the hand that lifts the latch, opens the door, but rather what wells up in a person so that one day they do the unexpected. She would like to know this because there's something welling inside her too, although she doesn't see it as clearly as we do.

The sound of a steel gate being kicked repeatedly clangs into the room from down the street and Jane groans into her pillow then slides it off her face. Those of us who were in other rooms come in and gather around her, our presence as invisible as the chutes of air drifting under the cracked-open window.

After a minute the alarm stops and London begins to rouse itself: delivery trucks rattle down the road, taxis ferry people to their jobs and businesses, the man in the brown corduroy jacket trots his beagle out to the adjacent green—doing so with such dependability we could set our watches by him if we had a need for watches. Across the street, morning light sifts through the clouds to give back the terraced row houses their eggshell colour; the neon signs on the chip and curry shops down the road buzz and flicker. Jane pushes the covers away and thinks about the tea set sitting beside her desk at work, the one that Gareth, the Chester's director and curator, said he wanted shipped a week ago.

And for a minute, caught up in the idea of simple tasks, caught up in the drift of the Whitmore and N, she doesn't remember what day it is or what will happen by the end of it; she simply thinks *work* and puts her hand out for her spaniel, Sam, who trots over to have his ears rubbed. Then it's there, in her waking brain: the fact that the museum is closing, that she will be unemployed in two weeks and that tonight she is going to see William Eliot.

The woods dreams are the ones Jane has most often, though in the past few months there have also been the usual sort about missed recitals and failed exams, about something bad happening to the dog, about her brother, Lewis, turning into a robot. And there have been dreams set in the museum where she works—though these are mostly about lost objects that turn up in the wrong cabinets or collections. We have our preferences, can behave like a pack of critics, sigh, 'Not that one again' when the dream about Jane's mother losing her in Marks and Spencer starts up, or turn away when the narratives become too strange, when they dwell too long on death or dying.

Sometimes when that happens we play a game. It's a child's game, but some of us are children. Besides, we know all games have a purpose: they prepare you for the world you are about to enter, inform the character of the person you are to become. We call this game 'Where Is It?' and we start by taking turns. One voice calls out a question: 'What's my name?' or 'Where was I born?' or 'How far have I travelled?' or 'What age do you think I am?' And those of us in the room begin to look for the answer in the things around us. We look on the spines of books; we look in Jane's picture frames, in the water glass on the bedside table. We look in the closet, in her yawning handbags, in the hollows of her pencil skirts and dresses. We skim the empty music stand, peer down the sound holes of the cello, repeat the question into the black slot of its *S* then wait to see if it will send back an answer. We finger the knotted ends of the blue rug, gaze out the window that looks over the city street. When we get bored, the one who asked the question will coax us on by repeating the question—'Where is it?'—and we'll move into the living room and run our eyes over the potted fig, the wingback chair, trace the swirling limestone fossil Jane's brother gave her one Christmas. Then we'll look in the gap between the sofa and its cushions, peer into the rubbish bin. 'This is easier in the museum,' we'll say, but shrug and keep going: inspect the Dutch jug from the market, the bird's nest Sam sniffed out in the park, the soft folds of the curtains. We'll stare into the blank screen of the telly, at the mirror above the dining room table, look into the rounds of the spoons in the drying rack—but we'll see and find nothing.

In the past few weeks we've begun looking under the far side of the bed at the box where Jane put her research papers, near the blanket the dog sleeps on. If we're feeling really brave we stay there, let Sam stretch his neck, sniff the air in our direction, his spaniel's face as white as a lamb's, his brown eyes curiously discerning. Yesterday he gave a low growl and those of us who were studying the box gave up and moved slowly back to our corners. That's when we saw Jane curled up and sleeping. 'There it is!' we said. 'In there!' Thinking, *Of course! Finally! We knew the answers must be hiding somewhere.*

At seven o'clock Jane comes back from walking Sam around the green. She sets his leash on the kitchen counter for Dora, drops some food into his bowl and starts to get ready for work. Standing in front of her closet, she tries to steady her thoughts, to focus on what she has to do in these next two weeks before the museum closes for good. Today is the last day of public admission, and tonight is the Chester's official farewell party, a gala timed to coincide with the annual Chester-Wood Book Prize lecture and reception. A month ago, William Eliot, botanical keeper at the Natural History Museum, was announced as the recipient of this year's prize for his non-fiction book *The Lost Gardens of England*. In less than twelve hours he will take the podium to deliver a lecture and talk about his work. Jane has not seen William since she was fifteen years old, and even though there is a part of her that wants to believe otherwise, she is certain he will not want to see her now.

Pressing the pads of her fingers against the puffiness under her eyes, Jane steps back to check her appearance in the bathroom mirror. She is thirty-four. She is not vain but knows she is pretty enough. Her mother was stunning—which is how Jane grew into her own self-assurance: by basking in the attention spilled onto her by men caught up in her mother's beauty. Tying her hair up, Jane thinks again about N, wonders if she was tall, if she was pale-skinned, if she had dark hair. In the dreams N always resembles her—not the girl Jane was at eighteen, but the woman she is now: high cheekbones, pert nose, a tendency to blush when self-conscious. Her former boyfriend Ben once remarked, just after he'd moved in with her, that Jane reminded him of a deer, all that nervous, pent-up energy. He was running a finger over her collarbone, imagined he could feel a tremor. She took his comment the wrong way, as she often did, swatted at his hand and got out of bed. She threw his trousers at him, forgetting that he lived with her now and had no apartment of his own to retreat to. He thought it was funny, tried pulling her back down, said, 'Come on, I love deer. What's not to love?'

We know what Ben meant, have come across deer at the edges of woods, along thickets—the pulse visible in their necks. Animals that will either bolt when seen or stand so still they can be right in front of you and remain unnoticed.

The morning unfolds like any other: we watch Jane get dressed, watch her eat toast and cheddar leaning against the counter in her yellow kitchen. Together we listen to the BBC news on the radio: flood warnings in the east, economic crisis in the west, a group of miners stranded underground in a country so distant some of us have never heard of it. 'They have sent up a note,' the man being interviewed says. 'We are drilling air holes, there is reason for hope.'

Six weeks ago Gareth came back from his meeting with the Minister of Culture, called the senior staff into his office and announced that the museum would be closing. We turned to Jane to see what that might mean. Until that point, we believed we were still learning who we might be: following Jane like a pack of hounds, staring at the files she read, the objects she held, sometimes saying, 'I know this!' Our days were spent huddling around astrolabes, stuffed tortoises, samplers, mustard pots, surgical tools, old diaries, photographs of estate lawns we might once have walked across. Some of us went back to the same objects again and again—a set of pearl hair combs, a galvanizing machine, the glass case of hummingbirds in the entry hall—stuttering toward our own names, sounds we thought might be familiar. But then Gareth gave everyone the news and a kind of panic set in.

For years we had been trying to mimic what we had seen Jane do with the museum collections: to catalogue, list and cite ourselves. We endeavoured to keep track of each other, tried to pay attention to who thought what. Most days this proved difficult. We have little in common: some of us are old, some young; the places or times we lived in feel different. And since we have no names to go by, we resort to epithets: The One with the Soft Voice, The Poet, The Musician, The Theologian, The One Who Sucks on His Teeth, The One Who Never Speaks, The Boy, The Girl, Cat, The Idiot. And then there are the transients, the passersby and the passers-through.

When remembering what documents or objects we'd circled or what things in the museum we'd returned to proved difficult, we braved philosophy. When that didn't work, we began our interrogations, asking each other quick sets of questions to try to find even a stitch of memory to build on. *What food did you like? What do you see when I say 'green'? What clothes can you imagine yourself wearing? Who did you love? What noises surround you? What is your name?* The answers, if they come at all, come slowly or in the form of further questions: progress in circles. We keep at it even though some of us are easily frustrated, some tired, sad or mean; even though some of us do nothing but run around the flat after Sam, barking like otherworldly animals.

Still, for those of us who want to make sense of things, there is constant learning. Time may have swept past us but we are caught in its gusting: we read the papers, watch the telly, listen in on conversations in cafés and tube stations, stand outside strangers' windows observing them as they eat alone in the quiet burrow of their thoughts. Some of us have even gone to school, studied particular jobs, ridden in ambulances; one spends nights following vagrants as they tread from the city's edge into the local park. In this way we have learned new words and new ideas, although the knowledge we gain is sometimes woolly. One of us can describe the spark that lit the universe, another knows clock workings, another listens to opera, one loves cowboy films, another the art of flower arranging. We understand the principles of radio waves and motors and satellite relays, even if we cannot say exactly how such phenomena operate. Meanwhile our own knowledge is lost or buried, our hands emptied of their work; even the accents that once shaped our mouths have been smoothed like stones scuttled on the banks of a whisking river.

We do not know what will happen when the Chester closes. Ask us what shape certainty takes and we will all point to a different corner of the museum: to the pendulum of the long-case clock, to the black stones of the birds' eyes, to the teacups in the upper gallery, to books, locks of hair, dress silk, to the computer in Jane's office, or the cabinet of milkweed and wild strawberry glass models made in a factory between wars. We do not know how to recover our histories, to identify what or whom we loved. We cannot see ourselves except as loose human forms— like those caught moving down the street in the museum's early

Victorian photographs, figures whose blurred shapes become clearer the longer you look at them. We only know that we are drawn to certain objects, places and people, and that we are bound to Jane like the Thale butterflies in the natural history hall—pinned to the boards in their long glass cases.

The sun is out when Jane leaves the flat to walk the three blocks to the tube station. It glints off the stand of bicycles, glides over the pastry shop window. At the end of the street we turn and follow Jane down the steps of the Underground through the short stretch of semi-darkness that divides the daylight above and the fluorescent light below. We feel a sense of having done this before every time, though we are uncertain whether this sense comes from the repetition of the act itself or an echo from some other point in our lives.

Below ground the station is crowded, and wedged together we shuffle onto the train, using the doors because even though they are unnecessary to us, they are a convention we remember. Once settled, some of us read the papers over people's shoulders, others watch the flares of tunnel light sweep past the windows. The boy amongst us flits the laces of a young girl's shoe; the poet sways in the aisle, caught up in a daydream. All of us aware of each other the way you are after becoming accustomed to a dark room. After all, every presence has a kind of weight, something felt: moods and shifts and feelings, a steady pulse of being.

Jane has found a seat in the middle of the car between a young man playing a game on his mobile and a tourist with a backpack wedged between his knees. There is a woman in front of them holding on to the rail, a plastic bag that smells of the apricots and peaches within it swinging from her wrist. We notice all of this but Jane does not. She is staring at the floor trying to imagine what exactly will happen when she and William meet.

When she is quiet like this, when her thoughts are steady, we can follow them almost the same way we do when we will ourselves into her dreams. It's like being in a valley in winter: the sound of a branch snapping, the *shish* of an icicle plummeting from a tree, amplified. This is why we're here: because Jane thinks about us almost as much as she thinks about herself, because the distance between her life and ours is not as great as with others and because we are lost and Jane is the closest thing we've got to a map. And she is a good archivist, has a willingness to navigate history, to consider its blank pages. But history is tricky. Jane thinks it is a buffer, a static place that sits obediently between now and then—something she can pass through, the way people walk through the natural history hall or the upper galleries of the Chester Museum. But we know she is wrong, and we feel bad about that. History is shifty; it looks out for itself, moves when you least expect it.

3 The last time William Eliot touched Jane they were standing in a field in Yorkshire at a gate that marked the start of the Farrington botanical trail. He'd placed his left hand lightly on the back of her bare neck, an adult innocently guiding his daughter's sitter through a passageway. It was 1991, and Jane was fifteen years old and wearing a blue fluted summer dress and new black ankle-strap shoes that she worried would be scuffed by the end of the walk. She was trying to catch a glimpse of the estate house that sat adjacent to the woods, craning her neck toward

a gap in the hedge, when William said, 'Come on, this way, we can walk by Inglewood House later,' his cool fingertips suddenly grazing her hot skin. She can still feel it sometimes: the light press of his thumb in her hairline, his body ghosting behind her.

That morning she'd spent an hour in front of the bathroom mirror tying her hair up, then down, then up again, putting on lip colour she hoped her grandmother wouldn't notice, changing her dress twice. When she was ready, she'd walked the two blocks between her grandparents' South Kensington house and the Eliots', trying not to bite her lip. William had answered the door in a collared shirt and beige trousers, a towel in his hand, his short brown hair still wet from the shower. He stood in the doorway longer than usual, as if over the span of a day and a half he'd forgotten what Jane looked like—her thick fringe and serious expression—and was trying to put her into context. Jane, flustered, had blushed. She'd wanted this exact kind of looking for the two weeks she'd been coming to babysit. Then he grinned at something, some private thought she sensed had nothing to do with her, and jutted his chin in the direction of the kitchen— 'Your charge awaits, Miss Standen'—ruffling his hair with his towel and heading upstairs.

Lily had glanced up when Jane came into the kitchen. The curtains on the French doors were tied back so the room was brighter than usual. The counters and sinks were spotless because it was Sunday and the cleaning lady William had hired while Lily's nanny was in Spain had been coming in on Saturdays. Seeing it was just Jane, Lily went back to running her blue crayon over the side of the ceramic milk pitcher, her cereal bowl half full in front of her, a few slices of apple scattered around the placemat.

'Need some help with your drawing?'

The girl tilted her head as if she was still unsure how much authority Jane had or how useful she was. She inspected the crayons spread out around her juice box, rolled the red one Jane knew she liked best under her palm a few times and then said, 'Okay.'

'Hmm. How about we do it on paper? Then we can draw something for your dad.'

Lily glanced toward the entry where she could see William. He was running up and down the stairs, dropping specimen bags and wellies by the door. The excursion was to be part fun, part field trip. William was finishing a research proposal on the Victorian plant hunter George Farrington and his estate gardens in Inglewood and wanted to take a last look at the original plantings along the old estate trail before he submitted the final application. He only had a week before the deadline and the drive was four-plus hours each way, so he'd invited Jane for a day in the country to help with Lily and to thank her for filling in for Luisa, who'd had a family emergency back in Spain.

Jane tore a piece of paper off the scratch pad that Luisa kept in the oak sideboard and gave it to Lily. Then she pulled up a chair and watched as the five-year-old drew a red sun and then a blue flower and a blue whale swimming through puffy yellow clouds. Lily pushed the drawing toward Jane when she was done and then took it back at the last second, adding five blue squiggles in the top right-hand corner.

'What are those?' Jane asked.

'A secret.'

'Oh. Can I guess?'

Lily nodded.

'Birds?'

'No.'

'Bumblebees?'

'No.'

'Airplanes?'

'No.'

'Drops of rain?'

'No.'

'Flying girls?'

'No, no, no.' She smacked her lips, satisfied.

'How about the flags of invisible cities?'

Lily, liking that, giggled.

When they first set out along the trail William stayed with Jane and Lily, pointing out various kinds of *Rhododendron* and *Chimonanthus*, cupping the glossy plant leaves in his hand and explaining that the shrubs liked acidic soil best, that they bloomed in winter and the flowers were pungent—'spicy smelling, actually; quite lovely'—which made Jane think of the cologne she'd found in William's bathroom cabinet, its woodsy clove scent. He'd started to give a brief history of the estate and of the Farrington family—'George was a great botanist, his brother an amateur geologist'—trying, and failing, to make it interesting to Lily, who kept interrupting to complain that she was too warm or thirsty. After ten minutes of walking together, he pulled out his notebook and said he was going to get started, that he wouldn't be far. Sometimes after that they'd round a corner and see him in the distance standing near a bed of fern, or just off the lake side of the footpath, a handsome thirty-five-year-old man in beige trousers and a navy jacket, two canvas specimen bags around his waist, wellies up to his knees in case he wanted to scramble down the verge, down the muddy ravine.

The trail was narrow but flat. The Farrington estate had been in the hands of the local Trust for twenty-some years and over that time the path had become a popular walking trail, as much for the three caves at the end of it as for the rare alpine and Asian specimens George Farrington had brought back from the Himalayas and planted in the late 1870s. The farther in they walked, the cooler it became, though the temperature was changeable: one minute Jane and Lily would be walking in shade and Jane would get goose pimples, then a few minutes later they'd come to a section of clear sky where sunlight blanketed the trail. The stickiness of the drive up and the summer heat followed by the blue coolness of the woods reminded Jane of summers at her family's cottage at the Lakes when their mum was between research posts or teaching semesters—summers full of walks and hill climbing. Jane had been twelve and Lewis ten and bratty the last time they'd gone up. Lewis's favourite pastime that year was sailing through the main room of the cottage to *thwap* whatever book Jane was reading with his hand before presenting himself to their mum and stating, 'Claire, we need milk,' or 'Claire, I'd like a microscope.' And Claire would glance up from the clutter of papers on her desk under the open stairs and say, 'Of course, Mr. Standen, whatever you want.'

About twenty minutes into their walk, the trees to Jane and Lily's left thinned, and Jane could make out the edge of a flat pasture at the top of a sloping rise, a ribbon of sun along its border. After a while a stone fence took its place, and every now and again one of the sheep in the upper field would *baa* and Lily would stop and stare at the ridge as if she expected to see a lamb standing there. William, by then, had gone even farther ahead, moving through the brome and couch grass, the troughs of fern. When he'd been gone for a while Lily started to pick up leaves and snatch bits of bushes, trying to imitate her father. Wiping her hands on her red overalls and traipsing along beside Jane, she asked a litany of questions that all began with *Why?* or *How come?* or *What if?* Jane tried her best to answer, to explain why some animals had stripes and some spots, why leaves float and why if Luisa said that Lily's mother was in heaven, then that was clearly where she was. Lily made a fish face at that and blew on the key that swung from a white ribbon around her neck. It was the key to Jane's grandparents' house. Lily had noticed it on the ribbon wound around Jane's wrist during lunch at the pub in the village; she'd gently tried to tug it off while Jane was doing her best to sit up straight and have a grown-up conversation with William over soggy cod and chips.

'Did your father put you up to the cello?' he'd asked.

'No. Well, sort of.'

'It must be difficult—the expectations people have.'

Jane had stabbed at a pea with her fork and missed, and the tine had made a scraping noise on the plate; she'd checked to see if William noticed. 'We don't see him much, unless he has a concert in London. Right now he's back in France.' She heard herself say 'back in France' and liked how important it sounded, liked how it made her father a busy man, famous, foreign.

On her second day minding Lily, when she'd started to look more closely around William's house, she'd rifled through the music collection and saw that he had Henri's Liszt recording and Paganini caprices, which were her favourite. There was a strange electric pleasure in seeing her father's image on the CD cover in William's house—it was a still from one of his Berlin concerts, the violin tucked under his chin, his black hair just long enough to toss back with effect and an expression she sometimes thought of as rage on his face.

'I've never seen him play—' William began, stopping when he saw Lily tugging at Jane's wrist. He reached across the table and gently grabbed her hand. 'Lily, stop that.'

'It's fine.' Jane smiled at William and loosened the strands of the ribbon until she could loop the whole thing off her wrist. 'You can play with it. Just don't lose it.' She handed Lily the key and the girl lit up, started spinning it. Jane glanced at William, hoping she'd done the right thing, that he'd think she was a good minder, that he'd go back to asking her questions about her life. Hoping, too, that this wanting to get to know her meant something, that it was a kind of affection.

William spent most of the walk taking samples and photographs and jotting plant names on a map of the trail. He'd walk ahead and wave at Jane before rounding corners, a signal that he was going farther along, that he wasn't scrambling down toward the lake or up toward the pasture, that he was only around the bend. Lily, bored, pulled the ribbon around her neck taut and held the key out in front of her chest, making up a singsong—*up, down, up, down*. She flicked the key again and again with her index finger while Jane stood in the middle of the path waiting for her: a five-year-old trundling along at her own pace.

Because Lily was dawdling, Jane tried to think of a game. If she thought up a game, Lily would forget the key and it would be easier to get it back from her. So Jane looked at the elm and sycamore, then over to the slope of meadow grass and ivy that rolled down to the ravine bottom, and then back to the trail. Every fifty feet or so on the edge of the path there were short brown posts with numbers painted in green on top. They lined the edge of the woods on the pasture and lakesides, marking the various bushes and shrubs George Farrington had brought back from his plant-hunting expeditions in Burma, China and Tibet. At the start of the trail, when William had told Jane and Lily about the botanist, he'd shown them *Paeonia suffruticosa* and *Viburnum farrington*. The Viburnum shrub was sweet-smelling with sprays of white flowers. Jane had picked a few of the buds when William wasn't looking, dropping them into her pocket so she could touch the petals with her fingertips while she walked.

The next post, Jane saw, bore the number 8. There was a tall, rubbery-looking bush behind it. She said, 'Let's play a game, Lily,' and the girl beamed up at her, expectant, her light-brown pigtails bobbing. 'Every time you see a post like this'—she took Lily's hand in hers and led her over to the side of the trail—'you have to tell me the number on it. If you get it right, we'll both shout hooray.'

Lily nodded and then stood there, waiting.

'Okay, we'll start at the next post. Ready. Set. Go.'

Lily broke into a little-girl run, elbows out, fists pumping furiously. She sped headlong up the trail and along the verge to search for the next post. Jane watched her dart ahead and then let her eyes drift up the trail to where William might be. Behind her she heard the sound of someone's footfalls, then a blonde woman in jeans and trainers passed her, nodding as she went, an old border collie trotting alongside her.

After a minute, Lily found a post and grabbed its top, which came up to her waist; she smiled so hard her eyes squinched shut. 'Nine,' she said triumphantly. She was right, so she and Jane both shouted hooray. Then Lily skipped back onto the path to find the next post and the one after that. She was always right about the numbers, and she and Jane always shouted hooray.

When Jane tried to shout William's name, her voice came out too quietly, too unsteadily, like the kind of voice you use to tell someone a secret. She wanted to make it loud, to scream, but nothing came. When his name finally did emerge it was jagged, in pulses, '*Wil-li-am*,' like a faltering heartbeat. She yelled it twice, three times, all the while turning circles and looking for Lily. He came slowly at first, then seeing Jane standing in the middle of the path alone, he started to run. Without asking what was wrong he began calling for Lily, and when she didn't appear he turned to Jane, his voice constricted. 'Where is she? Where did you see her last?'

Jane sputtered, 'I don't know, she was just here.' She pointed toward the bend he had just come from, to the post on the pasture side, and William took off, running up the slope, scrambling between the thin rails of the alder. When he came back down, flushed and angry, Jane said again, 'She was just here,' and her chest heaved into sobs. She wanted him to understand that it had happened quickly, that Lily had found the post and then run ahead to look for the next one, and that when Jane rounded the bend in the path after her, Lily was gone.

'Lily!' William turned away from Jane and shouted into the trees on the lake side of the trail. Jane tried to find her voice but when she called 'Lily' it broke and fell because everything had suddenly gone wrong, and even if it turned out okay, even if Lily appeared magically exactly where she ought to be, Jane had screwed up and William had seen that she wasn't a good sitter, that she had let him down.

'Lily!' William shouted again, starting down the slope to the lake, losing his footing and sliding a few feet. He picked himself up and ripped off his jacket, untied the canvas bags from his waist, tossing them up toward Jane, moving down along the bramble recklessly, panic in his voice, shouting, 'Lily!' again and again, tripping in the underbrush, losing and regaining his footing. Then suddenly he was shouting, 'Come out now!'—angry, as if this were a game Lily was playing, hiding somewhere close, crouching down in a patch of sage and staying very still. He was gone whole minutes, his shouts coming up over the verge to where Jane stood.

When his calls grew distant, Jane walked toward the trail edge, picked up his jacket and gripped it in her hands. The bird sounds were louder, William's voice barely audible, coming from back toward the lake. And then, there was nothing. It was there, in that span of time, that Jane allowed herself to imagine that he'd found her, that Lily was standing at the edge of the trail next to some post they'd already passed, that he was scooping her up in his arms that very instant and that she was saying the number, smiling fiercely at him and telling him to shout hooray.

Up ahead the woman with the collie reappeared. She'd turned around, and her dog was limping. A breeze sifted between them off the lake and lifted Jane's hair ever so slightly; she felt it brush against her skin just as she heard William's voice again, his distant shouts drifting up toward the spot on the path where she stood. The woman heard them too and began to walk quickly toward Jane, a look of concern on her face. William's voice coming closer and closer, Lily's name arcing through the boughs of the trees.

4   The tea set that Jane thought about first thing this morning when the grocer's alarm was blaring is sitting on a trolley beside her worktable. Gareth had stopped by right after she arrived to ask if she'd completed the exit forms, and Jane had lifted the Grainger file off the stack on her desk to show him that she was working on it. The set, one of the museum's most beautiful, consists of twenty-one pieces of china. The teapot and matching cups and saucers are a light green with gold leaf, each with an ivy band painted so precisely that it's hard for Jane to

look at the set without imagining the delicate wrist and steady hand of the artist. The Grainger, like the rest of the ceramic collection, was auctioned off last week, and Jane is supposed to have its deaccession complete so that the conservation department can pack it for shipping. But even now, lifting a teacup off its padding to check its catalogue number, she feels reluctant. She wonders if this is what it's like to lose the things you love in a burglary or house fire, is grateful that she's allowed to touch everything one last time.

Given the tastes of the day the Grainger tea set is relatively plain. It once belonged to a Duchess who was quite active in the Victorian land preservation movement, who liked to call herself a friend to nature. She didn't mind when the rose bushes grew too close to the windows, tolerated her husband's hound under the table, accepted his penchant for stag-horn furniture. Before washdays, she often let her girls run from the grounds into the house without taking their boots off, though she sometimes complained in her diaries about the mess. She had both a rigorous mind and a self-effacing quality that Jane finds refreshing.

The Grainger set was donated by one of the Duchess's granddaughters. Its supplementary information file consists of the original bill of sale, transfer of title, notices on two royal inventories and a roughly drawn place setting for an afternoon tea given in honour of the Duke's return from India—complete with a small crown designating the chair for the Queen. There is also a letter from the Duchess to her cousin B— written on a thin blue sheaf of paper and dated *11 May 1884 . . . The weather has turned for the better though the wind is bothering my hat. At present Minnie is skittering about by the gazebo waiting to take the*

tea service away. I fear I won't have so much as a teacup to hold on to
should someone come across the lawn. . . .

The phone on the desk rings and Jane glances at it. It has
been ringing all morning: other archivists sending their condo-
lences; Jane's brother, Lewis, calling to ask if she's okay. Angling
the teacup she's holding to copy the number inked on its base,
Jane turns toward the phone as the long beep of the answering
machine goes off.

'Janey, *c'est moi*,' her father says, his voice filling the airless
room. And then, as if catching himself, he switches to English.
'Pick up if you are there.'

There's a small *click* as the teacup hits the base of the desk
lamp, a sound so delicate it's like a pebble being tossed against a
stone. Stunned, Jane looks at her open hand and then at the four
pieces of china settling next to the ledger in front of her. In the
white noise of Henri's silence on the other end of the line she
can hear her father's steady breathing.

'Janey?' He sounds annoyed, as if he is trying to decide
whether she's there, staring at the answering machine. Jane
hears a nasally exhalation and then the sound of him taking a
drag of his cigarette before he begins speaking quickly. 'Listen,
Lewis telephoned. I know about tonight. I can fly in next week
if you need me to. It would just be for a few days. Inga and I are
in Vienna.' He's using the same tone she's heard him use with
waitresses and drivers and lazy violinists. For a second there's the
muffled noise of him speaking to someone else. Jane can make
out *semaine* and *mettre au point*. She wonders briefly if he is
going to say something real, say William's name, or *Everything
will be okay*, or *I'm sorry I haven't called in so long*, but when his

voice returns, he adds, 'Lewis has the number of the *hôtel*,' and then there's the old-fashioned clatter of a phone being hung on its cradle.

In the quiet that follows, Jane takes off her cotton glove, reaches down and picks up the largest piece of the teacup, the section with the scroll handle still attached. This is her first accident in the eight years she's been at the Chester. It is as if she's seeing the shard from a distance, as if the floor of her office has gone slant. When she finds her breath she sets the piece on her palm to inspect it, the handle suddenly absurd—its bone-china ear attached to a wedge that can hold nothing.

We did not break the teacup. When the phone on the desk rang, most of us were crowded into the office, standing or sitting against the walls, some of us with our invisible chins cupped in our invisible hands, the children stirring tufts of dust along the baseboard even though we'd told them repeatedly to stop. If one of us had broken it, there would have been a ripple of tension in the throng. Such overt acts—touching the hair of those sleeping, opening doors, turning pages or knocking things over, even lifting the drooping heads of flowers in their vases—are forbidden. When they do happen, by mistake, out of rage or hope or despair at the constant watching and wishing, the reverberation is called 'fluttering.' We have only fluttered Jane once—when she stood on the bottom step in front of a house we wanted her to enter, all of us wishing her forward as a gust of wind.

Jane puts the piece with the handle down and smooths her skirt. She is thinking, *If the museum wasn't closing, I'd be sacked;*

and *Queen Victoria has probably held this teacup;* and *I've just cost the museum three thousand pounds.* Jane cares about the Duchess and her tea set, but we do not. The Duchess's life is well researched; her portrait has been painted, and her peach-skinned likeness hangs in the imagination because of it. Even Jane, when she was copying the milk pitcher's catalogue number onto the bill of sale, conjured her correctly: a plump woman in a wide-brimmed hat and striped dress sitting in the middle of a manicured lawn trying to stretch the act of sipping tea across the hours. What we care about is Jane. Jane who has the ability to show us back to ourselves, to bring our own faces and clothes and jaunty hats out of the past, to place us on lawns and in gardens and on the stoops of houses, an apron of sun before us.

The last time Jane spoke to her father was three years ago; he'd come to London and they'd met at a sleek new bar on the Strand. He'd suggested it, explaining that it was near his hotel. She remembers how the maître d' and bar manager deferred to Henri, how this made it obvious that he'd been in town for a good few days. He was hungry even though it was late, so he ordered a cut of steak that came to the table so rare Jane couldn't look at it. She kept to martinis, because Claire had liked martinis and she was somehow trying to conjure the presence of her mother even then. It was almost ten at night by the time they met, and earlier Jane had gone to Harrods to buy a new dress for the occasion. She'd ended up with an expensive green silk scoop-necked piece with pearl buttons up the back—a dress that made her feel self-conscious, as if she were trying too hard to impress him. She remembers now that the conversation was lopsided, the news all his, as if she were interviewing him for some lifestyle article and he felt obliged to speak overlong on every topic. He'd mentioned 'Inga' twice in relation to his tour of Croatia, and it had made sense at first because Inga was his management team's tour organizer, an athletic-looking Swede only a few years older than Jane who had Henri's whole world on speed-dial. But the third time her name was mentioned it was out of context—she'd joined him on a side trip to Hungary where he'd been commissioned to work with a young composer—and Jane realized Henri was trying to tell her that he was *with* Inga, officially, outwardly, in the way Jane's mother had suspected a whole decade before.

At the end of the night Henri waited outside with Jane for her taxi. He kissed her forehead, and in that brief press, standing between the warmth of his lips and the palm of his hand cupping the back of her head, she was happy. As the late-night crowd dwindled behind them, the last of the men and women heading out through the glass door of the bar had looked twice at Henri, because even though he was nearing sixty and dressed casually in black jeans and an old sweater, he was still a commanding figure.

As usual, Jane thinks now, there's a kind of arrogance behind his phone call: the assumption that he can sail back into her life, after years of dashed-off postcards, and help her; as if what happened between her and William, what happened to Lily, somehow involved him; as if he'd risen to the occasion for her back then, when she was fifteen and needed him.

Flexing her neck, Jane tries to slow her breath, get her thoughts together. She picks up a thin shard of porcelain and touches the nib of its ivy to her wrist, the point lightly pricking her. She calculates, numbly, that the teacup is one hundred and twenty-seven years old, imagines all the clumsy maids and careless children, the repeated washings it has endured—not to mention being packed up and carted across the country numerous times before and after the war. A delicate slip of a teacup that has survived all this, but, Jane realizes with a start, has not survived her.

Gareth knocks on Jane's office door and then, as he has done since the day he hired her, immediately walks in. She's still testing the point of the teacup against her wrist when he steps toward the desk.

'Busy?' He rubs his thumb under the bristle of his moustache and eyes the teacup.

'Not really.'

'Is that the Grainger?'

'It is.' She clears her throat. 'Was.'

He pulls his spectacles out of his pocket and leans in, the white tufts of hair on either side of his bald spot falling forward. When he straightens up he smooths them back with his palms. 'Listen, I rang Oliver at the V&A about you. He says they'll put you on their inventory list so that if something short-term comes up—'

'Lovely. Thanks. But don't go to any trouble.' Jane musters a smile, clasping her palms in front of her the way the girls who come through the museum on school tours do when they are corralled into queues and told to behave.

The state of Jane's office hasn't changed much in the six weeks since the news about the closure came down, and Jane can tell that Gareth, leaning sideways to look at the stack of solander boxes lined up under her worktable, is registering that fact for the first time. The oak file cabinets have yet to be emptied, a tray piled with books and papers is mushrooming on a swivel chair in the corner, the glass storage case that runs along the side wall is still filled with objects waiting for their archives to be compiled and packed—parts of the Hendry shell collection on the upper shelf, Glauber's seventeenth-century mammal compendium beside it and a variety of anatomical specimens below. Gareth walks over to get a better look. He slides the glass door back and lifts one of the spirit jars off the shelf and up to the overhead light. Inside, a hairless cat with a bony spine and thin tail floats in formalin; its eyes are stitched into slits, its ears curled forward and as long as a rabbit's.

'Ah, the feliform hare—I wondered where this had got to. I might keep this chap.'

Jane doesn't say anything, and so Gareth sets the jar back on the shelf and turns to face her. His right eyelid is sagging slightly, which always happens when he's overworked. 'Listen, Jane, I know the last few weeks have been difficult for you—for all of us—but you'll find something.' He drops a paternal hand onto her shoulder as he moves past her. 'Failing that, at least be reasonable and hold off doing away with yourself until there's room to cart a body out.' In the doorway Gareth puts his hand in his jacket pocket and rattles his keys, a habit that Jane realizes she'll miss terribly. 'And don't worry about the Grainger,' he adds. 'See what Paulo can do with it, and then let me know and I'll call the buyer. Things break, Jane, you ought to know that by now.'

Jane first met Gareth when she was twenty-six years old. It was the first time any of us had stepped foot inside the Chester. She'd graduated the year before with a Masters in archives and records management and had been recommended to him by the senior archivist at the special collections library where she'd interned. Gareth agreed to interview her even though the vacancy was for a short-term position and he knew people who could fill it. It was winter and crowds were milling around the natural history hall in squeaky boots and woolly sweaters; the cloakroom beside the small museum shop was packed with puffy coats. Jane was early for her interview, and nervous, so she wandered across the hall and down a row of display cabinets, stopping when she reached a large glass case on thick oak feet. It contained a series of criss-crossed branches upon which Nathanial Hartford, Esquire, had supervised the wire mounting of two hundred and four hummingbirds in an attempt to display all the colours and designs of the species. The birds were caught in various stages of rest or flight, their wings closed or spread out like the slats of a fan. Most people paused here briefly, if they stopped at all, but Jane studied each bird in turn, the dark beads of their eyes, their long bills, flamboyant gorgets. Those of us who had followed her into the museum studied the birds too, and watched her, the care she gave each individual thing.

'When is a bird no longer a bird?' one of us asked.

The question was soft, hung in the air like dust in a shaft of light. We turned toward the woman's voice and could see some semblance of form, as if a stranger had arrived and was standing on the far side of a crown-glass window.

'Hello?' another of us called, and the one with the soft voice said 'Hello' back.

In those days we didn't speak; some of us didn't even know we could. Instead we moved around Jane, around the city and the country the way the living sometimes do, heads bowed, caught up in our own half-formed preoccupations. But when this thought came out, it was voiced and heard, so we moved closer together and closer to Jane, suddenly aware of each other the way a group of strangers roused by a near-accident or noise on the street might look up from the sidewalk to discover they are not alone.

Before Jane, before the Chester Museum, there had been a long period of silence. It hung like a pendel on a chandelier, a heavy glass tear. Some of us woke in the woods to William shouting for Lily, others to the search party that followed, to men and women crashing through the forest, their flashlights arcing across the places where we'd been sleeping. Others of us woke years later to Jane's footsteps in the asylum wards when she visited the Whitmore as a graduate student, her heels clipping down a long corridor.

It was, for all of us, like waking from a long and fevered sleep, the nature of the self we woke to slowly taking shape. One of us said he looked for his hands but couldn't see them; another said that she moved toward a door that was nailed shut. What sense can be made of such a world, emptied of everything that was once familiar? When those of us who were in the woods saw Jane standing there in a panic we went forward to comfort her; when those of us who were at the Whitmore found her moving through the wards, we followed her from room to room. We did not say a word, did not even know there were others like us there; each of us was wholly alone in the whirl of our own uncertainty. In the gutted hall of what was once the Whitmore's women's gallery, Jane stopped and dropped her satchel on the floor, and so we stopped with her, watched her pry a wood board off the old window and peer out across the lawn toward the woods. There was a notebook sitting in the open mouth of her bag and she pulled it out and then rummaged around for a pen. On the top line of a fresh sheet of paper she wrote the word *Whitmore*—a blue scrawl we all moved toward.

How, you might ask, do we see ourselves? How have we come to understand our predicament? Look around you: everywhere life forces wanting to get out, things unintentionally contained, baskets of energy. One of us believes we are like atoms with no centre; the one who likes clocks says we are lost time. Another believes we are poems, another thinks we are dreams meant to sort useless information, another thinks we are like sheets set out on the summer line, holding fists of air. We all believe we are *Here*. Here the same way a street lamp exists in the useless hours of daylight, here the way the codes scrolling across Lewis's laboratory computers equal a bird's DNA. Here like the blue-plumed kingfisher when Lewis touched the screen and announced the bird's name.

Over the past eight years we have come to know each other the way Sam knows the other dogs who traverse the green—as members of some disparate, unarticulated society, a loosely affiliated fraternity that never stays exactly the same. But those days are waning. We have become obsessed with fixity: we now do daily counts, march out for rounds, try to ferret out who came when; who among us might have shared histories. But accountability is a dangerous game. It demands fidelity—to the possibility of less-than-illustrious histories; to whom, exactly, we might have been.

Jane plays the message from her father again and fights the urge to call him. She wants to tell him to come, but the nuances of what she is feeling about seeing William would be beyond his grasp, and in any case he's too far away—as always—to make a difference tonight. Her eyes drift up to the black dress hanging on the back of the door, and then to the clock that's counting down the hours to William's lecture.

It was a month ago that the Board of Trustees announced William Eliot as this year's recipient of the Chester-Wood Book Prize. Jane was sitting against the back wall of the meeting room on a rickety Queen Anne chair that had once belonged to Mrs. Charlotte Chester, wife of the museum's founder. She was waiting to make a short presentation on the deaccession process, had been only half listening to Gareth going over the final budget.

'The prize money, of course, will be deducted—' he'd said, and one of the board members—a woman who'd come from the art history department of a small university—interjected to ask if they knew who the recipient was. Gareth didn't even glance up, his ruddy face bent close to his papers. 'William Eliot for that book on Victorian plant hunters.' He flipped a page of the report and the rest of the board members followed.

Jane felt as if the room's temperature had dropped ten degrees. She leaned forward, thinking for a second that she might be sick. The art historian glanced over at her quizzically, but then turned her attention back to Gareth. Sometime between discussion of the gift shop's sales figures and admission revenues Jane stood up and inched along the wall toward the door, squeezing behind the chair of one of the more portly members. Gareth blinked up at her, then went back to his report.

A few days after that, Jane began to see William's name everywhere—in book reviews in the papers, in a short article in the Sunday magazine, on posters in the Chester gift shop, on books propped up in store windows, the image on the back showing him greying at the temples and soft-jawed but otherwise almost the same. It took her a week to summon the courage to pick the book up in her hands, and another week to buy it, sliding it across the shop counter uncertainly, as if it were a gift for someone who was almost a stranger, someone whose tastes she didn't know.

There is some debate amongst us as to how best to understand the trajectory of a life—ours, or that of another. We understand that most people fail to recognize patterns, get caught up in new details, in allowing familiar situations to assume new guises. We can be guilty of this too. Those of us who have been with Jane the longest feel a constant swell of hope and a recurring ebb of doubt about what she can do for us and why we're here. Some of us believe that one day she'll open a file, or read a document or a book, and some particular scrap of information will fall out and the door of the cage that we imagine we're in will swing open. Most days we want this, but once in a while we hesitate, worry about what will happen when we know ourselves, whether we will Cease. Besides, we have come to know Jane, so much so that for some of us it is unclear where she begins and we end. William is part of that—because he is important to Jane he has come to matter to us too.

Jane leaves her office with her lunch bag and heads into the thrum and busyness of the natural history hall. Sometimes it's like stepping onto a fairground—people moving in all directions, small crowds gathered around the various cases and cabinets *ooh*ing and *aah*ing, expressions of pleasure or surprise on their faces. On good weather days Jane tends to take her lunch break across the street in the park. There's a low wood bench that's angled toward the grey facade of the Chester—its proper columns, plain pediment, notched cornices. Jane likes watching the visitors heading in and out of the main doors, strangers whose body language she can try to read. Sometimes it surprises her— who bands together and who moves off alone, like a planet slipping out of its expected orbit. Once she saw a boy of nine or ten standing on the steps and nervously glancing around, his hands twisting the straps of his backpack. When his mother came out and found him she went to hug him, but he pushed her away, wanting, Jane imagined, to have outgrown her concern, or ashamed of his own.

As Jane heads past the Vlasak cabinet and toward the front

doors she's thinking about that boy, and then she's thinking—
her hand on the brass plate that pushes the door out and into the
world—that soon William will be on the other side of this very
door, about to come through it toward her.

5   The doors of the Chester Museum first opened in the spring of 1868. The day was so stormy that the windows were lashed with rain and the street outside the museum was clogged with carriages whose horses had lost sight of the cobblestones beneath them. There was knock after knock on Edmund Chester's door as the foyer of the house on Brompton Road slowly filled with members of the scientific community, men who arrived in sopping top hats, soaked overcoats and trousers with wet hems. Edmund's first exhibit consisted of a selection

of fossils, beetles, shell and bird specimens informally displayed in his home on that blustery Thursday. Stones and mineral shards and passerines covered his dining room table—the most striking of which was a mounted bowerbird that Edmund had positioned strategically next to a lamp, its bright-yellow cap and wings gleaming.

He opened the meeting with a round of sherry and a short explication of the beetle collection. The Society members stood alongside the mahogany table while Edmund passed some of his samples around on cuts of paper. The men brought the specimens close to their faces for inspection, or moved the beetles up and down on their palms as if testing whether an insect's heft might further reveal its aspect.

'This one is from southeast Africa, from the family Scarabaeidae,' Edmund said, holding up a large beetle with a glossy emerald-coloured shell. 'It's known to feed on flowers.' He handed the specimen to Norvill Farrington who had come to stand beside him. He saw now that Norvill was taller than him by six or seven inches, and dressed more formally than the evening demanded, as if he'd come from somewhere other than his own house.

Norvill took the beetle from Edmund. 'That one was brought back by Nicholson last month,' Edmund added. 'He has about twenty of them.'

'I've seen one of his already,' Norvill replied, turning back to the table. 'He brought it to lunch in a snuff box.' Norvill angled the cut of paper toward the lamplight to better gauge the beetle's luminescence. 'This one's antennae are quite distinct—'

The door at the back of the parlour swung open and Norvill paused as Mrs. Chester strode toward the gathering in a bustled blue dress. She was carrying her hat in a gloved hand as if she'd just returned home, and her dark hair glossed in the candlelight. Edmund kissed his young wife's cheek, and then responded to Norvill's comment about the antennae. 'They're allegedly for fighting over the females.'

Charlotte nodded at the assembled men, taking in each of their faces quickly; she knew all but one of them. 'Gentlemen,' she said as she curtseyed. She squeezed Edmund's arm. 'I've come to say good night.' Norvill stepped back to let her by and she glanced down at the beetle in his hand, said, 'It's a pity it's so delicate; it would make a very interesting piece of jewellery.'

In the end it was Norvill who remembered Charlotte's comment about the beetle and who, three years later when the collections were first opened to the public, suggested that Edmund commemorate the event by presenting his wife with a bracelet featuring the glass-encased scarab. Charlotte mentioned this in her diary—her surprise that Norvill would have paid such attention to a trifling comment on the night they first met.

It is just past one o'clock when Jane comes back from lunch. She is thinking about Charlotte's bracelet as she crosses the marble floor of the natural history hall, and we traipse behind her through the crowds who've come for the last day of public exhibition: a woman in a beaded shirt shaking her son's arm for rapping the shell of the giant tortoise, a young couple peering into a cabinet of sea stars. When Jane reaches the wrought-iron stairwell that curves up to the first-floor gallery she takes the steps two at a time, then follows the narrow spiral up again to the galleries on the second floor, thinking about Gareth's earlier words. Sitting on the bench outside the Chester, they had come back to her—his comment about the feliform hare, the cat–rabbit hybrid that was part of a collection of early Victorian hoaxes, an anatomical impossibility stitched together by a taxidermist and passed off for almost a year as a new species. She saw Gareth holding it in its spirit jar and saying, 'I might keep this chap' as the cat spun slowly around. It hadn't occurred to Jane when he said it, or in the stress of the weeks before, that certain things might not go to auction, those bits and pieces of a collection with less determinable value. Packing the containers of her lunch bag back up it had come to her with a jolt: the Chester family archives and the dozen or so personal objects associated with Edmund and Charlotte would be exactly the type to fall through the cracks. If Edmund Chester's museum—his life's work—was no longer supportable, who would care about his walking stick and ivory letter opener, Charlotte's pearl hair combs or her scarab bracelet?

Charlotte's bracelet is on display in a small room that was once their maid's quarters. There are five galleries on the second floor: the zoological specimens are in the centre gallery, with the scientific, botanical, ceramic and print galleries in satellite rooms. The Chester cabinet is in an alcove off the print gallery. When Jane walks through the main archway she finds a half-dozen people looking at the wall of early Victorian photographs and a man studying the explorer Fitzgerald's hand-drawn map of the Kalahari Basin but no one at the Chester cabinet, so she takes out her key and unlocks its glass door.

The Chester family collection wasn't properly archived when Jane was hired, even though Gareth had been wanting a display for years and had been setting aside any relevant documents or artifacts he'd come across since he was brought on as the museum's director. The cabinet now contains some five shelves of the family's belongings including a handwritten copy of one of Edmund's Society speeches, his open ledger, an invitation to the museum's first public exhibit, yellowed newspaper clippings and old photographs of early displays. On the middle shelf are two facsimile pages of Charlotte's diary in which she describes the delivery of a pair of mammoth tusks, as well as a sketch she made of the natural history hall in the 1880s and a caricature of Edmund carrying a whale on his back. Her hand-held mirror and pearl hair combs are nestled on the lowest shelf next to a square of needlework, two smelling-salts bottles, a jet brooch and the scarab bracelet—the beetle mounted in an overlarge bauble of glass and braced like a cameo on a wide velvet band.

There is no official history of the Chester Museum, but Jane, as the compiler of the Chester family's archives, has sifted through a number of descriptions of the museum's early years. Most of the details come from Edmund's letters, although Charlotte's diaries and various Society announcements have added to his account, and objects in the collection—like the presentation notes Edmund wrote up on cards for that first night's exhibit— have added to Jane's sense of how those early evenings unfolded, the men usually staying late for a round of drinks and cigars that Edmund gamely provided.

In the eight months it took Jane to catalogue Edmund's

letters and ledgers she came to imagine him clearly, and often it was the ephemera that revealed him to her the most: the arrangement of objects for his first exhibit hastily drawn on the back of his wife's note to the maid about cleaning the wainscotting; the names of those he'd invited in his daybook, each attendee checked off diligently in a firm hand or crossed off in bold strokes. This is one of the marvels of existence, Jane thinks, as she takes the bracelet off its support and lays it gently over her own wrist: that so much can be recreated; that all the bits and snippets—the receipts for roses, inventories tucked into books, even sherry glasses or cigar boxes or the worn clasp on a velvet band—are enough to conjure whole lives.

Three years after Edmund Chester's first exhibition in the parlour of his home, his 'museum'—a roped-off arrangement of three rooms on the lower floor of the house—was opened to the public. Visitors could come weekdays from noon until two and all day Saturday with tickets at a half-shilling. Thursday evenings the house was open from six until eight for gentleman members of the various societies, and once a month, on the last Friday, it was open to those gentlemen and their wives—though the florid regrets tucked into Edmund's daybook indicate that the wives rarely visited a second time. The lower rooms of the house had, by then, started to take on a distinctive fetor from exhibits that were not always properly preserved, and from the constant traipsing in and out of what Charlotte called 'the rabble'—men on their half-day off, reeking of the pubs, or women carting their children and market purchases. Even the padded chairs in the breakfast room adjacent to the display suites had started to emit a fusty smell, despite Charlotte's weekly airing of the house and her attempts to beat the cushions into scentless submission. By the end of the museum's first year Charlotte gave up, and she, Edmund and their young children removed themselves to the upper floors, resettling the 'step girl' in the almost uninhabitable attic.

Charlotte was interested in details. She wrote eloquently in her diary about the minutiae of the collections, about arguments and making up, about Edmund's ridiculousness and his quiet, attentive virtue. If Jane ever needs to know how to remove grease stains from hardwood or how to pin the femur of a *Loris* skeleton onto its pelvic bone, Charlotte's diaries can tell her. It is, Jane knows, one of the reasons she is drawn to the bracelet: Charlotte's ability to tell a story; the woman's side of a man's world, glimpsed in an age of exclusion. Charlotte's caricature of Edmund carrying the whale on his back was drawn on the bottom of a letter to her sister, a letter in which Charlotte recounted an overture made by Edmund one evening after a glass of brandy with a professor of zoology from Brest. He'd pulled up a chair beside their bed after the professor had left and broached the possibility of purchasing a bowhead skeleton. Charlotte sat up against the pillows and stared at him blankly. 'A bowhead skeleton?'

'Hilaire has one,' Edmund said. 'It won't cost much.'

Jane has always liked to imagine this scene and so we see it in the same way she does: Edmund would take Charlotte's hand in his and kiss her palm, revelling in the lilt of lavender or lilac on her wrist after the fug of the cigars downstairs. Buoyed by expectations, he would glance up at her smart, pretty face only to be surprised at the tightening of her jaw. In circumstances such as these it was his strategy to bide his time, to drop the matter and ask again after the next success: a write-up in the paper, a visit from someone notable. He would demur, say, 'We can talk about it later. I shouldn't have woken you.' Then he would set her hand down on the quilt and drop his own over it.

'Recklessness doesn't suit you, Neddy.' We can see Charlotte saying this firmly while extracting her hand. Can imagine her yanking the sheets made in Edmund's textile factory up around her neck as she turns to the wall and demands a proper house in which children can be raised without being subject to fantastical sea creatures and pickaxes. Charlotte informing Edmund, finally, that she refuses to speak to him again until he puts in an offer on the terraced house next door—an offer that, we know, would have demanded considerably more than he could afford.

Edmund Chester did well in manufacturing. His company's linens, at the end of the nineteenth century, could be found in one out of every eight respectable English houses. At the end of his life he wrote that he had only one real regret— that he would've liked to travel more, to have been a man of adventure himself. In the Chester's early years he'd confessed to Charlotte that he sensed it wasn't the museum, but his engagement with, and support of, a particular breed of gentlemen that would be his legacy. He believed things ought to be remembered as attached to the people who held them in their hands. 'What we pay attention to defines us,' he wrote in a letter to his son, when Thomas was twenty and preparing to enter law school. Edmund Chester paid attention to what the men and women of his time thought mattered, to what they carried back with them from their forays into Africa, Asia, the Arctic, Europe and the Middle East. What they brought back in sacks, caught in traps, nets, cut with chisels, fashioned with their own hands.

He wanted, in those years, to do more than make sheets on looms; he wanted to capture the fantastic and strange, to live a life in the zealous pursuit of knowledge. *I did not collect to own*, he wrote in one of his last letters. *I collected to create a discourse between the men of my day, and the larger world*. 'For it is not only *people* that constitute a society,' he'd said in one of his early Thursday evening lectures, 'but also places and *things*, and this museum will explore the relationship between them.'

Edmund did eventually purchase the house next door so that the original site could be renovated and used wholly for displays. Walking through the front doors of the museum today one first enters the high-ceilinged natural history hall, the room's outer walls rimmed by display cabinets, its centre bare save for the shadow cast by the long sought-after bowhead skeleton, which hangs on near-invisible wires from the second-storey ceiling. The first floor was opened up at the turn of the century to form a gallery around the whale, and today a dozen curiosity-style cabinets dot its walkways. The whale's phalanges swim so close to the east and west railings that people sometimes lean out and try to touch the nub of the bones with their fingers, a small stitch of space that cannot be bridged.

—

The sound of a little girl's shoes clapping across the hardwood floor of the print gallery rouses us. This is the nature of the dream: one minute we are in the world and the next we are Elsewhere trying to understand who and what we see. *It is Friday*, we remind ourselves, *it is Friday, and today the museum is closing.* Jane takes a last look at the bracelet, placing it hesitantly back on its stand, and then she locks the cabinet and turns to go downstairs. Our attention is divided, and so some of us start to wander off on our own, to move toward the long-case clock, the Victorian photographs, the Bedford cabinet.

'Stay together!' one of us snaps.

'This way,' demands another.

We try to get our bearings, find each other, round up the stragglers.

'Where's the girl?' Cat asks.

'Here I am!' the girl calls from somewhere near the botanical gallery.

'I'll get her,' the poet says, heading off in the girl's direction—bowing at the stuffed cassowary when he passes it, and lifting a hand in benediction at the stacked bones of the moa.

Those of us who turn to follow Jane stop when the boy cuts across our path. '*Aaarrrrrrr, aarrrrrrgh,*' he moans, waggling his arms over his head, because last month he wandered down into the cinema and a film about zombies—and now he thinks it's fun to pretend he's dead.

The staff room across from Jane's office is an aggrandized cubby with a kettle, fridge and a microwave. When Jane sticks her head in to look for Gareth she finds Duncan sitting on the counter next to the sink eating takeaway noodles with her chopsticks. He'd been packing the Murchison trilobites all morning, so knee-deep in crates that his sandy hair and T-shirt are covered in bits of cardboard. Duncan is Australian, and although he's been interning at the Chester for six months he still looks like he wandered in off the beach.

'Have you seen Gareth?'

'Nope, I've been with the creepy crawlies all day.'

'Where's the Murch going again?'

'Auction. It'll probably end up in a law office in Japan.'

'Do you know anything about the stuff that isn't going to auction?'

Duncan shrugs. 'I dunno—. eBay?' He wipes his mouth with the back of his hand, slides off the counter and leans in to Jane. 'You still the only one with no job to go to?'

'Har har.' She pokes his chest with her finger. When he gets to the doorway Jane says, 'I broke a teacup—' and a sense of relief from the admission washes over her.

'Which one?'

'A Grainger.'

Duncan lets out a low whistle. 'Well, better you than me. Let's raid the bar at the lecture to commiserate.'

Those of us who are in the room stop skimming the newspaper on the counter, stop staring at the blinking lights on the microwave. We turn to see if she'll confirm whether or not she's going to the lecture. All morning we've sensed flight in her, a waver she pushes down by thinking about the tasks at hand: after the tea set there's the Bedford collection, then a group of astronomical drawings to prepare, Lord Dutton's Italian glass, a set of French and German clocks going to a buyer in India. In storage there's a crate containing the hunting weapons and personal effects of the last of Louis the XIV's menagerie keepers, which Gareth had asked her to re-inventory weeks ago.

'You in there?' Duncan waves his hand in front of Jane's face.

'Yes. Barely.'

'Chin up, it'll work out.'

'What will?'

'Whatever it is you're mulling over.' He pecks her on the cheek and she can smell the tang of soy sauce on his breath.

'Hey, start washing my chopsticks or get your own.'

Duncan glances over to the sink where he's dropped them. 'The museum's *closing*, Jane, it's not like I'll need them again.'

Heading back to her office Jane thinks about the day Gareth hired her, how he'd asked her to come in to sign some papers, suggesting they meet in his office at six p.m. when things wouldn't be so busy. When all the paperwork was done he'd taken her on a tour around the museum. By then there was only a cleaning staff of two and a security guard in the building. He'd already arranged for a temporary pass and let her swipe into the old elevator at the back of the natural history hall. When the door opened on the second floor he'd handed her a pair of cotton gloves. 'I've got all the keys and codes,' he said. 'Tell me what you want to look at and we can take it out.' Over the next hour she held the claw of a *Tyrannosaurus*, a pine cone that Darwin had brought back on the *Beagle*, a pocket compass that had belonged to Franklin and an original folio of one of Marlowe's abandoned plays. 'Edmund collected *everything*,' Gareth laughed. 'There was no subject—no aspect of science or art—that didn't interest him.'

In the science gallery next to a brass model of the solar system, Gareth had explained to Jane that the intention behind the design of the museum was to evoke the warm and cluttered feel of the parlour where Edmund had first exhibited his collection, to display the objects in the same half-light to which the men who first studied them would have been subject. He pointed to an ornate wall lamp and added, 'There was overhead track lighting put in during the seventies but I had it taken out.' He leaned in to examine the drawer of beetle specimens, saying, 'There's something to it, isn't there.'

And Jane had agreed there was, though she didn't mean the lucent quality of the beetle shells under the gauzy circle of lamplight, or the metronome of the grandfather clock in the corner. In that after-hours visit, she had felt something else, felt that she was in someone's home—that any minute its occupants might clamber up the stairs and find her gawking at their things, find her somewhere she didn't belong.

6 The electric shock machine sits in the middle of the science gallery in a room that was once Edmund and Charlotte Chester's bedroom. The wallpaper, a hunter green with narrow beige stripes, is faded where the back of a wardrobe once rested against it, and the dark hardwood floors are worn in a line from the doorway to the wall where the dressing table once sat, and in a halo in the alcove near the window. Visitors today are guided around the room by narrow carpets that wind past the outer wall cabinets before angling toward the two vitrines in the room's

centre: one containing eight astrolabes collected by the astronomer Jacottet and the other a display of nineteenth-century
medical implements belonging to Ambrose Bedford.

In her dissertation work on rural asylums Jane had come
across Bedford's name a few times, twice in relation to the
Whitmore Hospital for Convalescent Lunatics. A relatively
minor figure in Victorian medical history, he was known mostly
as an innovator of galvanizing, or 'electrotherapy,' machines,
though his practitioner's licence was revoked after the deaths of
two of his patients. His surgical implements and three of his elec-
tro-medical prototypes had been willed to the hospital nearest
his estate after his death at the turn of the century. The collection, some twenty items all together, included three galvanizing
machines, two trephines to bore into the skull, a hysterotome,
various saws with tiny pointed teeth, a half-dozen mouth gags
and two sets of restraining straps—one made of cloth and
the other of leather. They'd arrived at the hospital in a large
wooden crate and were promptly relegated to storage. In 2005,
when a new administrator discovered them wedged behind an
old X-ray machine in a corner of the basement, she'd contacted
a handful of curators at some of the larger museums. No one
was interested. Eventually a local archivist who'd done her MA
degree with Jane directed the administrator to the Chester, and
the Bedford collection became Jane's first acquisition.

We know that Charles Leeson was introduced to the electric
shock machine a week before his escape into the woods. He

turned forty-three years old the day it happened. If the Whitmore staff had consulted his casebook they would have noted that the day's date, the 26th of July, corresponded to the anniversary of his birth, which would have explained his boisterous behaviour in the day room and insistence at breakfast that he be given a collop of bacon off everyone's plate.

A month after Leeson began his tenancy at the Whitmore, it had been reported that he was improving, and his brother had come up to see him, arriving in a hack and presenting Leeson with a paper bundle of cured meats and ripe cheeses. That appearance had not been repeated for a number of months, although Leeson had taken special care to strike off the days as late July approached in the hope that another such visit would occur on the occasion of his anniversary. He had spent the better part of a week imagining it in vivid detail: Richard appearing in the day room in his smart hat and gloves, carrying a parcel bound in twine and stepping aside gallantly to present Emily. But this was where the daydream fell apart, because try as Charles might to change it, Emily's expression always crumbled when she caught sight of her husband: a gaunt-faced man folding and unfolding his hands, his eyes darting around the room even as he attempted to fix them. In this reverie, the gift Richard pressed into Charles's arms was heavier than expected, as if it were a whole rump or shank of ham. When Leeson dropped his nose toward it, something inside it gave a kick and the parcel moved, causing him to search his brother's needle-like face for an explanation. None was offered, so Charles turned back toward Emily, only to find her over by the games table stroking Wick's cheek with a palm leaf and laughing at his pursed lips and upturned chin. Then the rain came, falling inside the day room, and Richard spoke between clenched teeth, glancing Charles with spittle, saying, 'The dark forces are upon you—' saying, 'The Lord giveth—' saying, 'The country will rally against—' saying, 'At a fixed rate of two percent interest—' saying, 'You will never see her again.'

This was how the daydream always ended, although Leeson tried, day after day, from the windows that faced the front lawn, to imagine Richard arriving all over again: Richard in his smart hat and gloves carrying a parcel bound in twine, stepping aside to present Emily. The idea of Emily was the one surety he depended on, though it became looser around the edges as the weeks passed by. In truth, Leeson knew that he could do without his brother, could live complete even if he never set eyes on his sour face again. Richard's arrival in the dream was a formality, a tic he needed to move past, some mental obstacle that blocked the real thing.

The dimmest of the hospital attendants during Leeson's stay was a thick-necked man called Bream. His features were contradictory—eyes small but heavily lashed, nose pocked but noble, the lips under his patchy moustache plump. Because of this he appeared both dainty and brutish, the latter quality inevitably winning out when he opened his mouth to speak. Perhaps this was why it came as a surprise to Leeson that Bream, of all people, would have been aware of his anniversary, entering Leeson's ward as he did, carrying a mahogany box on a silver tray. And perhaps it was because Bream was smiling that Leeson believed he was being brought tea—not tea slopped from a pot into a cup as usual, but tea displayed in a proper tea box, one that, when opened, would reveal rows of canisters containing a variety of imported leaves. Never mind that the gesture did not make sense after Bream's behaviour following breakfast: the big man had chased Leeson around the day room for upending the card table, had crossed his arms over Leeson's so that he couldn't move, had walked Leeson back toward his bed step by step, as if they were a four-legged monster in a sensation play.

'I'd rather—' Leeson had entreated before sensing the futility of his overture. Still, a few scuffled steps later, Bream, sensing Leeson's resignation, had relaxed his grip and the solicitor had wriggled free, marching quickly toward his ward unescorted.

A short time later, Dr. Thorpe strolled into the ward. He conferred with a tall, sallow-looking gentleman with reddish hair and a trimmed beard. Leeson grinned, delighted at the possibility of a party in his honour.

'Charles,' Thorpe began, slowly and clearly, 'this is Dr. Bedford. He is going to help ease your agitation.' Having announced this, Thorpe turned to Bedford and began to reiterate in low tones his patient's predicament, listing off the symptoms he'd later record in his report: increased anxiety, troubled sleep, fleeting moments of clarity as to the exact nature of the harm he'd caused and demands at odd hours to see a commissioner who could release him to Emily so that he might plead forgiveness for his error.

After this, Bedford sat stiffly on the edge of the mattress and repositioned the box Bream had set on the side table. He made a few notes about his perception of the patient—an amiable-seeming man who smiled up at him with pleasure, an expression that was both unexpected and welcome. Bedford had thus far taken his galvanizing machine to three asylums and his patients had ranged from wary to hysterical. The last patient here at the Whitmore, Hopper, had gone so far as to wrap his hands around Bedford's neck, reddening the medical electrician's skin before the attendants managed to free him.

Now, with the air of a man about to conduct a chamber orchestra, Bedford extended his arms, lifted the lid on the box and pulled out the wires. The door on the far side of the ward creaked open and Herschel came in to sit on his own bed behind Leeson's.

'What age is he?' Bedford asked Dr. Thorpe.

'Forty-three,' Leeson answered, tilting his head to get a better look at the selection of tea. Bedford pulled the electrodes from their case just then and drew the wire transmitters toward Leeson's hands, nodding for Bream to fasten his wrists so that the transmitters could be applied to the base of each palm. The attendant's hand descended just as Leeson jerked his own away.

'Easy now,' Bedford said, smiling reassuringly.

Suddenly aware of what was coming, and unsure how to stop it, Leeson opened and closed his mouth, trying to find the words that would rectify the misunderstanding. Bedford leaned close, whispered, *Shhh* as one might to a child. Bream, taking two strips of cotton from the doctor's black bag, bound Leeson's wrists to the bed frame and then stood back while Bedford made a few more adjustments to the dials on the front of the machine. Herschel, in the whitewash of the room, began to hiccup.

'Ready?' Bedford pursed his lips, then nodded at Superintendent Thorpe as if to allay the doubts Thorpe had expressed that very morning. It was a nod intended to communicate that they were alike: *two men in a world of imbeciles.* He turned back to the machine and flicked a small brass lever ever so gently with his knuckle. Leeson looked at his arm as the electric charge scurried up it and a wave of nausea rolled down his throat; a hundred points of light prickled his eyes. His bowels loosened and he had to clench his buttocks for fear of what might come out. Bedford's face appeared then in the air above him, a finger and thumb forcing his eye open.

'The jarring disrupts the electrical patterns in the brain,' Bedford announced to the room as he checked Leeson's eyes. He pulled out his pocket watch. 'It is a process that is best carried out gradually and not in one instant. We will administer two treatments today, two tomorrow, and then evaluate his progress.' He stood and turned to Thorpe. 'You will see results, sir, believe me.'

Leeson closed his eyes. Emily was in the room then—or so he thought—her gentle face a few inches above his.

When Leeson opened his eyes after his second fit, the doctor's hawk-like nose and tobacco-coloured moustache came into focus. Then a hand appeared, its fingers snapping over Leeson's forehead, and Bedford, speaking slowly as if through molasses, asked, 'Can you say your name, sir?'

Leeson steered his gaze away. Over the doctor's shoulder he saw Herschel, mouth ajar, hovering near the back wall of the room, his fat hands in his black hair. He sensed someone else observing but couldn't lift his head to see whom.

Ockley, the attendant who had replaced Bream for the afternoon session, shook Leeson's arm. 'Give 'em yer name.'

'Charles,' Leeson said, his eyes darting across the room to meet Herschel's.

'Excellent.' Bedford clapped his hands and then rubbed them together. 'It's too soon, of course, to see the results, but we ought to press on. I'd like to do another round tomorrow.'

Jane has procured support material for the Bedford collection that includes a transcript of Bedford's one surviving journal, case reports, personal letters and his final medical censure. Leeson's full name is nowhere to be found in these documents, though there are records of patients from around the date of the Whitmore visit, patients referred to as 'JH' and 'CL.' Superintendent Thorpe, probably regretting his association with Bedford as well as his own brief susceptibility to a programme he sensed was dangerous, seems to have expunged Bedford from many of the Whitmore's records. Still, we believe the electro-shock machine tells its own story. The strap that the doctor would have carried it by worn to dullness even as the box's wood remains polished, as if it were oiled regularly and stored with great care. Some of us are fascinated by it and others are averse, giving it a wide berth when we come upstairs with Jane to watch her dismantle the collection. One of us gently clearing his throat as if he can feel his air holes stoppered, just as we imagine Leeson did.

Bedford's letters and his journal also say a lot. From them we know that in the early years of his practice the good doctor often relied on analogy. In his journal he recorded an exchange with a patient, 'MP,' who'd come to see him in his home against her husband's wishes. He recounted his suggestion to her that electro-shock therapy was 'simply a matter of relighting the lamp of the brain,' noting how she'd turned to the lamp on the table beside him, considering it from under the brim of her hat. 'More accurately,' he added, 'it is a way not only of *relighting* the lamp, but of *refining* the wick to effect maximal illumination.' She'd smiled at that—the word *refine*.

Bedford's surviving letters to prospective patients make it clear that he honed this writerly skill over the years, describing treatment variously as a renewing bath, a match strike, a dusting off and reordering of prized books on a shelf. These ideas, he acknowledged in his journal, were inaccurate, but he believed they had proved serviceable to those who were not able to grasp the complexities of the matter.

What words, we wonder now as we look at Jane setting the galvanizing machine onto a trolley, would Bedford have used on Leeson? What might he have suggested to usher him toward acceptance? What within the world of that northern asylum might bring the most pleasure? Afternoons in the airing courts? Feminine company? Perhaps to be told of an arrival, a long-awaited visit? Yes, that would be it—to convince Leeson that the treatment would be like opening a door to the person in the world he most wanted to see.

7   Because the upper galleries will be roped off during William Eliot's lecture this evening, some of the second-floor cabinets are being disassembled already. Earlier, Gareth had asked Jane to show two contract-based conservators around, and they'd jumped right into the work. It had surprised Jane to learn that there were companies you could hire to assist with this, specialists who came in at the end to help pack things up. The supervisor, Judith, was efficient to the point of brusque, which was fine with Jane, but her assistant, Thad, was overly chipper.

Discussing the Hoffmann fossil cabinet, he'd said 'brilliant' so many times in a row that Jane had considered wrenching the clipboard out of his hands and swatting him over the head with it.

By mid-afternoon two of the cabinets in the botanical gallery have been emptied, and there are notable holes in the science and ceramic collections. Each unoccupied space has been endowed with a small place card that reads: *Sorry, this item is currently on loan to another museum,* or *Sorry, this item is currently undergoing restoration*—because there are no signs that read, *Sorry, this museum is closing.* When Jane had gone upstairs a few minutes ago to see if the conservators had everything they needed, Judith was taking the Neanderthal skull and pelvis to the lift on a trolley and Thad was trotting behind her so determinedly it looked as if he were afraid she might try to lose him. Gareth had told Jane that another half-dozen contract workers are scheduled to come in on Monday to work alongside the staff for the two weeks he expects the dismantling to take. Getting up from his desk he said, 'Don't worry, Jane, they'll stay out of your way,' waving his hand like someone who could make a whole group of people disappear with the flick of a wrist. Still, it was deflating. Watching Judith and Thad wheel away the anatomist's collection Jane is reminded of those people in Hazmat suits contracted to clean up after pensioner deaths or murder scenes—someone entering your world and taking it in hand even though they'd had nothing to do with it when it was vital.

Jane stops on the landing on her way back to her office and surveys the mix of locals and tourists who are wandering around the natural history hall below. She spots a clutch of girls in navy kilts and monogrammed blazers staring up at the whale skeleton while their teacher explains something about it. Another group from the same school is standing in a cluster near the Darwin cabinet. The girls' kilts are hemmed above the knee, their long hair is thickly fringed and there's a tight, self-conscious look on most of their made-up faces. Jane knows that Lily would be in her early twenties now, but always imagines her stuck at the age of these petulant girls—fourteen, fifteen—on that precipice between childhood and adulthood.

In the years after Lily disappeared, Jane imagined that William must have believed he'd see his daughter again the same way that Jane, after her mother died, still expected her to be at her desk under the stairs of the cottage, or to pull up outside Jane's flat and tap the car horn. But such belief dissipates. In the beginning William must have thought he would spend the rest of his life imagining his daughter rounding a corner and appearing before his eyes: Lily at six, at seven, at eight. He must have looked for her in the parks he walked past, in the crowds of children on tours at the Natural History Museum where he worked—fifty faces staring up at the giant woolly mammoth— and he would have glanced at each one of the girls as he passed by. But then slowly his grip on her must have loosened; he would have questioned whether or not he would know the shape of her face, the exact shade of her light-brown curls. At some point he probably stopped calculating her age. He would pack up his day's work in the herbarium, then stop to stare out at the inner courtyard and down toward the ferns. He would be forced to work it out and hate himself for it: *she was five when she disappeared, it was 1991 . . . what year is it now?* And he'd have to look at his desk calendar or picture himself dating a letter to ground himself: the exact date difficult to determine because it fell into a larger swell of time without purpose, and his head was filled with catalogues, inventories, procedural systems. His life one of habits—habits that dictated when to wake up, when to eat, at what hour to switch on the telly, when to go to bed, what list from the collections to mentally flip through in the half hour between getting under the covers and falling sleep.

The research probably saved him. When Jane saw *The Lost Gardens of England* on the shelf in the museum shop she imagined the writing of it would have been a kind of solace. There'd have been little room for Lily in a book on plant hunters of the nineteenth century, in the classifications of species, in letters and dispatches from Ningpo or the Casiquiare River, the descriptions of *Amaryllis* and *Lobelia* shipped back from the Cape. So she had conceived of the book as a kind of escape for him—until two weeks ago when she read it and got to the last chapter on George Farrington and the alpine gardens he'd planted up north, and realized that to write that chapter William must have had to visit the estate again, to drive up from London on the same road he and she and Lily had taken together and to canvass the trail at Inglewood much as he'd been doing when Lily disappeared.

Jane puts her hands on the railing to steady herself, and one of the schoolgirls below, a blonde with pencilled eyebrows and a long aristocratic nose whom Jane has been absent-mindedly staring at, gives her the two-fingered salute and then stalks off toward the Nelson cabinet. In a few hours she and all the other visitors will be gone, and Jane will be standing in a black dress by the door, greeting guests, greeting William. For years she has imagined his life, how it must have changed, what it must be like now: the compactness of it, the self-imposed isolation—like the shells in the Moore collection, something small and hard a body could curl into. A lump rises in her throat when, descending the stairs, she realizes that it's not really his life she's been imagining, but her own.

From a distance, patterns are easy to discern and people are predictable. Most have a habit of circling back to what they know, to places that feel safe and familiar. Over the past eight years we've come to know what Jane will pay attention to when she walks through the museum: which cabinets she will ignore, which ones she'll gaze at, which she'll open. But the past six weeks have changed everything. Her movements and intentions are affected by collections going up for auction, by the need to assemble documents according to other people's schedules, by the fact that William Eliot will be here giving a talk about his book. Jane is thinking less about us, and more about him because of this.

Until the announcement of the museum's closure, our lives followed patterns of their own. We acknowledged one another as fellow passengers might do, like commuters on a train. We took up watch over Jane in shifts, sailing past each other almost wordlessly. This was partly because it's easier to keep track of each other when there are only four or five of us in a room, but also because watching Jane isn't easy. When Jane drops honey into her tea, some of us gaze at the spoon and yearn to taste what it carries; when she puts her hands over her mouth and begins to cry, there are those of us who ache to comfort her. Watching her work has always been best—there is possibility in it, in hovering around her, hanging over our own hoped-for histories like question marks. *Keep going*, we'd say. *Open that file; look there.* Sometimes we thought she heard us. Especially on those days when she turned her attention back to N and the Whitmore, when she sent out inquiries, dug into the archives, asked the right questions, when she gazed, as she did this morning, at the galvanizing machine and thought about Leeson, or dreamed of the woods—instances that allow us to say, *Yes, that is close to what happened.* But sometimes her papers got shuffled around or were crumpled into the wastebasket; sometimes days went by without Jane giving a thought to us, and so we'd grow restless, argue about what we were doing here and if we should leave, as if what concerned one of us concerned us all.

Even though it is not allowed, we know that we can flutter Jane, that there are ways we can effect change. A month ago, when she heard that William had won the Chester-Wood Prize and would be reading at the award ceremony, she spent a whole night staring through the dark at the ceiling. At half-five in the morning she got out of bed, threw on jeans and a jumper and took the tube to William's house with the idea that seeing him beforehand was the only reasonable solution. She stood at the bottom of the walk for half an hour, thinking he'd step out to go to work, or that he'd notice her from the front window, be the one to come outside, that he'd know what to do. But then an upstairs light came on, and Jane lost her nerve. So we started wishing her up the steps, willing her toward the pearly circle of his door chime.

Morality is not solely the terrain of the living—we argued about what we were doing as it was happening, unsure if what was good for us was good for Jane. Still, we wanted her done with it, we wanted her attention back on us, so we gathered together in the blue curl of morning, put our hands out and *thought* Jane forward as hard as we could. There were whole seconds when it seemed she might go, when she lifted her foot onto the next step, reached out her hand.

'This is it,' we said. And in our excitement we lost our concentration, saw her shake her head and turn around. Watched the wrought-iron gate swing closed behind her.

Sometimes when we are brooding, when our own progress seems blocked, we turn our backs on Jane and her work, on the museum things we've come to love, and look for distraction. We sprawl on the roped-off furniture in the upper galleries, watch people pee in the loo, follow random strangers, wander outside the building. Some of us have braved travel and left the city, some have even given up—were here one day and then wavered like light on water and vanished the next. On the bad days we leave Jane to her work, drift aimlessly past cabinets and museum visitors or wander up to the second-storey gallery windows. Once there, we stare out at the brusque efficiency of a city going about its business—the awnings rolling up and down over the shops near the corner, umbrellas opening and closing, peoples' clothing changing weight and shape with the season—so that when we shake our heads to clear the dream, we sometimes find weeks have gone by in a flickering instant. We have come to think of time the way we think about the museum: that being inside it is like inhabiting the past, the present and the future simultaneously. This is why we have to stay awake, be vigilant: we need to believe that we, like the museum objects around us, bear time with equal complexity, that eventually we might discover who we have been, what purpose we serve and what use we might one day be.

At four o'clock, Jacek, the museum's security guard, places a wrought-iron stand with a Closed sign outside the front door, and the last patrons, a group of well-heeled elderly ladies and an American family carrying shopping bags, begin circulating quickly through the collections. An hour later the caterers come in through the loading bay and begin setting up in the corner of the natural history hall. By the time the final visitor, a Japanese girl picking through the discount postcards in the gift shop, has made her way out, a long table draped in linen has been set up and a raised stage and podium erected at the back of the room.

Jane comes out of her office just as the musicians arrive. They set down their instrument cases to rearrange the chairs and music stands placed on the dais, one of the young men bumping into the tortoise display behind him when he bends to pick up his violin.

The main hall is the kind of impressive room Edmund Chester dreamed about: his whale skeleton is suspended between four marble columns and the ceiling is painted blue above it, so that looking up at its bowed jaw and notched spine you can almost imagine it whole, see it steering itself across the ocean. The cabinets and long-cases that line the west wall are accordingly nautical in theme: turtle collections, navigational instruments, a display of fossils brought back on the *Beagle*. The cabinets on the opposite wall contain flora and fauna. The largest, the Vlasak cabinet, is an old oak hutch filled with a variety of plant models made entirely from glass: moss, fern leaves, pine and cypress cones, lace vine, a rose replete with thorns, a sprig of wild strawberry.

When we gather back together as a group we find Jane in front of this cabinet. She is wearing the dress her mother, Claire, wore the night she met Henri, a cap-sleeved Chanel from the 1950s with a ribbon-cinched waist and bell-shaped skirt. A photo exists of Claire in this dress, taken on the deck of a friend's boat as it puttered on the Seine: the occasion was an evening party, a group of the nearly-famous holding martinis in their hands. Claire, seventeen but passing for older, was standing next to Henri, to whom she had yet to be introduced, and Henri was staring at the photographer, a woman he was dating at the time. The group's faces were brightly overexposed as if they'd been caught out at something, Claire's hand on the rail near Henri's, the lights of the city bleary dots between them.

Jane is looking partly at the cabinet display and partly at her reflection in the glass. All day she has been trying to remember something her therapist had once said about how one defines oneself, about the power of intention. She was twenty and wanted to give up the cello. 'Why?' the therapist, Clive, had asked, and Jane shrugged. She could have said 'to spite myself' or 'to spite my father,' but by then she was tired of the rawness of trying to communicate everything, of feeling like every failure or step forward had to be brought back to what had happened in the woods when she was fifteen. So she gestured at the cello case propped in the corner of the room and said, 'You try lugging it everywhere.'

Behind Jane the musicians start to tune their instruments. The caterers set silver platters down on the long table, unwrap the canapés. We hear the *ting, ting* of glass touching glass as a waistcoated server stacks the stemware into triangles, as if the world is stable and nothing or no one can knock things over.

'She's going to leave,' one of us sighs.

'No, she's not,' says the idiot.

'*Ttthhhhhtttt*,' says the one who sucks on his teeth.

We look at Jane's reflection in the cabinet glass to gauge her mood and see the aching space of our absence. Twenty-five rows of chairs are cast back at us, along with the lectern where William will stand and a tall ceramic vase stuffed with oriental flowers.

'I'll wager you,' says the musician.

'Wager us what exactly?'

'She took a diazepam in the bathroom,' the theologian says, 'while you were all out here gaping at the quiche.'

'Our mouths divined with heaven,' intones the poet.

'*Vrrrooooooom*,' drones the boy, as if he's a jet fighter.

'*Shhh*, everyone, give her a bit,' the one with the soft voice says, watching Jane study the glass-blown rose, the wilted edges of its thin petals.

❦

What Jane remembers most vividly about the last time she saw William was the constable's desk where she was told to sit and wait. It was in the part of the police station she had never imagined—a brown-panelled backroom area where the officers piled their everyday coats on racks and kept outdated family photos on their desk, where coffee mugs emblazoned with phrases like 'World's Best Dad' were clustered on a card table next to a well-used coffee maker. The nameplate at the desk said *Shaun Holmes* in brass, and this made her think of the Sherlock books that her brother, Lewis, liked, and so, to distract herself, she tried to remember if Sherlock was the character's real first name, the one his mother gave him when he was born, or some kind of nickname. Shaun Holmes had a frame on his desk with a photo of an Alsatian that Jane thought probably came from a calendar of dogs. Maybe October was Alsatian month, and if she opened the frame and peeked at the back of the image she'd find the squares of September with notes like *Sara's birthday* or *dinner at K's* written in the boxes. But then Jane rationalized that if 'Sara' or her birthday mattered to Shaun Holmes, he'd have a photo of her in the frame instead. Constable Margaret Mobbs, the woman who'd brought Jane to the desk after her statement on the trail, after it became clear that Jane couldn't stop crying, came by after a while with a book for twelve-year-olds, milky tea from a vending machine and a packet of plain crisps. She stood there a moment and then touched Jane's head, said, 'I'll leave you to it?' Instead of replying, Jane reached out her finger and tapped the last silver ball of a set that hung from strings on a stupid contraption on Constable Holmes's desk. The ball clicked with a light *tock* into the next ball, which *tock*ed its neighbour in turn, the effect diminishing as it moved along.

'Newtonian,' Mobbs said. She wiped what appeared to be a line of dirt off her sun-baked cheek and a strand of dull-brown hair slipped out of its ponytail. 'Inertia.'

Jane had to concentrate to remember what that was, because she knew that she *knew* it, but didn't right then. What it meant *then* was that Lily was out in the woods and Shaun Holmes and everyone from everywhere was looking for her, and that one click could lead to another and at the end everything would be okay.

'Or cause and effect,' Mobbs added, then shrugged. 'Actually, I'm more of a history of the ancient world kind of girl.'

Hours later, long enough that Jane's grandparents would have arrived if they'd driven straight up from London, if they'd been home to take the call and not out at the ballet and having a drink after with the director of the symphony orchestra, Jane looked up from the Alsatian—who was a real dog after all—and saw William. He was hunched in his jacket behind a desk on the other side of the room, a survey map open in front of him, a Styrofoam cup that was still steaming placed on top. His gaze was directed down at the cup, and it stayed there for a long time, and Jane both wanted and did not want him to look up at her.

To test the sound, the cellist with the cropped red hair begins to play from the music sheet in front of her. The guests will start arriving soon and the musicians have yet to check the acoustics properly. The violinist, a gangly man with a boyish expression, folds his legs under his chair and joins in. Jane recognizes the

piece: a Dvořák quartet her father had encouraged her to practise, suggesting once that if she got good enough at it they might
try to play it together. And it's this—the memory of her father's
dissatisfaction, and the aching swell of the notes the cellist is
playing so beautifully—that makes her start toward the front
door of the Chester. If she failed at Dvořák and at the cello,
and if what happened with Lily made her a disappointment to
her father and to her mother, why should things be any different now, with William? That day in the police station, William
had known that Jane was sitting across the room, and for more
than an hour he refused to glance up at her. By the time her
grandparents arrived, the room was so full of volunteer search-
party members being handed maps, flashlights and headlamps
that Jane hadn't known if he was still there. Besides, she reasons
now as she puts her hand out to the door, if she were meant to
see William it would have happened—there have been conferences and lectures, probably a hundred near misses. In the years
before her grandmother died Jane was in his end of the city
every Sunday, two blocks down the road. Jane grabs the handle
and opens the door onto the street. If Gareth sees her now, or
Duncan or Paulo, she'll say she's just stepping out, going for a
walk before the party.

As we move to go outside a second violinist picks up the
thread of music and the movement swells.

'I know this piece!' the musician amongst us exclaims, and
he begins to nod along. After a few bars he hums loudly, matching the violinist note for note, and even though the cellist has
stopped to adjust her music stand he keeps singing and whirling
around. We get like this sometimes, when what is happening

to Jane becomes less important than what we can learn about ourselves. 'It's number twelve! Listen, listen!'

Outside, the evening air is surprisingly cool. Jane stands on the pavement, lifts her chin and watches as the clouds pull their veils over the city. *Rain,* she thinks, and squints skyward. Unsure of what she'll do, a few of us start to worry, and we argue about fluttering her again. Then the one singing Dvořák picks up the melody, his voice swaying loudly as if he's remembering the best piece of music on earth.

'Shut it!' the theologian shouts.

'Leave him be,' says the idiot.

'I can't think with the distraction,' the theologian seethes.

'Folly,' says the poet, 'on the hill behind the seat.'

The theologian exhales, and Cat says chirpily, 'Right. I'm going to go back in and poke my fingers into the sweets.'

The girl amongst us whispers, 'Wait,' with little-girl urgency. She turns to Jane and tries to wish her back inside, but Jane stays where she is, and what we know of the girl—her brightness, the soft plane of her presence—turns to us for help. When we don't do anything, she takes Jane's hand, flutters her own fingers over the open curve of Jane's palm, tracing and retracing the same path with such focus we can almost see her bent into her work.

'What are you writing?' we ask.

Jane lifts her hands and rubs them together.

'Is it a letter?'

'No.' The girl sighs, and when Jane drops her hands back to her sides the girl returns to what she was doing.

'Is it a word?'

'No.'

'What is it?'

Two months after she quit playing the cello Jane told her therapist that she was thinking of a career in museums. And to Clive's credit, even with everything he knew about William's job, he didn't say a word, just cocked an eyebrow and scribbled something into her folder. Then he closed it and set it down on the table.

Less than a year later, when Jane was reading the casebook of an asylum patient for a class assignment, the image of Clive's blue folder, with its two-dozen sheaves of paper, dropped so casually onto his side table, came back to haunt her. What if *those* documents—the details of what had happened to her and how she'd struggled after Lily disappeared—might one day be all that was left, the one bit of evidence that defined who she was? Jane's mother, if she spoke about Lily at all, always referred to 'that thing that happened'—as if Lily's disappearance were an altercation Jane had had in the schoolyard or some childhood accident and not the defining before and after of her life. This was partly why Jane took to studying asylum archives for her dissertation, why she later took to N—she was drawn to the idea of what falls off the side of the page, what goes missing.

Jane was thirty years old when she finally stopped seeing Clive. She'd been skipping sessions now and then and not saying much when she did go. She'd started sleeping around a bit before she and Ben got serious, and with no other fodder—no recently dead mothers or on-again, off-again father complaints—Clive had begun to make an issue of the promiscuity.

'Absolutely,' he said when she told him she was done. 'Terms of service—the client decides when they've had enough.'

She remembers how he shrugged, and that the shrug stung. Then he picked up the stress ball on his side table, sinking into his chair in that slouchy fat-gut way she hated. He was still tossing the ball back and forth from one hand to the other when she lifted her scarf and coat off the rack in the corner.

'So, we're done then?' he asked as if expecting a summary statement or some expression of thanks.

'It's not a divorce, Clive, and neither of us is dying.'

'Right then, best of luck.' He stood up and shook her hand in that hearty well-done-us way that reminded her of politicians on the telly after a particularly depressing summit. Then he sat down and watched her open the door. 'Small everyday acts of bravery, Jane'—she could hear the ball softly hitting his palm behind her—'small everyday acts.'

When Jane opens the door and steps back inside the Chester, we breathe a sigh of relief even though we're unsure what turn of thought has led her back in. While we were outside someone adjusted the lighting, and now the hall is glowing in lamplight, the marble floors gleaming, the bowhead fixed above us like a celestial being. The hummingbirds, the tortoise, the sixteen cabinets are all where we left them—our eyes settle on each display as if we are passengers on a train compulsively counting our bags to confirm that all our belongings are here. The girl is still beside Jane.

'What did you draw?' we ask her.

She shakes her head as if it's a secret.

'A picture?'

'No.'

'An arrow?'

'No.'

'What then?'

'Invisible cities,' says the girl.

8   It's almost seven o'clock when Jane gathers enough nerve to leave her office and enter the natural history hall. There are already a hundred people milling about, and the crowd is so noisy that the sprightly notes of the quartet's Vivaldi are almost lost under the chatter. Jane's mother liked to call rooms like this, filled with wealthy arts patrons, 'philanthropic rooms'—said disdainfully, because to Claire forging a career as an academic or a musician was something one *did*, whereas having money was something that happened to you. Claire came from old money,

but after she met Henri she sidled out of it, acted as if every success, every honour she earned, was achieved despite some vaguely difficult upbringing. At parties or conferences when people asked if she was Andrew Standen's daughter, she would say, 'the cabinet minister?'—then light up a cigarette and laugh bitterly as if the suggestion were ridiculous. It was the same for Jane except that Jane couldn't escape her lineage: at university she was Claire Standen's daughter, at social and charitable events she was Andrew Standen's grandchild and for the eighteen years she studied cello she was Henri Braud's offspring—even though her father had toured through most of her childhood and then left for good when Jane was sixteen.

Jane's mother had visited the Chester only once—three years after Jane started working there as the full-time archivist, and four or five months before Claire died. From where she's standing by the glass wall of the gift shop, Jane can almost track Claire's movements in the natural history hall that day. By then Claire had lost over a stone and had cropped her hair into a pixie cut so that its loss wouldn't be so noticeable. 'Look, I'm Twiggy,' she'd said, twirling around by the Nelson cabinet. Claire had loved unexpected parts of the collection: common seashells, flints, a Royal Worcester vase in over-bright colours, the Canopic jars secreted back from Egypt. She'd stopped at the mounted aardvark and touched his bristly snout, looking straight into his glass-bead eyes. The prognosis by then wasn't good—a few months, the doctors said, a year at the outside—and Claire had retreated, as she always did, into her intellect, filtering everything through irony and her sense of the absurd.

—

Duncan, scrubbed clean of cardboard dust and wearing a tuxedo, sidles up to Jane. She's already on her second glass of Chardonnay.

'Break anything this afternoon, Janey?'

Jane rolls her eyes at him even though she wants, irrationally, to unbutton his black jacket and bury her face against his chest, hide in the space between his lapels. It occurs to her, as she leans into him and he casually drapes his arm over her shoulder, that it was ridiculous not to take Lewis up on his offer to be here with her. A month ago when they'd met up at The Lamb and Lewis suggested he'd come to the lecture, she had said, 'No, no, I'll be all right, I can handle it.' No one at the Chester knows about Lily, and that's probably why she told Lewis she'd be fine—she didn't want anyone watching her, watching her and William.

'Big crowd for a book about gardens.' Duncan takes a sip of wine and surveys the audience, most of them standing and socializing around the empty seats. When he spots a pretty twenty-something in a black cocktail dress he lifts his arm off Jane's shoulder and straightens his bow tie. 'You ever heard of this guy?' His eyes follow the girl until he loses her.

'The author?' Jane stalls. To her relief, Duncan doesn't notice.

'That Judith's a bit of a ball-breaker, isn't she?'

'Sorry?'

Duncan glances at Jane. 'The conservation supervisor. I saw her come out of Gare's office and the look on his face—I swear I thought he'd had a stroke.'

'That's not funny.'

Duncan turns and gives Jane his full attention, leaning his right shoulder against the glass of the gift shop wall. 'You okay? You're acting a bit odd.' When Jane doesn't reply, his gaze drifts down to take in her dress and the heels she's wearing. When his eyes come back up they stop overlong at her chest. 'You look great, by the way. Your—'

Jane interjects before he says something crass. 'Have you read the book?' There is a large pressboard mock-up of *The Lost Gardens of England* staring down at them from over Duncan's shoulder.

'Nah. You?'

Jane nods.

'What's his name again, anyway?' Duncan takes another sip of wine and squints into the distance. 'Is it Wallace?'

'William,' Jane says, scanning the crowd. She can feel the muscles of her face trying to approximate indifference. 'William Eliot.'

Names are the most valuable things. We have always said this. They are more valuable than the clocks, books, photographs and objects we find ourselves circling; more important than the tortoise behind the musicians, than the logbook and slivers of wood from Nelson's ship in the nautical cabinet beside us. Names are pronouncements, entries, claims. Where things hold secrets—ones the people passing through the Chester do not always seek out—names state. They say, *I was, I am.* When the Chester first opened, it was the things that were highlighted: the wadded birds that could be stroked so that their feathers' remiges and vanes might be felt under the tip of a finger, the sea sponge modelled in glass that could be lifted toward a lamp and turned over, its latticework marvelled at. The pickaxe the explorer Hoburn carried on his expedition north was once swung through the air by the nephew of a Society member, one swift *swish* that startled everyone. Back then, names mattered less because the men attached to them still lived. But Edmund Chester knew better. He forecasted a future rife with forgetting. As much as we love his museum, as much as we love Jane, we must admit that if we thought in terms of currency, and if fluttering were allowed, we would pick up the gold astronomical clock in our hands, we would secrete Jane away, and we'd hold them both ransom for names. To have lost the thing that you have carried with you the whole of your life is no slight thing. This is why we stand around Jane's desk and crane our necks when she flips through censuses or logs, church registers, hospital records or ship manifests. We are looking for the slightest scrap of a signature, any blotted bit of ink we might know. Some of us mouth the names she writes down to see if the form they take is familiar, to see if we can slip into them like we would our own coats or favoured pair of shoes.

A day or two before Jane met Lewis at The Lamb to tell him about William Eliot's lecture, the suggestion arose that we should all take names. It was evening, and we were in Jane's flat and still reeling from news of the closure. One of us said that taking names would help us sort out who was who, be an expedient way to reference the speaker. He was over by the bookshelf perusing the spines, and after a minute he said, 'Call me John.' Most of us are superstitious and so we hesitated.

The theologian said, 'No.'

'I think we should all have a say,' John countered.

'Ah, democracy, excellent choice,' said the idiot.

It was almost ten o'clock and Jane was curled up on the sofa. There was an old black and white film on the television and she'd been drifting in and out of sleep. The dog was flopped down by the door, nosing the draft from the landing.

'What exactly is the motion?' the theologian asked from the window.

'That we take names,' John said, 'like I just did.'

'Pseudonyms,' the theologian corrected.

'What's that?' asked the girl, who was sitting on the floor watching the tail end of a commercial for mobile phones.

'It's sort of like a nickname, like the one the poet gave me. Except that it's an *assumed* name, an alias,' Cat said.

'You mean made up?'

Cat glanced at the television. The movie had come back on and the two main actors were facing each other, a man and a woman pretending to be real people, pretending to be in love. 'Yes,' she said, 'made up.'

'It's a false name,' the theologian added warily, not even bothering to turn around.

'What's the harm in voting?' John asked. 'Who's with me?'

A few of us raised our voices, started to argue. The poet cleared his throat.

'Stop talking!' the boy shouted. 'We're trying to watch the telly!'

Sam stood up and gave a low growl.

'Now look what you've done,' Cat said.

'Who started the dog up?' the theologian asked.

'My point exactly,' said John.

'Pay attention!' the boy seethed, turning back toward the screen.

We stopped talking and gathered around the television. The couple was now in a convertible driving along the coast. The woman had a silk scarf over her hair, the tip of it flapping lightly in the wind. They started to argue and the man jerked the wheel, pulling the car over to the side of the road under a cloud of dust. The woman threatened to get out. When the dust settled the man knocked his cap back with his knuckle and drew the actress toward him. She turned away and the music rose a notch.

'Haydn!' the musician shouted, figuring it out at last.

'It was better during the car chase.' The boy sighed.

Over by the door the dog slid his forelegs forward, his chest hitting the hardwood with a *thump*.

'What about the names?' John asked.

'Let's wait a bit longer,' we said, still watching the movie. 'See what happens.'

'Right,' John said tersely. 'Meaning wait and see what happens to me.'

It was the next day, or maybe the day after, that we went with Jane to meet Lewis at The Lamb. We remember the day almost as clearly as Jane does because of what she said at the end of it. She'd arrived at the pub early and instead of entering sat on the heath across the road to pass the time. A few of us lay on the green beside her, watching the clouds sweep overhead like lantern slides. Others sat by the pond and drifted into elsewheres: parks from childhood, village squares, meadows in some other when.

It was a Sunday, and when we went inside the pub it was quiet: a few couples finishing lunch by the windows, two men at the bar. Jane bought a pint and slid into a snug surrounded by diamonds of stained glass.

'Right,' one of us said, picking up the thread of the conversation we'd been having on the heath, 'so if everything Ceases eventually—'

'Not a hypothetical,' the theologian interjected.

'*If* everything Ceases, then why are we still here?'

'Because,' the theologian snapped, 'we've *chosen* to be here.'

'To what end?' John asked.

'Love,' sang Cat.

'Fear,' the poet ventured. 'The alternative being unthinkable.'

The one we call the idiot sighed and said wearily, 'Listen. Matter is equivalent to energy, it cannot be lost; it can only be transferred. The physical system, endowed as it is with an unobserved quantity—'

The theologian clapped his hands together. 'Who's up for today's pub quiz?'

'I am!' Cat said.

'Fine. Ready? Tell us something you like. First thing that springs to mind.'

'Cats,' she shouted. This was her usual answer.

'Excellent. Anyone else?'

'Chopin!'

'Good, next?'

'Those white sweets with green inside. What is that?'

'Mint,' we said.

'Anyone else?'

Beside us Jane lifted her glass and took a sip, wiped a daub of froth from her lip with her finger.

'Stout!' a gruff old voice shouted, a voice we rarely heard. And, happy for him, we cheered.

Duncan excuses himself to head to the bar and Jane stays where she is, at the edge of the gathering, the door that leads to the staff offices a quick twenty paces behind her. Some of the crowd are migrating to their seats and the music has become more sombre as if it is trying to lull the audience into a more attentive state of mind.

From where she is standing Jane can sometimes see Gareth's head as he moves around the room shaking hands. He doesn't have anyone with him, which means that William isn't here yet. Twice Gareth has moved in the direction of the front door and Jane's pulse has started racing—but in both instances he then steered toward another circle of people. The second group includes a tall redhead with a glint of diamonds on her neck, a woman who Jane realizes is Dr. Osborne, the science director William works with at the Natural History Museum. If Lewis had come, if Jane had let him, Dr. Osborne is exactly the kind of person he'd be interested in talking to. He'd have launched into some specialized topic with the good doctor—phylogenies or evolutionary convergence—forgetting that it is his job to protect Jane.

What Jane remembers now about the day she met Lewis at The Lamb is how relieved she was to talk with him. He'd tossed his car keys onto the table and leaned down to kiss her on the cheek, his face smelling soapy and clean.

'Sorry I'm late. Natalie just got back from yoga and I had the girls.'

Jane hadn't seen him in two weeks and he had a new haircut, his brown locks cropped in a vaguely Roman style with a short horizontal fringe. 'All hail Caesar,' she said as he flopped onto the bench.

He stretched his long legs out under the table. 'You look good.'

Jane crossed her eyes and made a face. Lewis was playing nice. He always played nice—the little brother with the big house, lovely wife and brilliant kids, trying to bolster his cloistered sister.

After the first round of pints Lewis broached the situation with the Chester. He put his feet on the bench beside Jane and said, 'Well, the upshot is, if the museum closes and you don't find work right away, we'll probably see you more. The girls miss their auntie.'

Jane mustered a smile, wanting him to believe she'd been sufficiently encouraged. 'I was thinking I might go up to the cottage if I can't find anything straight away, air the place out, go through mum's things. We have to start thinking about selling it.'

'I know. But if we do—*if*—I'd still want to wait until the market's better. You want the Merc?'

'If you can spare it.'

'Gran left it to both of us.' Lewis tapped his fingers on the table; clean white crescent moons.

'So how goes the—?' Jane narrowed her eyes trying to remember what bird he was on now.

'Pigeon?' he offered.

'Wasn't it a starling?'

'We finished that weeks ago. Now we're on to passenger pigeons.'

'Very sexy.' She plucked a petal off the daisy hanging out of the finger vase in front of her.

Lewis picked up his coaster and flung it at her head. 'I don't make fun of your narwhal horns.'

'It's a narwhal *tooth*.'

'Actually, you'd like this pigeon. We got it frozen—from an American zoo of all places—so we're working from that.'

'Aren't passenger pigeons the ones that carry little scrolled-up messages in tubes around their neck?'

Lewis tilted his head, trying to decide if she was having him on. 'Leg, Jane, around their *leg*. You're thinking of the *carrier* pigeon—or a St. Bernard. The passenger is extinct. Ka-put. Gone.'

Most of us paid attention when Lewis spoke about work. We had enjoyed the field trip we took with Jane to his new lab outside the city, recalled the strange feeling we had watching computer screens in white rooms sequence creatures we only knew as corporeal things: bodies we saw flit through woods, peck across lawns, ones we saw wired in the cases of the museum. We were like the school kids who came to the Chester, overwhelmed and giddy; the theologian like an obstinate teacher asked to surrender control of his class. While the rest of us wandered in our little group from lab to lab, the theologian paced along a walkway that overlooked a clipped lawn bordered by tear-shaped hedges. In the atrium, Lewis had introduced Jane to a colleague called Shiro, who bowed stiffly before escorting her toward the aviary. His guided tour was rehearsed. He recited a string of statistics and findings, said that there were five international teams vying for the full genome patents of each avian species. 'Every day is a race,' Shiro added, swiping his pass to access a room at the back of the facility, 'and right now we are in second place.'

When the tour was done, Jane rejoined Lewis in the lab where his team was working. He pointed to a multicoloured pattern of squares running down his computer screen and said, 'This is the kingfisher.'

One of us whistled three times and then flapped both arms in the air.

'*Whoosh!*' shouted another from a different computer, as if the bright pattern on that screen had suddenly swerved into a bird wing and the bird had lifted off.

'*Cheep cheep*,' said a third—for no reason we could discern— and soon we were all flitting about and cackling with laughter.

That day at The Lamb, listening to Lewis talk about his work, most of us felt happy. We liked to think about the afterlife of birds, the idea that a scroll of data on a computer might one day bring the passenger pigeon back into the world. The theologian was less enthused. He turned to those of us standing around the snug and said grittily, 'I would like the record to show, once and for all, that birds, like all living things, are tangles of DNA and that we, to the best of our knowledge, are *not*, so we ought not to care about whether Lewis's lab maps the genome of every living thing on the planet or makes toasters.'

'*Atomus*,' said the idiot, 'from the Greek for indivisible. Matter being what it is, it *is* plausible that we—'

Cat yawned loudly. A ruckus broke out by the cigarette

machine. The one who never speaks began waving his arms up and down vigorously.

'See?' John said, 'we're not so unlike Lewis's pigeons.'

'I fail to see the analogy,' the theologian said stiffly.

The arm waving increased and the flurry of commotion drew closer. The daisy bobbed its head in its vase and Jane's napkin drifted off her lap and onto the floor.

'Enough!' the theologian snapped.

'Who put you in charge?' John asked.

All of us stopped what we were doing except for the one flapping over by the wall. Jane picked up her napkin.

'Are you saying *you* ought to be in charge?'

'Maybe,' John said.

'And you actually think you're fit for the job?'

'As fit as you.'

'As fit as me? Sorry, but we are not equals, *John*,' the theologian said. 'I am not like you.'

'Meaning?'

'Meaning I'm not mad.'

A woman in a light-pink summer jacket who'd been sitting at a table by the door walked through the group of us towards the loo. We shuddered, could smell the laundry soap on her clothes, the trace of a lemon wedge on her fingers. Whenever a physical form moved quickly through our throng—or we through it—a feeling of disarray came over us.

'What's "mad?"' asked the girl.

'Or who,' said the poet.

'It's a kind of preoccupation,' said the one with the soft voice.

'It's everything-all-at-one-time,' Cat added.

'Well, we have *that* in common,' John said, watching the door the woman in the pink jacket had gone through. 'We're all susceptible to moving forms, which means we're all—'

'*Twoo, twoo,*' insisted the voice by the cigarette machine.

'Dear God,' said the musician.

And the arm waving started again, except this time Cat joined in, and then John, and even the boy cried *caw-caw* as he staggered around the pub like a monster.

Jane takes a glass of white wine from a waiter's tray and wanders to the back of the hall to stand by the Vlasak cabinet while she waits for the lecture to start. She can see Gareth milling around by the bar, sipping Mortlach from his private stash and chatting up Randall Wood, the Chester Prize's co-founder. A few acquaintances from other museums come by to talk with Jane, stay for a minute or two asking after work prospects, and then, finding Jane anxious and distracted, excuse themselves to circulate amongst the crowd. When no one is looking, Jane turns toward the side of the mahogany cabinet and drains the last half of her glass of wine, closing her eyes at the calming effect.

'Brilliant,' the theologian says. 'Here we go again.'

'Wouldn't you?' Cat snaps. She moves toward Jane, has an overwhelming desire to put her arms around her.

A few minutes later, Gareth passes through the crowd near Jane and raises a hand in greeting; his tufty white eyebrows flare up as if to say, *What are you doing back here?* Then he slips between a woman in a red jacket and a man in a grey suit, moving in the direction of the main door. Jane calculates that he's probably seen William arrive and is going to greet him. She starts for the bar.

'What do we do?' Cat asks.

'Abandon ship,' the musician says.

'*Ka-pow, ka-pow*,' shoots the boy, and the girl standing next to him whispers, 'Stop it.'

'And the handbook says?' This is the theologian's favourite quip, his way of taking pleasure in our confusion, as if there were a handbook, as if we could even open it if such a thing existed.

'We stay with her,' the one with the soft voice says, and the poet throws his arms overhead and intones: 'And so to enter the last chamber of the ungated world.'

When Lewis came back from the bar that day at The Lamb, dropping a last round of pints on the table and plunking himself down on the bench, Jane closed her eyes tight and said the one thing she'd been holding back. 'William Eliot's written a book.' Then she opened an eye to gauge the expression on his face.

When Jane was growing up, Lewis was the only person other than Clive who'd let her talk openly about what had happened with Lily. But ever since he and Natalie had the girls, she'd been unsure how the mention of Lily would sit with him. As soon as William's name was out of her mouth, she was sorry she'd said it.

'A book on what?' Lewis looked peeved.

'Victorian plant hunters.' She moved the pint Lewis had set in front of her closer and a dollop of stout slopped over the side.

'And?'

'And nothing.' Jane tugged a few napkins out of the dispenser to wipe up the spill, and then, without looking up, added, 'He's giving this year's lecture at the Chester.'

'Oh. I see.' Lewis tilted his head to try to catch her eye; it reminded her of when she'd go to his house for curry night, how she'd notice him trying to calculate whether she was on her third or fourth glass of wine. 'You want to talk about it?'

'I'm sure it'll be fine. We'll say, "Heya," there'll be a load of *Rhododendron* prattle, that kind of thing.'

'Naturally.' And that's when Lewis asked if he should come, and Jane said she'd be okay without him.

'Mostly it's just got me thinking,' she said. 'I've got all that research on rural asylums—you know that paper I was working on? Maybe *I* could write a book.'

'A book?'

'On the Whitmore and the mystery of N. You know, the problem of the historical record.'

Lewis placed his head in his hands. As if he was tired, as if he had been listening to her make things up for a hundred years, as if he was bored of watching her try to copy everyone else; as if she'd never find something of her own.

'I could do it,' she said.

Lewis drained his pint and then patted his jacket pockets to locate his keys. He said, quietly, 'I didn't say you couldn't.'

We remember the exact moment Jane brought up the idea of the book. We remember it because we thought it would change things.

'Did you hear that?' John asked.

And those of us who'd wandered away from the snug turned our attention back to the conversation. We had been distracted by a couple at the bar having a row about where they wanted to holiday and if they could afford a five-star. The boy, who was fluttering the specks of salt on the table, stopped when the theologian stood over him.

'Hear what?' we asked, some of us still weighing the pros and cons of a beach hotel in a country whose name sounded like white sand.

'She was talking about the Whitmore; she said she might write about it.'

'How long ago was the Whitmore?' Cat asked, trying to splay time into a chronology. 'And what came first?'

'A waterfall,' the boy said.

'*Tweep tweep,*' called a voice from the other side of the room.

'Magpie!' shouted the musician.

The theologian interjected. 'I think the woods were first.'

'Was it a hundred years ago?' we asked, because we easily forget numbers.

'Once again, time is relative,' the idiot said, and the theologian grunted.

'The dates are in Jane's book,' the one with the soft voice said, and then Lewis stood up and we stopped our bickering.

'I wish,' Cat said, looking at the receipt Lewis had left on the table, 'that we could write things down like people do. I forget sometimes what matters to me and what matters to everyone else. How can we figure anything out if we all start thinking we like stout, or—' She gestured to the girl, who'd wandered off toward the bright flickering keno lights. 'That we like bedtime stories, or—' She lifted her hand toward the boy kneeling on the bench near the window.

'Dogs. I like dogs.'

'Exactly.' She sighed. 'See? I think I like dogs too.'

'Maybe you do,' John said, 'maybe we all do. Suppose it's the *why* that matters.'

'*Why* I like dogs?'

'Yes. Why.'

'Terriers,' the boy said, staring out at the playing field through a pane of yellow stained glass, 'I like terriers.' He turned toward us. 'Have I said terriers before? Or just dogs?'

'Terriers,' we all replied.

'Which is why we have Jane,' John said, watching her as she shrugged on her cardigan. 'Even if we could write "terrier" down on a scratch pad we'd probably forget we'd done it or where it got put.'

'Writing is against the rules,' the theologian intoned.

'Na-na-na-na,' the musician chided before drifting over to the dartboards.

'In the meantime—' Cat reached her arm out toward the boy, who was watching two teenagers kick a ball back and forth over the green. 'In the meantime,' she repeated, when he didn't feel her shape trying to touch his, trying to show him that everyone was going, 'we will all try to remind you every day—okay, everyone? *Terriers.*'

'One terrier,' he said, as the teenagers, in their brightly numbered jerseys, moved farther into the field. 'Dock.' He turned to us as he said the name.

'Dock?' we asked. 'Is that the dog's name or what they called you?'

'Dock,' he repeated. 'Dock,' saying it quietly. 'The dog's, maybe? I'm not sure.'

Lewis put on his jacket, pocketed his wallet and said, 'Walk you to the tube?'

Jane slipped her arm through his and squeezed tightly. We could tell she was relieved to have told someone about William, even if the conversation hadn't gone the way she'd wanted.

We turned to leave. If we lost track of Jane we'd have to make our way back to her flat on our own, which meant there was a chance we might get lost, spend hours or days making mistakes in direction. The boy suddenly called out, 'It was the dog's name! He was brown and white and he liked crusts of bread and *I* named him.'

So out we went, giddy from our progress, the boy imploring from the back of the group, 'Can we please, please, please try not to forget.'

We haven't forgotten the dog. And we haven't forgotten what Jane said about writing a book. But things are different now. We bristle when the subject comes up. The night a few weeks ago when she pushed her Whitmore files under the bed, some of us stormed out, and some of us stood over her while she was sleeping and called her a liar. So now, when Gareth steps onto the stage to place a jug of water and a glass on the low table beside the lectern, and Jane goes up on her toes to see if William is standing in the crowd nearby, some of us are wishing her well and some of us are just wanting the production over with. The boy, full of pent-up energy, is zooming around, while the girl walks in circles around Jane the way children sometimes do, running their fingers around the bell of a skirt or along the silky waves of a curtain.

'Come here, sweetie,' the one with the soft voice says, and the girl wanders back to us.

'Who's that?' the girl asks when she's back in the fold, and we turn to where she's pointing, to the marble bust of the museum founder sitting on its pillar at the far side of the stage.

'That's Mr. Chester. Edmund Chester,' we say, and his name feels good coming out of our mouths, the sure shape of it.

This is the wonder of names. Like the press of a footprint in the snow: proof that someone has been there.

9   There is a scattering of applause during Gareth's introductory speech when he mentions that the Chester Museum has been exhibiting the work of individual collectors for one hundred and forty-two years. He waits until the applause subsides, nods to acknowledge it, and then continues. 'Edmund Chester was a man of his time, of the Industrial era, in that he valued and upheld the two most prevalent ideals of his age: progress and mastery. For Edmund, society's ability to move forward and look back simultaneously was a wonder. The men that

he admired, those he surrounded himself with, strove to understand the world in new ways, to mechanize it, simplify it and
coordinate it, while also preserving and revelling in the past and
in the fortitude of the elements. Men of his generation didn't
rest on their inheritances; they used their money and titles to
ferret out new possibilities, business models, technologies, rem-
edies and inventions, formulae that could be shared among all
kinds and classes of people, that could affect how all members
of society lived their lives. The associations to which Edmund
belonged, the fraternity to whom we—as inheritors of this collection—owe a debt of gratitude, believed that they had come
of age in an era of optimism and vitality, one that was a means
to a new kind of power, a power that was not exempt from
accountability. Those who didn't invest in factories or inventions supported local homes, schools and civic institutions. Like
Edmund they believed that knowledge mattered, that our history, values and society were reflected in how we regarded and
understood the material world—a material world that wasn't
limited to the creatures and specimens found in nature but one
that extended to those things we made ourselves.'

Jane can detect a hint of anger in Gareth's voice, a gruff-
ness that she's only heard a few times, most distinctly when he
announced the museum's closure. He has been the director and
head curator at the Chester for almost thirty years, and he helped
vote in the very government that is cutting museum funding.
Jane knows that when Gareth was a young boy his mother
brought him here once a summer, packing sandwiches and a
canister of tea. After they wandered through the museum they'd
lunch in the park across the street because it wasn't gated then

and anyone could use it. Seeing his interest in the diorama of exotic animals—the mounted wolf and the moose whose great antlers had been hung with pondweed—his mother bought him a book on mammals. In the year that followed, whenever he was stuck inside the house because of pollen counts and the cotton that seemed to puff up in his chest, she'd give him quizzes on the mammals' Latin names, on their subspecies, diets and habitats.

Gareth had told all this to the Minister when he'd invited him to tour the museum a month ago. As Jane trailed behind them, she heard Gareth explain that he knew what it was like to visit a museum and carry the experience back into the world. Even back then, Gareth said, he knew that the scientific instruments and plant models he saw in those cabinets had applications and counterparts in the landscape he walked through every day to school. The Minister seemed to see it otherwise: he thought of museums like the Chester as a series of dimly lit rooms where things that were interesting but no longer relevant were shelved. He barely glanced at the displays, seemed to take more interest in the walkway carpet. 'Cutting the museum's funding is a mistake,' Gareth had said. Jane knew he thought it was a poorly conceived cost-cutting measure by a government that specialized in being shortsighted, that was ignorant about the finite nature of resources, whether natural, man-made or ephemeral. Gareth understood the black and white economics, but not the sense of it. He had done his best to appeal the decision, but no one in power had budged.

What, Jane wonders now, would Edmund Chester make of the museum's closing? Of the long-case clock auctioned off to a private buyer in the south for a coastal home he'd hardly set foot in, of the birds going to a lawyer, the Darwin collection to a bank executive, of the whale bones being shipped to a failing aquarium halfway around the globe? Even the specimen jars that were part of the original collection had been packed into padded cases and would soon be driven down the road to the Natural History Museum, where they'd be left in storage because that museum did not have room to display them.

Edmund had not been ashamed to admit that he loved *things*. In his letters and journals he praised everything from a piston to a pendulum, a cluster of mushrooms in the woods to his factory—a place he loved for the way it expressed a work-ing order, a procedural seamlessness, though he also knew from his own encounters with misfortune that order was an illusion. Jane thinks that the museum was his refuge in this way—a per-fect expression of the largely mysterious world, of the gaps in mankind's knowledge, of the delight of the newly discovered, all under the shelter of one roof. For Edmund, the collection must have been like a giant puzzle, and he'd occupied himself with fitting one piece into the next, whole years spent expanding the imagined frame. The museum was his way of capturing the accomplishments and wonder of men's lives in rooms that testi-fied to their efforts and erudition—men like Arthur Nicholson and Perry Humphrey, men like Norvill Farrington, who, in those early years, held up the scarab beetle on its card of paper and explained to those gathered how the wings made a chirring sound, a mode of vibration that caused the body to sing.

What would Edmund Chester have said he'd accomplished, if he'd had time to say so on his last day on earth? Jane thinks of him as a man of science. His pleasure was in the 'how' of the world, its palpability, its reverberations. Even when lifting Charlotte's chin with his hand in the happy years of their marriage he had probably marvelled at how her eyelids lowered the slightest bit; how her lips parted in anticipation. His life was one of constant study: measuring inches of cloth by hours, assembling fossils bone by articulated bone, weighing his grief against his joys, his discoveries against his losses. In the end perhaps he would have said he had offered people a glimpse of the wonder of the world; he'd helped expose its mysterious workings.

A year or so before his death, Edmund wrote a letter to his son about what he called a series of 'disagreements' with the house clock. This letter is one of Jane's favourites. Sitting on the landing, his shirt sleeves rolled up to the elbow, the guts of the old longcase clock on the floor around him, its pendulum stilled, he found himself thinking, *This is the symbol of the age*: the world's workings laid out before us, and those of us with the patience to sort through the intricacies casting about its parts. He admitted that on some nights he'd wake with a start and hold his breath until he could make out the clock at the base of the stairs ticking. How even though the maid wiped its brass bezel and glass regularly, he often took a cloth to it himself because it gave him pleasure that the cut of cloth he used came from his own factory, and that the clock face was aging as he aged, that it too needed tending.

Edmund also liked a good gathering. If he were here tonight to see his museum closing, the collection dispersed, Jane thinks he might have been pragmatic enough to enjoy the champagne, to take his wife's gloved hand in his and say, *Let's begin again.* He might have reinvented himself, bolstered himself by dwelling on what was possible. Jane is under no such delusion about herself. She took up the cello and then gave up the cello; she went to university to study archive and records management and then came to the Chester to work. Standing in a hall full of people bursting with enthusiasm about their own careers she finds herself with no secret or special skills, no hidden reserve of optimism, and little imagination for reinvention. Instead she has a paralyzing numbness, a sense that whatever she gets close to dissipates or breaks. What Edmund Chester touched made him feel alive; what Jane touches makes her feel absent, as if there's a life force in everything but her, as if she's on the outside of a world twitching with possibility.

As Gareth nears the end of his speech, he directs his gaze to the front row, a few seats in from the end. From where Jane is positioned along the side wall she can make out the back of a man's head: short, sandy-coloured hair, William's long neck and narrow shoulders. 'We all live in history,' Gareth concludes, 'because it is history that shapes us.'

While the audience claps—some of the staff members from other museums standing up in a show of solidarity—Jane moves slowly along the wall toward the first row. She stops beside a marble column where she has a good view of William—out of his line of sight because he's watching Gareth, but able to observe how his eye-glasses are now thick brown frames instead of the wire-rimmed ones he used to wear, how his face is softer, his lips thinner. Jane feels a twinge, a mix of sadness and surprise, that she remembers his lips, her fifteen-year-old desire to kiss them.

What she thinks will happen, what she *wants* to happen, is for William to read and for the lecture to end and for him to turn at some late point in the evening when the room has thinned, and see her talking with Gareth a short distance away, and to come over. When Gareth introduces them, William might smile and shake her hand. And maybe Gareth will say, by way of context, that Jane is a good archivist, and they'll talk about his lecture or Jane's work on the Whitmore archive, and it will be okay that everything that matters between them goes unsaid.

After she bought *The Lost Gardens of England* Jane had thought about not reading it. She returned to her flat, set the book on the side table and stared at the cover—a Marianne North painting from nineteenth-century Jamaica with a green assemblage of cabbage palm, breadfruit, cocoa and coral trees. It was as if she was waiting for the book to do something. Then, two weeks ago when she finally did set herself down on the sofa and pick it up in her hands, she read the whole thing in one sitting. But she didn't follow the stories—the steamship sinking off the coast of Madras with a whole cache of specimens collected in Ceylon, the murders of two Scottish plant exporters along the Yangtze— so much as imagine William doing his research, working on the problem of the missing specimens he described, the lost lives. She convinced herself that she was reading the book with an archivist's eye for how one uncovers and arranges historical events, for the ways in which what one knows and doesn't know can be shuttled between the struts of fact and extrapolation. But she knew she was lying to herself, and the farther into the book she read, the more exposed she felt. By the time she finished the last page describing George Farrington's legacy—his alpine and *Rhododendron* plantings in the woods at Inglewood, the very woods where Lily, and N too, were lost—she was shaking. She closed the book, pulled a wool throw across her lap, turned her face into the sofa cushion and cried like she hadn't since she was a child.

When she woke up the next morning she thought about calling her therapist, but didn't. Instead she remembered how Clive had suggested, during one of their last appointments, that Jane had to let go of the idea of William. He'd said, 'Grief is different for everyone.' Later he amended the statement: 'Actually, what you have is not grief, it's more like sorrow. You're sorry that this happened to Lily, and sorry that it happened to you. Grief can be shared,' he said gently. 'What you have in common with Mr. Eliot is more like guilt. And that is always individual.'

What little we know about ourselves we know because of Jane. Our task as we see it is to wait: wait through those weeks and months when her thoughts have nothing to do with us, days when we have to force ourselves not to make ripples in the living world to gain her attention. Days we have almost risked Ceasing to be able to work a keyboard, switch on the History Channel, put a fist through a wall. We have, in our own way, been waiting for William too, for something to be repaired or unconditionally broken.

When William takes the stage, the applause peaks and then subsides. He adjusts the microphone and places his book and lecture notes on the podium; he pushes the bridge of his glasses up with a finger. 'Thank you, Gareth, for that wonderful reminder of the value of museums like this one, and for the warm introduction. I must confess to feeling a bit intimidated. I see so many colleagues here, so many people doing wonderful work in museum science. To have a book—especially one that started out as so much scribbling—be so well received is, frankly, unexpected.'

He pauses and takes a sip of water and his hand trembles as he puts the glass down. 'When Gareth first called me about the award, he very clearly stipulated that new work was expected in terms of the lecture. I happily accepted because there was a thread of information, a tiny confluence, if you will, that I had uncovered during my research, but which had no place in the final book. This has to do, of course, with the wonderful museum we are privileged to be sitting in tonight. Many of you may not be familiar with the name *Norvill* Farrington, but hopefully by the end of this talk you will be. He was an important reformer of museum science in the Victorian era, a geologist of some note, an early supporter of the Chester and friend to its founder, Edmund. He also happens to have been brother to George Farrington of Inglewood—the Victorian plant hunter who features in the last chapter of my book.'

While William pulls his lecture notes out from under his book, we turn to Jane. Her face is impassive save for two red blooms on her cheeks. We know that she is wishing to be elsewhere even as she is relieved to be here; that she is trying, as she has always tried, to put the idea of William into an equation so that she can say 'he is X' or 'we owe each other Y' and leave it at that. Instead, the idea of him slips constantly out of every box she tries to put him in. We sense her anger welling too—because William has announced that he is going to be talking about Norvill. Norvill, whom Jane knows through her work on the Chester family archives. Norvill, who she irrationally thinks is *hers*.

'Norvill Farrington was born in London in 1843,' William begins. 'By the time Norvill was twenty he'd become acquainted with Edmund Chester through a mutual friend, the collector Roger Cain who was also a member of the Royal Society . . .'

The details in the first part of the lecture are all facts that Jane knows, information gleaned during the months it took her to organize the Chester display upstairs, months spent going through the museum's records and the trunks of material she found when Gareth sent her to Edmund's great-granddaughter's house on the coast, boxes of ledgers and letters pulled out of her attic along with Charlotte Chester's diaries, writing desk, hair combs and scarab bracelet.

At first, listening to William speak, Jane feels strange. It's uncanny, this doubling: Jane's knowledge of the Chester family set against his, the confluence of their interests and thinking. Even the steady rhythm of his voice is unsettling, although there's a wooing quality to it too, as if he's reading a bedtime story, as if at the end something will be *said*, a moral tale delivered that will make the world more coherent, easier to live in.

Jane leans against the marble pillar and its coolness kisses the space between her shoulder blades. Listening to William, she can feel longing seep over her. She registers it as if from a distance, thinks how the feeling is like being overtired as a child—thinks of Claire eight months pregnant with Lewis and hauling a two-year-old Jane across the university quad, trying to find some secretary of undergraduate services or assistant to the assistant registrar who'd watch her *just for a few hours*. Jane had wanted that too—a large office chair in some out-of-the-way corner, a place she could curl up in.

William may be right about Norvill and Edmund's friendship, and about the two occasions in the 1870s when the Farrington and Chester families met, but gradually Jane registers that he's skipping over other key facts entirely, and as she follows the thread of his lecture she tries to guess if he's overlooking them on purpose. What about the details in Charlotte Chester's letters and diary, details that Jane had noted: brief remarks in a feminine hand that read 'N.F for dinner,' 'N.F for tea,' 'discussed contemporary novels with Norvill'—Norvill's name scrolled over the pages even as the names of other guests, ones noted in Edmund's own daybook, were overlooked? William hasn't mentioned Charlotte by name at all. He is focusing instead on how Edmund Chester helped secure funding for one of George Farrington's Himalayan plant expeditions, how Edmund himself funded George's last trip to Tibet—an agreement that was reached after a weekend shooting party at Inglewood. An event that Jane has seen referenced in the archive.

When he is finished and the applause subsides, William slips into the crowd and Gareth gently ushers him down the centre aisle to the book-signing table at the back of the hall. A dozen people are already holding books for William to sign. It is obvious that William is new at this; he is overly formal with the first few people who press their copies into his hands—Hamish Andrews, a senior member of the board who congratulates him heartily, and a botanist maybe five years older than William who inquires amiably about his research sources for the chapter on the Madras shipwreck. William glances up at his publicist, a woman in bright-red lipstick and a metallic dress who is monitoring the process, as if checking to see whether discussion is allowed.

Jane stands by the hummingbirds, not sure what she's waiting for. Her black dress, reflected back at her in the cabinet's glass, suddenly seems like something one would wear to a funeral. Her thoughts are muddy: she looks from bird to bird and can't separate the impact of seeing William from the contents of his lecture or the fact of the Chester's closure. One moment of clarity emerges: William, at least, is *making use* of the things he knows—things *she* knows.

To Jane's left, reflected in the glass, a girl in a white gossamer blouse and long blue skirt appears. She is coming over to look at the hummingbirds, and the effect of these two images blended—the semblance of the girl and the nimble hover of birds—is so beautiful and unexpected that Jane can't bring herself to turn around.

'Mina?' A blonde woman in a green strapless dress appears in the reflection behind the child. 'Where are you going, darling?'

Mina turns around and says something too quiet for Jane to hear.

'Yes, they are. All right then, a quick look, hurry up.' She smiles at Jane in the reflected glass—two women of childbearing age catching each other's gaze and therefore complicit, sharing what it is to have children, or what it must be like.

Mina walks toward the cabinet and the woman takes a mobile phone out of her beaded clutch purse. She checks its little rectangle of light and then turns away from the ruckus of the main hall, presses some keys and puts it against her ear.

Jane looks down at Mina and makes a silly face. The girl is eight, maybe nine; she has the kind of mousey-brown hair that gets blonder in the summer, a heart-shaped face, a chicken pox scar on her brow just above the bridge of her perky nose. Because she has manners and because her mum has let her come over, she mouths, *Hi* to Jane and then she turns and studies the hummingbirds, counting them under her breath.

'Mina?' It's a man's voice this time.

Mina glances over her shoulder at William, and Jane watches as he comes toward them, touching the blonde woman's waist as he moves past her, the mobile phone still pressed against her ear.

'Sweetie, it's time to go, it's past your bedtime.' He reaches down for Mina's hand and she threads her fingers through his. Then William stands there for a few seconds registering what she's looking at—something Henri or Claire would never have done for Jane—taking it in as if it matters. 'That one's lovely,' he says, and he points a fraction of an inch off the glass at one of the birds on the middle branch, a broadbill with a blue throat and green chest. He doesn't look at Jane.

'I like this one.' Mina identifies a grey bird with splayed wings and a ruff of purple feathers around its neck, her finger pressing against the glass so that for an instant after she moves her hand away, there's a faint round print there.

William turns to Jane and his eyes flick up into hers. The small red centre of pressure that has been in her chest all night balloons and moves up to her throat.

'Sorry to interrupt.' He smiles at Jane and places his hands on Mina's shoulders to steer the girl, who Jane can now see resembles Lily, toward the woman who is putting the phone back into her bag.

'Sorry—' Jane turns toward William and tries to steady her voice. 'Have we met before?'

It's obvious she's speaking to William, but instead of replying he turns first to his wife so that she can register his confusion, see that despite what these sorts of things sometimes look like, there's been a mistake. Then he turns and looks directly at Jane.

'I don't believe so.' His voice is even, but his brow is creased and his lips are pinched in a vaguely baffled expression. He is looking at Jane—Jane, who everyone says *hasn't changed a bit in all these years*, who in all the essential ways still resembles *that Jane*—and he doesn't know her.

How ridiculous it suddenly seems—the monastic life she'd imagined for him, the amount of space she'd believed she occupied in his everyday existence, an expanse she'd thought would equal the space he and Lily consumed in her. Jane can feel herself begin to shake, William staring at her blankly now, a stupid passive expression on his aging face.

'Will?' his wife asks, standing behind Mina and moving her arm protectively over her daughter's chest.

It isn't even a thought. It takes Jane two steps to reach him, to place her left hand gently against his cheek and slap him sharply with the right.

Part II

10 September had swept in, and Inglewood House, when Norvill Farrington arrived, was colder than he'd expected. He stood morosely in his old childhood room—a panelled suite that felt claustrophobic compared to his own bright and well-appointed accommodations in London—and rang impatiently for the footman. There was, he saw now, something too rural about the house: its dark, stocky furniture, grey flagstones, thick wood-beam ceilings, heavy curtains and mahogany shelves; the tiger and deer skins in his room becoming more motley every

year. It had been a shooting lodge before his parents purchased it in 1847, and in the intervening thirty years the only substantial improvements seemed to have been made to George's gardens. When Norvill was young, the house had fascinated him; he'd grown up with dead pheasants displayed in terrariums, stag and fox heads mounted along the hall outside his room, a stuffed bear in the entry near the stairwell. He'd spent whole hours contemplating the animals' wet-seeming noses, the muzzle of white fur around the roe deer's snout, the fox's yellowed canines. But now it all seemed oppressive and disingenuous and *cold*—the wildebeest, cheetah and buffalo heads imported, fixtures that, like the brass telescope on his desk and the globes on his bookshelf, seemed to say *the real world is elsewhere.*

In Norvill's absence a large mirror had been hung to the left of his bed, its frame a Baroque monstrosity. He recognized it from the room of his mother, Prudence, and imagined it had been moved because of the patina that had developed on its reflective surface—or perhaps because replacing things and shuttling objects around the house were two of Prudence's abiding pleasures. Norvill took off his hat, jacket and shirt to change for George's reception and surveyed himself briefly in the marred mirror. He almost didn't recognize the figure blinking back at him: his face was more sun-kissed than expected, his cheeks ruddier, moustache thinner. There were patches in his sideburns and on his chest that, upon close inspection, were flinted with strands of white. Standing there, the brown and amber hues of the room cloaking him, he felt as if he were a stranger, or if not a stranger, a kind of double: a brother to himself, a 'George' observing his sibling's return to the nest, his awkward attempts to settle into it.

Norvill mentioned the mirror in a letter he wrote that night to Charlotte Chester—secreted to her through his footman and the lady's maid Prudence had assigned to her. He felt a frisson of excitement over the daring of the note, its physicality and possible interception, in the downstairs gossip he knew its passage would elicit. The letter was written on George's monogrammed house stationery, and the envelope bore the inky scratch of Charlotte's given name. The top slip of paper inquired after her quarters: were she and Edmund happy with their rooms? Was the fire sufficient or would they require extra bedding? The second slip confided that although the prospect of her company made the journey north desirable he felt a growing agitation at finding himself back in Inglewood, his countenance reflected in the obscenity of his mother's mirror in a room and a house that were resolutely his, but wholly belonged to George.

William Eliot's lecture at the Chester—his references to Norvill and Inglewood, to the gardens of the estate—had helped us conjure an image of life there. Some of us remembered the great lawns and the elaborate flowerbeds, glass hothouses and peacocks; some of us remembered a mirror and Norvill's description of how he felt looking into it. The mirror was larger than the room's windows, its frame a sea of gold waves, though up close you could discern carved sprays of laurel and *Acanthus*, bevelled curves where the dust always settled. One of us remembered the feel of the frame under her hand, could see herself running a cloth over its furrows, too busy with work to study her own reflection.

What we liked most about William's lecture was how the simple act of making a statement allowed us access to an image. When he said 'Inglewood' and 'lake,' some of us could see a boat tethered to a rock by a fraying length of rope; when he said 'manor,' one of us saw a library of windows to wash and drawers of cutlery to polish. A vision of Prudence Farrington appeared vividly to some of us at the mere mention of her name—one of us saw a stern and stubbornly uncorseted woman with streaks of grey ribboning her brown hair, another pictured her striding along an Indian carpet in a yellow-striped walking dress she'd had made for the shooting party, her pursed mouth relaxing enough to form a series of words that took the guise of a favour, though such appeals were usually closeted demands. The morning's work put away because of this request, and the pattern of the day unexpectedly changed.

When the party reached the lake it was announced that Norvill would row the guests to the picnic spot on the opposite shore in two groups—announced by George on the grounds that he himself would then be able to identify points of interest in the dale, although Norvill believed it was simply a matter of George not wanting to pick up the oars. George had taken to calling their excursion an 'exploring party,' and as such wanted to be at the front of the group at all times in order to draw their attention to various flora on the trail and to regale them with stories from his last plant-hunting expedition in the Orient.

There were six in the first group: Edmund and Charlotte

Chester, their three children and one of George's housemaids—
a milk-faced girl whose name Norvill had already forgotten;
and five in the second group: the Suttons of Helton Hall sitting
stiffly on the bench in front of Norvill, George and Prudence
behind, the Hindu and George's prize lurcher Cato at the stern,
the hound leaning into the wind and working his nose in the
direction of the swans. The Hindu, Rai, had ostensibly been
brought along to haul the hampers and carry the guns, although
Norvill suspected that George preferred his valet's company to
anyone else's. As much as their mother enjoined her elder son to
the role of congenial host, and as much as George embraced it,
Norvill knew that his brother would, in every instance, rather be
scampering up the ledge of some Yangma rock face beside his
former porter than leading a group of bustled women across the
estate's grounds. Rai, wedged behind the hampers, was appar-
ently of the same mindset: his brown face was impassive above
his light-wool *gho* and his eyes stared drearily at the approaching shore. Loading the boat he'd said nothing, as usual, though
when pushing off he'd levelled instructions at the dog in his
native tongue—the velvet lilt of his voice causing the Suttons to
sit even straighter.

It had been a slow morning, with the guests still adjusting to their accommodations, the rooms in Inglewood House
draftier, Norvill imagined, than they were probably used to. The
large east-facing windows in the guest wing let the sun in early,
which would have woken anyone whose curtains hadn't been
secured, provided the noise of the servants lighting fires and
rustling through the corridors hadn't already done so. Norvill
would have done things differently, of course—ensured no one

was disturbed, sent breakfast to the rooms at a later hour. But, as the older of the two brothers, George resided on the estate, an act with which he staked further claim on both his authority and their mother's affection. When he wasn't away on his expeditions, he continued in his role as sole executor of the family's diminishing fortune, which was why Norvill was rowing across the midriff of the lake, and George was sitting in front of him pointing up to the rock face that backed it, explaining how the prickly white stalks of the *Spiraea ariaefolia* rooted themselves in the nooks of such a vertical plane.

Norvill leaned sideways to press the right oar into service and the prow angled toward the sandy ledge of the shore. Really, when he thought about it, George ought to be rowing. After all, the exploring party was a means of getting everyone outdoors so that George might show off some of his recent plantings, an entertainment wed to his desire to procure expedition funding from the Suttons and his need to appear to all as a man to whom things came easily, a man who could make an afternoon tea worthy of a monarch appear by a lake without so much as a hint of sweat above his scarred and bristle-covered lip. But, Norvill had to admit, it suited him, this delegation of duties. He had rowed briefly at university, and still had some trace of an athlete's physique. The rowing required him to remove his jacket and roll up his shirt sleeves. He felt himself wholly present in that, at least, in the act of moving things forward by will, stroke after stroke across the waveless water.

The weekend had been Norvill's idea. One night at the club Edmund had mentioned that he was travelling up to Keighley to look at a small cotton mill, and Norvill had suggested that Charlotte take the journey with him; they'd be welcome to stop up at Inglewood and stay with George. George, sensing an opportunity, had then invited the Suttons. Roger Sutton owned a successful ironworks business and his wife came from plantation money; they'd helped support one of George's first trips to the Himalayas and always enjoyed a bit of society. They, too, had heard of Edmund's growing collection and thought the idea of his museum 'quaint.' Once Sutton and his wife had accepted, Norvill decided he'd rather not be left out, after which Charlotte asked permission to bring the children. That settled, Norvill presented himself at Kings Cross station on the appointed morning and he, Edmund, Charlotte, the children and their governess caught the first train to Leeds. The plan was to alight there and to lunch at a hotel along the river that George had recommended and then to take the branch line on to Moorgate, and a carriage from there.

The hotel in Leeds turned out to be quite popular. It was bustling and bright with round, linen-clothed tables and high-backed chairs dotting the main room, and white wicker chairs and low tables set up in the conservatory. The waiters carried their silver trays at such a height one could see oneself reflected on the polished bottoms. By the time they had set their napkins down and Charlotte and the children had rustled off to peruse the sweet shop little Celia had noticed on the high street, Norvill had confirmed that things were progressing exactly as he'd hoped: Charlotte was, once again, responding positively and almost openly to his gestures of affection while Edmund, distracted by the prospect of investing in a new mill, seemed completely unaware of where and how his wife was bestowing her attentions.

Earlier, sitting across from her in the train carriage, his knees inches from her skirts, Norvill had at first sensed nothing. Charlotte was tolerating him as if he were a stranger, as if the fervid kiss in the museum months before, as if two years of stolen moments—moments that both exhilarated and humiliated him—had never occurred. And so, to distract himself, he'd spent an hour trying to engage young Thomas with lessons on the formation of mountains and valleys, only half attending to the boy's questions and therefore unsure whether or not the principles of lateral continuity and vulcanism were being properly grasped. He'd quoted parts of Lyell's *Principles of Geology*, pointing out the window at the sloping valleys, and had stared overlong at Charlotte over Thomas's head, raising an eyebrow at her when she turned from the window to chide Celia and Ned for jostling each other for the better view. To his mind he was demonstrating a kind of paternal attention toward Edmund and Charlotte's eldest, though truth be told he preferred the younger children. There was a clamminess about Thomas, a veneer of constant effort, as if even the simple act of getting his brain to properly register the age of the earth involved expending a prodigious amount of energy. When they came to the topic of the transporting power of running water Norvill almost imagined he could see turbines start to spin under the glistening furrow of the boy's brow.

A half hour before they alighted, the issue of sub-marine forests behind him, Norvill began to talk himself out of furthering his relationship with Charlotte; he decided to imagine that he had misread her intentions, or that it was possible he had not been clear in his. During an overdue conversation with Edmund about implementing a board of trustees at the Chester he even began to feel a fissure of guilt, a creeping nausea from the idea of what the break in faith might do to Edmund. The thought of putting Charlotte in such a predicament unnerved him too, though every time he imagined having her to himself, doing certain things to her, these thoughts abated.

They were almost at Inglewood—Norvill gazing out at the cottage houses and trying to imagine what being liberated from his obsession might mean—when Charlotte leaned across the carriage, dropped her gloved hand onto his knee and brushed away a feather that had flitted down from her hat. Norvill looked at his knee and then up at her face, watched as her gaze dropped lightly onto his. A darting glance confirmed that Edmund was deep into his papers beside her, the children following a story the governess was reading dully. Every muscle of Norvill's body was held in check against his desire to grasp Charlotte's pearl-buttoned wrist, to fasten her hand with his. Charlotte watched his face studiously, as if to measure her effect. And so he held her gaze as if from a dare, moved his neck against his starched collar, remembering the nick he'd suffered that morning at the end of his razor, willing himself not to reach up to check it for blood.

William, in his lecture, did not mention Charlotte by name. Some of us were ogling the canapés, and some of us were studying the guests, but we all noticed the omission. Those of us closest to Jane were marvelling at how she inserted her own version of events into William's, how when he said 'they travelled by train on the Friday,' Jane immediately placed Charlotte across from Norvill in the coach, and anticipated how the presence of Edmund and the children would force them to behave a certain way. Even then, after the lecture, as we struggled to untie William's banal account from Jane's embellishments, and both their versions from the hazy dream that is our own, we were conflicted. There are truths and there are the stories one *wants* to hear, though we crave both—share a desperate need to locate ourselves in a place, to understand why William's lecture could so vividly evoke a row of chestnut trees or a bedroom mirror or the view over the lawns from George Farrington's private library. One of us is convinced that he was once a guest there. Some of us knew only the woods, how the edge of the Farrington property ran right up to the asylum, Farrington's trees waving their arms at us over a stone wall while we walked in circles over the viewing mound.

The way that William's words turned into images reminded us that once, at the Whitmore, there had been a magic show. The preparation took weeks, with various permissions needed in order for the inmates to perform certain tricks. There was to be no sawing of anyone in a box, no escape from shackles, though Professor Wick was allowed to rehearse privately with his own top hat and one of the farm rabbits. The best deception was the sleight of hand, when Hopper made billfolds, pipes and a pocket watch disappear, only to have them turn up in the hands of his assistant. This is what it was like for us at the lecture: it was as if we were a magic show audience asked to pay attention, every ounce of energy we had expended in concentration. But a pocket watch is easier to follow than a story; it has a chain one can see as it slips into the magician's sleeve.

—

We know that it was Norvill who suggested that photographs should be taken, souvenirs of the weekend compliments of the Farringtons, who had, once or twice a year for the last six years, employed a photographer from a nearby village to take portraits of the family and once, the previous summer, a postcard of the house and gardens. We suspect that the Chester children were allowed to play by the lakeside that afternoon because there is a photograph of them in that year in the archives at the Chester Museum: a small ambrotype of the children in flouncy swimming costumes, their arms roped loosely around each other's waists, Celia's hair wet and plaited under her bonnet, its ribbons untied.

The photographer's name was Thwaite and we can envision him appearing just after lunch on the trail side of the lake, hailing the party self-consciously and waving his hat back and forth to garner attention. Norvill and Rai would have rowed over to assist him with his tent and equipment while Charlotte, artfully arranged in a blue dress under the uplifted arms of a hazelnut tree, might have called the children out of the water and instructed them to dry off as best they could. The photograph of the children is the only one that Jane has seen, although some of us know that Thwaite also took the obligatory group photos under the long face of the cliff, the gentlemen standing, George with a rifle over one shoulder, Rai behind him staring out of the shadows and Cato sprawled in front of the blankets. In one of them, Charlotte's hand is a blur on the dog's neck as if she was petting him, and Norvill is beside her, his gaze meeting the camera but his body oriented in Charlotte's direction as if they had been conversing and, on being called to pose, he simply turned his head. In what would have been the last photograph of the day, taken after Thwaite had returned to the trail side of the lake, the group appears small, as if forgotten, as if glanced at over one's shoulder when one is already too far away to discern faces and relations. In that photograph the rock face above them is an almost sheer sheet of limestone already bearing traces of the plants George had brought back as seeds the previous winter: alpine anemones set against his prized mosses, the tiny white stars of the *tubergeniana* gawping beautifully out of their crevices.

Once Thwaite had departed, George, in the role of congenial host, turned his attention to Charlotte. She was sitting on the blanket nearest the water, the skirts of her dress spread flatly around her from the lack of crinoline or bustle, which she had been told to leave off if she desired to venture into the cave at the end of the walk. All morning George had been noticing his brother's darting looks in Mrs. Chester's direction, but rather than judge him, or the two of them, he decided to walk over and see for himself what the fascination was.

Charlotte smiled up at him as he approached, and when he stood in front of her she tilted her head in inquiry. Up close he could see that she was lovely in a young motherly sort of way, with the slightly frazzled look of one who doesn't rely on her lady's maid. Her bodice was overly snug as if she'd recently put on weight, and her breasts bulged slightly above her neckline because of it. She had a mole—as perfectly circular as the brown centre of a *calderiana* he'd once seen blooming in

Bhutan—that peeked out beside the gauzy frill of her vest, and George, surprised at himself, had to fight the urge to touch it. Her conversation thus far had been expected and conventional: the positive qualities of vernacular architecture, the value of schooling the poor and the merits of an icehouse. Earlier she had also started to engage the Suttons on the politics of sugar but one look from Edmund had put a stop to that. For the past hour she'd been working idly at a sketch, and George's shadow fell over it as he studied the quick strokes she was making with her gloveless hand.

'May I?'

'Of course.' She handed her papers up to him.

He smiled politely at her landscape and then turned the page to a fresh sheet.

'I did tell you this was a shooting party, did I not?'

'I believe you called it an *exploring party*, Mr. Farrington. You indicated we were to take a long walk, a cave was promised and some of your—' She searched for the words he'd used and then settled for 'alpine gardens.'

'Have you travelled much, Mrs. Chester?' He sat down beside her and glanced around for Norvill.

'If you are asking me if I'm worldly, Mr. Farrington, I couldn't say.'

'Why not?'

'Because I'm unsure of the categories or means by which you'd gauge it.'

George smiled thinly at her. He liked her calling him Mr. Farrington because he knew that is what she would call Norvill when they were not alone, which meant that in some small cleft of her thinking he and his brother might be interchangeable, even fleetingly the same.

'Allow me to explain.' He smoothed a clean cream page with his hand. 'By shooting, I meant, of course, pheasants, but I also meant seeds. By projecting the seeds from the shotgun into the rock face I have discovered a means by which to better integrate my alpine species into the landscape.' He dipped the nib of the pen she'd been using into its inkpot and then dashed out a few black lines to form a cliff and a lake. 'In Wallanchoon,' he continued, 'the natural order of things is to see flowering plants like the *Rhododendron* and yellow rose thriving on the lower part of the pass while the heartier tenants take up residence in amongst the lichen and sedge.'

Charlotte watched studiously as the cliff he'd outlined was endowed with inky smudges and crevices.

'At first I attempted to plant my seeds here in a similar fashion, in two bands on the mid and upper ledges of the cliff, but few of the plants took and it cost me three-quarters of my supply. Last summer, I had a better idea.' He set the sketchbook down, leaned back on his palms, and looked over his right shoulder at the Suttons, who were craning their necks up at the rock face above them. 'Rather than climb it again, scattering the seeds as I went, it occurred to me that *shooting* the seeds toward the cliff might better mimic the dispersal of the wind.'

Charlotte tilted her head, trying to picture George climbing the cliff, imagining him first in some sort of harness, and then climbing a laddered rope, though attached to what she couldn't say.

Returning to the paper in front of him, George drew, in

five sure lines, a rowboat, then added a dashed-off human form and a shotgun from which ten lines of India ink sprang. 'Shall I demonstrate?' he asked, leaning intimately over Charlotte's lap to set the sketchbook down beside her.

'Please do,' she replied with a teasing expression that seemed to indicate that she knew exactly what George was doing and why.

George stood and called for Rai, and then, bowing, swung a last look at Charlotte Chester, thinking that he would have pursued her too if she was to his taste, if he wanted a woman at all.

George went over to the rowboat and Rai followed, carrying two of the shotguns they'd brought for the pheasants and a sack of seeds. The valet hiked his tunic up as he manoeuvred the back end of the boat into the lake. Cato ambled after him to the waterline and then barked when Rai, without a backward glance, stepped into the water and hopped on board. Edmund and Sutton, long engaged in a discussion about efficiency in manufacturing, moved toward the rocky outcrop that jutted into the closed end of the lake for a better view, their forms blackening against a stand of fir trees. Charlotte turned back to her sketch and frowned, thinking it flat somehow. She remembered a criticism of Turner she'd read once in a woman's magazine, the critic arguing that without the human form, no landscape could ever be sublime.

Balancing her sketch pad on her knee she thought to try a bird, a swan perhaps, but when she glanced up for a model there were no swans in view, only the boat cutting across the lake, its oars knitting the water. Gathering resolve, Charlotte dipped her nib into the inkpot and attempted to add her husband and the insufferable Sutton into the scene. She would have liked to draw Celia, but the children, bored with the protracted nature of the photographic exercise, had taken off 'on an expedition.' Bess, their governess, had been sick all morning, Charlotte feared to think with what, which meant that one of the Farrington maids had been charged with minding them. The girl was bright enough, and pleasing to little Celia because she'd taken her to investigate the chest of toys in the old schoolroom after they'd first arrived. When Charlotte had last seen them, Thomas was constructing a catapult out of a Y of wood and one of Celia's ribbons. Charlotte had told him to stay close if they were going into the woods and to watch his younger brother and sister. She'd also allowed the maid, whose shoes were too soft-soled for the forest, to stay within earshot of them near the first clump of trees. This, Charlotte confirmed, was where she was presently stationed.

Before George's first shot, Charlotte stood with her sketch pad and moved toward a flat-topped rock jutting out between the limestone crag and the picnic spot, trying to subdue the annoyance she felt at Mirabelle Sutton, who had hefted herself up to join their husbands, thus ruining the integrity of Charlotte's composition. Norvill, seeing that Rai hadn't done it, had taken it upon himself to pack up the lamb and was bent over his work a few feet away. He'd been growing restless since lunch, swatting at flies one minute and then brushing off the tufts of dog fur that had fastened to his trouser legs the next. His jerky gaze finally moved from his leg and boot to the cut of lamb that was drawing the insects, then on to the wicker basket where the food belonged. The maid, standing stupidly by the trees, appeared to be of no use, and his mother, reclining on a chaise a few feet away, was seemingly oblivious. Charlotte alone was following his actions, observing him in a way he could feel, so he turned to her and gazed brazenly at her figure, bound as it was in a dress he'd once said was becoming, a pleated and vested thing that was too heavy for the afternoon, her chest flushed and splotchy because of it.

Prudence Farrington coughed politely and Norvill swung around. He glanced at the needlework on her lap to assess the extent of her occupation. 'Is anything the matter, Mother?'

'Of course not, darling.' She peered at him from under the straw of her hat and then gently tapped her chest under the pleated bow of her striped walking dress. 'Do I seem unwell?'

'You appear both perfect and content.'

Prudence smiled up at him in the same polite way she probably smiled in rooms with no one else in them, the corners of her lips lifted tightly in feigned tolerance. Together they watched as a fly of considerable size landed on her skirt and began to inch over the silk of her knee, Norvill admiring its daring, its proximity and permission, envying it almost, until his mother adjusted her position on the folding chair to gain a more direct view of the rowboat and it flew off. Prudence would be fifty-five this year but she had kept both her figure and her quick turn to temper. As a boy, Norvill had never been sure what would set her off, though he was usually quite certain it was a direct consequence of an act that emanated from him. She'd been in great spirits, however, since the guests arrived— thinner and frailer than when he'd come at the start of summer, but more congenial.

Aware that his gaze was still on her, Prudence shifted again and stared sternly back at her son, puffing up slightly in her chair. The gesture reminded Norvill of George's description of a hooded snake he'd once encountered in India; how it seemed to sit up and waver at its intruders, widen its body.

'Would you bring me some lemonade, Norvill?'

'Of course.' He poured and handed her a half glass and the tips of their fingers met briefly.

She took a drink from it and returned it to him. 'It's good to have you both home at once,' she said finally, but her eyes were on the boat by then, on George, as they'd always been.

Seeing that George was almost in position to shoot at the upper ledges of the rock face, Norvill crossed the divide to fetch Charlotte. She was well out of danger but it was within the realm of possibility that small stones or rubble could skitter down and reach her. He picked up the lap blanket she'd dropped earlier and placed it on the rock next to her, then, with more urgency than he intended, he said, 'You should come back to the picnic area where it's safe.'

'Am I in peril?'

He winced, unsure of the possible allusions. 'It's not for me to say.'

Charlotte breathed deeply, gave him a bemused expression, and returned to her sketch. Norvill remained where he was at her shoulder, taking in her scent under the pretense of admiring her drawing. In the dark coil of her hair he believed he could detect the same lavender notes he remembered finding on her pillow in the early years of the Chester when the house doubled as a museum and, sent on an errand for Edmund, he'd happened past their bedroom.

'The sketch is charming,' he said, leaning closer.

'It's tedious,' she chided. 'The lake is wanting, and there are no swans to fill the space.'

'Why not draw the boat?'

Charlotte flipped the page to show Norvill George's caricature of a man with a shotgun in a skiff. 'It's already been drawn.'

'Are you afraid of repetition?'

Repositioning the inkwell she'd set beside her, Charlotte returned to her sketch. 'One always ought to be wary of being unoriginal.'

Norvill studied the perfect line of untouched skin that marked the part in her hair; hair that, in this light, was the colour of the Arabian mare George had shipped from Spain last year. 'Does my admiration for your accomplishments offend you?'

Charlotte laughed, perhaps at the huskiness of his voice— a mocking laugh that made his skin prickle. 'And if I gave the sketch to you?' she asked, smiling clearly and easily up at him, 'what would you do with it?'

'Have it mounted,' he said, anger welling in his throat.

11 After the first hour of driving, the motorway is mostly empty. It's pitch-black outside and other than the ambient light from the dashboard we are tunnelling through darkness. Jane has yet to relax her grip on the steering wheel and she's shivering, though we're unsure whether that's because she's using the cold to stay awake, or because Lewis has yet to fix the Mercedes' heater like he'd promised. Our thoughts are scattered; we retrace William's lecture one minute, then circle back to our concern for Jane the next. Her thinking has been

hard to follow—there's a prickliness about her, a distance. She switches lanes to pass a car numbly thinking, *Indicate, accelerate,* then *Breathe, slow down.*

A taxi had dropped Jane off at Lewis's house just before midnight. She'd thought about knocking on the door but hadn't wanted him to see that she was upset, so she'd jotted down a note about taking the car on the back of a receipt folded up in her wallet and slipped it through his post box. When she got back to her flat she parked her grandparents' old Mercedes in a No Stopping zone and put the hazard lights on. Inside the flat she threw a handful of clothes into an overnight bag, left her mobile phone with its four missed calls from Gareth on the kitchen table, changed out of her dress and collected Sam, remembering to leave a note for Dora, who lived in a flat upstairs, saying that she wouldn't need to walk the dog. She had her seat belt on before it occurred to her to go back for the box of files—pulling the Whitmore research out from under the bed and stuffing it into the boot next to a fuzzy grey jumper that probably belonged to Natalie or one of the girls.

Those of us who were there, who had followed her when she ran out of the Chester, tried to sort out what she was doing; we broached whether one of us should stay in the flat and wait for the others to return.

'Attendance!' shouted the theologian, but everything was moving too fast for voices to be sorted.

By the time the Mercedes surged onto the motorway headed north, we were divided, at odds about what to do, unsure where we were going.

—

After she slapped him, after the conversations in the radius around William and Jane stalled, everyone had turned and stared at her. This is the scene she keeps trying to suppress while she's driving: the publicist rushing over and putting her hand on William's arm, saying, 'Mr. Eliot? Is everything all right?' and William just standing there, rubbing his cheek and staring at Jane with a shocked expression that either meant he'd finally recognized her or that he was baffled at the seemingly random act of a stranger. And so she had run—pushing through a group of six or seven people holding wineglasses, and past Jacek, the security guard, who she was sure would reach out and stop her, force her to turn around. An expression of concern clouded his face; perhaps he'd assumed she'd had a row with a date and was rushing out to get some air.

No one was on the street when Jane burst through the door, and not knowing where to go she'd slipped into the park across the road, ducking behind the boxwood and moving along the hedge, her heels spiking the grass. There was a bench in an unlit corner along the far side of the green and so Jane made her way there, her hand on her mouth to keep the sound in her throat from escaping, though it came out anyway, a yelp she didn't recognize as hers, a sound like the one Sam sometimes made in the middle of the night, his back legs scrabbling the floor.

City sounds travel differently at night, and sitting on the park bench Jane became as aware of the din as we often are: the *whoosh* of the nearby traffic drifting over the park only to slide back down over the sloping roofs of the terrace houses; the weight of her own ragged breath rising in the air and then cascading around her. Sound becoming like movement or waves of light—which is how we sometimes see it, as if the human cacophony is a spectrum of colour: Jane's jagged breathing an ice blue; the woodsy thrum of the string quartet, who had picked up their instruments again on the other side of the Chester's windows, a burnished yellow-brown.

Hearing the music start up again, Jane had turned toward the park gate and dared to imagine that the space she and William had occupied, the stillness and silence that had followed the slap, might somehow be blotted out by guests moving toward each other and rejoining their conversations, by the quartet taking up their instruments and playing again as if nothing had happened between movements. But then, on the other side of the boxwood, she heard a car stop in front of the museum, its tires slick on the pavement. A few seconds later a man's muffled voice stated a destination and the driver replied, 'No problem.'

Jane could have peered around the edge of the shrub to confirm that it was William and his family getting into a taxi. She could have stepped out and tried to explain herself, tried to justify in some semi-coherent formulation what had just occurred, but she didn't. The taxi doors opened and people got in, and the driver sped away.

When she gets tired of driving, of the quiet of the near-empty roads, Jane switches on the radio. The music is so loud we're barely able to converse, to confirm who is with us and who is missing. The theologian shouts at us to stay awake, to focus, because this is one of the ways he believes you can Cease—by being lulled into the complacency that comes with travel. So the musician hums along to Ravel, and the idiot watches for cars sweeping by in the opposite direction, christening each set of ghosting headlamps with a name: 'Electron,' 'Proton,' 'Neutron,' 'Nucleus.' Cat asks repeatedly, 'Who is missing?' and John shouts, 'Stop asking that!' even as he tries to ferret out who got left behind. There is something strange yet ordinary about it all, as if we are a family heading out on holiday—our excitement almost frantic, the lot of us talking over each other and then sulking in silence.

By the time we pass the exit that leads to the family cottage at the Lakes we decide that Jane must have known where she was headed from the moment she left the city. Most of us assumed that she would do what she'd mentioned to Lewis in The Lamb weeks ago—hole up and regroup, go through the last of Claire's things. But we are wrong. Instead, Jane takes the exit toward Inglewood. She is focusing on the notes of the final movement of Brahms' fourth symphony as she turns, and then she follows the broadcaster's voice as he relays the news: austerity measures abroad, the high street in peril, monks setting themselves on fire, the miners still trapped underground. Jane thinking, *Boccherini String Quintet in E Major* when the music starts playing, thinking that by the time the rescuers drill an air hole down far enough the miners will all be dead.

❧

As she drives into Inglewood village Jane is strategizing about where to leave the car so that it won't be conspicuous. The locals probably expect a few unfamiliar vehicles parked around the inn, whereas a car left by the trailhead in the early hours of the morning might raise questions. Jane knows that there's been a volunteer search-and-rescue group working in the area since well before Lily went missing, a handful of residents who can be called out to assist climbers or spelunkers lost or in trouble in the caves at the far end of the botanical trail—people who might take seriously a car sitting in the hikers' parking lot at five a.m.

The last time she'd come here with William and Lily they'd parked down the road from the pub along the narrow river that forms a channel through the centre of town. The limestone cottages lined up on either side of the water are grey and nearly identical, as if the whole village had been built in a fit of industrial prosperity. Inglewood had been pleasant that day, the sun out and the main street in bloom. Ceramic pots bursting with pansies were lodged outside the shops next to welcome mats and boot scrapers; bells rang above the doorways when people walked through.

This morning, the sky is a dusky grey as Jane drives down the street. The porch lights on most of the houses hunkered along the river have yet to be turned on. At the top of the street Jane sees a church, its tower lit by a dozen spotlights hidden in the shrubbery. There's a parking lot at the rear with two cars already in it, so Jane pulls up next to the one closest to the road—an old Vauxhall with a layer of leaves matted against its windscreen. She cuts the engine, gets out and opens the back door for Sam.

The rumble of the waterfall that winds down from the lake on the botanical trail is audible from the parking lot, which means that Jane has guessed correctly and the start of the woods is a short walk around the corner. Opening the boot of the car she unzips her bag and roots around for her jumper, while behind her Sam spins in a circle and barks as if he is expecting a ball. Jane shows him her empty hands, says, 'Quiet,' and he diligently studies both palms before trotting across the road and into a grassy field, where he lifts his leg beside a boulder.

Jane steps onto the road and her eyes adjust to the landscape, to how the early dawn light gives the asphalt a slick hue and the field across from her a denser texture; to how the woods on either side of the field bristle against the heavy grey drift of the clouds. If she turns right she knows that she will come to a stone bridge flanking the falls. Lily had insisted they stop there, and William had lifted her up carefully, holding her tightly by the waist so that she could throw leaves into the cuff of frothing water at the bottom of the twenty-foot drop. George Farrington, William had explained, had engineered the whole system in the late 1860s—narrowing the river in parts, damming the valley to form the lake, carving out the falls with the idea that they could eventually provide power for turbines that would serve the village. Jane remembers William marvelling over it, how one man's desires could control so many things.

It's only when Sam wanders farther into the field across from the church and Jane moves to follow him that she realizes she is standing between the woods where N went missing and the trail where Lily disappeared. The chimneystacks, hipped roof and lead dome of Inglewood House are silhouetted to her left above the row of chestnut trees that divides the estate grounds and the field; the Whitmore would be a ten- or eleven-mile walk west beyond that. She calculates that if she turns right and walks twenty minutes in the opposite direction to the Whitmore, past the waterfall and along the Farrington trail, she'll be at the spot where Lily was lost. And it's this knitted thought—of Lily lost and N missing—that startles her. All of her adult life she's used the word *lost* for Lily and *missing* for people like N. As if Lily's accident, death or kidnapping was an act of negligence on *her* part, and hers alone, one that William, the police, the man or woman who may or may not have snatched her—that Lily herself—had nothing to do with. Lost, like one loses a mitten, a book or a key, something entrusted to you and lost through a lack of attention.

Jane turns toward the botanical trail and walks quickly. Her nose is dripping. She wipes it on the sleeve of her jumper, shocked that she has just blamed a five-year-old girl for messing around and running in and out of eyesight in perfectly ordinary woods on what should have been a perfectly common day.

Even in the wooded dusk it takes Jane only fifteen minutes to get from the gate to the place where the woods open onto the lake. On that day with Lily, with the slow progress they'd made, it had seemed to take hours. But Jane is walking quickly because even though the sky is slowly steeped with blue, the woods are rustling, and the shapes of the bushes and beech trees change as she gets close to them. There's a push and pull to what she's doing. On the one hand she's acting purposefully for the first time in almost twenty years; on the other hand, she's afraid of what she's moving toward. Lily's disappearance taught her that there is malevolence in the world, and that it can come at you unexpectedly, pass its hand over your body like a magician: *abracadabra*, you're gone.

Walking along the trail behind Jane the theologian does a roll call, though it takes some time to sort out whose voice says, 'Here.' John uses his name and is smug about it, and Cat says, '*Meow*,' and the one with the soft voice calls, 'Yes, I'm coming, I'm coming, and I have the girl.' The musician, the poet and the idiot raise various kinds of cheers, and the boy *vrooom*s, and the one who rarely speaks hoots softly like an owl.

'The old man?' the theologian asks, and no sound follows.

The poet makes the slurping sound of someone sucking on his teeth but fashions it into a question.

'Also gone,' the theologian says.

Our rank is depleted, but even as we try to identify the others we'd felt travelling with us over the past few years—those stragglers who seemed like a caste of distant relations—we are at a loss as to how to describe them. The shape of our group is new again, its edges uncertain. This reminds some of us of what happened at the Whitmore: most days the breakfast tables would be lined with familiar faces; then suddenly, two or three would be gone and a stranger would appear out of nowhere—though looking up from your plate you couldn't always say who was new and who was missing.

When we arrive at the part of the trail where Lily disappeared, it is the blue hour, the trees soaked in stillness, the lake as slick as a lacquered plate. Some of us are sure that we know this place—and not just from the images William's lecture inspired, from his talk of shooting parties and garden plantings, but because some of us have stood here before, can remember Jane, fifteen and terrified, rooted near the very spot where she is currently standing.

'Once there were peacocks here,' the theologian says. He turns from Jane and looks up the trail. 'They'd wander off the estate grounds and into the nearby grotto. There's a path off that way that leads to the largest of the caves.'

We watch him move along the trail to where he thinks the path begins, but a few minutes later he is back, deflated. Either he is wrong, or the path is gone—the intervening century hiding it under a wood-fall of twigs and leaves.

Jane edges her way down the slope that leads to the lake just as she'd watched William do that day on the trail. Her right foot slips on her first step and she has to grab the branch of a tree, move down in increments. When she gets to the shoreline she finds a flat rock that juts out of the bank above the water and sits on it, wiping her face with the heel of her palm.

'Is she crying?' the musician asks. And those of us who have already made it down the slope sit beside her and study her face.

'Wouldn't you?' Cat asks.

'Hardly,' he replies—though we can all hear the tenderness in his voice.

The lake, to Jane's surprise, is beautiful: the line of pink sky ribboning the gap between the trees at its far end mirrored on the water, the cliff gazing down at its own bleary reflection. She always thought this landscape would be instantly recognizable, fixed in her brain, but now she finds she can't be sure if William came from the part of the trail that runs up above where she's sitting, or if everything happened farther along. A laugh bubbles up in her throat: where *everything happened*? She sounds like her mother—always referring to Lily's disappearance as if it were a natural disaster involving citizens in a country difficult to pinpoint on a map. Sometimes Jane would count the weeks or months between any references to it at all, as if it weren't a weight she was living with daily, as if, in those first few years, she wasn't startled every time by the phone ringing in the cottage or in her grandparents' entry hall, as if one call couldn't change everything. For years, Jane believed that some trifling piece of information—the physique of a stranger, a colour or gesture, a sound or a word—might stretch the frame of that day, bring a barely glimpsed hiker to mind, reveal an image of Lily orienting her body back toward the gate or to the lake. But her memory of what happened is always the same: she is half watching Lily, half peering up ahead for William; the game continues and Lily has missed a post, so Jane stops beside it and, after a minute, calls for Lily to come back around the bend, smoothing the petals in her pocket while she waits.

The worst part of not knowing is how the imagination fills in the blanks, how it tries to ferret out an answer from all the possibilities and how, in doing so, it settles on the most terrifying. In that version, Lily is abducted. And sometimes she is murdered, and sometimes raped, and sometimes she is still alive and suffering.

Clive once told Jane that what she really had to live with was the not knowing. *All kinds of accidents, Jane, are very real in a place like that.* Sitting by the lake, the early morning light coming up over the stiff-necked trees, Jane thinks, *Accident* and she can see some version of it, the long muddy slope William had slid down when he was calling for Lily, the gap in the boulders around the shore side of the drainage grate, the relatively short distance from the trail to the water. This lake, her grandmother told her years later, was the first place they thoroughly searched. Within twenty-four hours they'd brought in divers and two days later they dredged it from one end to the other, but they found no trace of Lily.

Because William refused to see Jane or her grandparents, Jane came to believe that if, in the years that followed, someone found a shirt, a shoe or a body, they'd call William, but no one would think to contact her. The key to Jane's grandparents' house had been around Lily's neck, which meant that for months Jane had nightmares about the person who might have taken Lily appearing in their house in South Kensington, waiting in Jane's bedroom for her to come home from school or rehearsal. Clive had wanted to know what 'he' looked like when Jane confessed this, because if any leads came out of Jane's sessions it was agreed that he could pass on the particulars. But the intruder was never the same: sometimes he was a version of some movie actor, sometimes a stranger, and sometimes he looked like her father or like William.

What Jane wants now, sitting on the rock, the waves of the lake lapping in front of her, is a sign or a ritual. If she had something of Lily's she would send it off on a leaf over the water or dig it down next to the roots of a plant. But she has nothing—just as she found nothing in William's face when she walked up to him at the gala: a vacancy where she had hoped for more.

—

Turning away from the lake, Jane listens for Sam. The last time she saw him he was running between the trees along the shore, probably on the trail of a wood mouse or a squirrel. When she doesn't hear him she whistles and starts back up toward the trail. She is thinking about the shooting party William described at the lecture, about how the Chesters had stopped on their way to Edmund's prospective mill to tour the Farrington grounds and walk out to the caves. They'd probably inched down the very slope she was now climbing on their way out to the lake. The rock that she'd been sitting on still had an old mooring ring mortared into the stone, and it was flat enough to use as a jetty. William had mentioned how Prudence Farrington's diary described in great detail the preparations at the house around the time of the Chester–Sutton visit but said little of the occasion itself. It seems to Jane that William's lecture, too, was full of gaps—the fact of Norvill and Charlotte's relationship chief among them. In the latter part of his talk he'd focused on the state of the gardens that summer, and on George's autumn trip to Sikkim, for which he'd procured funding from the Suttons. William had been fixated on the story of the plants—the retrieval of seven *megalantha* specimens from Kangchenjunga; the discovery of *Campanula grandiflora* and *rupestris*.

This, Jane realizes now, is where his attention has always been: not on the people in the story but on the withering plants sealed in terraria and Wardian cases. The fact that Norvill had received a commission to survey fault lines along the east coast shortly after the shooting party, and then went away for the better part of a year, had been a quick footnote in William's lecture. But it was something that Jane hadn't known, something that surprised her. The Suttons, William had said in conclusion, returned to Helton Hall. Edmund eventually purchased the mill up north and the Chester family went back to their museum.

The pieces of the puzzle clicked into place, Jane thinks, and everyone was back where they had started—except Norvill.

By six a.m. the sky that zigzags above the trees has turned a cloudless blue. It is still too early for a B&B, but Jane supposes that by seven the local hotel staff might be up and making breakfast, which means that she can see if there's a room available. She can picture it, a narrow single with awful floral paper and a costly in-room phone from which she can call Lewis to make sure it's okay that she's taken the car. But then she imagines Lewis saying, *Gareth called*, followed by an awful hanging silence.

At the gate Jane stops and whistles for Sam again. For the last twenty minutes he has been darting in and out of the treeline. She stands there listening, waiting for him to come barrelling toward her, but he doesn't. Leaning against the wood slats in the cold, she whistles again, her fingers in her mouth this time, like Lewis taught her. She whistles this way twice and then puts her hands in her pockets thinking, *Okay, it's been a while since he's been allowed off-leash, he's nine years old, this is the last of his wild oats.* And then it dawns on her: *Maybe this is how it works: you do what's expected of you all of your life and then one day this loses its lustre and you stop what you're doing, take off into the woods and disappear.*

We watch Jane whistle again, turn her ear toward the humming woods, scan the dawn-lit lip of pasture and the crumbling stonewall behind it. We know she is willing herself not to be scared but her heart is pounding. She can hear birds, the falls, a car engine turning over on the main road, even the distant *shush* of cars on the motorway. Time stalls, then hitches forward: Sam comes bounding through the alder. He skirts a post at the edge of the woods and runs straight for her, his wet and glistening body wrapped in night smells as he leans against her legs, the happiest she's ever seen him.

12 The first time Jane met William Eliot he was standing in her grandmother's overplanted South Kensington
garden in a crisp white shirt with his sleeves rolled up to the
elbows. His hands were caked in dirt and he was listening while
Jane's grandmother, Meredith, carried on about the crested
irises. There were two freshly planted pots of lavender at his
feet and a snake of ivy he'd cleared from the overgrown trellis.
When Jane stepped out of the glass door of the conservatory
to ask if she'd missed breakfast, Meredith ignored her at first,

concentrating on what William was saying about the *Botrytis*. It was a Sunday and Jane had slept in; her bare feet warmed on the flagstone while she crossed her arms over her nightdress and waited for her grandmother's attention, an eleven-year-old who was not yet self-conscious in front of strangers.

'Jane?'

When Jane looked up, both Meredith and William were staring at her, William with a bemused expression, Meredith tight-lipped. A bee had zigzagged up from the lavender and was hovering around Jane's elbow, and she had been following it, the insect lightly touching her fingers before veering off toward the verbena.

'This is Mr. Eliot. He lives down the road. He's the botanist I was telling your grandfather about.'

William bowed over-formally and winked at Jane on his way back up. 'Lovely to meet you, Miss Standen.'

Meredith waved Jane toward the kitchen as if reading her mind. 'There are scones in a brown bag on the counter. But get dressed first, please, and run a brush through that hair.' She turned to William, smoothing a grey curl at her temple. 'It's easier to take the children out of Cumbria, I'm afraid, than it is to take the Cumbria out of the children.'

It was Meredith who, four years later, organized Jane's babysitting. She'd run into William at the local produce shop, commenting, as he tried to unload a basket of groceries at the till with Lily hanging off one arm, that she hadn't known he shopped there. Meredith took the girl's hand as William explained that the nanny's father had had a stroke and she'd flown home to Spain the night before. He was going to have to call an agency, he said, and find someone for the week—maybe just until three each afternoon because he was in the process of making arrangements to get off work early.

Meredith relayed the conversation to Jane as they sat in the Mercedes in stop-and-start traffic that was about to make Jane miss her cello lesson. If she arrived even five minutes late Mikhail would already have left and they would still have to pay him. Jane had only made that mistake once in the year she'd been studying with him, but for at least two lessons after that incident he had been gruffer than usual and Jane wasn't anxious to work through his distaste again. As she edged along the turn lane that led to the academy, Meredith asked Jane what she thought about helping out with Lily, just for the week, and Jane, craning her head out the window because the lorry in front of them was impossible to see around, said, 'Fine, yes.'

Lily was, according to Meredith, a sweet girl, and Jane figured she'd probably be easier to mind than Lewis was when he was eight and Jane was ten and she'd been left in charge at the cottage. And she liked Mr. Eliot, had met him a handful of times in the four years since they'd first been introduced in the garden. He'd always been warm and friendly, though in the year after his wife died he'd seemed bewildered, almost glassy, as if something else was going on behind his eyes. Some months after the funeral, he'd stopped in for tea, sitting stiffly on a tall-backed chair while Meredith offered him biscuits. Jane and Lewis, noticing snowflakes outside, had raced down the stairs to put on their coats, and Jane remembered pausing for a second, watching William curiously from the entrance archway before stepping into the first faint fall of snow.

—

There are two memories from the weeks of babysitting Lily that Jane circles back to. In the less complicated one William had come home from work with bags of groceries and Jane was helping him put them away. Halfway through he stopped and hopped up onto the counter to direct Jane as to what went where—'upper cupboard,' 'crisper'—while juggling three mandarins to amuse Lily. When everything was put away, Lily invited him over to a spot on the dining room floor where she and Jane had organized a teddy bear birthday party. There were six stuffed bears, with varying degrees of wear, set up in a circle around a dishtowel. The birthday bear was wearing a napkin ring for a crown and all the bears had little plastic cups in front of them. Lily handed her father the small green cup that belonged to the brown bear with the chewed-on ears and then expertly tilted a plastic teapot with a mermaid decal on it to pour him tea.

'What kind of tea is this?' He put his nose into the empty cup.

'Chocolate.'

William took a fake sip and said, 'Mmm, lovely.' He called over to Jane, who was packing up her cello in the living room. 'Miss Standen, would you like some chocolate tea?'

'No, I should get going.' Jane picked up the score she'd propped against a stack of hardcover books on the coffee table and dropped it into her bag.

William stood up and came over with the plastic cup still in his hand. 'What were you playing today?'

'Just practising. A prelude I'm working on for my exam.'

He inclined his head. 'Will you play something for me before you go?'

'What would you like me to play?'

'Surprise me.'

William waited to see where Jane would sit and when she chose the brocaded bench under the back window he picked up the Hope chair beside the bookshelf and moved it into the middle of the room.

Jane watched him settle in as she checked her tuning. When she was satisfied, she put her bow down and reached into her pocket for a hair elastic and said 'Sorry,' because she didn't mean for him to be watching her tie up her loose hair, fixing the strands so that they wouldn't fall forward while she was playing.

'Are you going to play the piece you were practising?'

Jane laughed. 'No, I'm not that good at it yet.'

'What then?'

She lifted her bow. 'I'll play the *sarabande* from Bach's fourth cello suite. I like it better.'

Jane was used to being looked at when she performed but there was something different about playing for William and the gentle way he studied her face. Mikhail mostly followed her hands, and Jane's father—when she was eight and nine and he still made time to listen to her—had mostly gazed at the floors or out the cottage window, as if gauging the music he was hearing by its effect, as sound pared off from the physical act of its production. Usually Jane looked down at her bowing hand or closed her eyes, unless she was in lessons, in which case she mostly watched Mikhail's face, because she could tell by the set of his mouth whether she was succeeding or failing—and because secretly she was always anticipating the moment he'd shake his head, say, *Stop*, and instruct her to go back and do it again. The previous week, in the middle of the very *sarabande* she was playing for William, Mikhail had snapped his fingers and interrupted her, chiding her for a decision she'd made. 'Lighter!' he said. 'How do you walk through your house?' He stomped in place. 'Like this? All the time? You're always storming off? In the *bourrée* we think of steps, no?' He tapped the ground with his foot like a dancer. 'But in the *sarabande* the accent is on the second beat.' He picked up a piece of chalk and wrote a line of music on the board behind him. 'Ornaments are *here*,' he said, 'and *here*—unless you are indifferent. Start again.' She started again and he stopped her before she even got to the crescendo in bar seventeen. 'It's a *decision*, Jane. It's a decision about what phrase is swallowed by, or swallows, the rest. The slur is too long technically to obey. So: decide. It's the swell of it, okay? Like this—' He arced his hand up and let it fall. 'You can play like everyone else *da-da-da-dee* if you want, but I thought we agreed you could start making decisions of your own now. No rushing through it. No thinking. Just feel.'

Jane made two minor mistakes in the *sarabande* she played for William, which wasn't bad because the piece was technically above her skill level. It had almost no easy phrases and an emotional ambiguity that made Jane think of a scene from a ballet—the wood nymph who was up to no good stopping on his way to mischief to admire the beauty of the moon. Both times she hesitated she glanced up to see if William had noticed, but his expression didn't change—he was watching her in a way that seemed completely free of judgment. She played everything after the *crescendo* with her eyes closed and when the last note lifted up and dissipated she opened them to find him leaning forward in his chair. When he didn't applaud or say anything or do any of the usual stuff, Jane stood up, flexing and unflexing her left hand, her face flushing even as she willed it not to.

William walked over to her, shaking his head in disbelief. 'That was absolutely amazing. Seriously, Jane, I'm stunned, I had no idea.' When she looked down at the rug—at its border of green leaves and butter-coloured flowers—instead of meeting his gaze, he took her chin gently between his thumb and forefinger and guided her face up toward his. 'You should be very proud of yourself.' He held her face like that for whole seconds before he turned and walked into the kitchen.

The next day when William was at work, Jane put Lily in front of the telly and went upstairs to see if there was anything to read in the study. It was a Friday and William had asked her if she could stay late because he had a dinner to go to.

His study was a cluttered room with a sloped roof just off the master bedroom. The walls were painted in what Jane's grandmother would have described as 'Oxford grey' and the furniture was a darkly stained wood that matched the built-in shelves on the supporting wall. Jane perused the spines feeling wholly uninspired because she'd been hoping for a novel, though she did pull Darwin's *The Expression of the Emotions in Man and Animals* off the shelf because Claire had read it and said that it was wonderful.

Without quite meaning to, Jane opened up William's desk drawers. She ran her hand over the business cards and paper clips and the elasticized receipts, sifted through the papers stacked next to his computer, feeling a pulse of pleasure at moving his items a few inches, in reading the notes he'd left sticking out of the books he was working through. In the bathroom she found a bone-handled shaving brush and razor, a bar of soap that smelled like cinnamon, a half-used tube of ointment for cuts and scrapes, paracetamol, plasters covered with fairies in pink dresses, and a paddle hairbrush in the back of a drawer that was probably his late wife's. In his bedside table drawer she found a photograph of her—Camille, she was called—in a silver frame, her hair long and damp and her shoulders bare except for spaghetti-thin swimsuit straps, a blue beach parasol poking up behind her. Jane studied the image and then blankly and stupidly thought, *And then she died,* as if the woman in the photo were just a romantic affectation abstractly attached to William, a character in some novel you could easily put away and not a human being who had slept and dreamed and woken up in the very bedroom Jane was, at that moment, standing in.

Jane suspected that William was going on a date, because after he'd come home from work and organized pasta for her and Lily, he changed into a nice suit. He came down the stairs flipping a burgundy tie into a knot and then, having checked it in the hall mirror, turned and asked Jane, 'How do I look?'

She laughed and said, 'Very handsome.'

By the time he returned that night, Lily was tucked into bed and Jane was asleep under a throw on the couch with the television on. This is the memory she goes back to most often: a dream within a dream that begins with William bending over her to wake her up, gently shaking her arm and saying her name. Jane drowsily thinking, *I hope it's all right that I fell asleep,* worrying that everything is okay upstairs. The canned laughter of the comedy she was watching coming in waves in the background, which meant that she couldn't have been asleep that long. His face above hers because she can smell garlic or onion, the faintest trace of cigarettes, even though she'd thought he didn't smoke. His hand on her shoulder to wake her and then on the blanket, his fingers trailing slowly over her T-shirt and across her breast as he gently tugs the blanket down.

By the time Jane sat up, she was already unsure if it had happened. She remembers trying to clear her head, trying to formulate a question. William seemed in a hurry to get her home.

'Ready?' He folded the throw she'd been using in quarters and dropped it over the back of the couch.

'Yeah.' Jane stood up, trying to shake the fog of sleep. She glanced around for her bag, conscious that her eyes were welling up.

'You all right?'

'I can't remember where I left my bag.' She wiped her eyes and walked into the kitchen, only to remember that she'd dropped it by the front door when she came in. It was lying next to her cello at the foot of the stairs, and when she bent down to pick both up, William reached in, saying, 'I'll get this,' his hand around the cello-case handle before she could even think to say no. He walked her the two blocks to her grandparents' house in a light rain without a word and handed her the cello at the gate, waiting at the end of the walk to make sure she was safely in before raising his hand to say good night.

By the following Monday evening Jane was convinced she'd made everything up. William had acted normal that morning when she'd appeared at the door, and when he'd come home from work he was harried as usual—running late because he'd been trying to get support letters for his grant and had accidentally left the office without the files on Inglewood in his briefcase and had to go back for them. During the first week Jane wouldn't have minded, but now Lily was starting to act up. She was smart enough to sense that Jane would let her get away with a lot more than Luisa did.

That summer Lily was interested in fish, and William had gamely gone out and bought her an aquarium with two blue dolphin cichlids and a scuba diver figurine whose chest of buried treasure contained part of the water filtration system. He'd also helped her cut a dozen pictures of fish from a *National Geographic*, awkward frontal photographs and cropped images that she later sellotaped onto the headboard of her bed. Lily had given them all names—'Rusty' and 'Lucy' and 'Misty' and 'Fritz'—names William said she'd imported from last year's fascination with ponies, the spirit of 'Fritz' the Shetland pony somehow reincarnating into a photograph of a blue tetra. He'd explained this to Jane while rifling through Lily's dresser drawer after work one day, searching for a favourite purple T-shirt Lily wanted to wear to bed. Jane was looking in the closet under the folded pile of clothes the cleaning lady had left in the basket.

'Did you tell Jane about the Gourami?' William asked.

Lily put her thumb in her mouth and shook her head no.

'Hey,' he said, tapping her fist, 'what did we say about that?' He put his hands on his hips and turned to Jane. 'Any luck?'

'Nope.' Jane pointed toward the top shelf of the closet where a row of stuffed animals was lined up. 'Could it be up there?'

William came and stood beside her and started pulling the soft toys down two at a time. Lily grabbed the donkey she liked before it hit the floor, and he glanced down as she caught it. 'Show Jane the Gourami, Lil. She'll like it.'

Lily climbed up onto her bed and pressed a finger against the cut-out of a spotted orange fish with a black stripe down its side, the back end of its body almost translucent and flaring like a veil.

'It's called "Jane" now,' William said. 'What was it called before, Lil?'

Lily made a squirting sound with her mouth and then laughed and hid her face behind the donkey, peeking over its head to say, 'Luisa.'

On the trail that day in the woods, Lily had made a dozen fish faces, sometimes just with her lips, sometimes by opening her mouth and hanging out her tongue, and once, probably imitating something William had shown her, by putting her hands next to her ears and swishing them back and forth like fins. Jane thought, during the whole of that walk, of almost nothing but William, of how she must have imagined that he'd touched her that way—imagined it because it was something she thought she wanted, because a touch like that would mean he saw her differently: the way she thought she wanted to be seen.

13   On the walk back to the village, Jane runs the tips of her fingers lightly over the shrubs that border the pathway, thinking about the flower petals she plucked at the start of the trail two decades ago, how they were in her pocket all those long hours at the police station when William had gone back out to search and night was falling and she'd sat at a stranger's desk. Jane had touched those petals again and again, saying each time her finger felt their crushed silk, *Please find her, please find her*, offering all kinds of behaviours, all manner of pacts—*If they find*

her I will always . . . or *If they find her I promise to never . . .* —to whichever god might be listening.

Turning toward the church it occurs to Jane that coming up to Inglewood is the most intentional thing she's done in a long time. Even the split from Ben four years ago had been ambiguous, almost an accident—a fight over nothing that ended with him moving out. They had been at his brother's art opening in Chelsea, and Jane had reached out to straighten Ben's already straight tie and he'd swatted her hand away. Ten minutes later they were out on the fire escape having a go at each other—'You always—' and 'You never—' and 'If you'd just—' And Ben had shouted, 'I don't know what the fuck I'm doing with you.' Without a word Jane slipped the ring he'd given her for her thirtieth birthday off her finger, tucked it into his jacket pocket and turned toward the railing. There was a streak of orange left in the sky, the outline of the buildings across the river uneven against it. She counted the seconds in her head: *one thousand and one, one thousand and two.* By *one thousand and five* he was gone.

What surprises her now about what happened with William last night isn't that she'd run, but that running away also feels like running toward. Neither her mother nor her therapist, nor Lewis for that matter, thought she should come back here. But returning to these woods—not just for herself or for Lily, but to sort through the story she has started to piece together about N—seems exactly right. Files, books and computer searches are all well and good, but these are the actual woods that N walked through, this is the village she must have come upon the day her new life began.

—

The church where Jane left the car sits at the top of the main road. Its crenellated tower is from the fourteenth or fifteenth century, but the rest of it is early Victorian, probably rebuilt in the throes of the Industrial Revolution when most of the nearby cottages went up, or a few years later when the Farringtons first moved to Inglewood, taking up residence in the house and bringing their money with them. There is a cemetery plot on the west side of the church, its old stones jutting at angles, and on the far side of the parking lot is the field that acts as a brace between George Farrington's botanical trail and the walled estate with its surrounding woods. Jane skims along the grassy sway with Sam in tow, thinking about the Whitmore trio and how they might have passed under the church tower on their walk to or from the Farringtons'. And then it occurs to her that the Chesters would have passed this way too, only a little later, on the weekend William lectured about. Edmund, Charlotte, the three children and the governess they'd brought on the train with them. Passing under the thumb of the church tower's shadow, Jane has to work at imagining this. Despite all her reading, until William's lecture she had never pictured the Chesters *outside* the museum or the city, never imagined Charlotte bounding energetically across the hump of a field or stopping, as William said they did, at a riverside hotel for lunch, the world around them noisy, bustling and brightly lit.

As she crosses the parking lot back to the Mercedes, Jane cycles through the facts: William said that the Farringtons and Chesters had met twice at Inglewood House: in September of 1877 for the shooting party; and in the summer of 1879, after Norvill's return from the coast, when Edmund had made enough money with the mill to fund a substantial part of what would become George's last plant-hunting expedition. Sitting in the car with her hands on the steering wheel it comes to Jane that there is something too tidy about that fact, about their paths crossing here at Inglewood *twice*—as if the research William had done could summarily limit the extent of their interactions, as if he'd perused all the relevant documents and could say without reservation that those were the only instances upon which the two families properly met at the estate. It seems unlikely to Jane that the Chesters wouldn't have been at least *occasional* visitors, especially if Norvill and Charlotte had the kind of relationship that Charlotte's diaries suggest they did.

Jane starts the car and puts it into reverse. Whether William is right or wrong, it is the certainty with which he made the statement that they'd met twice that's bothersome. Perhaps the same could be said for Jane's assumptions about N? Perhaps her disappearance into the trees at Inglewood wasn't an isolated incident based on a chance encounter but part of a series of connected events. Perhaps Jane's mistake all these years as she picked up and put down the Whitmore story has been the same one William may have made about the Chesters and the Farringtons in his lecture: presuming that there were few previously existing ties between those gathered at Inglewood House for the weekend; presuming that people's lives—even those of the Whitmore patients—are ever simple or small, that there is no traffic of the heart or transit between one kind of place and another.

The doorbell at the village inn is answered by a woman in a long burgundy cardigan and jeans, her dark hair lit with grey. She glances down at Sam but Jane can't tell if the glance means *no dogs allowed* or *dogs welcome.*

'I'm hoping for a room. Just a single.'

The woman opens the door and Jane and Sam follow her into the reception area, the smell of sausage and eggs drifting out of the nearby breakfast room. 'How many nights?' As the woman pulls a ledger out from under the counter, the silver bracelets she's wearing jingle and she pushes them farther up her arm so they stop.

'Dogs are all right?'

The woman tilts her head as if to say *depends on the dog*, or *you tell me.* 'He's an extra five.'

'That's fine.'

'Right, fill this out. It's seventy a night unless you stay for five nights. Then it goes down to sixty-five.'

'Five nights is perfect.' Jane glances over the form: name, address, licence or passport, contact number, credit card.

The woman comes around the counter and pets Sam's head the way he hates, small taps with flat fingers. 'What's his name?'

Jane hesitates for a second, and then without knowing why exactly, she lies: 'Chase.'

'Hiya, Chase, hi there.'

Jane surveys the registration form again, taps the pen against the paper. 'Do you have any information on the caves?'

The woman roots around behind the counter but comes up empty-handed. 'Let me have a look in the sitting room.' She swings her curtain of hair over her shoulder and pushes open the nearest door and the voice of a BBC radio host—'*Up next we've got one hour of back-to-back*'—floats through from the other room.

For 'Name' Jane writes *Helen Swindon*. Helen was a girl she'd gone to university with and Swindon was the last name of a short-term boyfriend in the last orchestra she'd played with, an oboe player she'd broken up with when she quit the cello. She scribbles down a fake address, a made-up driver's licence and a mobile phone number that's close to hers but with a different digit at the end; she has a pile of crisp bank-machine notes on the counter by the time the woman bustles out of the sitting room.

'Right.' The woman drops a stack of pamphlets on the counter. 'Here's a brochure on the caves, one on the trail and a map of the village.' She picks up Jane's form, flicks her eyes over it and then hands it back to Jane, tapping a finger next to a line that asks for her signature. 'What brings you up this way?'

'Just a holiday.' Jane signs *Helen Swindon* quickly, in a dense cursive, and is surprised by how legitimate the signature looks.

'I'll just take two nights now, you can pay the rest later.' The woman counts out the required number of notes and slides the remainder across the counter toward Jane. 'Do you need help with your bags?'

'No.'

'Car?'

'Yes.'

She hands Jane a parking disk and her room key, and then slips Jane's form into the ledger and puts it back under the counter. 'The car park is at the side of the building. Breakfast is seven till eight through those doors—if you'd leave the dog in the room. Public lounge is just through there, though it's usually quiet. Shower's tricky—you need to give the tap a good heave to get it open. I'm Maureen, my husband's Andy. Just ring the buzzer by the front door if you need one of us. And help yourself to a cereal bowl in the breakfast room if you want to leave water out for the dog.' She tugs her cardigan closed and then rubs the corner of her eye with a knuckle. 'You all right, Helen?'

'Yes, fine.' Jane perks up. 'Just tired from the drive.'

Jane pulls her bag and the box of files about the Whitmore out of the car. Her room on the second floor is larger than she expects, with modern wallpaper in green and tan stripes, and a view of the river that cuts through the centre of the village and the grey stone houses on its far side. There's a trestle desk in the corner and a small stand on which sit a kettle and packets of ginger biscuits. On the bed there's a plush robe folded into a neat square and tied with a thick yellow ribbon.

Sam noses the empty rubbish bin, the bathroom tile, the area under the window, drinks loudly from the water bowl and then settles down on the mat just inside the door to scratch his ear with his hind leg.

'I know you're hungry, pal, but let me just get two hours of sleep, okay?' Jane sets the alarm beside the bed, changes out of her damp clothes and slips under the thick white duvet, the Whitmore box next to the desk in her direct line of sight. Sam takes up watch from his mat on the floor.

Because it is day and because we do not trust ourselves to rest, we gather around and watch as Jane settles into sleep. That we once took sleep for granted! That we dropped onto our own beds or cots or idled langorously on our sofas and didn't savour the escape! How the body unflexes itself into a state of compliance, frees the mind to travel.

'I miss beds,' Cat says. 'I think I had a white ceiling. I can almost picture waking up and looking at it; it had decorated squares—'

'Coffers,' the idiot offers.

'Decorated squares with an oval in the room's centre and a hanging gas lamp—'

'That's the Whitmore,' John says. 'The ceiling in the men's ward looked the same.'

'Hark the soft pillow of her hallowed mount,' the poet says. 'There is no greater pleasure than falling asleep on top of a woman.'

'There are children present,' the one with the soft voice says, and the one who rarely speaks snickers. We turn our attention back to Jane.

Under the plush duvet of the inn Jane is dreaming nonsense. So we sift through the flickering residue of her day: Sam running out of sight, the hours of driving, the mobile on her kitchen table blinking Gareth's name. After an hour or so she works her way back to the knot that is William. She sees him and Mina at the hummingbird cabinet, their faces reflected in the glass. But then the dream shifts and the birds twitch to life. Some flit up off their mounts, some get caught in their wiring. After a minute all two hundred and four of them are flapping wildly, trapped in the case like a swarm.

'Do something,' the girl says, turning from the dream and imploring us.

'We can't,' the theologian replies.

'Why not?' John asks.

Those of us who were drifting off into our corners come forward, ready to take sides if we have to.

The birds knock against the glass.

'Help,' the girl says again. 'I mean it.'

'Let's try,' the one with the soft voice says. 'It's only a dream. They hardly ever make sense anyway.'

In the dream the hummingbirds are dying; they crest and fall with broken necks, the flurry of one colliding with the arc of another. Jane does not know how to break the case, she cannot move to save her soul, and William and Mina are oblivious, the little girl saying, 'I like this one' and tracking a hummingbird as it flits into the glass. In the end it is N who hands Jane the key, who loops it off the ring in her pocket and presses it into her palm. Jane standing back as the birds pour out of the opened panel in a fluster of sound.

'Thank you,' the girl says quietly, and someone claps from the far side of the room.

'Who's that?' the theologian snaps, not recognizing the figure.

Some of us leave the dream then, and some of us stay, watch Jane touch the bodies of the birds that litter the case, her fingers stroking their ruffed feathers, righting their bent wings.

Once, when we were at a play with Jane and Ben, we debated the validity of Ceasing. The theologian liked to tell us that death was the end for everyone and that all of our flapping about wouldn't change the fact that we would eventually stop Being.

The argument started at the end of the fourth act when the actress playing the mad woman climbed a stepladder in a gauzy white dress and hanged herself by the neck. Blue floodlights made fake river water below her and all of us turned to Jane, who had clenched her eyes shut. The rope went taut as the lights dropped to black, then blazed back on to reveal an empty stage.

'Where did she go?' the boy asked.

'Trap door,' the idiot answered.

'She was pretty,' said the girl. 'I liked her hair. What's a trap door?'

'It's a hole that opens in the floor,' the one with the soft voice said.

'Is she stuck?' asked the girl.

'Nope,' we said.

'Actually it depends,' said the idiot. 'It is, conceptually speaking, possible for matter to pass through matter, and therefore possible for matter to become stuck, one thing inside the other, the woman and the floor, for example, the surface of things being—'

'Stop—' the theologian hissed.

'—the surface of things being an *illusion* and the particulate nature of the universe such that gaps and fissures exist between all things. If we take molecular models—'

The theologian cleared his throat.

'—and apply probability, which granted precludes—'

'Shut it,' said Cat, 'or else.'

The audience shuffled toward the bar.

'Shall we?' the musician asked, and he stepped forward to conduct us up the aisle.

At the bar the girl wanted to know, 'If the white-dressed woman—'

'Ophelia,' we said.

'If *O-felya* isn't trapped then is she Ceased?'

'Define your terms,' said the idiot.

'No one is talking to you,' Cat snapped.

We turned our attention to the same place we always did.

'Yes, she is *Ceased*'—the theologian flourished a wavery hand in the air—'for all intents and purposes.'

'Excuse me,' someone said—a woman in a black turtleneck and tiger-print scarf—speaking to the queue of people in front of us at the bar. Because it was a weekday matinee the theatre had only opened one of its three lounges and it was packed. We always felt pinched in these situations so we moved out onto the balcony to stand beside the crowd of men in suit jackets and women in blousy dresses holding a cigarette in one hand and a drink in the other. Through the glass doors we could see Jane and Ben still arguing about whether or not the performance was any good, Ben's eyes flitting over Jane's shoulder to the women walking in and out of the loo.

'So is she stuck or is she Ceased?' the girl asked again, eyeing the cup of ice cream an elderly woman was handing to her husband, the side of it lightly shimmered with ice.

'Not stuck,' we all say.

'Again—' the idiot interjected, but we shushed him.

'Ceased. We will all Cease eventually,' the theologian repeated, clearly annoyed by the topic.

Bored, the boy made the Indian powwow call he'd been perfecting and circled a nearby couple.

'We may Cease eventually, sweetie, but we are not Ceased yet,' Cat said. 'At least, not exactly.'

'And what's *griefes*?' the girl asked.

'Where did you hear that?' the one with the soft voice asked.

'The man with the sword said it.'

'*Ka-pow, ka-pow!*' shouted the boy as he fired a few shots and then turned on himself and released an arrow.

'Formes, Moods, shewes of Griefe—' expounded the poet.

Cat leaned toward the girl. 'It's a kind of sadness.'

'—my inky cloak,' the poet sang, 'trappings, suits of woe.'

We think now that Ceasing might be as wrong as everything else. We entered Jane's dream and changed things and nothing happened; John took a name and he is still here. Even fluttering, in the understated ways we have done it, has gone unpunished. When pressed it's hard for us to remember where these rules came from, if they were something we were born with or if they came from the theologian.

'There's someone here,' the theologian says, and he looks from Jane's bed toward the window. The rest of us, weary of his declarations, try to concentrate on what he's perceiving, but we can see nothing but daylight streaming in through the window, the wind lifting the long grass that banks the river, and Sam, his paws twitching on the mat.

Jane pushes off the duvet and Sam stands in the square of sun where he'd been lying, shakes his fur and stretches. It's almost noon, so Jane slips into jeans and a sweater to head to the shops for something to eat and to buy a notebook and pens so she can start into the Whitmore box, see if there's anything she overlooked when she dipped into it last.

In the corner shop she grabs a sandwich, dry dog food for Sam, a cheap squeaky toy he'll probably chew a hole in within minutes and some stationery. While she waits in the queue a young boy and his sister race up and down the candy aisle, and the flap of the boy's jacket knocks a handful of chocolate bars onto the checkered floor.

'Phillip!' The boy's mother glares at him from the till where she's paying for two juice cartons and a newspaper. 'Put those back right now.' She smiles apologetically at Jane and says sorry to the cashier. Philip puts the candy bars back, then falls in line behind his mother. As soon as he does so, the boy and the girl who are with us run up and down the aisles just as the other two had done. '*Zoooooom*,' airplanes the boy, and the girl races alongside him imitating his engine sound, the two of them zipping up and down the aisle so fast they flutter the chocolate bars the boy had set on the edge of the box back onto the floor. The clerk looks up when they fall, Jane glances over and the mother frowns. She walks over to put them back: a small everyday slippage of matter.

Back at the inn Jane slides the Whitmore box over to the bed and sits on the carpet with her back against the wood frame and mattress. She pulls out the casebook pages she photocopied almost a decade ago when she was doing her MA. Riffling through them she decides to start with Leeson—her best source for what happened the night of the trio's escape and visit to Inglewood House. Wanting, in more ways than one, to go back to the beginning.

14 The Whitmore patient casebooks always follow the same formula: basic statistics followed by descriptions of the individual's symptoms upon committal to the asylum, and supporting statements from two doctors. *Charles Leeson, age 42, solicitor, married.* Jane sits against the wood frame of the bed in her room at the inn and rereads her copy of Leeson's file, picturing him the way she always does, as the type of gentleman found in a crowd scene in a painting by Manet: his hair peppering into grey, his clothes fit and proper. Under 'Symptoms' a doctor

with spidery handwriting had penned: *Believes he has murdered his infant and that he is to be put on trial. Hears animal noises at night. Is convinced creatures are trying to get into his house. Claims there is a man inside the statue in the city square watching him . . .* And even though Leeson's name is at the top of the page, some of us standing around Jane are confused, because it seems we both know and don't know the man being described.

This kind of information—clinical and without context—can be found in the other files Jane reads: *Eliza Woodward, 22.* Admitted: *June 2, 1877.* Occupation: *Button seller.* Status: *Single.* Whether first attack: *No.* Duration: *2 weeks.* Cause of insanity: *Unknown.* Symptoms: *Believes she was being held captive in her own home. Disobeys her father. Invents mischief. Claims that she has thrown candles at the minister during mass and set him on fire. Injures herself by hitting. Will go out without a bonnet. Unpicks fancy work she has just completed. Has fits of laughing, crying and kissing people.*

Alfred Hale, 36. Admitted: *January 25, 1877.* Occupation: *Instrument repair.* Status: *Single.* Whether first attack: *Yes.* Duration: *3 weeks.* Cause of insanity: *Blow to the head.* Whether suicidal: *No.* Whether danger to others: *Uncertain.* Hallucinations: *Believes himself to be a renowned composer. Maintains that he has performed for the Queen in her bedchamber. Claims to have powers in his hands and that it is dangerous for anyone to touch them.*

Jane stands up and puts on the kettle and Sam stretches his back.

'What's wrong with kissing?' Cat asks. She makes a loud *mwah* sound and then moves around the room—'*Mwah, mwaaah, mwaaah*'—pretending to kiss all of us.

When Jane sits back down to her files and notes, we gather

around her again, though sometimes she reads too fast for us to follow because even a quick glance at a word like *button seller* can call to mind a shop with a wall of oak drawers along its length; the smell of the wood polish applied every morning before the doors were opened for business. We see *teacher* or *joiner* or *clock repairer* and suddenly some of us can feel the grit of chalk dust, or see holes bored into wood, hear a broken chime drag its heels across the hour—some version of our selves appearing in these notices, a hint of relation, though the details are so scant they don't make room for the person we are starting to feel we were: someone who may have taken delight in snowfall or a child's curtsey, the canter of a horse or the efficiency of stamps, or the rough ardour of a washerwoman. These files say nothing of generosity, playfulness, the wing-collared jacket one of us believes he preferred, the bowl of ripe fruit one of us remembers painting in art class, a fly sitting on the leaf of the strawberry.

At the end of each casebook there is a square box for patient outcomes. Inside some are the phrases *discharged cured* or *discharged uncured* or *died of illness*; occasionally the note says *transferred to—* followed by the name of another institution. In John Hopper's case there is a letter from the supervisor at a clockworks factory affixed between pages: . . . *thought it prudent to appraise you of J. Hopper's progress over these past two weeks. Overall he has shown a high degree of conscientiousness—both in work and personal command.* . . . Charles Leeson's casebook has no such letter. Instead, in looping writing the last entry states: *Died 5 September 1877.* Then, in a hand that Jane thinks might be Superintendent Thorpe's, the added words: *at the Whitmore Hospital for Convalescent Lunatics.*

—

By the time Jane gets up to go out for dinner she is almost half-way through her Whitmore file box and has written two pages of notes that don't connect the pieces of the story in any meaningful way. She has what she had a year ago—names and a web of relationships between the patients convalescing at the Whitmore in 1877, but no mention of any woman's name that starts with *N* outside of the 'missing' reference in the hospital logbook.

Jane pulls her bag over her shoulder and Sam stands up and wags his tail. She leashes him and then stops to check her bag for her mobile, rooting around in it until she remembers that she left the phone on the kitchen table back in London, deliberately, so that no one would know where she was.

The village fish and chip shop is lit yellow by dingy overhead lights and smells more like grease than the sea. Sam waits outside while Jane sits in a plastic chair listening to the deep fryer gurgle over her haddock and the kid behind the counter laugh at a video on a computer screen.

Jane takes a sip of her fizzy drink and then plays with the straw, poking it around the hole in the can while she tries to decide if she should call Lewis or Gareth, or both. It's possible that Lewis still doesn't know what happened and that Gareth has stopped calling. Maybe William explained how he knew her, or maybe Gareth decided it would be best to wait until Monday for Jane to explain herself—Gareth assuming that the work week would start as usual and that Jane would simply show up.

From the picnic table outside the inn, Jane can see down the road to the pub, its outside lamp hanging over a knot of

Saturday-night drinkers. When a group goes back in and the conversations diminish, the village goes back to its humming: the sound of power lines and the steady drone of a generator out the back, the river shushing underneath it and, somewhere under that, the churning falls.

Sam drops his chin on Jane's knee and she feeds him one of her chips. 'Because you're on holiday,' she says, and he drops his chin again and blinks up at her. She glances down the road to the pub one more time, craving a glass of wine or an off-sale bottle she can bring back to her room—but it's late and she decides it won't kill her to go without, so she wipes her hands on a napkin and gathers her rubbish. Sam barks and, when Jane gives him a stern look, wags at his own audacity.

'We'll go exploring tomorrow, okay? Provided you can behave.' She rubs his ears, still as soft as when he was a puppy, and puts her head down, touching his cold wet nose to hers.

By eleven Jane is in bed and we are settling into our corners, attending to how her thoughts move between the files she's been reading and what she could have done differently with William. The best part of the evening, for us, was earlier when we watched her leaf through a file of programmes and invitations to various hospital entertainments. We crowded around the photocopies she'd made of the events that took place the summer N went missing: sheets of carefully inked names and intended performances, formal invitations to recitals and plays. Some of us could call up snatches of songs or forgotten faces as we looked at the handbills: 'Mr. Tom Underwood playing street piano!' 'Miss Florence Donlan singing "Now Ever" by Mattei!' 'A recitation of Tennyson's "Tears, Idle Tears" by Mr. Samuel Murray!' 'An ensemble performance by the Whitmore Players of *The Rosebud of Stinging Nettle Farm: A Melodramatic Pastoral in Fifteen Gasps!*' 'Dr. Thorpe and Matron Montgomery performing a duet by Mendelssohn!'

'Oh God,' the musician groaned, 'that woman couldn't play pianoforte at all!'

Memory being what it is, we sometimes remember backwards, or sideways, or inside out. We will read the name of a song and instead of its melody some of us might experience a tightness around the ribs, a corseting. Or we might recall the notes but instead of seeing the musicians playing will picture the diamond pattern of a floor. Applause spilling out from an audience might equal heartache; a leaflet for the Fancy Fair might put the taste of toffee in our mouths. History is never perfectly framed, although the photographs in the museum may suggest otherwise. In Jane's file tonight we saw the notice for Dr. Thorpe and Matron Montgomery performing a duet, and one of us felt the heat of a room and another felt a bump on his forehead and still another saw a man in a wooden chair tapping his hand on his leg out of rhythm with the song. We saw the Matron's thick fingers fall clumsily on the keyboard a beat behind the doctor's bowing, and it pleased us to believe that someone with keys to rooms we could not open could do something so poorly.

—

An hour after Jane has switched off the light she sits up in bed and pulls the cord on the lamp. The bulb flickers back on. We rouse ourselves as quickly as children who have only been pretending to sleep. Jane gets out of bed and goes over to the file she left on top of the Whitmore box. She thumbs through it, not exactly sure what she's looking for. Stops at one of the programmes she'd photocopied a decade ago when she was doing her dissertation, one for the Whitmore's 1877 asylum ball.

'Lancers,' Cat says, peering at it.

'Punch,' says the musician.

'The Captain is here,' trills the poet.

Jane scans the programme, then leafs back through the file folder to see if she'd made a duplicate of the invitation. Near the bottom of the file she finds it—a grey-scale copy of an ornate and perfectly typeset card, more formal than the usual billets done by patients practising their calligraphy.

THE WHITMORE HOSPITAL FOR CONVALESCENT LUNATICS

RESPECTFULLY INVITES YOU

TO OUR ANNUAL SUMMER FESTIVAL AND BALL

ENTERTAINMENT & LIBATIONS PROVIDED

GLEES BY THE SINGING CLUB BEGIN AT 3

READINGS IN THE RECREATION HALL AT 4

TEA ON THE GROUNDS WILL BE SERVED AT 5

DANCING ON THE LAWNS COMMENCES AFTER

THE FORMAL BALL OPENS AT 7

CARRIAGES AVAILABLE FROM THE STATION

Jane's dissertation work had been a survey of the types of records and documents kept by rural asylums in the Victorian era. Although she'd written a chapter contextualizing the intended use and consequential applications of these documents, most of the work had been dull—about 'kind' and 'type' more than content. She'd categorized programmes and entertainment broadsheets as 'ephemera' and hadn't spent much time thinking about them. As she pulls out the invitation for a closer look she finds she can't say exactly what a ball at an asylum might look like, although she knows it was part of the enterprise of normalizing and reviving patients: to provide them with formal occasions where they could dress in their best suits and gowns and practise behaving the way society expected them to. Such rehearsal was especially important in a convalescent hospital like the Whitmore, where the patients were presumed to be curable and often enjoyed greater freedoms in anticipation of release.

Jane reads the invitation again and tries to picture the hundred or so souls at the Whitmore spinning on the hardwood floors of the recreation hall she'd walked through all those years ago. Closing her eyes she adds papier-mâché streamers to the walls, delicate bouquets on thin-legged tables, candle chandeliers and music from a band made up of patients and staff. The patients who weren't in refractory care, who weren't, as she'd read earlier in a casebook, 'banned from the ball and all other social engagements for a fortnight,' would have been present, wearing their best clothes and dancing with—. And that's when it occurs to her: with the public. The invitation was an invitation to the *public*, not just family or friends, but members of *society*. *Carriages available from the station*. Asylums and convalescent hospitals, she knows, regularly invited the public to their institutions so they could see how well the patients were treated, recognize their progress and the value of the hospital's work. Slowly, she reasons it out: if balls weren't just for guests of the patients, if they were for members of the community, then George Farrington, who lived a mere ten miles away, would probably have been invited. As one of the wealthiest landowners in the area, he would have known the Superintendent, or at least have been familiar with him.

I hope they did not suffer from their long walk. The letter Farrington wrote to the Whitmore after Leeson and Herschel showed up at the manor wasn't warmly or personally addressed, but it seems to indicate that Farrington wasn't a stranger. He mentioned Inglewood by name but didn't feel the need to con-textualize himself or his estate. Jane does a quick calculation: he was moderately renowned as a botanist in 1877, but not so famous that he might eschew the convention of declaring himself and his relationship to the Whitmore at the start of a letter if he were a stranger to those with whom he was corresponding. Instead he *presents his compliments.*

Jane gets back into bed and turns off the lamp, sure now of her conclusion. George Farrington *knew* the Whitmore—he *must* have been familiar with it; he stated in his letter that it was a long walk to his estate. And if Herschel, Leeson and N had found their way to one of the most famous residents in the area, maybe that resident had also, at some point, made his way to the Whitmore—as a member of the public invited to the summer ball some two months before N went missing.

'Lancers!' shouts Cat, 'and galops. I think she's on to something now!'

The musician turns to Cat and slides his right hand out in front of himself, making a buzzing sound with his lips and then the *waa-waaa* of a brass instrument.

'Is it what you expected, Mr. Farrington?' the poet demurs, mimicking a woman's haughty tone.

'Who said that?' Cat asks, and the poet clacks his teeth like a wild animal.

'Punch,' the musician shouts again, 'in crystal glasses,' and some of us can taste it: the pleasant fizz of soda and the tang of fruit, bits of apple settling lightly on our tongues.

After a short debate, we decide that Jane was right about the orchestra and Cat was correct about the dances. While Jane sleeps we imagine ideal versions of possible selves: hair coiffed and held perfectly in place, an evening so cool we did not feel the sweat pooling under our shirts. All of us so hungry for memory we will take it any way it comes, even see it as Jane envisions it: the papier-mâché banners and profusion of candles, the wood floors gleaming. Those images are set against the fragments we think we can remember—bits and pieces we puzzle over as we move into the long night ahead. The boy says, 'I've never been to a ball,' and the girl whispers, 'Me neither,' and Cat air-kisses their heads and says, 'But it is such a lot of fun!' She whisks around the room so they can sense her dancing while Sam sits up to *oouuff* at us in the dark.

15   In the summer of 1877 the orchestra was more spirited than it had been the year before, in part because it was made up of more patients—Alfred Hale among them, wearing a large paper collar and playing an admirable trombone. There had been the usual round of dance lessons in the weeks preceding the ball for those who were untrained or who lacked confidence. The men and women had been allowed to practise together in the final week after instruction in their own gendered wards. Now, let loose under the high-ceilinged, rose-festooned

room on the actual evening, there was some confusion about roles—some women taking the lead as some men rested their arms lightly on top of their partner's. The warders in their dark-blue uniforms stepping in to send overenthused gentlemen on their way, intent that no advantages be taken. Noble separated us when it suited him. Bream was tolerant, going so far as to join in for a spin when the fancy took him, though he gripped so tightly on the turns with his sausage fingers some of us worried he'd leave behind a row of bruises lined up like the keys of a flute.

Before he took the quadrille with Sallie Herring—who had plucked out so much of her hair she'd been given a bright yellow felt cap to wear—Superintendent Thorpe had been stationed at the head of the receiving line. Leeson had stood beside him briefly, bowing and shaking hands with the first few guests and introducing himself as a commissioner, winking hopefully at the Superintendent as if it were all in shared fun. He was quickly relieved of this assumption. Shortly thereafter, a dapper gentleman in a frock coat with a velvet collar and a bright yellow boutonnière came in through the double doors. By the time he and the older woman accompanying him reached Thorpe and the Matron, Leeson was hiding farther down the queue, the super-intendent having stuffed a cigar into his pocket in exchange for better behaviour. Leeson bowed at the woman, who was ahead of the gentleman in the processional, and she nodded her head hastily in his direction, the peacock feathers nestled in her hair arcing toward Leeson so that he had to restrain himself from reaching up to bat them away.

Ask us what we remember of a night like this and the women will tell you about the feel of gloves on their arms again, about the shift of a corseted dress, the weight of the bustle, about how the men's starched collars lifted their chins so that they seemed to be looking down their noses at you when they presented themselves for a dance. The men remember how the candy colour of a dress hung in their eyes, how there was a promise of brandy, how the true choreography of the evening lay in trying to arrange a secret meeting with the woman of their choice.

By nine Hopper had started to follow Eliza Woodward, eventually stealing a kiss from her behind a potted fern, the pillow of her lips a pleasant surprise. Hale was less lucky: he spilled his punch on Sallie's skirt and Sallie pulled his ear in return. The night was a mix of distractions: the fit of new shoes, the increasing warmth of the room as the dancing continued, squares of cool air radiating off the glass panes of the windows along with our reflections. The room casting us back in our best suits and dresses, colouring the body back in.

Sitting on the floor beside Jane's bed, head bent in concentration, Cat can see herself in sea-green satin, can remember her lips on John Hopper's in an alcove behind the fern. John, sitting beside her, is aware suddenly of his own former body: his hair stubbly but growing back after another enforced shaving. The two of them side by side as Jane goes on dreaming and we go on remembering the ball. The shape that is Cat whispers to the shape that is John, 'How did you guess your name?'

We gather that we knew some of the guests personally, and others by reputation: the Magistrate and Commissioners existing in name only, as was the case with most of the local businessmen and their wives. The poet knew George Farrington because the week before the ball the Superintendent had placed a slim red volume of Farrington's poetry into his hands, suggesting that he might find it interesting. 'The book,' the Superintendent had said earnestly, sliding it across his desk, 'exudes a quality of liminal thought of the sort presently admired in literary circles. . . .' This statement was, of course, pure condescension—the Superintendent thoughtlessly implying that due to his incarceration, the poet had no access to the pulse of current conventions. Sensing his mistake, he tried again. 'It's simply that as a *fellow wordsmith* I thought you might feel a kinship with the man and his work.' The poet, however, found Farrington's work banal, bordering on trifling, and he barely gave it a second read, though he prided himself on being open-minded. His own offerings had, in their infancy, been widely misunderstood and even mocked in the pages of some of the better magazines. When he'd still been free—which was how the poet termed the period of time before his marriage to the succubus—he'd often been chastised by his friends for continuing to write when the evidence against his having talent weighed so plentifully against him.

It was *The B–*, an upstart magazine favoured by the new generation of writers, that changed the course of things. Upon the publication of his second book the editors of the magazine had sought out and reviewed his first, which most of their brethren had blighted. It was found, in the eyes of the new reviewer, to be 'a marvel,' 'a heralding cry of the new age.' Suddenly the poet was lauded, and just as suddenly he was married to a woman of society who had tricked him into the union through false claims of pregnancy. Within weeks he stopped being able to write at home, and then, after months in a *pensione* in a country he remembers only as ripe with oranges that bled when you ate them and with women whose nipples were dark as mud, he stopped being able to write at all.

Standing by the window in Jane's room as the ball unfolds around us, the poet remembers his wife articulating the situation to the Superintendent on the day he was committed: 'Imagine, sir, that there are strings that connect us to the world. It's as if my husband's are slowly being plucked away.'

When the ball was formally underway, George Farrington asked the Superintendent about the poet. They were standing at the far end of the room near the French balcony doors, George stroking with one finger the arc of a scar hidden by his moustache.

'I have some interest in poetry,' George explained, and the Superintendent smiled.

'My wife and I are familiar with your work, Mr. Farrington— botanical *and* poetical—though I fear I am not qualified to discuss either. I enjoyed the lake sonnets tremendously.'

'Has he continued to write?' Farrington asked, glancing around the room as if he expected to recognize the poet's visage.

'He engages in the odd recitation, and occasionally we find a stanza or two pencilled on paper in the art room. Sometimes there are snatches of verse in the letters he sends to his sister.'

'And is he much recovered?'

'He is improving, though he still has the habit of sitting for hours staring at objects, at blades of grass or pieces of fluff cast off by the hens. He fancies that he has an army that inhabits an underground city. A city he spends, I dare say, much of his time "visiting."'

'And his wife, the Countess? How does she fare?'

'She comes once a month to visit. You'll see her there by the tall windows in the crimson dress. He wants nothing to do with her.'

Farrington found the poet's wife staring out the window at the airing courts. He bowed as she glanced over her shoulder at him—a quick flash of dark eyes and high cheekbones, a slight equatorial earthiness to her skin.

'The poet's wife as an object worthy of attention?' she asked. 'It will get you no closer to him, Mr. Farrington. I have, you see, no access.'

George tilted his head. 'I beg your pardon. Are we acquainted?'

'The world feels oppressively small some days, does it not?' She faced him directly, gave him a formal curtsey and then glanced around the room. 'Is it what you expected, Mr. Farrington? The madhouse?'

'I came without presumptions.'

She put her arm through his and turned him toward the crowd. A gentleman in a double-breasted green jacket and a woman with thick lace cuffs and a wide collar waltzed by. They were followed by a dapper gentleman with long side-whiskers and a white cravat, and a plump woman in a tulle gown. 'One of those two men jumped off a bridge and one of the women set fire to her house. The other man is the local draper and the other woman is the Superintendent's niece. Dare I ask whom you perceive to be whom?'

George shifted uncomfortably and tried to retract his arm without revealing his distaste to anyone who might be watching.

'I just wanted to say how much I admire your husband's poetry.' He disengaged his arm stiffly and bowed again.

'As a poet yourself?'

George hesitated. 'Yes.'

'Do you know what they say in here, Mr. Farrington?' She levelled her eyes at him and he stepped back, ready to take his leave.

'I do not.'

'That we're the mad ones—the ones outside. That it's our actions, our slights, strategies and resentments that are so unreasonable.'

'And is that what you believe, Countess?'

She smiled at him for the first time, but the expression dropped away as quickly as it had taken shape. 'He's over by the pianoforte. He was here skulking around the curtains when you first presented yourself.' She lifted her wrist and her fingers fell in the direction of a short, balding man in a cream-coloured jacket standing in front of the piano and within hearing range. 'He's in a mood. Mind he doesn't bite.'

By the time the windows were opened a little while later to let in some air, Leeson was waltzing with a commissioner's wife and Hale had put away his trombone to stand at the punch bowl next to the red-haired girl from the laundry who had stolen into the chapel with him once for a lusty half hour. Herschel had excused himself to one of the chairs along the wall and was seething at a perceived slight—a glare—received at quite some distance from the Matron. N was fiddling with the ribbons she'd braided into her hair, feeling common compared to the wives of the local businessmen, the robust sisters of the wealthier patients, the pink-cheeked daughters of lawyers and doctors and bankers. She'd been asked to dance numerous times, and had laughed through a catastrophic quadrille with Herschel, only to be told by the Superintendent as they partnered for the *schottische* that she danced quite commendably. For that she tripped purposefully and stepped on his toe. When they were finished he escorted her off the floor, only to find Farrington waiting for him.

'Superintendent Thorpe.' Farrington bowed at the girl and just as quickly dismissed her. 'I beg your pardon, there's a matter that I believe might merit your attention.'

'Of course.'

Farrington bowed again at the girl, this time regarding her more fully, her face uncomplicated in its youth, pleasing and open. He gestured toward the back of the hall and said to the Superintendent, 'Please, this way.'

Farrington led Dr. Thorpe along the wall. With the slightest nod of his head the Superintendent soon brought Bream and Ockley into step behind him; he would need their assistance if anything unsuitable was occurring. He had his list of suspects already, and as he strode through the ballroom he mentally noted those he could and couldn't see of the troublemakers present: Hopper was by the grated fire, Hale by the punch bowl, Leeson sniffing around a woman in a blue-ribboned dress, albeit at an acceptable distance, Greevy sprawled miserably in a chair. He couldn't see Herschel anywhere.

'Through here.' Farrington opened the panelled door to the patients' library and together he and the Superintendent entered the room, along with Bream, Ockley and, because she'd tacked on behind them, N. The library was dark save for the corner, which was lit by a short candelabrum gripped firmly in Herschel's hand. The poet stood behind Herschel, his eyes closed as if in a trance, in mid-recitation: '. . . and enter the ground / to find ourselves / dwelling in the city beneath it, / our bodies bald, backs clean / wings grown within us . . .'

Gathered in the room were seven or eight individuals, including Commissioner Mullan and his wife. The Countess was standing behind Mrs. Mullan in the shadows.

'And feign again / the kiss of sun, / and wander farther from it. . . .'

In the candlelight the poet appeared as little more than a soft-lit face with half-moons under his eyes and a waxy sheen on his forehead, but his voice and the words were magnetic, some thoughts solidly said and others whispered as if secreted from his mouth to the ears of those closest. Those listening were mesmerized, and even Herschel, who normally could not keep still, was standing fixedly beside the poet, his fist gripping the centre of the candelabrum, though his eyes darted from face to face as if he expected an attack.

The poem, dark and otherworldly, made only a kind of half-sense—talking rats, kings who ate shoes, flowers that bloomed only when you looked away from them—but as those present allowed the words to wash over them, the work started to take on a fuller meaning. It was like listening to the most dysfunctional of the patients: their words took on weight if you dropped your notions of what was acceptable or logical.

Just when the poem was about to reach its peak, just when the gates between the upper garden and the underworld had been bashed by those above in order to bind the two worlds forever,

Ockley coughed noisily into his hand—perhaps out of spite. The poet opened his eyes, saw that he was not alone, and stopped speaking. For a second or two his gaze settled on the face of each person present, as if to see with whom he'd been intimate, and then without a word he fled past all of them out of the room.

His words, as some of us remember them—and as the poet standing watch beside Jane's bed recites them—seemed like a dark art. For some of us, listening to him was like being pricked repeatedly with a pin—the sensation a discomfort radiating out from its point of entry. A poem of nerve ends, of images that stitched you up in a zigzag pattern and then scissored you open again.

If George Farrington had been less obsessed with the scraps of the poet's new work, he might have remembered N standing behind him in the library, remembered that he and she had danced in the same quadrille earlier in the evening, and that during the course of the dance he'd had cause to move past her a few times, her gloved hand settling briefly in his, the delicate bones of her fingers palpable under his thumb.

Instead he was preoccupied with whether or not the poet had set his work down on paper, and if he had, how it might be recovered and sent to a publisher, previewed perhaps in a magazine, delivered to readers who had been waiting for a new title to appear. As he discussed these matters with Thorpe, Farrington became aware of the Countess's eyes on him, how she was glaring at him from her place at the window with a gaze so unrelenting that he eventually begged his mother to go over and distract her.

The limits of our attention being what they are, only small strains of the evening remain with us: Herschel obsessing about the Matron, who was watching Hale—puffed up at being in the orchestra—to make sure he didn't harass the red-haired girl from the laundry. Leeson at the long drinks table watching the commissioners from a distance; Wick obsessing over who had been rifling through his personal things: someone had taken two cigars from a mahogany box under his bed and his book on *The Systems of Chemical Philosophy*. Old man Greevy watching Leeson stare idly as the gentleman with the boutonnière, who was a head taller than any other man in the room, walked over to join in the commissioners' conversation. The old man mumbling, 'That one is master of the estate at Inglewood, I've a nephew works for him.' A room that is filled with people stuck in the web of their own complicated narratives: Leeson turning his attention to N as she wavered there, to the shine of her ribbons as she left the drinks table for a chair, catching glimpses of her between other bodies as she slipped her feet out of her shoes to flex them under the blossom-pink folds of her skirt.

This is our problem with time and its knots and bows: our impressions are muddled, and as Jane is sleeping we say, 'The night sky was B minor,' 'My feet felt pink,' 'The music was punch,' 'The panelled room was a woods I felt at home in.'

Yes, we would like to remember exactly, to whisper to Jane that this or that transpired, to slide one piece of the puzzle into the next, to assure ourselves that the conversations we eavesdropped on, the sprung looks between people, actually occurred. We would like to bring together hardwood floors and medallion ceilings and window-glanced sky, would like to say with surety that Hale played well and Hopper was kissed, that Wick was vindicated and that N wished, because of Bream's groping advances, that she was elsewhere.

But there are only a few things we all agree on: that Leeson at one point noted the man he would later recognize as Farrington, that Farrington was watching the poet, and that the poet—like us—was watching the ghostly figures of his invented world.

16 Leeson had been walking in the woods around the lake for almost an hour, but he'd had to double back when the ground became too quaggy as his shoes were already the better part of ruined. He was, by this juncture, lost. He had been looking for N in the forest, accidentally coming out past the Farrington estate house when he'd meant to retrace—*exactly*—their steps from the month before.

For weeks now he'd been trying, from his ward-confinement at the Whitmore, to deduce what had happened on the walk up to the Farringtons' house. He'd been asked numerous times by Superintendent Thorpe where the girl had gone—only to have the good doctor suddenly drop the topic a week ago. Today, during the four hours it had taken him to retrace the route to the estate, he'd rehearsed the events of that August afternoon, reciting the facts as he had to Thorpe: the door was left unlocked, Herschel had walked out, Leeson had followed, then the girl. It had been the three of them in the woods, and then it was just him and Herschel taking tea in the house of the gentleman he recognized from the ball.

After the trio's excursion, Leeson's privileges had been revoked and he had been under constant threat of transfer back to a less convivial institution. These threats had been most disconcerting in the first two weeks after their adventure, though their power waned once he was given leave to go as far as the airing courts. At the end of the third week, having been on his best behaviour, he had been allowed to return to morning duty in the greenhouse, where he was given the responsibility of refilling the watering cans. He'd passed time in the afternoons playing a game he called 'evens and odds,' jotting down figures in his notebook: evens meaning that the girl was still in the woods and odds that she was elsewhere and he'd never find her. According to his calculations the lace doily on the day-room table had five hundred and eighty holes, the wood planks in the ward corridor amounted to one thousand and forty; there were fifty-eight patients in the men's wards and forty-eight in the women's; there were two balding attendants; the rug had twenty knotted sections of tassels, the first grouping consisting of three hundred and sixty strands. The cutlery was five—odds—and the number of the confraternity at his breakfast table evens every morning except Sunday, when Professor Wick ruined it by plopping himself down and knocking over a singular cup of tea. The tomato plants, shrivelling in their beds later that morning, were even, which was a small consolation; the cards in the games room even; the magpies odds one Monday and a subsequent Friday, and evens the rest of the week. And so it went in favour of his finding her, somewhere, he decided, between the pollarded oaks and the estate itself.

Leeson's second escape had been well orchestrated. On his last day of greenhouse duty, the attendant Bream had appeared on the other side of the glass with a wheelbarrow. He'd rubbed his thick neck with one dirty hand while pointing to the gatehouse with the other. *You're to weed along the walk.* He'd waited to see if Leeson would obey and how quickly, because he was known for enjoying the task of *inspiring* complicity as much as he was known for the clotted stupidity of his preposterously slow thinking.

After an hour Bream handed Leeson off to Noble so that he could go and skulk around the Superintendent's garden. It fanned out in a V shape between the gentlemen's airing court and the ladies', and if one stood on the mound under the flagging pear tree one could sometimes observe the women circling the lawn under their parasols. Noble watched his charge half-heartedly from the wall of the gatehouse where he was having a smoke. Leeson saw them then: the hall porter's keys which dangled off of a large hoop from his belt—keys that Leeson knew he hung on the back of the door in his quarters when he went to bed. It followed that if a search party was to be mounted, if he and Herschel—or whoever else might be willing to be counted in their number—were to escape to find N, the keys would need to be pilfered or something would need to be bartered—though Leeson couldn't think of what he had to offer Noble that might earn him a half a day's grace.

Before Leeson's first 'day out' there had been talk that suggested he might soon be ready for release, though Leeson suspected this had more to do with his letters of complaint to the Commissioners about Bedford's shock treatments and less to do with being cured. The Superintendent's refusal to look for N and Leeson's irate reaction to his confinement—a total of three incidents that twice involved restraints—soon put a stop to Thorpe's talk of Leeson being allowed to 'return home.' This suited Leeson perfectly, for 'home' had become a remote idea, a stuffy and enclosed particularity that had started to lose the draw it once held for him. Still, if he wanted to venture out again, if he wanted to become the kind of patient who could come and go more freely, he would need to be 'better.' Any progress he made after that revelation was, of course, a ruse—actions undertaken in order to gain back his privileges. The more he focused on the questions Dr. Thorpe lobbed at him and on the responses of the others in Thorpe's care, the greater his insight into how to fool the doctor into thinking he was making progress.

'Did you sleep well?'

'Very well, thank you. I haven't felt this rested in years.'

'Do you want pudding today?'

'Pudding would be delightful.'

—

Now, as Leeson stood in a thicket by the lake, he remembered that it was these very same woods that had, a month ago, restored him to himself, stirring up memories he had long been avoiding: the excessive demands of work, his wife's diminishing affections, the ineptitude of his very being. Cutting across a nearby field that August afternoon, Herschel and the girl ahead of him, he had marvelled at nature's inherent symmetry and its embeddings: a whorl inside a whorl on the side of a tree. Touching his hand to the bark's welt he'd been reminded that he had secrets, undisclosed debts his brother had discovered before his confinement. In a copse of alder he'd spied a moss bed that seemed to be growing out of some older bed of lichen, and stroking the two textures with his fingers he remembered having relations with the sour-smelling woman who came to sweep out the offices in the evening, though it had happened only twice, hurriedly and awkwardly, and late in Emily's pregnancy when she refused to let him near her. And, too, he had remembered why he was at the Whitmore in the first place. Remembered it not in the way one tries to remember something another tells you, facts or words that hang like banners over some unseen reality; but remembered it in the body, as if it were happening again: Emily in bed in her nightshift saying, 'Please, Charles, just take her,' imploring him over the baby's cries. Leeson walking back to the rope on the wall, pulling at it harder this time, straining to hear Rose's steps on the landing. The infant, six weeks and still ruddy, nudged toward the edge of the bed so that Emily could pull her shift down, press her hot face into the coolness of her pillow. The thought that she might die had lain unspoken between them since her return to bed, though once, in a fever, Emily told Charles that she believed the infant was stealing whatever strength she had left, a leech clamping on to its parcel of blood. The birth had not been at all what she'd expected—the baby caught in there so that more than once the doctor's hands had come out empty and covered in her blood, the stench of her own body revolting her. And then there had been nothing, a perfect black hum that lasted two days. The ache was far off at first and then closer, arriving one note at a time, like a change in season, until it was over her and around her with its buds and sprouts, open mouth and tiny wings. When she had almost regained herself, the constant needling of the baby threatened to undo her all over again: its hands little curled things Emily both loved and wanted to slap away. Charles coming in to annoy her, to fawn and act stupidly and move around the room picking up and putting down books and coverlets, winding up the music box he'd bought her once on a whim. His manner as incessant as the infant's: *how was she feeling, had she slept well, should he send for the doctor again,* asking, asking, asking.

'Please take her,' Emily had repeated into her pillow, her back to the screaming thing beside her. 'Give her to Rose.'

But Rose had not come, despite his repeated pulls on the rope. She was the only person in the house other than Emily to have held the infant. Unsure how to proceed exactly, Charles bent over the swaddle that was his daughter and carefully took the bundle in his hands; one of the baby's arms came free and scrabbled in the air. He glanced toward the door again for Rose, and when he did not see her he pulled his daughter up toward his chest, surprised at her lightness. He had imagined she would be weightier, as if already filled with the materials required to turn her into the adult she would one day become.

'Rose—' he called from the bedroom doorway, trying to make his request sound firm. She'd only been in their service for two months and Emily already suspected her of pilfering, first the pearl from a pair of her earrings and then a few coins from her purse. 'Rose!' he called, louder this time. And then Leeson had stepped onto the landing to survey the hall and the entryway to the sitting room below. The runner at the top of the steps was untacked in the place where he'd asked Arthur just the day before to fix it. The baby was now blinking wide-eyed and silently up at him, which made him think that Emily might take her back, might allow her to remain in the room. Turning, he caught his foot, and unable to lift it over the bulge of carpet, felt himself going down. For a brief and amazing instant Charles believed that he might be able to correct himself, was falling forward slowly enough that it seemed he had whole minutes to plan his adjustments, angle his shoulders so that he might reel backwards instead and take the brunt of the fall. Sets of instructions spun through his mind even as he tee-tered: free your right arm, keep the baby firmly in the crook of your left, use your hand to break the—. But his right arm did not do as instructed and so he tumbled sideways on the land-ing, meeting the floor with his shoulder, his eyes on his child's fluttering lids as the soft cup of her head angled toward the hardwood and then lightly hit. Emily was in her nightdress in the doorway before he could even sit up, and the baby screamed so loud her face passed through two shades of red and into a mottled violet.

In the month before they found her dead in her cot she often screamed like that, and Emily, unable to meet Charles's eye, would by her very silence imply that *he* had done that, that something was not right with the baby and that this fault, like all the other faults she'd found in the world, was his.

In the end it didn't matter that Herschel hadn't come with Leeson when Leeson had wagged the keys in front of his face victoriously; Herschel was indifferent to the fact that N was not dead, but missing. Or, if not missing, then a kind of changeling who had walked so long in the woods she'd turned into hair-grass or foxtail, into a tree or fern or fawn, invisible to anyone who didn't know to look for the part of the meadow that moved against the current of the breeze.

Standing in a bower a stone's throw from the lake, Leeson remembered what old man Greevy had said about his plan: that if Leeson found N and brought her back he would be made a king, and could set a national holiday, and would be given keys to the kitchen where they could all have as much butter and jam as they desired, jar after jar they could take for themselves or give to anyone. And Leeson had agreed, adding that N could be queen and guest of honour at the next annual ball. 'If she isn't *ffffft*,' Greevy added, miming someone hanging from a rope. Herschel had gone along with that, had slung his tongue out of his mouth in an enthusiastic parody. For a second, Leeson had tried to imagine the girl that way, her neck stretched and bruised. The awkward nature of the image convinced him that she couldn't be dead, and he said so, and Herschel shrugged and returned his attention to the Greek alphabet that Professor

Wick had scratched onto the chalkboard. '*Alpha, beta, gamma, delta, epsilon*,' Wick said, instructing his fellow inmates to follow along. But none of the other patients cared, and the words made no sense to them, so Wick went on with his lesson, and the others, one after the other, got up and wandered away.

Above all else, Charles valued tenderness. He knew, as he made his way towards the shore to get his bearings, that his wife wasn't coming back, that she had excised him from her concern, that she would recoil if he presented himself to her, even cured. He knew, in full account, what he was and what he'd done. He also knew that more than anyone it was the girl who saw him, who had given something of herself by touching his head in the clearing in the woods that August day and saying, 'There, there' after she heard about Bedford and his shock therapy.

All of which meant there was nothing to do but look to a new set of possible futures, futures that he could unfold like a sheet of sums, a sheet that said 'one plus one equals two,' that said 'evens': go and find the girl.

The first shot from the boat resounded around the lake and Leeson's head jerked up. The crack was followed directly by a light clattering of pebbles falling high over the rock face to the right of where Leeson had stopped. The noise of children calling out to each other ensued—'Thomas! Celia! This way!'—and then the bushes not too far from Leeson's station parted and a lanky blond boy leapt through, brandishing a stick and shouting, 'Beware! Here come the invaders!' as he whacked at the foliage. Leeson ducked and held his breath and the boy charged on toward the path Leeson had come in on, the white glimpse of his shirt receding from view as he hacked his way through the low branches. Leeson listened for more voices. He had been drawn this way by the convivial sounds of a picnic, but not wanting to be discovered he'd decided to stay a respectable distance from the clearing. After a minute of silence Leeson stood to go. He would circle back to the woods that led to the estate and leave whomever it was on the other side of the bushes to the comfort of their privacy. He was about to turn back to the path that led away from the lake when he saw the little girl: a young thing with a rope of wet hair and pleasing features marching toward him, her complexion as bright as that of a porcelain doll he'd once seen in a shop window. Her eyes were to the ground so that she didn't slip, hands holding up the hem of her frilly skirt.

'Celia!' a boy's voice shouted from the nearby verge of the woods, and the girl glanced up and ran directly into Leeson.

17 No one is in the breakfast room when Jane comes downstairs, so she takes a seat at the table set for one by the front window. The lace curtains are pulled aside and offer the same view of the river that she saw from her room, but lower to the ground so that she is now level with the short bridges that arc over it. She'd stopped in the lounge on her way through and had spotted a dog-eared book on the history of Inglewood, written in the 1970s by a local historian. While she waits for Maureen to come out of the kitchen and take her order she thumbs through it.

Inglewood House was built in the 1840s as a shooting lodge for Walter Finley, a pineapple importer who wanted a rural retreat. The original structure was a modest two storeys built in the imported classical style by an Italian architect. When it was finished it represented many of the Italian's Palladian values—strength, austerity, symmetry, dignity, reverence—and, according to the less-than-charitable local historian, none of Walter Finley's. Within two weeks of the last paintings being hung, Walter was dead. The local doctor ascribed the suddenness of his departure to a strain of the heart. When Mrs. Finley arrived from the city the next morning she found her husband laid out behind his bed curtains, completely naked. In the kitchens below she found no fewer than twenty pheasants taken in the previous afternoon's shoot lined up on a long work table for plucking. Within a month, the house was in the hands of the Finleys' son Lawrence, who was in the process of bankrupting himself overseas; he sold the house almost immediately, never having set foot in it.

Hugh Farrington purchased Inglewood House intending to use it as a summer estate, but on the family's first foray up from London, his wife, Prudence, fell in love with its remove. They stayed for the better part of eight months, during which time Prudence oversaw various improvements and added feminine touches to make the rooms less austere.

❦

We know that George Farrington's early years in Inglewood were as delightful for him as they were miserable for his brother,

Norvill. William Eliot had alluded to this in his talk at the Chester, citing a short twentieth-century monograph of the family written by a local headmaster who'd been acquainted with the Farringtons. Norvill was caned regularly by his tutor, had no friends to speak of and was forced to stay home and take extra lessons, while George, three years older, was allowed to travel with his father when he visited the House of Commons. One spring Norvill gathered the nerve to enter his father's study to complain about the inequity, and Hugh, in a bout of unpredictable anger, struck him in the head with the sheaf of papers he was reading. Thereafter he refused, out of shame, to allow Norvill to bring up either issue again. Norvill that year was made all the more miserable by George's happiness with village life, by his friendship with the head gardener's son and his tireless enthusiasm for the outdoors. This misery he exhausted by setting snares in the woods for hares, taunting the blacksmith's daughter and, once, catching a grass snake by the river and releasing it in the scullery.

Norvill had only been away at university a year when George wrote to tell him about being offered a spot on a botanical expedition to the Himalayas. He would be gone eight months and Norvill would need to stay the term in Inglewood to manage the house and property and look after their mother, who had begun to suffer from stress again. Their father, he wrote, was required too often in the city to make lodging in the country house a reasonable option for him.

We know it was in that year, as George dispatched letters from canvas tents perched on cliffsides—the hands of the porters who delivered them to British ships so dirty the envelopes arrived at Inglewood with a crust of earth—that Norvill began to imagine his brother dead. Their mother read the missives to herself at the breakfast table, the hand holding the paper visibly trembling, the other flat on her neck. As he watched her lips move silently, Norvill invented a catalogue of misfortunes: cholera one day, rockslide the next, a parasite or botched robbery in a village on another. His mother would smooth the spotless white table linen in front of her when she was done, and Norvill would glower at his grizzled bacon, shoving his fork into the pale flesh of the melon brought into the village by cart, fantasizing that George was, at that very minute, expiring on a gravelly hillside. His mother, her face lit up, asking once, 'Whatever, darling, are you smiling at?'

Neither George nor Norvill had children, and after Prudence died the estate fell into the hands of her nephew Archie, the only son of her younger brother. He had the house emptied and the household dismissed almost immediately but held on to the property. During the bombing in the Second World War, Inglewood House was used to lodge schoolchildren from the south, as was the nearby Whitmore. The estate's gardens were already ruined by then, according to the local historian, and further demolished when volunteers dug up some of the plots near the house to plant vegetables.

After the war Inglewood House sat empty. Then, in the 1960s, long after anyone had set foot in it, Archie's daughter listed the house with a property agent in London along with the furniture Archie had kept, and a good portion of what, by then, had become 'unfashionable' art, as well as the books, the textiles and the moth-eaten menagerie of stuffed mammals that had been stowed in their coastal attic. The property was advertised for ten years before a group of investors from the Inglewood area managed to form a Trust and purchase it, hoping to find the capital to restore the gardens as a means of bringing tourists into the village. By the time of the book's writing in 1976, the estate was falling apart, though the author felt sure—in the way hopeful local historians tended to—that the estate would 'soon be returned to its former glory so that it can take its place as a unique representative of the houses of its age.'

When Maureen comes out to clear Jane's plate, Jane says, 'Thanks,' then 'Sorry,' because she can tell from the dwindling sounds of the washing-up on the other side of the swinging kitchen door that she is the last of the five guests to have come down for breakfast and that Maureen has been waiting for her to finish up.

'We make the rooms up between noon and two,' Maureen says, the red apron she was wearing over her blouse replaced by a simple grey jacket, a pink shimmer on her lips as if she's going out. She collects the cutlery and then angles the Inglewood book on the table so that she can see it better. On the cover there's a black and white photograph of the estate house from the turn of the century, the Doric columns of the front portico looming over a half-dozen gardeners in white shirts and waistcoats clipping hedges or hand-mowing a lawn that seems to sprawl endlessly in front of them. 'My grandfather was a delivery boy there,' Maureen says. 'Never once set foot in the place.' She pauses. 'Do you need anything else?'

'No thanks.'

She bends sideways to get a better look out the window behind Jane. 'It's nice weather for your walk to the caves.'

'I might go over to Inglewood House, actually.'

As Maureen heads toward the kitchen, she says over her shoulder, 'It's not open to the public, I'm afraid. They've been doing some work there on the weekdays, taking up half the village parking.'

To get a better look at the estate Jane puts her hands up onto the mossy ledge of the stone wall that runs along the field, its flattened top lined with a carpet of lichen that furzes under her fingers. With the toe of her left shoe jammed into a crevice, she tries to haul herself up. On her third go she gets high enough to rest her torso on the ledge, the flat width of stone pushing into her abdomen, her legs dangling and Sam barking and turning circles below. From up here she can see the back of the manor: a row of floor-to-ceiling windows that look onto the gardens, four narrow balconies spaced evenly above those, and then the roof, gabling up to its six chimneys. There are ceramic pots of juniper on the patio stones clustered next to a dozen bags of fertilizer and a wheelbarrow; the air is claggy with the smell of manure and mulch.

When she drops back down onto the grass near Sam, he jumps up on her, his paws dirtying her jeans, tail wagging madly. For a second or two she thinks she will carry on with their walk as planned, but then the image of Leeson and Herschel meeting Farrington in a parlour on the other side of the stone wall pulls at her. This is followed by thoughts of N, by what it might mean—at a time when everything else in her life is going so badly—to find her.

'Right, then, Mr. Coleridge'—she claps, bending down to Sam and hooking one arm under his forelegs and the other under his bum—'you wait up on top. Do you hear me? *Wait!*' And once up, having pushed himself off her chest with his back legs, he does wait, all two and a half stone of him balanced sideways on the flat top of the wall, inching down into a sit while Jane hauls herself up again.

Inglewood House, when Jane peers into its windows, is in a strange state, as if mid-restoration. Looking through the tall windows that line what was once a library Jane can discern a half-dozen pieces of furniture covered in drop cloths and stacks of boxes lined up on either side of a large marble fireplace. The far wall of the room is completely taken up with empty book-shelves of gleaming wood. Heavy silk curtains hang on either side of the windows, gold tassels banding the cloth; the ceiling has an ornate set of panels with motifs from the Orient. The library is uncarpeted except for ratty grey runners laid over the hardwood—the kind movers set down at every venue.

Sam whines and Jane glances over to find him sniffing along the flagstone by what would have been the servants' entrance, beside a trap door for deliveries. The delivery door is flapped open on one side and Sam wags madly as he tracks someone's coming and going. 'I don't think so, bub,' Jane laughs, pressing her face back to the library window. When she turns to him again a minute later, he has toddled down two stairs and his back end is sticking up out of the entrance. 'Sam! Get out of there!'

The steps Sam is sniffing around on are worn in the middle from over a century and a half of use. Crouching down Jane can see that they lead into what looks to be the washing-up part of the kitchen. The open access is a permission she doesn't think too long about. As a precaution Jane calls, 'Hello?'—and taking this as a kind of consent, Sam bounds all the way into the kitchen and around the corner and out of view.

The washing-up area is spare, block-walled except for the plastered area near the pipes, most of which are post-war add-ons that terminate, open-mouthed, near the corner. There are two large metal basins along the far wall, old 1930s things, with wood counters on either side. A plastic Tesco bag is sitting on one of them. Jane goes over and opens it gingerly to find a freshly wrapped sandwich, a bottle of water, a bag of crisps and an apple. Hearing the plastic rustle, Sam trots back from the other part of the kitchen and wags his tail against the metal legs of the basin.

'Shhh,' Jane whispers.

As Jane wanders from room to room, she muses that Inglewood House seems just like any old house that a new owner is moving into—boxes and crates everywhere, workboot prints on the hardwood, cans of paint and drop cloths, a battery-operated radio on the floor of the main hall next to a dustpan and broom. The look and feel of the place is still mid to late Victorian: the rooms dark wood and richly painted, the details around the archways intact, the Gothic embellishments on the banister handrails just as the Farringtons would have had them. The library Jane had surveyed from the window is dark blue, the carved armchairs under the sheets probably Chippendales. Opposite the fireplace

Jane lifts a sheet and finds a satinwood cabinet with Wedgwood plaques depicting hunting scenes on its doors. The dining room adjacent still has what looks to be its original wallpaper—a faded grey Asian print sprigged with cherry blossoms. In the study that she imagines would have been George's, Jane lifts a sheet's corner to find a dark-red scroll-armed sofa, threadbare where one might have rested one's arm, and then a mahogany secretary and a worn black leather armchair. Under a sheet stamped with the name of a turn-of-the-century hotel she finds a cabinet filled with glasses and decanters. The boxes and crates in each room bear inventory stickers—ovals stamped *FT* and bearing a London address, their designations handwritten in marker underneath: *GFS 60-122, GFS 123-140*. The system reminds Jane of the work she should be going back to, although what's here is infinitely more appealing because it seems to be about recreating, not dispersing, a world.

Walking past marble pillars and carpets wrapped in plastic, Jane thinks how strange it is that she has tried and failed to properly imagine this place. She recalls what she knows of George and Prudence, of Norvill, and can't even decide if the waist-high pillar in front of her would have hosted the sculpted head of a beautiful girl or Theseus slaying the Minotaur. At the end of the hall she opens a heavy wood door and is shocked to find a deteriorating wall-to-wall animal mural in what must have been the nursery or schoolroom. Ten wild animals are arranged around its perimeter: a shaggy lion in full-toothed roar, an elephant with his trunk trumpeting toward the ceiling. There's a sanguine giraffe drawn out of proportion, a gorilla in a top hat and a mean-looking tiger so faded from the sunlight streaming through the window that he looks as if he's receding into a far-off dream. Jane thinks about the young George Farrington as William had described him in the last chapter of his book: a self-conscious child, singular in his focus, constantly at his mother's knee. And Norvill as a boy? Nothing that she has read would say. Charlotte's diaries stick mostly to the details surrounding his visits to the museum or to the house to see Edmund, with little reference to what kind of man he was, let alone what kind of child. The Chester archives and Edmund's accounts state when Norvill did and did not appear for meetings at the museum, what contributions he made by way of geological specimens, but offer nothing about what it might mean to spend formative days surrounded by tribes of wild animals—the painted ones in the schoolroom or the stuffed ones under plastic in the main hall.

When she finds the parlour near the front of the house, Jane lifts the sheet off the horsehair sofa and sits. The black leather is split on the curve of the arm so that she can slip her fingers into its seam and feel the bristled fibres. There are a half-dozen inventoried boxes along the wall of the parlour and a stuffed grouse shrouded in clear wrapping, a mahogany longcase clock beside it. The ceiling is lower than she expected, and the wall where she imagined a set of watercolours hanging from ribbons is bare. The view from the window is of the great expanse of the front lawn. This room, or perhaps George's study next door, would have been lit up on the night of N's disappearance— would have cast the light Leeson and Herschel and N were drawn toward after their long walk from the Whitmore.

Some of us have been in Inglewood House before, can conjure the objects that lined the shelves and cupboards, the pastoral oils that hung from the walls, embellishments we once touched or were responsible for. *The plate was kept here, this book cabinet was locked, flowers were to be placed on this mantel, an armoire was located in this nook, the gun room was down that hall, this was the larder, the scullery; the laundry was pushed down this chute to be collected in the morning.* We are like inventors, staring at a machine that isn't there, that we seem to make exist out of the whirl of our own ardour. This, after all, is what we have been after—bits and pieces of stories we've lived, images that sail back to us as we enter a room, even if what we glean is the kind of knowledge that comes from village gossip—how one year the season's bag of pheasants exceeded three hundred and George complained that it was more trouble to find mouths willing to eat so much bird than it was to go out on horseback and procure it. And so we see him here in this room, greeting a visitor or hastily reading a letter; or we glimpse Prudence upstairs in her cotton nightdress with her hair braided—recall how, in her last years, she insisted on starting each morning with three tinctures, how watching her open her mouth to receive them was like watching a baby bird.

You might ask what it's like to conjure such moments, to say that Herschel once sat where Jane is sitting and that Leeson stood in this very room and bowed for Prudence with a Romantic flourish she secretly liked. To suggest that the three clocks plunged on with their awkward ticking, each half-second announced like some fissure in physics the idiot thinks we can slip into. To remember N at the door watching the footman, then darting away when he went to find Farrington. To know that Farrington, assessing the situation quickly, took over before the footman realized that the number of the party had changed.

'*Twoo*,' one of us says, and Cat sighs and air-kisses a circle around all of us.

The poet wanders off to the study, the theologian stares at the grouse, and the one with the soft voice sings a song that must be what the living call a lullaby.

Is what we are conjuring guesswork? Or a kind of love? We know that Norvill once stood in the door to his childhood nursery, his face clouding over as he read a letter from Charlotte. We know that he crumpled the note and threw it against the wall, and that he was made desperate because of it. Admittedly some of our knowledge is conjecture, but some is fact gained by access and some is understanding human nature, our dispositions imposing themselves on the maps made by others.

And, too, one of us happened to pass him in the doorway in the way that people constantly pass by each other: the seen and the unseen, the preoccupied and the perceptive. The body is a miraculous thing: an assemblage of struts and muscles and nerves; two hundred and six bones placed exactly under a corset of muscle and ligament; and eyes to see, ears to hear. The hand that curls around a leaf of scented paper is a marvel to watch, and so too is the arrangement and rearrangement of lines on a face marred with unhappy thoughts.

18 When the young man who has been working in the gardens walks down the servants' steps and into the kitchen of Inglewood House, Jane is thumbing gently through a box of books in the library. She doesn't hear him, but Sam cocks his head and turns toward the sound, then trots across the main hall to the top of the stairs. They've been in the house nearly two hours. After the first fifteen or twenty minutes Jane had relaxed, realizing they weren't going to trip any alarm wires or walk into a security guard; the house is clearly

in a state of suspension, the Trust probably local enough to live up to its name.

Jane notices Sam's agitation and thinks he might need to go out to pee. She takes a last look around the library and follows him down the stairwell. When she gets to the bottom step she sees a young man, in a T-shirt and dark trousers, standing at the sink with his back to her. He's rinsing his hands with water from a plastic bottle. Jane can make out the fuzzy interference of music playing in his earbuds. Stuck on the bottom step, she glances at Sam, who is standing ten feet behind the stranger, undecided whether she should sneak across the kitchen to the exit or go back upstairs until he's gone. She's about to step down and cross between the built-in pantry and the sinks when he turns around.

'Whoa, Jesus!' He plucks out his earbuds and says, more politely, 'Sorry, you scared me.'

Jane smiles. He's eighteen, maybe nineteen, has a mop of dark hair and patches of stubble on his chin. She can see now that he's wearing navy overalls, the upper part cinched around his waist and the knees caked with dirt. There's a company patch in the knot where his belt would be. She tries to sound casual. 'I didn't know anyone was working today or I would have said hello on my way in.'

He looks her up and down quickly, the way boys his age tend to do—interested because she's a woman, but vaguely dismissive because she's older—and then he taps his thigh to call Sam over, and the dog bounds up to him without so much as a backward glance at Jane, leaning in with his full weight while the kid kneels down to pet him. The boy angles his head toward the back gardens, says, 'We're running a bit behind, and it's my dad's company, so two of us are doing weekends. I thought you lot weren't coming back till Monday?' He reaches into his pocket to turn his music off and flinches when he catches the cut on his hand on the seam. He lifts up his hand to inspect it. There's a smear of blood across his palm.

'Are you okay?'

'Yeah. I just nicked myself rewiring the trellis.'

Jane slowly lets out the breath she's been holding and steps toward him. 'Let's see.'

He meets her halfway and shows her a three-inch cut between his thumb and index finger. It's long and narrow, but not too deep.

'It probably just needs a plaster.' Jane tries to sound apologetic and authoritative at the same time. 'I don't really have anything with me.'

He shrugs and looks again at Jane; his eyes are glassy and bloodshot. Jane realizes with a start that he's totally stoned.

'Spit on it,' he says.

'Sorry?'

'It'll help clean it.' He grins at her.

'Listen—'

'Blake.'

'Listen, Blake, I'm just finishing up, but I think that cut needs to be cleaned properly, so maybe you ought to dash over to the pharmacy.'

The kid narrows his eyes. He can tell that she's speaking to him differently now. 'I'm not as high as you think.'

'Right. Well, I'm just going to check off a few more boxes—' Jane jabs a thumb toward the stairs to the main floor and clears her throat. 'You should really clean that up.'

He nods but stands there, and Jane feels sure he's going to call her bluff. Does she have enough on him that he will be less likely to out her? Maybe he's just stoned—hardly a serious offence—but he's probably the one who left the delivery door open, so why would he want to attract attention to that fact by claiming he happened upon a break and enter? Besides, she hasn't *taken* anything, doesn't have a stack of books or a vase under her arm.

'It's Helen, by the way.' She sticks out her hand to break the silence.

He offers Jane the hand with the cut, and when she doesn't shake it because it's still bleeding, they stand there awkwardly.

'Brilliant,' he says, 'see you around, then, Helen.' He presses his earbuds back in, gives Sam another head scratch, and walks up the steps, throwing one last look at Jane before he's gone.

Back at the inn, Jane runs into Maureen re-stacking magazines and travel guides in the lounge and asks about the restoration work at the house.

'I think the Trust got some last-ditch money from an investor in London to redo the house and gardens as Farrington left them, though there's talk that the investor plans to turn the upper floors into some kind of swanky hotel.' Maureen straightens her back, clearly stressed at the thought of competition, and drops a guide to Five Best Local Walks on top of a pile of brochures. 'You hear a different plan every week. If you ask at the pub, Lucy will tell you—she's one of the local Trustees. Everything all right with your room?'

'Yes, great.'

Maureen picks up the remote control and turns on the tele-vision in the corner. It's an older model that flares before the picture of an outdoor concert takes shape. Jane recognizes the orchestra playing in the summer performance series, the stage lit up with blue and white lights, Battersby conducting. Reflexively, Jane scans the string section for people she might know.

'You like classical music?' Maureen's tone makes this more a statement than a question.

'My dad plays.'

'Oh, what's his name?'

'Henri Braud.' Henri's name is out of her mouth before she realizes what she's done, but Maureen doesn't seem to recognize it and she's already moved on to tucking the throw cushions on the sofa back into their appointed corners.

'Anything else I can do for you?'

'No thanks.' Jane lifts the plastic bag in her hand. 'I forgot to pack a hairbrush or moisturizer, went out for supplies.'

Maureen takes a last look around the lounge and turns to go. 'Right then, see you in the morning, Helen. I've a roast to see to now.' She looks down at Sam, 'Good night, Chase.'

Climbing the steps to her room Jane tries to sort out what she's doing. She's running away, exactly like she did when she was twelve and her mother rang up to say she wasn't coming down to South Kensington to fetch her for the summer holiday. Furious because her bags were by the door and she'd already spent hours waiting for Claire to pull up outside her grand-parents' sitting room window, Jane took off. It was a ridiculous effort. She made four cheese-and-chutney sandwiches and took the tube to Leicester Square, ending up in a five-screen cinema where she spent the last of the birthday money Henri had sent from Prague watching one film after another, movies she didn't even want to see. Her grandfather had raised his hand in a solemn salute when she returned at midnight, then picked up the phone in the hall to call Claire and report that Jane was fine, all without a reprimand.

Jane knows she is repeating herself, hiding again. Not only because Maureen and her husband are of an age that means they might once have helped search for Lily, might still remember Jane's name, but also because she might really want to escape this time, fall off the map for good.

The Whitmore's concert announcements and entertainment programmes are spread out on the floor of Jane's room where she left them last night. After the run-in with the kid at Inglewood House she'd been too wound up to come directly back here, so she'd driven to Moorgate—the largest hub in the area—and she and Sam had window-shopped the chain stores on the high street because it was Sunday and almost everything was closed. Tomorrow she'll drive over there again to go to the local records office, where she had done some of her dissertation research. The original Whitmore ball invitation should still be there and she'll be able to check the exact date. The office will likely have some of the Farrington estate archives as well, if they haven't ended up in a private collection or with Prudence's side of the family.

Outside Jane's window dusk is falling. The street lamps blink on although they're not yet needed. Across the river a group of hikers is traipsing back into the village, their heavy outer layers tucked under their arms or strapped to their packs. They pass a spry-looking gentleman in a tweed cap tossing crumbs to the ducks, and Jane watches them laugh at the brown-and-white-speckled forms congregating below him. There are a dozen cars situated around the church up the road, and when Jane presses her face to the window she can see that the clock tower reads half past five. After a minute she turns back to the Whitmore box, picks up the page of notes she made last night, puzzles over it again. She can see no patterns or leads in what she's written; N is not mentioned, a hole in the middle of everything.

Jane had told Maureen yesterday that she would stay until Wednesday—three days away. Three days isn't a lot of time, but it isn't unreasonable. She decides that if on Wednesday she has no solid lead as to who N was or what happened to her, she'll give up, head to the Lakes as Lewis expected her to, call Gareth and explain herself. She'll clear out the cottage to sell it, and sift through the last of her mother's things.

Out of habit we tilt our heads. We consider Jane's predicament, how hard she is being on herself. We are sympathetic, but even our sympathy is outweighed by our determination to keep hold of the larger truths we are learning.

'What about the Whitmore?' we ask. Inglewood House is all well and good but some of us have never been there. As we walked through its rooms with Jane some of us felt as if we were dropping in on strangers with whom we had only one tenuous connection.

'We have until Wednesday,' John says, watching Jane rummage through the bag of clothes she'd packed hurriedly in London.

'How much time is that?' asks the boy.

'*Arpeggio*,' answers the musician.

'Not enough,' the theologian snaps, preoccupied with what pressed on him in the small parlour at the manor, a word or a set of words, a circumstance on the tip of his tongue.

Jane is changing to go out for dinner, and as she pulls a thin blue angora sweater over her head, we bristle because the cloud of it begs for touching and because we don't want her to stop what she's doing when there are still files to go through. Thinking about the ball gave some of us a semblance of self, the tour of Inglewood House did the same for others, and we are all craving to feel that way again. But Jane has turned away from the Whitmore box. She straightens her skirt and dabs her lipstick, and the cluster that is us rises to follow her out the door.

'I'm going for a walk,' the theologian says irritably.

'Don't,' Cat replies. 'You're the one who's always saying "stay together."'

'Perhaps I overestimated the company.'

'There's no need for—' John begins, but before he can finish the theologian has slipped out the door.

There is always a sense of gloom when one of us leaves. Few who wander off come back. For this reason, for a very long time in our first years of solidarity, hardly any of us went off on our own unless absolutely necessary. We don't know what happens to those who disappear. Maybe they get better leads and head off to follow them; maybe they learn things they want or don't want to know and, full to bursting with the knowledge, close their eyes and Cease.

'What now?' asks Cat.

'Dinner,' says the musician, and he raises his arms to conduct us, whistling as he ghosts through the door.

The idiot once told a bedtime story to the children that began with a great black sea that doubled as an ink-dark sky. When you looked, it was filled with stars and seashells lined up together.

'Stars *and* seashells?' the girl had squealed.

'Absolutely,' the idiot confirmed. 'Caught in the great net of time.'

'Where are *we*?' she asked, hoping we were the fishermen.

'Where do you think we are?'

'On the water?'

'No.'

'In the moon?'

'I'm afraid not.'

She smacked her lips. 'A spaceship!'

'No, we're the house the sea-sky lives in. It's in our heads twirling around; a spiral galaxy that's shaped like a snail.'

'*Ewww.*'

'Why not?' He laughed. 'Think of the breakfasts the mind can eat: Sands of time! Acres of now! Parcels of eternity! Tasty stuff.'

'Don't listen to him,' the theologian said, calling out from the wingback chair under Jane's sitting room window. 'The sky is the sky, and the sea is the sea, end of discussion.'

But it was too late. We'd all listened to the idiot's story and something in what he said as he carried on shaped how we started to think of ourselves, led to a sense that we were stuck together in something that could not be flattened out in ways that would otherwise be perfectly sensible. It was as if we were knots in a net that could take different shapes at different times. As if we might, one day, loop back on ourselves, come so close to the past we'd be able to taste the dust of our history in our mouths.

The pub at dinnertime is packed and smells of spilled beer and curry. Jane has avoided coming here until now because she doesn't want to have the *you're-not-from-around-here* conversation. She takes a seat at a low round table. A waitress comes over and drops a plastic menu in front of her, asks what Jane would like to drink.

'White wine, thanks.'

The girl taps the wine list and Jane scans it.

'The Chenin.'

'Small or large?'

Jane glances at the two tables nearest to her: plates of fish and chips, roast and potato, pints, a couple sharing a bottle of Malbec. 'Large, thanks.'

The pub is almost exactly as she remembers from twenty years ago. The red-and-gold-medallioned carpets are the same, the leather stools and wood-backed booths, the belled lamps over the dining area tables. But there is a row of coin-operated games along the far wall now, flat-screen televisions recapping the day in rugby, a snooker table that may or may not have been there before. The customers are a mix of locals and tourists: a group of men in heavy boots and jeans at the bar, a few couples out on the smoking patio, the shop cashier from yesterday chatting up two girlfriends over by the far window and hikers tucking into dinner, their Gore-Tex jackets hanging off a nearby coat rack. At the far end of the bar there's a cluster of twenty-year-olds standing around a high table, the kid from Inglewood House among them.

Jane watches him, curious in spite of herself. His back is mostly to her but sometimes he shifts around the table to talk to the girl in the miniskirt on his right or the guy in the hoodie on his left. There are at least two rounds of drink in front of them, a mix of pint and shot glasses. One of the three girls, the one with the dancer's posture, who Jane thinks is the prettiest, is already swaying, her cheeks flushed and her gestures theatrical. The girl next to Blake, the loud one in the spangled silver top and large hoop earrings, leans sideways to say something in Blake's ear and then turns her head, narrows her eyes at Jane. This reminds Jane of the young girl at the Chester, glaring at her from under the bones of the whale.

'Helen?'

Jane looks up from her almost empty glass of wine to see Blake holding a pint glass, a smart-ass expression on his face that she'd like to wipe off. This is what kids do, she thinks, when they get bored of their village bollocks. If, as teenagers, she and Lewis had stayed in the Lakes they'd have found whole new ways to push the envelope too. She smiles up at Blake, probably unconvincingly.

'How's the hand?'

He pulls it out of his jeans pocket and displays the plaster. 'Saved.'

Jane glances back at his table of mates, sees the girl in the silver top seething. 'I think you're wanted.'

He pulls a stool out with the toe of his boot and straddles it, places his pint on the table.

'I meant *elsewhere*,' says Jane.

'They'll live.'

Jane leans back and before she can say anything more he has leaped up to the bar and is getting her another drink. One of the workmen asks him a question and pats him on the back, and Jane hates herself for noticing how attractive he is. He's wearing black jeans and a white long-sleeve shirt. She glances down at her own clothes—a black A-line paired with a light blue sweater. Ben used to call it her librarian-wear.

'So where are you from?' Blake swings a leg back over the stool and slides a glass of wine toward her. It is so topped up he must have told the barman he was trying to get her drunk. 'London?'

Jane raises her eyebrows in a noncommittal fashion before realizing this probably looks like flirting. 'Why do you want to know? So you can send birthday cards?' She can hear herself trying to sound tolerant, trying to sound like someone engaging in playful banter because it is the polite thing to do.

Blake spins the pint in his hand and looks over at his friends as if gauging whether or not he should pack it up and go back. 'Listen, Helen, you have beautiful lips. I mean, the bottom one especially, there's a kind of'—he narrows his eyes—'luscious thing happening there, and I am completely fucking horny and a little bit drunk, but I am also a nice guy and a good conversationalist. I like music, I like books, I read the paper *daily*, I can name, I don't know, like fifty varieties of roses, and animals like me. My mates over there are talking about a YouTube video that shows two yobs eating their own feces—' He takes a breath. 'So I'm asking you to save me.'

Jane glances around the room. She feels like she's part of a spectacle, but no one other than the spangled girl is watching them.

She looks at him again. 'How old are you, Blake?'

He grins. 'You remember my name.' He pushes her wine-glass closer with the tips of his fingers. 'Nineteen. Why? How old are you?'

She debates how to handle this. 'The proverbial too-old-to-be-having-this-conversation?'

He shifts forward and his knees touch hers under the table. 'I'd like the record to show that *you* just called this a conversation.'

'My mistake. Clearly.'

'So, Helen,' Blake drums his fingers on the table, a chuffed expression on his face as if the lads he was sitting with bet him that he wouldn't make it past two minutes. 'What do you want to be when you grow up?'

'Hmm, this is a serious question?'

'I have to say that you strike me as a very serious woman. So, yes.'

Jane thinks about this. She wants to come up with an answer that is pithy or maybe even a little bit honest; she wants, almost, to say her name *is actually Jane*. But what wells up in her instead is something she can't quite articulate. It has to do with the fifteen-year-old version of herself that she can see across the room in the booth that she shared with William and Lily, a girl in black shoes that are too fancy, a girl whose ankles are crossed under the table, whose knees sometimes glance William's.

'Have you ever been in love?'

Blake blinks at her. The question is unexpected. 'Well, Helen'—he pauses and picks up a coaster, taps it on the table—'assuming you are engaging in a *real* conversation, I will answer you honestly. I have never been in love.' When Jane doesn't say anything, he cocks his head. '*Is* this a real conversation?'

'Three times for me,' Jane says. 'Different kinds of love.'

He nods. 'That's a respectable number.'

For the next half hour we sit in the pub with Jane and some of us pace the room and eavesdrop, and some try to remember if we know this place, try to fathom how long it has been here, wonder if the man at the bar is the son of the son of the son of a man or woman we once knew. Those of us who have been with Jane the longest want to whisper to her, *Look how that boy is seeing you.* To show her how open he is to the possibility of who she might be, how attenuated he is to her gaps and omissions. Ben was never like that; he held his ideas of Jane up in the air between thoughts of himself, of the wife he'd left for her, of the woman he wanted her to be. When they made love Jane closed her eyes and Ben looked at his own flexed arms as he propped himself above her. Even when she was in charge he thought, *I'm fucking her,* and 'her' was always the girl he saw at the Portrait Gallery in a Prada dress, the daughter of Henri Braud and granddaughter of the renowned Standens.

'And then what happened?' Blake is leaning forward, laughing the way you do when a story has turned so tragic it's funny.

'She hung herself.'

'Jesus.'

'From the top step above her desk. A neighbour found her. Mrs. Greeves.'

'Grieves? Like grieving? You're kidding.'

'No, Greeves with two *e*'s; I never thought of that, actually.'

Blake shakes his head. 'My mum is one of those boring-but-nice mums. There's four of us and we're all little bastards, which is why I wouldn't be surprised if she did something crazy one day: drowned the cat, set fire to the house.' He shifts his position and his leg falls against hers more deliberately.

'Do you like being a gardener?' Jane asks.

'It's all right. Do you like estate management, or reno work or whatever it's called?'

'I do.' Jane smiles. 'You know, it's late. And I've gotta let Sam out and I swear your girlfriend over there is going to come over and drive a fork through my throat, so I'm going to say good night.'

Blake stands up and Jane stands too, and she says, 'It was really nice chatting with you,' and is surprised by how much she means it.

'Let me walk you out.'

'Um, I think you need to get back to your mates.'

'Helen, look at me.'

She does. He is staring at her intently, one side of his mouth lifted in a nervous smile, a chop of hair hanging over his forehead in a way that probably drives his mother crazy. There is a thumbprint-sized patch of stubble on his jaw that he missed shaving, an acne scar on his chin. She can tell the ridge of his nose has been broken, probably in rugby. She wants to put her finger lightly on the bump of it.

'I'd like to see you again.'

Jane laughs. 'That's very flattering, and I mean it, but probably not a good idea.'

19 As the woman at the local records office in Moorgate enters Jane's information into the computer, Jane has to fight her anxiety about using her real name—Helen Swindon doesn't have a reader's card but Jane does.

'Right, here you are,' the woman says, squinting at what must be Jane's particulars. 'I just need to see two pieces of ID.' She glances down at Jane's driver's licence and bank card, says, 'That's fine,' and then slides a temporary pass across the counter. Jane slips it into her pocket and the woman goes back to the

Sudoku puzzle she was working on. A few minutes later after Jane has emptied her things into one of the lockers in the cloak room and checked through a window to make sure the car is all right—Sam still sleeping off his morning run through the woods in the backseat—Jane walks past the woman again.

'Don't forget to sign in,' the woman says, tapping the metal part of a clipboard with her pencil.

Jane writes her name illegibly, a false signature that feels like the physical form of a lie, and then she walks through the nearby door and into a bright but soulless reading room. Of the eight plywood tables lined up under the windows only two are occupied: one by a woman in a fleece jacket sifting through a folder of newspaper clippings, the other by an elderly gentle-man reading what appears to be a turn-of-the-century will. The whirling progress of a microfiche on the other side of a short supporting wall and the *peck-peck* of the archivist's typing are the only noises in the room. Jane pulls out a banquet chair with tatty upholstery, sets her notepad down on the empty table and then takes her reader's card up to the archivist, a woman her own age with cropped blonde hair and a small diamond nose-ring.

'How can I help?'

'I'm looking for the index for the Whitmore Hospital for Convalescent Lunatics.'

'Right. Have a seat and I'll bring it over.'

The Whitmore index is bigger than Jane remembers. The Whitmore was only one of five county asylums whose archives she'd surveyed when she was writing her dissertation. It hadn't been until she found the hospital logbook and the startling

reference to 'girl, N–, missing' that she'd properly paid attention back then, stopped seeing what she was reading as 'types'
and 'categories' and instead saw a specific place and a particular person. Her eyes had jumped to the next line and the
next to see if N had been found, stopping in shock at *Letter
from G. Farrington received*—the name so immediately familiar from William's tour-guiding on the day Lily went missing
that she'd had to get up and leave the room, splash her face
with cold water.

By noon Jane has called up a dozen sets of files and boxes,
has gone through the Commissioners' reports, the admission
books and the records of transfer for the years 1876–78. She
can find no record of a woman patient at the Whitmore whose
name started with the letter *N*, and no further references to the
trio's outing except for a cryptic set of recommendations from
the Commissioners for stricter regulations in relation to supervised groundwork and permitted excursions outside the asylum's
gates. She spends the next two hours trying to decipher Medical
Superintendent Thorpe's angular scrawl and his shorthand for
injuries (*I*), incidents of restraint (*Res*), or complaints by patients
(*Comp*). She finds Herschel and Leeson noted briefly, Herschel
complaining of *Cons*, remedied by *Prs*, and placed on short-term
supervision; Leeson suffering from a bout of *Ma*—which Jane
takes to be 'mania'—in late July and placed under stricter observation. Bedford's name and the electrotherapy treatments she
believes he performed do not appear at all.

Within an hour we are dizzy with Jane's work, but we focus as
best we can: sit on the table, lean over the books, read what we

see aloud. The boy dive-bombs loudly around the older gentle-man working on the far side of the room until the theologian demands he stop. There's panic rising in us because Jane isn't writing much down, because we suspect this stretch of days may be all we have, our last chance to see ourselves, our last chance to grasp the shape of who we have been before Jane gives up on N and on us, before she is forced to choose a new direction.

Jane runs her finger down a list of patients attended to by the Visiting Physician and those of us who think we can imagine a sickroom, who might know what it was like to lie in a narrow cot behind gauzy curtains, scan the list, chant the names to see if the saying changes us: 'Amelia Sowerby, Annie Witt, Matthew Tippings, Frederick Vine.' Most of us ignore the columns of symptoms and diseases, though Cat whispers them quietly. 'Cholera, cholera, seizure, cholera, influenza.'

In the afternoon, after Jane has taken Sam to the park and walked briskly along Moorgate's high street to unknot her back, she opens the casebook records for 1877. When she'd come up from UCL to do her research on northern asylums she'd photo-copied Leeson's pages and a handful of others—of patients who were at the Whitmore around the time of the trio's walk in the woods—but because she'd fallen behind in her dissertation, she hadn't read the casebooks thoroughly.

It happens now that as Jane reads through some of the casebooks she hadn't photocopied she feels as if she is *re*read-ing them, as if they are stories about people she has come to know and can imagine, as if the jottings and spare details are the transcript of a dream. *Samuel Murray, 40.* Admitted: *March 2, 1877.* Cause of insanity: *Overwork. Marital strain.* She comes to the casebook of a Mr. H.J. Morley and realizes with a start that this is Herschel's. She either hadn't noticed it as a student, or hadn't thought to copy it, had relied instead on the hospital logbook, Thorpe's case report and Leeson's more voluminous stack of notes to frame the events of the day. Now, suddenly, here he is in inky blue calligraphy: Age: *32*. Admitted: *May 17, 1877*. Occupation: *Farmer*. Status: *Unknown*. Degree of Education: *Unknown*. And then in a different hand, under the notes of admission: *Refuses to work farm equipment or tend field. Complains of pains in limbs, exhibits swollen digits and capillaries on face. Was found on roof of neighbouring cottage; refused to be brought down. Consistently mislays or removes various items of clothes. Claims that his wife is an impostor. Lets crops foul when they are the sole means of income. Believes he is losing power of tongue.*

The daily reports over the next three months are typically cryptic: *agitated* one day, *compliant* the next, *morose, found naked by attendant in greenhouse, idle, behaviour improved, found picking at walls, refuses to speak, found with sewing scissors, found without shoes in garden, treated with cold bath, improving, wants to be read to, has difficulty sleeping, will not speak, gestures to throat repeatedly, admitted to hospital at B–, returned to W–, refuses meat, agitates fellow patients, broods.*

On the 1st of August Herschel is *improving*, and then there is a gap of six days that corresponds with the start of his walk to Inglewood.

In Leeson's casebook there were more notes than ever after his and Herschel's return, as if Thorpe wrote down everything Leeson had to say about their adventure. But there is nothing in Herschel's—just a quarter page of white space, as if he'd said nothing at all.

Despite her training, Jane is not an overly organized archivist. Gareth once said he couldn't reconcile how good she was *procedurally* with the mess of her desk. 'I have a system,' she'd scoffed, but she was lying—her system was more like a technique: tossing everything onto a table to see what overlapped, what connections might be made when the edges of two disparate pieces of paper met.

There is a photograph in a plastic sleeve next to the Whitmore's *Servant Engagement and Discharge Book* that Jane, busy in other ledgers, has yet to study. It shows thirty-six members of the Whitmore staff in a semicircle on the hospital grounds: the male attendants in stark uniforms with polished buttons, the women's staff in black dresses and white aprons. The Matron is at the centre of the circle in a striped dress with puffed sleeves that all but obscure the assistants on either side of her; the Superintendent sports a bushy moustache that had already gone out of fashion.

We know some of those faces, but not by name; we know, too, that these gatherings were rare, that the photo was taken in autumn because a number of the women wear shawls, that there would have been the fuggy smell of cigars weft into the Superintendent's suit. We know that the men and women in the photograph were in some cases kind and in others insufferable. So we pause over the composed expressions of these figures, and wait for ambivalent or wishful feelings to flit over us. The man with the side-whiskers, we decide, is a bully; the woman in the plain apron must be the cook; this is a girl from the laundry, her stringy hair tied in a simple knot. We lean in to study a furtive-looking man in a bowler, and wonder suddenly if it's Noble; we decide that the tall man with the clippers must be the gardener, sense that the dark-eyed woman with the chatelaine is a nurse. The seamstress is on the grass between them with a basket of needles and yarn resting beside her knee, as if she, along with everyone else, had been called out to the lawn in the middle of work.

Before Jane finishes at the records office, she asks the archivist with the dyed blonde hair for the index binder for the Farrington family so that she can see how much material she'll have to sift through to find any record of the night George Farrington met Leeson and Herschel. The family archive, when it arrives, is more substantial than she expects, and for a moment, flipping through the long list of the index binder, her resolution wavers. She knows it will take her weeks to sort through the relevant categories—the legal records, estate accounts, letters and household notebooks—if she's to do a proper job.

'Are there any diaries?' Jane asks when the archivist drops off the household ledgers she requested. 'I thought Prudence Farrington kept one?'

The woman glances at the clock to gauge how close they are to closing, then says, 'I think there's a separate index for Mrs. Farrington, but let me double-check.'

The household account book for Inglewood that runs from mid 1876 to late 1877 is typical of its kind. There is a cramped signature across the top of the first yellowing page: *Martha Stroud, housekeeper.* This is followed by entries that reflect domestic commerce and concerns: *twelve loaves of bread ordered from Hargraves, blankets aired, firewood delivered to the main house and cottages . . .* There are inventories of kitchen pots, rotations for cleaning the silver plate, twenty-seven pages in which nothing unusual seems to have occurred. In September of 1877 there is a note about funerary costs but no mention of the person being buried, so Jane jots the date down so that she can compare it to the Farrington family death certificates when she looks at them tomorrow.

Before she packs up, she leafs through the large red book dedicated to household staffing. Every staff member has their own page with the individual's position, pay rate, advances made and a note as to whether or not board was included. There are addendums at the bottom of each, detailing when people resigned or were let go, and these are mostly in the housekeeper's writing: *Mary Margaret Teems removed 26 July for pilfering flour, no reference given*; *Wilson Penfeld retired with a gift of five pounds.*

Jane is startled when she finally looks up and finds the archivist standing beside her chair. The woman smiles as if she's used to this, as if it's one of the job's small pleasures.

'There's a note on file that says Mrs. Farrington's diaries are on loan to the Trust. I believe they have George's Tibetan notebooks and sketches as well.' She lifts her shoulders apologetically and turns to go.

'Sorry—' Jane interjects. 'Do you mean the Trust that's restoring the estate?'

'Yes—the Farrington Trust in Inglewood. In all honesty, between them and that gentleman from London we've been moving those boxes up and down from storage *a lot* lately.'

'Gentleman from London?' Jane can hear how thin her voice sounds, so she clears her throat, tries to sound assertive. 'Do you remember his name? I think he might be a colleague.'

The archivist purses her lips. 'He was finishing a book— something about Victorian gardens? A nice man—bit posh—he was up here a lot in the spring and then again a month ago.' She juts her chin in the direction of the stack of material on Jane's table. 'Looking through most of the same things that you are.'

Jane glances down at the archives she's been working through: it's all Whitmore material save for the Farrington household books and index binder. 'Sorry, do you mean the Farringtons? Or the Whitmore?'

'A bit of both, same as you.'

To clear her head after she gets back to the inn, Jane takes Sam for a walk in the field that runs along Inglewood's stone wall. On her way back she stops at the spot where the wall slumps a bit, the section she'd climbed over yesterday, and peers across the lawn to where the gardeners are working on a series of freshly dug beds. She has never liked the waste of large estate grounds, the kind that seem to exist solely for the purpose of having an expanse of lawn to gaze across, but she can appreciate the beauty of a good garden: the bright explosions of pink and white flowers the gardener in the wide-brimmed hat is carrying on a tray, the twitching green reeds around the pond she'd glimpsed earlier on the far side of the wisteria arcade.

Without quite meaning to, Jane scans the pair of gardeners packing up by the stables to see if one of them is Blake. Eventually she spots him near the ivied enclosure off the back of the house just past the library, a gated space that would have been the family's private garden. He turns toward the stables, stretching his back as he goes, and Jane ducks and heads for the road before he is close enough to see her.

Turning back toward the inn, Jane whistles for Sam, who has been tearing around in the treeline, then she picks up a skinny branch and whisks it through the long grass in front of her, all the while trying to convince herself that the archivist in the records office must be mistaken about William looking through the Whitmore material. There's something more than territorial about her discomfort, a resentment she can't quite shake off. This feeling isn't like the one she experienced listening to his talk on Norvill, her sense of *that's mine*; this has more to do with the whole of her life, with feeling like a fake. She can still see Clive's face when she said she was going to take an MA in Archives and Records Management at The University of London, how he held his pudgy features perfectly still as if he didn't want to give away his belief that this was just another move in a series of moves that involved replicating the lives of others. Music because Henri did music, archives because William did archives. She'd seen the same tight-lipped expression on Lewis's face at The Lamb when she said she might write about N and the Whitmore. As if she was trying to be Claire, as if getting her research published would somehow create a meaningful connection between them.

Watching Sam zigzag across the field, Jane realizes that there is something else bothering her: the possibility that William has already made a connection between Inglewood and the Whitmore. Maybe George Farrington had business with the hospital? If Farrington attended the ball, as Jane suspects he did, in what capacity had he done so? Was he a patron? She circles back to her revelation from the first evening at the inn: his letter to the Superintendent said, *Mr. Farrington is glad if they in any way enjoy'd themselves here*—a courtesy, and an indicator that he was familiar with the hospital or at least sensitive to the kinds of patients who moved through there.

Back in her room, Jane fills Sam's water bowl and he drinks all of it, then flops down happily inside the door despite the mess of burrs in the white fur along his hocks and under his belly. Her new hairbrush is still in the shop bag so Jane takes it out and settles down beside him, stroking his ears and running her fingers through his soft curls before gently working the tangles out, one knot at a time.

Later in the evening we go to the pub with Jane. Most of us like the closeness of a public room, the chatter of everyday conversations. We can tell, when Blake saunters in, that he is looking for 'Helen'. He's taken care with his clothes, is wearing a pressed shirt with a collar, black trousers and polished boots.

He spies Jane reading at one of the low tables along the bench wall where they'd sat the night before. Her pint glass is empty so he heads straight to the bar to order her another one, striding past us and stirring up a waft of rosemary chicken from a nearby table.

'I thought I'd catch you at the house today.' He puts a full pint down beside her empty one, avoiding her papers, and stands waiting for her to offer him a seat. When she doesn't say anything, he straddles a low stool, tugs the corner of her pile of papers toward his side of the table and asks, 'What're you working on?'

'Just some Farrington stuff.' She places the Whitmore papers on the bench beside her and then changes her mind and tucks them between the straps of her handbag under the table. 'Thanks for the pint.'

Blake leans in to say something, but hesitates as the waitress from last night appears. 'Heya, Blake.' She smiles warmly at him and then flicks a quick slit-eyed look over toward Jane. 'Can I get youse anything to eat?' She reaches across the table to take Jane's empty glass and her long blonde hair swings forward and her midriff touches Blake's arm. 'Curry's on special.'

Jane shakes her head, smiling at the girl's territorial exercise.

Blake keeps his eyes on Jane. 'No, we're great, Katie, thanks.'

Katie wends her way through the crowd back to the bar. Blake checks to make sure she's gone and then turns back to Jane and says, 'Sorry,' as if he owes Jane the apology, as if he is protecting her—as if he thinks something is happening between them.

Around ten, Blake's dad, who's been up at the bar, walks past the table to say good night. He grins awkwardly at Jane and pats his son's shoulder. By now Jane is used to the idea that everyone in the room seems to know Blake and is watching them, though when Blake explains to his father that she's part of the restoration team from London, her lip twitches and she sits up straighter. Embedded in the lie is what happened less than a week ago with William, and a whole other world she is trying to ignore. Still, despite the lie, Jane finds to her surprise that there is a lot she can say to Blake: that she has an MA in archives and record management, that she used to play cello, that her father is a famous violinist, though she won't give his name, that she has a brother who is a geneticist, and, when Blake presses her for details about her relationships, that she lived briefly with an architect.

'That's one,' he says.

'One what?'

'You said before that you'd been in love three times.'

Jane laughs. 'Well, the other two weren't quite reciprocated, so they might not count.' She drinks the last of her pint and he watches her set it down as if calculating the likelihood of getting her to stay for another.

'But you live alone now?'

'I do. Well, me and the dog.'

He is watching her mouth move and it makes her self-conscious—because she likes it and because it makes her feel like some twenty-year-old version of herself that she never got to be.

'What about you? I'm guessing you live with your parents?'

He stands up, takes their empties in his hand and put his lips to her ear. 'If I lived on my own, do you think we'd still be here?'

When they leave the pub Blake holds the door open and lets her go through first. Then he drops his hand to her waist to guide her to the right before she can say good night and head left toward the inn. He jerks his chin toward the church and the falls, says, 'It's nice out,' and just as Jane is about to say, *I should probably go, it's late*, he threads his hand into hers and pulls her gently along. When they get to the field that divides the falls and the Farrington trail from the estate he takes the path up along the stone wall that runs beside Inglewood House.

All night Blake has wanted to touch her. Jane sensed it, and she saw that his father noticed it and was uncomfortable with it, that Blake's neighbours sitting next to them had picked up on it too. The woman, dressed up for dinner, had caught the clasp of her bracelet on Jane's sweater when she rose tipsily from the bench and tried to move between the tables, had laughed nervously as she tried to release it. Jane blushed and looked at Blake and shook her head because she knew what his neigh-bours, what everyone, was thinking.

Halfway up the path, near the spot where Jane had climbed the wall, with the sloped roof of Inglewood House's stables sil-houetted between oak trees, Blake stops and kisses her, his hands in her hair, body pressed against hers. She doesn't pull away, and when he senses that she is letting it happen, when she kisses him back, he kisses her even harder.

Jane closes her eyes, feels his warmth against her, tastes the tang of beer in his mouth. This is how it begins, she thinks: a door opens and you step in or out of it, or you stand still with a bar of unexpected light at your feet and you wait to see if the sun inching over your legs, your arms and your face, feels good; if it does, you go in.

They end up on the grass. He moves on top of her for a second and then he pulls away, says, 'Wait here.' He's up and over the wall before she even knows what's happening; when he comes back two long minutes later, he has a blanket from the stables.

'Listen, Blake—' She stands, presses her fingers against her temples. It's ridiculous: he is a kid, she is a grown-up, and when he cleared the wall she had a feeling he'd done this a dozen times before. That makes this encounter seem an even worse idea than it already is.

He drops the blanket around the back of an oak whose low branches span the field on one side of the wall and the grounds behind the stables on the other. Then he stands ten feet away from her undoing the buttons of his shirt. Underneath his shirt he's wearing a white T-shirt; a spiky black tattoo is banded around his left arm just above his elbow. He loops the T-shirt over his head and then unzips his trousers and when he is down to his underwear and socks he just stands there in the cold night air looking more grown-up than he should. When Jane doesn't move closer or move away, he comes over to her and lifts her sweater over her head. He kisses the front of her neck and under her chin, traces her collarbones with his thumbs. Then he leads her over to the blanket, lifts her skirt and runs a track of kisses up her thigh, the woods pulsing around them, a salt taste on her lips from his skin. He has a condom in his wallet and that surprises her, but when it takes him a few tries to tear it open with his teeth, he says, 'Go ahead and laugh,' and she does, and everything between them slows down, becomes more intentional.

There are human experiences that we can remember, and sensations we can sometimes glean. We often lean toward or away from things because of a desire or unease.

When Blake kneels in front of Jane and Jane puts her hands in his hair, one of us goes for a walk with the children, one of us wanders into the woods to be alone, and some of us stay to watch, the poet behaving rudely even as his voice lets slip a kind of grief. Those of us present are trying to remember our own wants and needs, the ways we were loved, what acts, or what kinds of touch shaped us.

When they are finished, Blake leans over Jane to keep her warm, rubs her arm with his hand, stopping to trace her nipple with his finger. 'I can get another blanket.'

She kisses him because he is a good kisser, because he is sweet, because for the last hour she has only been *here*; and because he is a gentleman who wants to bring her another blanket that will smell of dust and old straw, who paid for their drinks with the only ten-pound note left in a wallet that had a strip of Velcro on it.

'It's okay, it's late, and I have to get back to Sam.' Jane slips into her skirt. We watch her and think, *Yes, it is late, late for us too.* We also want release: we are tired of scattering ourselves into todays and yesterdays, tired of being in this woods now and a hundred or so years ago all at the same time. How long have we been trying to concentrate? For the last hour Jane has been aware of nothing but what it feels like when a finger trails down your spine, when a chest reverberates against yours with laughter, when a twitch turns into a tremor inside of you. She has had what we want: to be wholly in one place with no thought outside of it. Though once, pushing into her, Blake called out 'Helen,' and she quivered, put her mouth against his ear but remained silent.

This, we thought, *is how you reinvent yourself. This is how you disappear.*

PART III

20 The summer of 1877 was the wettest anyone at the Whitmore could remember and the strain of the confinement was felt by everyone. In June the kitchens were low on meat one week and short of sugar the next. In July the Commissioners did not come by to register receipt of the patients' complaints, and so a revolt against flock-picking ensued. The poet's wife had visited to advise the poet that he would soon be released, and he'd upended a table, smashed a vase and was sent to the refractory ward for a week. Those who enjoyed his poetry brooded.

All summer there were rumours of cholera in the village, which meant that no escorted walks were permitted, although walks under parasols had been promised. The world was topsy-turvy: the countryside was soaking wet, yet the ferns in the Whitmore's front gallery were dying of thirst. For a fortnight the patients lined the windows, quietly seething.

In the middle of those weeks of endless rain, Superintendent Thorpe conceived of a competition that he hoped would enliven the general mood in the hospital and motivate the patients to behave. The idea was to create a series of pleasure gardens—twenty small plots to be assigned to selected patients who would be given sole care of their budding tenants. By early July the garroted vine had been dug out of the hillside by two perpetually soaked attendants, and by mid-month the plots were bordered with box and further divided by narrow gravel walkways, each gardener's name to be painted on a zinc plate and hung from a wood post at the entrance.

We know that the assignment of a plot was deemed a privilege because the patients had to apply for one and these applications were noted, and occasionally pasted, into the casebooks. To be granted a plot one had to be well into recovery, to have gone at least a month without incident, to have demonstrated the attainment of some skill—whether pillow-making, plain sewing or fancy work, shoe repair, clockwork or upholstery. Supplicants were also required to have eaten their meals without complaint and to have made a formal application in legible lettering. Those who were deemed suicidal were prohibited from applying because the gardens were outside the walls of the airing courts and beyond the gate that led to the infirmary. The farthest plot crested the top of a grassy rise that sloped down toward a shunting river, a river those in danger of self-harm were never allowed to see.

A list of the first group of recipients was drawn up a week before Herschel slipped out of the door, followed by Leeson and N. The Superintendent had announced that the names of those selected would be posted in the day rooms of the men's and women's wards. This was his first mistake: the public nature of the act, the assumption that the success of the few would inspire the many.

Alfred Hale was pretending to read a newspaper in a wing-back chair when the men's list arrived. The moment it was pegged up he moved toward it. Eliza Woodward was working on a sampler by the window. She stood when the Matron swished in, abandoning the last red stitch in the *A* of *Amen*.

Both their names were on the list.

That night, someone set fire to a curtain.

Thorpe, having underestimated the strain the weeks of rain and detention had been causing, was forced to conceive of a second reward, an event that would include everyone. A second list was drawn up, dividing the patients' names into groups of eight, and it promised a late-summer outing. Posted next to the garden plot awards, this larger notice announced 'A Carriage Ride and Walking Party!' in a female attendant's best calligraphy, under which Herschel had been requested to sketch a stand of trees in fine weather. 'To exotic gardens in a magnificent wood!' the poster read. 'To observe strange and wonderful plant species!' Under this last line Herschel had inexplicably drawn a toad, but by the time Thorpe saw it, the squat creature could not be removed. Three dates for the outings followed; they would go in two omnibuses lent by a friend of the Superintendent's, so that the only cost would be for drivers. The names of the staff members assigned to lead the parties were noted in block print, though some reassignments were demanded. To quell the dissent over the garden plot allotments even further, the Superintendent consented to allow the genders to mix.

Alfred Hale liked to refer to the Whitmore as a country house. He'd suffered from a blow to the head at the hands of a thief, and there were whole weeks during his confinement when he believed he was a guest at a grand estate; that he had been invited here to play the trombone with a renowned ensemble. Because of this he had a habit of entering every door as if it were the boundary between the outside world and a great hall: he doffed his hat constantly, looked searchingly for a doorman to take it, sought coat stands that did not exist. Once, he plopped his bowler on Noble's head because the hall porter had the misfortune to be standing inside an entry. He behaved in a similar fashion when he returned to his ward at night, saying, 'Good evening, it's delightful to be here,' before engaging in a round of handshakes with those already turned in to their beds.

Hale was now assigned to a walking party that consisted of so many names he became unsure as to who they were and how, with so many bodies, their instruments might be delivered to the estate. He took Bream aside and went over the list, asking, 'Is that the French horn player?' 'Is that the violinist?' Bream walked away, shaking his head, and Hale shouted after him, 'Will the instruments precede us or follow on?' He wrote to the Commissioners about the injustice of being separated, even briefly, from his cases, but the Commissioners failed to respond. He spent the intervening days considering which of his 'fellow musicians' might be left off the omnibus in order to make room for his trombone. According to the billet posted over the card table, his walking party was to consist of himself, old man Greevy, Professor Wick, Charles Leeson, three women he could not place, and the one called Eliza Woodward whom he'd seen kiss Hopper at the summer ball. He'd watched them dance afterward, noting that she had fine-looking lips but absolutely no sense of rhythm. The poet had snickered watching them, said that she had a habit of pretending to strike herself with a knife through the heart, but that due to her anatomical ignorance she always thumped her closed fist against her collarbone. And so, thinking only of a seat for his trombone and his need to have it with him, Hale got it in his mind that after an evening meal, as soon as was feasible, he would lure Eliza out of the women's half of the dining hall to relieve her of her misinformation.

Eliza Woodward's casebook states that she had come to the Whitmore complaining of fatigue, an exhaustion that made the Whitmore's usual constitutionals—the forced ingestion of meats, the rhubarb purgatives—feel like constant and torturous supplications when all she wanted to do was sleep. In late July of 1877 her casebook states, *Does not seem to mind the rain*, as if this were so anomalous it merited an attendant's notation.

There had been a time when she was well, and muzzily Eliza knew this. There was still colour in her cheeks when, during a lesson in comportment in the wood-panelled sitting room, the Matron produced a looking glass.

'Who do you see?' the Matron cooed, smoothing Eliza's hands so they did not grip each other so forcefully.

Eliza peered closely but she did not understand the question. Instead of answering she touched her neck with her fingers, the delicate cording of it visible to her for the first time. The ligatures were akin to the strings of an instrument, and Eliza thought, as she considered them, of the ones belonging to the idiot Herschel, how they must have been nicked or severed.

'I see a *lovely* young woman,' the Matron chirped. 'Can you say her name?'

Eliza stared at the Matron. She did not know if she should say her Christian name, or her pet name, or the one her father had thrown at her.

'Eliza?' Her lip twitched. She wanted to get the answer right; if she did they wouldn't take away her garden plot and when the rain stopped she would have an oval tag with her name on it above a bed of flowers.

'Well done,' the Matron said, and she moved with her looking glass across the sitting room toward Sallie Herring, the mirror's refracted light cleaving the walls and ceiling. When the Matron sat down, Sallie stopped pulling at her hair, sliding away the tuffet of strands that were already nested on the bench beside her.

The night before Alfred Hale assaulted her, Eliza stole out of bed with a blanket and a pillow to lie down in the far corner of the women's ward where there was space enough between the last cot and the wall to breathe. To help her sleep she sang a lullaby her sister Julia used to coddle her with: '*Pussy, Pussy, where have you been today? In the meadow asleep in the hay.*' When the widow in the cot beside her swatted her for singing, she prayed quietly for her sister and brother—whom she had loved, her father once said, to excess. When praying didn't lull her she resorted, as she sometimes did, to whispering her own name. This was dangerous, because in the blackened room, the grey curtains blotting out even the moonlight, she could sometimes hear herself call back. The saying of her own name shifting from a query to a conversation; how in the gap between the pulse of saying it over and over again a transfer occurred, so that it was as if she were standing in her best dress on the far side of a seamless field, hearing someone at a distance—some lost version of herself—anxiously begging her home.

No two people saw the August 1st event in the dining hall the same way. Hopper refused to be complicit, and so Alfred Hale enlisted Herschel, who, having finished his bowl of rabbit stew, waved at Eliza across the oak divider until he had her full attention. When the patients were all getting up to leave, she crossed the room toward the waist-high partition and Herschel and Hale approached her. Hale was hiding the knife he'd prised the evening before from the rump of ham sitting inside the kitchen on a sideboard.

Greevy would say later that it was Herschel who had ruined the promise of the walking party. That had he and Leeson not gone off into the woods the morning after the event in the dining hall, the rights and privileges promised the patients, and the expedition to the gardens at Inglewood, would have been ensured. But in truth it was Hale who ruined things—who brought the knife to Eliza's throat after she crossed the divide to greet him.

What was lost that month was not only the promise of a walking party and the sight of exotic gardens whose plants had been transported from countries that sounded lush and mountain-crowned, but an element of trust amongst the patients. Any sense they had of independence was gone, for suddenly in the wake of the various crises, it became clear that the actions of one impacted the others without any gaps or omissions. Hale had brought the blade up, Leeson had moved to intervene, and Herschel had *cluck*ed in excitement and drawn Bream's attention.

Eliza had watched them all assemble, peering down at the heavy bone handle of the knife at her throat, laughing as if she'd been enlisted in a pantomime. Bream barely had his hands on Hale when Eliza wrested herself from the musician's grip, turning to kiss her assailant on the cheek. He was bundled off with his hands behind his back and not seen by any of the other patients for a week.

In the aftermath of the attack Herschel was chastised and censured. Superintendent Thorpe retracted a number of privileges, reading them off a list as Herschel sat in the doctor's damp office with his mouth open. 'No garden plot for you,' Thorpe said, 'and no walking party. And no escorted rambles in the bloody woods.' The sound of the pencil whisking across the paper, striking off one form of contentment after another, was almost more than Herschel could bear. 'You may have drawn Bream's attention,' Thorpe snapped, 'but I have witnesses that saw you lure her over.' He leaned forward in his chair and Herschel flinched. 'She could have been killed, you know.'

It was the woods that had made the confinement during the weeks of rain bearable for Herschel. If he stood under the lip of the hospital roof in the airing court he could still see the trees bristling wetly beyond the stone walls, hear the *proo-proo* and *brrrk* of the birds in their shelters. A desire rose in him to see the birds and confirm that they were real; also a desire to make himself known to them, to consolidate some sense of community. A week before the rain started Herschel had been given spadework in the potato beds, only to be reassigned to art class when Bream found him at dinner tending to a shirt-pocket full of worms. In art class the patients were encouraged to suggest assignments: paint a tree, attempt a portrait, replicate an aspect of hospital architecture. When it was the poet's turn he said that everyone had to paint an image caught in the eye of an animal. He requested it in verse and then bowed deeply at Herschel. During the day in the woods with Leeson and the girl, Herschel was still seething at the rights and privileges Thorpe had taken away, but he was also looking for that stillness: a dunnock or a resting tit, a crow on a low branch who might cast back his likeness.

At first Herschel had been unhappy when Leeson joined him in the woods, had watched with dismay as he came briskly through a clearing and flailed a hand overhead. The two men were friends because of the nature of their circumstances and the proximity of their ward beds, but, Herschel felt, Leeson did not understand him. By the time the girl joined them, he had reconciled himself to the fact of company, though it was the poet he would have preferred to be with.

As Charles and the girl walked ahead, Herschel busied himself tracking the patter of the birds as they took to their shrubs and branches, their own poems arcing out of the flutes of their throats. Theirs was a language he could speak, their twittering complaints and warbled praise braided with his own twiney thinking. Herschel understood that he did not see the world as others saw it. He saw himself as being like the poet in this regard, although the poet had a means to speak of his purgatorial travels whereas Herschel did not. In the weeks before the walk his problem had been getting worse. He would recover his voice in therapy only to lose it again, and because of this he had started to pluck grievances from grounds where there were none, to revel in bitterness. He could savour the weight of his silence only when he was amongst the others, and so he started to take the most prominent seat in the games room or in the ward in order to perch there, his face slack and his mouth gaping open like a purse.

We know that when Jane read Herschel's casebook she was able to see how his progress varied. One week there would be talk of his release, and the next there would be a threat of removal to one of the stricter asylums. He oscillated from *improving* to *having fits* to *privileges returned* within three hastily written lines. What Jane doesn't understand is that this is only part of the story, gleaned as the hospital staff tracked patients over the course of a day or two and jotted down exaggerated acts or volatile aspects. The hours of selfhood between fits in the bath or dining hall rebellions went mostly unrecorded, and no one but Dr. Thorpe was tasked with asking 'How do you feel?' or

'What are you thinking?' No one but Thorpe was willing to read Herschel's body language, watch him flit his hands and arms as if they could speak for him on the days his voice failed.

The lack of a proper voice, the silence, wasn't Herschel's choice. A trap door had closed in his throat one morning and refused to open again. He'd been walking the cornfields of his farm, watching the crows settle between the stalks. He had opened his mouth, intending to disperse them, but instead of a human word a serrated sound came out. He squawked at himself with surprise. That night under the rough blankets of his bed he could feel a tingling in one arm; then, days later, he felt a prickliness in the other. The soles of his feet became itchy and his clothes nettled his skin. His body grew strange and worked against him—his arms so heavy that although he became fascinated with the contours of his own limp sex he stopped being able to touch it. He walked purposefully into town but when the chemist asked him to describe what salve he sought, a guttural sound emerged. When he tried to modify it, it assumed the *whoot* of an owl. At first he recoiled from his disability, hid in out-of-the-way places when his woman came around—on the sloped roof of his barn, on the guttered lip of his neighbour's house. But then he realized what was happening: it wasn't that he couldn't speak; rather, he was acquiring a new language, and his physical discomfort was part of the required change. Some days, if he concentrated, he believed he could feel his metamorphosis—his vocal fold closing and his esophagus opening into a swelling crop, the crop opening onto a blooming gizzard.

It suited Herschel that the physician called to the farm to assess him believed he was an imbecile.

When asked by the young doctor if he was a danger to others, the woman who claimed she was Herschel's wife—but who did not, in reality, live with him—gazed at Herschel with hooded lids and said, 'Yes.' She sat primly in the front room when the second doctor came and testified that she lived in constant fear of her husband's self-harm, pointing to the grey space of the adjacent kitchen where she said duty had required her to lock up the knives. Herschel *caw*ed in reply. He knew there would be some other man in his bed before he exited the carriage at the hospital. Still, even in his fledgling state, Herschel knew that, no matter the cost, he wanted other than what he had. He was tired of meagreness and petty ways of thinking; he wanted a larger view of the world, wanted to get out of the poverty of his own life, out of the insularity of the village he had been brought up in. The second doctor, at least, had studied him with a certain degree of open-minded patience, as if he discerned a mind at work under Herschel's feathered thinking.

If Thorpe had asked Herschel what he remembered about that day in the woods, and if Herschel could have voiced it, he might have said the cast light of the forest, the sun broken by branches as if by the struts of a window, the dew palpable and settling. The poet's words covered everything he saw like a gauzy web: recitations netted overtop of the spindling trees, crawling over the thick veins of the leaves like a caterpillar. *Caught in gusted exaltation! / Tooth-tipped we slip / under the grazed skin of the mottling ground.* The green noise of the poems and the woods surrounded Herschel: leaf-mouths and nattering grasses, the low hum of the pan of moss he put his ear against. The throstle in the forest understorey saying *hello* in its *tweep* and *burble*; the poet singing, *Come under, come under and know you are not alone.*

In the latter part of the day, Leeson and the girl started to trail Herschel at a distance. From time to time, Herschel would turn and glance around for them, sure that they'd become separated. His own face was slick with sweat from the exertion of the walk and he resented his companions when they caught up to him because they did not appear to be suffering as he was. Leeson had been distant earlier, in the hour when they'd walked three abreast, absent-mindedly gravitating toward even the faintest tread of a path as if he needed to course a route others had forged before him. Herschel had been mulling over a stanza the poet had composed weeks ago in the potting shed while observing turnip roots dangling over the edge of the work surface like little phalluses: *All our ghosted pities / all our sorrowed births / bursting like seeds / in the blackened womb of earth.* Herschel had never seen before that the earth was like a womb and he did not like to think of it. It changed the entryway of a woman's sex into a door to an incomprehensible chamber, and it turned the place where the horizon met his farm's fields into a fertile slit. And so the Whitmore girl's sex was a fact he was aware of as they entered a stand of oak. Leeson walked between him and the girl as if he were a partition. As if he thought Herschel were some kind of animal, catching whiff of his prey.

Later, what Herschel would remember most clearly about the girl was her absence—how after the three of them had passed through a clearing bobbed with flowers, Herschel had lost her.

He'd wanted to communicate his happiness at the good weather, had wanted to try a word, to say 'open' or 'yes' or 'glad,' to point to the lifting arms of the shaggy trees, but when he turned he saw nothing but bird-flit and the scrabbling of a small mammal in the root-hem of an alder. Suddenly lonely, he'd doubled back in the direction from which he'd come, finding the girl and Leeson in a sunlit sward at the edge of a clearing. The girl was sitting on Leeson's jacket, resting against a tree. He'd watched them for a minute, then chirped, and both of them glanced in his direction. The solicitor offered the girl his hand so that he might help her up, holding it in his as he led her over a fallen oak. It was a trifling gesture that Herschel knew he ought to ignore, even as he felt petty jealousy take root.

In the week after his return from the woods Herschel had not been subject to the same degree of interrogation as Leeson. The solicitor had been ushered in and out of Thorpe's office at least once a day until the matter seemed miraculously resolved, like a cloth wiping away all trace of a stain. By then, Herschel mostly recalled the Farrington paintings—a variety of land-scapes inside of a landscape broken up by walls—and the roe deer they'd happened upon in the copse wood, how it matched and did not match the one whose head dipped down from an oak board in George Farrington's parlour.

Eventually he went back to painting class and to listening to the poet's words and to his own tongue's *chirrup*ing indeci-sion. Words or no words? Sound or silence? He wondered what he would want to say in a human language if he recovered the tools with which to engage in it. His thoughts becoming more birdlike every day: *tree, roost, lift, flight.*

There is a photograph of Herschel on a card tucked into the back of his casebook. When Jane discovered it yesterday she set it aside on the table at the records office while she continued to work. The photograph is one of forty studies made by a physiognomist called Merrifield who had sought to prove that muscular and cranial indicators could be used for diagnostic means. Herschel appears in the painting smock he was most fond of, his dark hair messy, eyes pouched with exhaustion, nostrils flared.

When Jane first saw it, the one who never speaks whistled, and understanding that he meant *Look*, we gathered around him. We felt one thing slide into the other: Herschel's knowledge of himself alongside our knowledge of him as he was before and as he has been with us. Our growing knowledge of Eliza Woodward and Alfred Hale and John Hopper is almost the same even if it isn't captured in a photograph: 'That's me!' Cat had said when she saw herself in the dining hall, when together we remembered our old mischief. And the musician standing beside her had faltered, and John had gone to stand beside him so he would feel less alone in his shame. A sheet of sums that seemed to add up perfectly.

There is a trick to looking at an image. Jane may have seen Herschel's unblinking eyes and twisted mouth but she was still not seeing him as we do. We see him as if he is passing through the photograph: a man who was escorted to the stool and who sat on it, who arranged his features into a question. We see the farmer who was permitted to leave after the work of the dark hump behind the drop cloth was done. We understand how that particular afternoon unfolded into days and weeks and months and a year or more of thoughts and deeds and reveries. It doesn't matter that memories can sometimes be misshapen, that there are a hundred ways to fix or lose a sense of self.

When Herschel bristled at his photo we turned to him and said, 'Yes, but that is not who you were; that is not all of it.' Cat air-kissed him and we made an effort to think of her as Eliza; John looked at the clock on the wall of the reading room and we remembered with him that time was once his life's work. That afternoon at the records office is the kind of time that we exist for: one in which we are brought back to some semblance of self. Jane only had the photo, while suddenly some of us could remember Herschel lumbering in to dinner in a top hat, making wood benches in the workshop, marvelling at lantern slides, offering Greevy his allotment of meat. A few of us saw Herschel in his best suit on Visitors' Day, greeting the poet's wife and pretending through mimicry to be the poet while the wordsmith hid behind a high-backed wicker seat and snickered at the Countess's annoyance. One of us saw him as he stood in the woods in a stream of light, cupping his hands under it. As if light might pool there, containing a world of wonders, the kind most people never see.

A fortnight after the trio's escape a bout of cholera erupted in the village, and shortly after that the hospital logbook states that two attendants and fourteen patients, including Alfred Hale, became ill.

In those weeks of fever and quarantine, we longed for the kinds of distraction that had come with the summer ball: for music and movement, the declarations of the poet, a sip of ginger beer or elder wine. It was suggested by some that it was more pleasant to be at ease in the world than to rail against it, and so a number of patients gave up trying to make themselves well.

When the worst wave of fever pressed through the wards some of us believed the building was on fire. Those who had glimpsed the river through the iron bars of the infirmary gate dreamed of it constantly. Whether ill or not we all thought about the gardens we had missed, what it would be like to ride to Inglewood in an omnibus, to walk the trails with the fresh afternoon air swaddling our faces. Sometimes lying in our beds we thought of N, believing as Leeson had that she might still be out there, lost in the gathering night. Though it is difficult, even now as we stand at the hip of the woods waiting for Jane to leave Blake and walk back to the inn, to remember what night meant to us. Not night the way Jane knows it, with its electricity, street lamps and neon shop signs, the ambient glow of distant cities; but night as we knew it then: its bale unfurled overhead. Hours so dark and moonless not even the needle holes in the sky could guide you home.

21 Blake promises to walk Jane back, but says he wants to show her something first. And even though she feels self-conscious about what has passed between them, Jane agrees to go with him, caught up in his infectious happiness as he takes her hand and pulls her under the hoops of light cast by the street lamps and toward the start of the trail. When they reach the gate he stops and kisses her, pressing her back against the wood stiles as if he wants to start all over again. She pushes him away, laughing, and he carries on through the gate, doing a

slow jog backward down the trail, cocky and enjoying himself. It's only when she insists on knowing where they're going—uncomfortable because he is pulling her into the dark, past the short, numbered posts and the moon-glossed plants that she and William and Lily had once passed—that he turns to look at her fully, aware of the tug of resistance in her hand.

'The grotto.'

'Why?'

'You'll see. It's just a little farther along.'

Those of us who had stayed with Jane follow her and Blake down the trail. Our attention is divided between them and the woods because that's where Cat took the children when Jane's sweater came off, and they have yet to return. They were playing a game as they wandered across the waving field, Cat asking, 'What sounds do you hear?' and the girl answering, 'Crickets.' A dog had barked in the distance, and then the boy said, 'Dock.' And the theologian had called after them that they shouldn't wander too far.

If Jane remembers correctly the grotto is about a ten-minute walk along the trail past the last ledge of the upper pastures. You have to cut up through the woods to get to it. It isn't impressive: just a small recession under a curve of limestone with cobbled stones mortared around its edges. It had been tall enough for Jane to stand up in when she was fifteen, though it arched down from its apex so sharply that only a few people could take shelter if it started to rain.

When Blake says that he is taking her there, she remembers that in its centre two decades ago there was a stone plinth displaying a weathered marble bust. Jane had assumed, walking up to it with Lily, that it would be a sculpture of George Farrington, but when they got close they saw it was a woman's head—a Greek sculpture of a girl with ringlets in her hair and drapery across her shoulder, stains from lichen and moss mottling the folds.

Now Jane passes the spot along the trail that leads down to the lake and the rock where she had sat three days ago, but Blake doesn't stop. His hand is warm around hers as he pulls her gently forward, singing an old Oasis song about all the things he would like to say to her even though he doesn't know how. He grins at Jane as he launches into the chorus, a daft and off-key nineteen-year-old doing whatever he can to keep the night going.

In the darkness Blake overshoots the narrow path that forks up from the main trail and they have to go back for it, using the light of his phone to find the tread where the two paths intersect. Jane remembers how Lily had announced that she needed to go to the bathroom at this point in their walk, and Jane, not sure what she should do because William was still ahead of them, took Lily up the narrow trail to quickly pee in the woods, thinking that it would alarm William if they turned around and headed all the way back to the village. Back then Jane hadn't anticipated the grotto or the limestone cliff above it. Lily had seemed surprised too, though it was the sculpture that excited her the most. The trek up the trail was, in Lily's mind, a diversion that she had caused, which meant that their discovery—a classical bust appearing miraculously in the midst of the monotonous woods—was also hers.

Jane and Blake stop along a slope of alder three quarters of the way up the trail, and from there Jane can make out the glow of a fire. The grotto's roof is lit up: an orange waver visible through the rails of the trees. Blake takes Jane's hand again and leads her farther up, breaking twigs and kicking aside fallen branches as he goes. Toward the top the easy chatter of two men's voices cuts clearly through the night air, while a radio news report runs underneath their conversation.

About eighty feet from the clearing Blake stops, still within the cover of the trees but level to the men, who sit on fold-out chairs in puffy coats, a pit fire between them. Jane turns to ask Blake what they're doing up here, and in turning realizes that it isn' the pit fire lighting the grotto but a carpet of votive candles laid over the grotto's floor—dozens of them, flickering under the limestone. The man in the tweed cap gets up and pulls a can of lager out of a nearby cooler, tosses a bag of crisps at his mate.

Blake whispers in Jane's ear, 'It's a vigil for the trapped miners. Half the village has been taking turns. The big guy on the left is a friend of my dad's.' He inclines his head toward the grotto. 'Wanna say hello?'

Jane shakes her head no and rubs the sides of her arms to warm herself. She can see that the plinth and sculpture are gone and that a sagging placard leans against the grotto wall. *Day 14* is written on it in black marker, the *13* and *12* beside it crossed out. Jane recalls the news report she'd heard on the drive from London: the days it might take the rescue workers to drill an air hole, the months it might take to bring the men to the surface. Her own problems suddenly feel small.

Watching the men keep their vigil, Jane thinks about her own choice to hold on so tightly to what happened to Lily. She has chosen to live in the past, just as she's chosen to lie to Blake, to lie—through omission—to almost everyone.

Over by the pit fire one of the men laughs heartily at something his companion has said, and their ease with each other, and the ease Jane feels with Blake, is strangely comforting. She drops her head onto Blake's shoulder and he turns and kisses her forehead, says, 'Tell me when you're ready to head down.'

The cottages that back onto the falls are a poorer version of the limestone houses that sit along the river: one-storey structures that would have been built for the men who ran the Farrington properties—the stable manager and head gardener—or for the local headmaster or a village merchant. Most of the houses are dark as we walk past them, their tenants sleeping, and so Blake has to guide Jane along the pavement until they get to the farthest house, the one with a light in its back kitchen.

For us there is often no difference between what we see in the world and what we watch on the telly. Actions set in motion by the living can feel like scenes so far removed from us that any act of intercession on our part seems impossible. In this way, the window in the cottage at the end of the road is not unlike a film screen, one on which a girl of fifteen or sixteen appears in flannel pyjama bottoms and a T-shirt, opening a kitchen cupboard at the back of the house to pull out a box of cereal. This is where we find Cat and the children—peering between the gaping curtains as the teenager roots around in the refrigerator for milk.

'Cat found the twooms,' the girl says when she senses our presence behind her.

'The *twooms*?' the one with the soft voice asks.

'Headstones,' Cat explains, 'up from the gate in the woods. Not very big. Probably the Farrington family's dogs.'

'*Ruff-ruff*,' barks our girl, watching as the teenager scoops cereal out of a blue ceramic bowl and deposits it in her mouth. 'I'm hungry.'

'Me too,' says the boy, which is what he always says when the girl mentions food. Even though he knows that what he feels is not actual hunger, he likes the idea that his needs concern us, that because we are adults, all forms of provision fall under our sway.

John leans toward the boy. 'You're not hungry. At least, not in the way that you think you are.'

'The cottages have changed,' the theologian states, tired of the tenor of the conversation. 'There used to be wood-beam ceilings here.'

We bend forward to look at the ceiling, even though we are tired of indulging the theologian. He's been making emphatic statements since we arrived at Inglewood: *These houses are new; the old stables are gone; the pub has a different sign.* His proclamations were exciting at first, but now, as there's little to set them against—no facts, no dissenting opinions—they've become tedious.

Even in the dim light from the kitchen we can see that the ceiling is plaster. We can also see the reflective sheen of a flat-screen television, the blinking dots of DVD and CD players, a stereo with large speakers—various signs of modernity.

On the mantel there's a digital photo frame sliding a series of bright images across its screen, like a magician shuffling a deck of cards.

'There was ivy here,' the theologian continues, 'all over the front of the house.' And maybe because we want to believe him, or maybe because there once was, some of us picture rustling vines covering the cottage, imagine this whole row of houses hunkered alongside the falls in shaggy green coats.

'I remember ivy,' the boy says.

'*Hedera helix,*' the idiot chimes. '*Helix* from the Ancient Greek—' and he stops because he expects to be interrupted, even though no one opens their mouth to silence him.

Inside the kitchen the teenager stands up. She places her empty bowl in the sink and switches off the light. A second light goes on in another more distant room before a door shuts and drops us back into near-darkness.

'Where'd she go?' the girl asks.

'To sleep,' the poet says.

'I want to sleep,' the girl says, 'I'm sleepy too.' She fake-yawns.

'You *are* sleeping,' the theologian replies.

The girl shakes her head; she doesn't like to be told this. She moves up to the window and taps it lightly with her fingers.

'Don't—' the theologian commands, more sharply than he should.

Over on the mantel the photo frame is still lit up and the girl watches the years slip across it: the teenager we just watched morphing into a chubby eight-year-old holding the handlebars of a bicycle with pink streamers. Then she is ten, and standing on a bristly field in a football shirt; then thirteen or fourteen in a peach-coloured dress, under a cluster of green balloons; then a young girl again: she and her mum holding up cake beaters covered in batter in a floral-papered kitchen.

'I want to go *home*,' the girl says, and she turns and waits for one of us to do something.

But none of us steps forward because, like her, we have no sense of how to get there.

We like to believe in the resilience of children, and sometimes, watching them—our own two, or the boys down the hall in Jane's building, or Lewis's daughters—we marvel at the vibrancy of their imaginations, their ability to cordon off one version of reality from a preferred alternative. In the real world children grow. They learn to toggle between the actual and the imagined in new ways, eventually settling in a domain that allows them to walk to the corner shop on their own, master multiplication tables and graphs, write letters and essays, make their own decisions. We are less sure about how knowledge is gained here, in the half-light of our existence, or how such knowledge will serve the boy and the girl, though we agreed long ago it would be wrong to lie to them. Even at the gravestones that bear the moss-clad names of the Farrington pets—'Beck,' 'Duke,' 'Cato,' 'Cicero,' 'Tip'—Cat had asked the children if they knew what the markers were for, if they understood what *buried* meant. The girl said yes, but the boy wasn't listening; he was tracing the weathered letters, trying to find a familiar name.

We plod back toward the inn caught up in our own concerns. Jane and Blake had gone ahead while we dallied at the cottages and we let them go—the boy distracted by the falls and the rest of us not wanting to leave him. Now, as we walk, the girl is worrying her way around the contradiction we've set up: the idea that she is both awake and sleeping. The poet tries to make it clear to her, explaining that just as her hunger is not *real* hunger, she is not sleeping in the way she used to sleep; this is a different kind of dream. She shakes her head at this and he tries again, saying sadly that the girl with the cereal bowl is *alive*, 'whereas you, little flower, are dead.'

In the early days of our interrogations the question we were most afraid to ask each other was 'How did you die?' It held in its husk the possibility that some strain of suffering might be remembered. It was more pleasing to ask what kind of music one preferred, what kind of food one favoured, if a spouse or children came to mind when we said the word *family*. It was easier to tug out of the mind memories like 'terrier' or 'clockworks' or 'a wall of drawers in a long narrow shop' than the last thing the body remembered.

One of our final interrogations took place at the museum. Jane was collating the Lyell glassware archives for auction and we'd wandered upstairs. The one who never spoke was in the alcove in the science gallery by a tall window, and having just asked the poet a set of questions and getting no response but metered verse, we turned to the figure in the nook.

'What clothes can you see yourself wearing?' we asked. 'Where is your house?' 'Are you old or young?' A dozen more questions followed: 'What colours do you like?' 'Are you of faith?' 'Have you seen the sea?' But the figure stayed mute.

The theologian grew impatient and snapped, 'How did you die?'—as if this were an equally weighted question. To which the figure by the window *cawk*ed and then released a long slow whistle, as if falling from a great height.

The idiot once told us that learning is not the same as knowing. '*Integer non scientes*,' he'd groaned when the rest of us exclaimed *aha* at a trivial detail that Jane was reading in her office. We made no distinction back then between those bits of information that drifted through us and the larger ideas we could retain, the kind of knowledge we could build on. We always asked, 'When will we know ourselves?' never 'When will we know ourselves *enough*?'

When the poet told the girl that she was dead, the boy overheard. Now the girl is walking dolefully beside Cat and the boy is scuffing his feet, though he keeps turning to look back at the field. We have dispelled their happiness before, but it never gets any easier. Once, in Jane's flat, the girl shrieked loudly during a game she and the boy were playing, and Jane turned her head to where the girl was standing. It was a game the children liked: they chose a letter, and whenever the radio announcer said a word that started with that letter, the girl or the boy won a point; the first to reach a score of fifteen won the game. That day, the girl picked *P* and the boy *M*. It was a frosty winter weekend and Jane was gathering her things to go Christmas shopping. The broadcaster was interviewing an astronomer called Peter. At one point a whole sentence of *P*s—'extrasolar planet,' 'parsecs,' 'Outer Earth Project'—erupted and the girl shrieked in delight. Jane stopped, keys in hand, on her way to turn off the radio, and glanced to where the girl was standing beside the kitchen counter.

'She heard that,' the boy said. 'Do it again!'

And the girl made the happy sound, but not as loudly as before.

We all turned to Jane. She clicked the radio off, opened the closet and shrugged her coat on. In the kitchen Sam padded through us to inspect his bowl. Wrapping a wool scarf around her neck Jane glanced once more at the spot where the girl was standing, then ran her eyes over the newspaper folded on the end of the counter, the coffee mug in the sink, as if she were forgetting something.

'She saw me!' the girl said, and the boy leapt off his kitchen stool and went to stand next to the girl, windmilling his arms.

'No she didn't,' the theologian sighed, but some of us weren't convinced, wanted to believe the children.

'Are you sure?' Cat asked.

'Of course I am,' the theologian said, and he walked right up to Jane, close enough to see the flecks of mascara under her lash line, the fine baby hair on her cheek.

'Because?' the girl begged.

Jane opened the door and we moved to follow her.

'Because,' the theologian said gruffly, 'the living only see what's useful.'

Just before we reach the inn the boy runs ahead and the girl follows him. The rest of us discuss whether Blake will be in Jane's bed when we get to the room, and the musician hums, and the poet grunts the way he did earlier, like a rutting pig. We debate whether Jane will stay in Inglewood longer than she said she would; we can sense that she is light-headed at having slipped away from the world of accountability. When she thinks about the Chester and the work she dropped there, about what happened with William, she pushes the thought out of her head and instead thinks about Inglewood House, and the Whitmore, and us. This makes us happy, even though we know it shouldn't. But we also know it won't last. We know this just as we know Gareth will have phoned Lewis when Jane didn't return his calls or show up for work on Monday. Just like we know that Lewis will have tried calling the cottage by now, will have gone round to Jane's flat and found her mobile. Lewis is probably up at the Lakes already, trying to find her.

Two tunnels of light from a car's headlamps swing over us and we stop squabbling. The car cuts its engine in front of a stone house near the top of the village and the heavy *clunk* of the car door is followed by the wooden *thump* of a front door closing. For a second the sounds of the street fall back into the pulsing *whirr* of the nearby woods. And then, just as the boy turns toward the door of the inn, a ragged unhappiness palpable in his movements, we hear the same high bark we've heard before, a sure and sharp greeting. Some of us look to the field, and some of us to the house at the top of the street, imagining a dog in the yard uncurling himself to salute his master's return. The dog barks again, behind us this time, and the boy turns and stares up the road past the church to the woods beyond it. Without a word he starts to run.

The boy is clearer to us in that moment than he has ever been, his eight-year-old arms working, legs moving furiously: a boy with a shock of brown hair, a child's luminescent skin; a large plum-coloured bruise on his back. The theologian runs after him and is almost astride when the boy picks up speed and throws his arms out like an airplane, banking left for the field before he wavers and vanishes completely.

Jane is drying off from the shower when Sam starts barking. Some dog outside has set him off and Jane has to come out with wet feet and dripping hair to *shush* him. *Fair play*, she thinks; she's left him alone longer than usual this evening. She taps the mattress, 'Come here, Bubby,' and Sam jumps up. Jane scratches his head, runs her palms over his white and wavy spaniel ears. For the last half hour she's been puzzling over the evening's unexpected events: Blake, the craziness of the two of them—how good it felt; and the vigil at the grotto, the sudden appearance of the larger world's concerns in a place that has always been so closed, so loaded in her mind.

She pulls on a T-shirt and slides into bed, thinking about all the opportunities she had to tell Blake about William and Lily. The sound of the falls was a cue that brought back that day, and the earthy smell of the woods, its mushrooms and resin, and the weight of the weather hanging over the field.

22 During the two weeks when Jane was watching Lily they had a number of conversations about love. Lily was obsessed with pairs: *This fish swims with that one; my best friend is Bronwyn; these horses ride together.* On the Wednesday of the first week William had suggested that Jane walk Lily over to the Natural History Museum so they could have lunch with him. At the stone steps that led up to the main doors Lily had stopped abruptly and announced that her nanny, Luisa, didn't have a boyfriend. She studied Jane's face as people milled around them,

trying to register if Jane found that fact as unsettling as she did.

They arrived early and William wasn't in the main hall waiting for them, so Jane gave William's name at the information stand. A nice woman in a navy blazer called upstairs and then came around the desk to say that he was still in a meeting but that they could wait in the exhibition hall. She bent down to talk to Lily, who seemed to know her, and said, 'Well, aren't you looking smart today?' Then she stood up and added, 'You must be Jane.'

Jane nodded, feeling a frisson of excitement she didn't quite understand—the thrill of an adult acknowledging that William had spoken about her.

The woman left them in the hall where the museum mounted temporary exhibitions. That summer it held a display on early human settlements. Lily immediately made up romances: the *Homo erectus* pictured above the partial skeleton was married to the *Neanderthal*; the wax models in the cave diorama were a royal family—*This one's the King, this one's the Queen*; the mammoth is in love with the ox, this is their human baby. Jane enjoyed it so much—the crazy menagerie Lily was inventing—that she didn't bother telling her that half of her pairings lived in different millenniums or belonged to different species. Standing behind a velvet rope that surrounded a cast of early human footprints, Lily glanced at the parallel trails—the fleshy indents of a smaller set of tracks following a larger one—and then turned her attention back to Jane. 'Do *you* have a boyfriend?' She pursed her lips in a kissy fish face and Jane laughed and said no, wondering if Lily thought that she was closer to Luisa's age, twenty-two and not fifteen, trying to remember if, as a child, she'd also organized the world of adults into a large, undefined category.

A week and a half later, at lunch in the pub in Inglewood, Lily had asked if they were going to see the caves at the end of the Farrington trail. This was partly because she'd liked the dioramas that day at the Natural History Museum—wax models of shaggy-haired *hominids* staged around a campfire—and partly because William and Jane had been talking about caves on the drive up. William had said that one of the reasons the Farrington trail was so popular was the caves at the end of it. The larger one was a draw for spelunkers and tourists, although most people only ventured a hundred feet in, to the railings that bordered the first chasm.

Lily was in the back seat of the Saab dancing a pony on her knee but quietly listening; for the first part of their conversation William was using a tenor Jane had come to recognize, a pitch that meant he was speaking to both her and his daughter: simpler words, uncomplicated sentences. He mentioned the caves in Lascaux, moving the conversation tangentially to fill the space that Jane tended to leave open, and she told him that her father had taken her and Lewis to see their grandparents in Toulouse the previous summer and they'd made a day trip up to see the cave paintings at Font-de-Gaume. William, who'd been watching the road, the intermittent traffic, turned and looked at Jane in the way that always made her feel like he was *considering* her. She liked the heat of that kind of attention, how it demanded reciprocation, how it made her push through her uncertainties in order to find something to give him.

The Dordogne was greener and lusher than the parts of France Jane had visited before. As they drove toward the caves in the early morning a mist was lifting off the fields, clouding the drowsy heads of the sunflowers, dissipating around the stocky bulls grazing in their pastures. It was the first time Henri had taken Jane and Lewis anywhere without Claire. She'd backed out of the trip at the last minute because of a deadline, saying she'd meet them in Paris, though by the time they'd packed their things in Toulouse even that was in doubt. Jane had overheard them having an argument on the phone the morning they left for the caves and Henri's annoyance had been palpable the first part of the drive, but by the time they exited the motorway and started heading east, wending through a series of compact villages and driving under the rocky overhang of the Dordogne's cliffs, he'd softened. He began talking about his own childhood, how his father had brought him here when he was ten or so, just a little bit younger than Lewis.

There were no tickets left for the English tours of the cave so Henri bought tickets for the French. Jane's French was tolerable but Lewis's was almost non-existent. Henri said he'd translate, and ruffled Jane's hair as they walked toward the bridge where the tour started. 'But Jane will understand everything perfectly, *n'est-ce pas?*'

The tour guide was a man in his fifties in a baggy knit sweater. He introduced himself as Marc, and midway through his preamble he stopped and smiled at Lewis. '*Anglais?*' Lewis blushed, and Marc turned to a couple in blue rain slickers. '*Et vous? Vous parlez français?*'

The man replied, 'We are German.'

'Okay.' Marc smiled. 'I will try to do French and English if that is acceptable.' He surveyed the French speakers—a family of five and two young women with daypacks—to make sure they didn't mind and then clapped his hands together. '*Parfait.*'

Before he unlocked the iron door that led to the cave Marc explained the rules of the tour: *no bags past the entry, no touching the walls, not even with shoulders; we move quickly and stay close because our time inside is limited.* He looked at the German man and at Henri, and explained that there would be narrow passageways, and a Rubicon where it would be necessary to crouch down. 'You see?' he said to the German in English. 'Ducking?' And he bowed his head to make sure the man understood. Jane was closest to the large iron door that had been set into the cave wall, and as Marc took out his ring of keys to unlock the six bolts that crossed it he smiled at her. '*Vous êtes prête, mademoiselle?* You ready?'

What struck Jane about the caves was how difficult it was to see anything at all on the walls until the marks were pointed out. The lighting was dim to preserve the paintings and her eyes were slow to adjust. At a short railing, Marc stopped the group and gestured overhead. 'I will give you a moment,' he said. 'See what you see.' Jane scanned the convex limestone above her, the layers of rock yellow at her height but a brighter eggshell white above. There was a pool of brown to her right, but no shape she could distinguish clearly. Marc lifted a laser pointer to the brown stain and he used its red beam to trace the head, hump and chine of a bison. 'Look here.' He moved the pointer a foot to the right. 'And here.' The French girl behind Jane, the one whose perfume smelled like sweets, gasped, and Jane understood—she, too, was startled. How suddenly clear they were: two bison face to face, their delicate heads and rust-coloured horns bowed in front of their thick brown bodies.

'Look,' Marc said, running the pointer over the bison's thin legs. 'The artists are using perspective. Dimensionality, *non*? We had it and then we lost it.'

When her eyes had adjusted more fully to the subdued light, Jane could see that the bison were both painted *and* carved. Their backs and bellies were incised, their eyes scored into the stone; pupils the size of tuning pegs seemed to follow her when she shifted back and forth.

Marc smiled at her. 'Yes, good. It is almost like it is moving. The whole herd is running. Imagine the flame of a torch as our ancestors passed through here.' He moved his hand back and forth under the curl of the bison's stomach. 'How it would catch the folds and curves of the cave wall. Undulating, *non*? They are alive, you see.'

Marc stood back and let everyone take turns standing underneath the two bison. When Lewis, the last of the group, went up, Marc asked him, 'How many do you see?' and Lewis glanced up the corbelled vault of the cave and answered, 'Two? Maybe three?'

'Come close, everyone.' Marc ushered the group together. 'Look again,' he said, '*regardez*.' And he passed one of the floor lights over the upper reaches of the chamber to where a dozen bison grazed along a horizontal plane. 'You were surrounded,' he said cheerfully, 'this whole time.'

After Jane had finished telling William about the cave she turned to him and saw that he was grinning. She'd been talking for ten minutes, maybe more; it was the most she'd ever said to him. She'd been trying to articulate a thought—about what it was like to be shown something, to have a person wave a red laser over a russet stain, trace the lines of a reindeer's back until its thick black antlers and gentle face materialized. 'In this one there is kissing,' Marc had said, and although he was joking he wasn't exactly wrong. It was one of the clearer paintings: the incised tongue of the larger reindeer touching the head of the one with red horns kneeling before it.

Shortly before they got to Inglewood, Lily spilled the last of her juice over the Saab's back seat. She announced the accident and Jane unclipped her seat belt and turned around. She took the plastic cup from Lily's hand and used a fistful of tissues from the box on the floor to dab the bib of Lily's red overalls, mop up the puddle that had gathered around a button on the upholstery. She felt the car slowing down.

'Do you want me to pull over?'

'Nope, almost done.' She tapped Lily on the nose with her finger. 'Better?'

Lily lifted up her plastic pony; there were beads of apple juice in its glossy pink mane.

William was still driving slowly. 'I'd feel better if you were buckled up.'

Jane dried the pony, wiped Lily's booster seat around her legs, then swivelled back down onto the passenger seat. She lifted her hips to smooth the clump of her sundress and refastened her seat belt. When she glanced down to see if her hands were sticky she noticed that the front hem of her dress had settled a few inches above her knees, the half-moon scar she'd earned in a riding accident when she was seven noticeably white against her summer tan. She left the hem where it was and looked out the window at the patchwork of farmers' fields. A test, she thought. To see if what she wanted to happen, what she *thought* had happened the night William woke her on the sofa, was actually occurring.

Jane rolled down the window when they exited the highway. At the first sign for Inglewood, William, his eyes on the road, asked, 'How did you get that scar?'

Jane told the story about the cave twice that day, first to William on the drive up and then, later, to Constable Mobbs. An hour before Jane's grandparents were due to arrive, Mobbs reappeared, pulling a chair up to the desk where Jane was sitting. Mobbs's face was red as if she'd been running and for a second Jane thought there might be some news.

'You holding up okay?'

Jane felt her chin wobble and her eyes begin to well so she turned back to the swinging spheres of the contraption on Holmes's desk and knocked the end ball with her knuckle.

'It's called Newton's Cradle,' Mobbs said. She jabbed a thumb over her shoulder. 'I asked Oliver. Something about the transfer of energy.'

Jane pulled back and released the first ball, and watched the last swing out. The three balls in the middle didn't move.

'Right then.' Mobbs patted her cheeks with her hands as if she were aware of how flushed they were. 'Listen, I need to ask you again if you can think of anything else that might be of use, not just what you saw or didn't see—' She ducked her head lower to get Jane's attention. 'But anything that you and Lily talked about on the trail, anything she said. If Lily's wandered off'— Mobbs pursed her lips and glanced across the room to where William had been sitting before going back out with one of the search parties—'you're the only one who can help us understand what she might have been thinking. Okay? Can you do that?'

Jane nodded and Mobbs pulled out a notebook and a stubby pencil. And for the next half hour Jane recounted the story of the cave at Font-de-Gaume, telling Mobbs how Lily had been listening to her describe it to William, and how later, when Lily had to pee and she and Jane discovered the grotto, Lily had mistaken it for a cave. She'd thought they could go inside it, that they'd find painted bison and mammoths and oxen and horses. 'She kept going on about the reindeer,' Jane said, because the kissing reindeer was the part of the story Lily had liked best, that and the part at the end about the domed cavity at the back of the narrowest tunnel, the wall that was marked, almost like a finger-painting, with the splayed fingers and narrow palms of human hands.

23   The archivist helping Jane is called Freddy. He's a paunchy and bald middle-aged man who spends the first hour of the morning moving fussily around the local records office reshelving books and indices from a squeaky trolley. When Jane walks over to his desk to request a biography of George Farrington, he produces a slip of paper from under a stapler and flusters, 'Miranda left a note for you. Sorry, I forgot it was here. She thought you might like to look at Lucian Palmer's journals. Do you want me to call them up?'

'Sorry, who is Lucian Palmer?'

Freddy lifts the piece of paper to indicate he's told her everything he knows.

'Why not?' she says. 'Thanks.'

Palmer, Jane discovers, is *Dr.* Lucian Palmer, and his medical journals—two deteriorating calfskin booklets with marbled endpapers—show that he was a village doctor who was occasionally engaged as a Visiting Physician at the Whitmore. His notebooks list his patients by a coded system that includes their initials, the location where they were tended to, their symptoms, treatments and outcomes. Some entries reference hospital visits and certificates he's signed: *B* for births, *D* for deaths, and *S* for statements made on behalf of those committed. Jane leafs through a hundred yellowing pages of tight, almost illegible handwriting looking for capital *W*s, for *Whitmore*, which Palmer tended to mark with a flourish.

The seventh reference to the Whitmore says *Whitmore patient* where the deceased's initials usually go, and *INGWD* for the location. Jane checks the page twice. She's been connecting the two places in her mind for so long that it is strange to see proof of it. A short paragraph follows in which Jane can only glean *called upon* and *G.F.* and 'death by—' She tries a few more times to make out Palmer's microscopic cursive, then takes the journal up to Freddy. But after several minutes with a magnifying glass he can only add *carriage to—*.

'May I get a copy of this?'

Freddy examines the delicate binding. 'What pages?'

'Just that one for now. Is the other archivist—'

'Miranda.'

'Is Miranda coming in today?'

'At noon.'

There is nothing else in Dr. Palmer's journals that references both Inglewood and the Whitmore, and the best that Jane can discern, after she comes back from a quick and early lunch in the parking lot with Sam, is that the coded entries take place in or around 1877, the year N disappeared. She wades back into the birth and death records in the Farrington folder, but finds nothing related to 1877 there. George died in Tibet in 1881, and Norvill in Scarborough in 1890. Prudence lasted until 1912, still tucked in at Inglewood House, and died at the ripe old age of ninety from pneumonia.

Jane scans the material she has amassed on the table and picks up the *Biographical Sketch of George Farrington, Esquire*, by S.B. Atkinson, which Freddy had dropped off last: an exaggerated turn-of-the-century account that hadn't seemed credible when Jane glanced through it. She places it on the book support, gently opens its flagging millboard and skims the contents again. It is the kind of biography that was typical of its day— embellished and flattering, with enough anecdotes of a personal nature to cement the authority of the writer. Some of the details she recognizes from the chapter in William's book on George and from his lecture at the Chester: George's birth at Buxton House, his father Hugh's rise through government, the move to Inglewood, Hugh's death in India, George's growing renown as an importer of rare species. She turns to the last few paragraphs of the book—a book that she now knows William must have read—and tries not to picture him in this very same room with George's death unfolding in eloquent detail before him, his thumb on the corner of the nicked page the same way hers is now.

In *The Lost Gardens of England* William describes George's death in what was then a closed-off region of Tibet. William's version is less florid than the Victorian biographer's. Unlike the drama posited by S.B. Atkinson—brimming with details he'd likely never have had access to—William is matter-of-fact: George was climbing along a steep crevasse where he'd heard there was an unusual strain of poppy. His Sherpa, moving up ahead, came into some kind of difficulty and George misstepped in his rush to reach him. He fell some distance down a cleft in the rock. The Sherpa survived, though he was days getting off the mountain, and two weeks later returned with ropes and men from his village to retrieve George's body. George was given a sky burial in the Buddhist tradition, as he'd instructed—his corpse left to the vultures—though his Sherpa honoured his request that a lock of his hair be sent home to Prudence.

When Miranda comes in and settles behind the desk to relieve Freddy, Jane walks over with Lucian Palmer's journals and asks what made her recommend them. She knows an archivist can't reveal information about other patrons, but she asks anyway— was this one of William Eliot's sources? The gentleman who was up from London?

'I really can't say if the gentleman *read* it during the course of his research. Was it of any use?' She smiles, and her arched eyebrows give her away.

'Yes, it was helpful, thanks.'

Jane moves slowly to her table and sets Palmer's journal on top of the stacks of material she still has to read through. Her hands are trembling. Sitting down she tries to sort out what exactly is unsettling her—it's more than the way that William's name recalls the scene she caused at the museum; it's more than just the hazy sense of his presence here with her again as she's going over the Farrington material. Jane smooths her hands over her hair and takes a deep breath. No, it's more like anger; anger at the possibility that even here, doing the only piece of research she's ever chosen wholly for herself, she's following in his tracks again: William up ahead in the woods, William ducking in and out of view, William turning the corner. What if Jane doesn't find N? What if William has already found her?

The old pay phone in the hall takes credit cards. Jane nestles her notebook between her knees and swipes hers before she loses her nerve. When the operator answers, Jane asks for the Natural History Museum number. 'The botanical division if you can find it.'

The phone at the museum rings three times, and when a woman answers Jane's chest hitches with relief. 'Hello, sorry, I'm looking for William Eliot's number.'

'I can transfer you. Who's calling?'

Jane pictures the woman in the blazer at the information desk who'd called upstairs when she was fifteen, a public relations smile on her face. 'Helen, Helen Swindon.'

It takes two tries for the transfer to go through and both times as the phone rings Jane can feel her stomach churn.

'William Eliot.' His voice is brusque.

Jane glances at her watch: it's quarter past twelve so he's either just back from lunch or trying to head out.

'Hello, Dr. Eliot, my name is Helen Swindon. I'm with the Inglewood Trust Restoration Project—' Her voice goes up airily at the end as if she's asking a question. 'I know you've recently written on the Farringtons and I'm wondering if I can ask you a few questions.'

'Where are you calling from?'

Jane doesn't know how to respond, wonders, irrationally, if he recognizes her voice, wants to know where she is so he can ring the police, have her arrested for assault.

'Are you here in London?'

'No, I'm up in Inglewood.'

'Sorry, I'm just finishing a meeting.' His voice is neutral, efficient.

'If it's a bad time—if I'm intruding . . .'

'How pressing is it?'

Before Jane can answer, William moves his mouth away from the phone and she can hear him say, 'See you at three.' Then he comes back, says, 'Sorry, that was the last interruption,' sounding more relaxed, like the William of twenty years ago.

'I've really just one quick question, if you wouldn't mind.'

'Try me.'

Jane presses her forehead against the hallway wall. 'Well, the Trust, as you probably know, is currently researching the Farrington archives, and one area I've become interested in is the relationship between Inglewood House and the old Whitmore.'

'The convalescent hospital?'

'Yes. I think George Farrington visited there and had dealings with the Superintendent.'

'It's Helen?'

'Yes.'

William lets out a breath as if he's trying to remember what he's read. She can see him in his black leather chair exactly—although she's picturing him at thirty, not fifty—a plate-sized fern fossil sitting on the corner of his desk with a framed photo of Lily beside it. 'Are you asking about the monies Farrington left the hospital, or about something else?'

Jane shifts her position and the notepad drops from between her knees. 'There was an incident in 1877 involving three patients who showed up at Farrington's estate. I'm wondering if you know of it.'

'Not offhand, but I can see what I can locate—most of the material is indexed on my computer at home. What's the number there?'

Jane looks up at the hallway ceiling, realizing she's stuck. 'We're in and out of the office mostly during the day. Would it be all right if I call you?'

'Fine.' His voice is muffled and she can picture him tucking the phone under his ear. 'What's your e-mail in case something pops up?'

Jane squeezes her eyes shut. 'I'll send it to you this afternoon.'

'Right.'

'Sorry—William?'

For a few seconds he doesn't say anything, and Jane realizes with a pang that she shouldn't have used his first name, that whoever 'Helen' is, she wouldn't have.

'What is it?' He sounds annoyed.

'Do you know anything about a Whitmore patient who died at Inglewood? It's referenced in Dr. Palmer's notebook.'

'Yes, that was the man caught trespassing. A Gleeson, I think, something like that. You'll have to look yourself. The details are in Farrington's private correspondence.'

Jane parks the Mercedes on the pavement in front of the inn four hours later and sits in the car, resting her head on the steering wheel while Sam thumps his tail expectantly against the back seat. Even though she stopped at the pharmacy on the way back from the records office and downed two paracetamol and a bottle of water, her head is pounding. She's stunned by the conversation with William and by his assertion that Leeson died at Inglewood. All afternoon, sifting through files and journals, she'd tried to sort out what she was feeling about it, about hearing William's voice so privately in her ear and about his casual reference to Leeson and the story she was trying to unravel. This is the first time since leaving London that she feels a desperate need to self-medicate with more than wine.

Upstairs in her room Jane finds an envelope addressed to 'Helen' slipped under her door. She sits on the edge of the bed and opens it. On a scrap of ruled paper Blake has printed: *Meet me at the pub at 8.* And beneath that, underlined: *please.*

We watch Jane fall back on the bed and put her hands over her face, and we debate whether she will meet him. After what happened with the boy we are under strict orders to stay together and that means we have to tag along with Jane. 'No more lollygagging,' the theologian had snapped, as we crossed the parking lot outside the records office this morning. He turned to the girl, who was already lagging behind. 'That means *you*, little miss.'

When Jane gets up and starts her bath, we move to various corners of the room. Some of us drop our heads on our knees in an approximation of exhaustion. We have learned a lot today and are trying not to lose any of it. The idea that William has been thinking about us, that he might know something about the Whitmore, about the world we inhabited, feels as strange to us as it does to Jane, even if his interest in us is peripheral.

Jane slides down into the tub and closes her eyes, trying to still her thinking, and in the calm that follows, the room becomes quiet enough for us to hear Sam's easy, regular breathing and the lapping of the water as it fills the tub.

Leeson, standing in a thicket near the lake, blinked dumbly at Celia Chester. He thought *child* and then *soap*, as if she belonged in one of those sudsy advertisements inked onto the back pages of magazines, a thought immediately succeeded by the knowledge that he should not be by the lake or out of the hospital, that he had no experience with children and could not be trusted. Still, he noted the pleasing pink blooms on the child's cheeks, how her lashes flitted up when she saw him, though the soft expression on her face quickly rearranged itself into wide-eyed terror. Before he could even declare himself she emitted a high-pitched shriek. Leeson, stunned, put a hand out to calm her, but before he could reach her she dashed off into the bush. In the seconds that followed Leeson heard a commotion, heard Celia calling out and others calling back to her. He smoothed the front of his waistcoat, then tapped the flat of his hand to his head. *Think, think, think,* the hand said, as if he were late for an appointment and only had to remember where he ought to be going. He raised his chin in the direction of the voices— one shouted, 'Present yourself!'; another cried, 'Edmund!'—and took a few steps toward them. It was clear: there had been a mistake; the girl had been startled; he was to blame. He would make himself known so that he might clarify the situation.

Within minutes the rustling on the other side of the bushes grew louder.

'Show me where!' a man shouted.

The man's voice was the kind that Leeson imagined men in the military would have: brusque with resolution. Instinctively, he hunkered down beside the hazel thicket the girl had dashed around, debating whether or not he should raise an arm above the foliage or shout 'Here!' Instead, overwhelmed by a vision of men in red tunics brandishing rifles, he slipped back into the welt of the marsh grass and moved through the loosestrife toward the mud bank of the lake. He had heard the group early on when he'd first lost his way, and drawn by the resonant voices of the men, the bubbling-up of a woman's laughter, he'd tried to listen to their conversation through the trees, retreating when he heard a dog bark the way dogs do to announce a visitor who is not threatening. He'd wondered if the laughter was N's, wondered if he'd remember what hers sounded like, if he had ever, in fact, heard it before.

—

After the voices, and after the trampling steps of two men passed the glut of reed in which Leeson was hiding, he got up off his haunches and, stooping to keep his head below the level of the nearby bushes, moved toward the lakeside where the voices had originally come from. He calculated that if he was there and waiting, sitting calmly in the open, the conversation might be between gentlemen divested of the urge to shout.

What he would always remember was the feel of the sun on his face when he came into the clearing and saw George Farrington, how surprised he was by its warmth after hours of walking through the spun nets of the trees. A summer sun in autumn—as if brought out for the tea, arranged by the host to please his guests. Leeson, never one to shy away from a direct gaze, peered up into the orb of it to assess whether it was the same sun as always or if its commission had made it perceptibly different. Its searing whiteness was so unlike the version in the watercolour Farrington had shown him a month before in the small parlour at Inglewood—a circle so theatrically delineated it failed to resemble anything other than a button of yellow.

The shot was a colour too—a bright burst that kissed his arms and chest and passed through the left lobe of his lung. His eyes were still speckled with sun but had cleared enough that he could see the shape of a man, of men, rushing toward him, even as the ground rose up to meet his back. A commotion of voices hovered over and around him while his own throat bubbled up a confused apology. He thought briefly that it was Bedford again looming over his face intimately, but Bedford proved to be George Farrington, his scarred lip giving him away. Things could, Leeson thought, be better. Thorpe would want an explanation; Leeson could imagine him in his dark-panelled office already—jotting details into his book.

'Look at me!' George shouted, his face coming into focus, his hands on Charles, in Charles, pressing down. What to say to such an audience? That he had been wilfully detained these past months? That the stump of meat he received at lunch was often overcooked and that the kitchen staff did this to him intentionally? That sometimes the body is nothing at all and other times it is like the pulse of a frog's throat: ghostly thin and vibrating? *Ribbit*, he wanted to say, or *Pardon me for*—but the botanist was shouting 'What were you thinking?' over his shoulder at a man with long side-whiskers wearing a black hat. Bubble and spit came out of Charles's mouth when he tried to speak of an old favourite hat of his own, a silk topper with a narrow brim that he had recently been missing because it fit him so perfectly. The botanist in a rage above him, while a cushion of some sort was placed under his head.

And then she was there, wiping the mud off his cheeks with the corner of her shawl, her fingers in his short greying hair. 'Shh,' she said, and he could see that she was crying. 'Shh, Charles, I'm here.' He counted the number of times her lips opened and closed, tried to work one word apart from the other. One of the men pulled her away as she said, 'But I know him, please, sir—' Charles's attention wholly on the progression of each word: odd, even, odd, even, odd, even. Then everything thickened and went silent; Charles was both in and above himself, observing his form as indifferently as his doctors had done. N beside him on her knees, her hair duller than he remembered, though otherwise she was exactly the same.

Jane stands up in the bathtub and reaches down to pull the stopper. She watches the water swirl away until Sam pads into the bathroom and *woofs* lightly to gain her attention.

Those of us who were waiting in the main room start towards her, but the theologian interrupts us, says, 'I have a confession.'

'Go on,' Cat chides.

The theologian clears his throat and announces, 'I realized something yesterday at the cottages. I think I know who I was.' He pauses and turns towards us, and we can feel the full force of his attention. 'I believe I was the local headmaster.'

What the theologian had remembered as he stood outside the long row of cottages by the falls was the sensation of being inside one of those rooms, of watching a grey wall of fog thickening outside his front window. He could imagine himself in a wingback chair with weak springs, the sitting room warm in the ambit of the fire. He recalled an evening that was over-quiet because the bird he'd kept had died—a linnet gifted to him by a former pupil. He'd considered, in that hour, in the form of his former body, the nature of fog—how quickly it can roll in and recede. He'd thought he ought to use the idea of fog in the lesson he'd planned for the next day's class—a metaphor to illustrate what God does, and doesn't, allow us to see. He was so deep in rehearsing his analogy that he didn't hear the sound of a horse approaching until it stopped outside on the cobblestone street, and George Farrington appeared suddenly outside his window, as if he'd stepped through a curtain.

When the theologian tells us that he was the local headmaster, we move toward him to ask if he remembers any of us, if he can see us as we once were.

He says, 'I think I remember the boy. He may have been a pupil. It seems to me that his brother might have worked for Farrington in the stables.'

'Do you remember the ball?' Cat asks, because she has been obsessing about that event.

'No.'

'But you remember the picnic,' the one with the soft voice says. 'The day Leeson died?'

The theologian wavers and moves toward the room's only chair. 'I remember the fact of it, gossip, but I was not there.'

'And your name?' John asks.

'Bernard,' the theologian sighs. 'Bernard Hibbitt.'

We have always imagined that knowing who we once were would enact some kind of completion. The theologian's revelation dissuades us of any such conviction.

'*Tweeet?*' Herschel asks.

'I don't know,' John shrugs. 'He's still here.'

'You thought I would Cease,' the theologian says.

'Pretty much.' John replies. 'I think we've all been expecting it. As if we only have to learn a certain amount about ourselves and then—'

'*Whoooo,*' Herschel says.

'Exactly.'

'You're not even *a minister*!' Cat exclaims, and she throws her arms up in the air.

The theologian takes a deep breath. 'So what then? I'm still here. As are you—' He waves his hand at us and says our names almost disdainfully: '*Eliza, Alfred, Herschel*—'

'Samuel,' adds the poet, bowing. 'Samuel Murray.'

'Which means . . . ?' the musician asks.

'That we were wrong,' John surmises.

'About Ceasing?' begs the girl.

'About everything.'

While Jane dries off and sorts through her limited wardrobe, we concentrate on what we know. We ask the theologian to tell us his story in the hope that he will be able to recount the details that matter, find intersections between his life and ours. We decide that we will call his story 'Bernard,' because all of our stories get titles—words that we use as clues to help us remember.

'Dock,' says the girl, before the theologian starts, because it is one of the words we have asked her to be responsible for.

'Yes,' we say. 'Good, the terrier,' and our hearts sink because we realize that she doesn't fully understand that the boy is gone.

'And roses,' she adds, and Cat remembers that in the button shop where she worked it was her job to put fresh flowers in the vases on either side of the doorway. When they started to wither she was allowed to take them home.

'Stout!' the girl calls, and we turn and applaud her lightly, even though the one who loved stout is gone.

'Ha . . . Haydn!' she says, and the musician starts humming.

'Clocks!' she shouts enthusiastically, and we applaud again, and John says, 'Thank you,' because that is his word.

'And . . . Dock!' she repeats, enjoying being the centre of our attention.

'You said that one already.'

'Shoes of grief!'

'*Shewes*,' the poet mutters, and we all laugh; we would ruffle her hair, swing her around if we could.

'Evens!' she says. But we aren't sure where the word comes from, and for a second we waver, the way a parent would if their child came home with a toy that did not belong to them.

'Jane,' she says finally, breaking the spell, and she turns to where Sam is sleeping by the door and says as sweetly and studiously as any five-year-old would: 'Sam! Good dog. Nice dog. Good Sam, stay.'

Before she leaves for the pub—going early because she's hungry now that her headache is gone, and because she's not sure she wants to commit to meeting Blake—Jane sifts back through the Whitmore files and finds her copy of Leeson's casebook. Despite what William told her on the phone, the casebook clearly states that he died at the Whitmore. She pulls the photocopy of Palmer's notebook out of her bag and tries again to decipher his scrawl. She reads his scribble taking into account what William told her, and she thinks she can discern the word *shot*, thinks that the phrase *death by* may end in *exsanguination*.

After she'd hung up with William, Freddy had confirmed that George Farrington's personal letters were in private hands—which means that William, in researching his book, had access to them, and, for this week anyway, Jane does not. It's not that there are pieces *missing*, she thinks now; it's that the lines between scattered bits of information have yet to be firmly drawn.

By the time Jane closes the door of the inn behind her and turns toward the pub she has decided that the undertaker's fees in the Inglewood household account book for 1877 must have been for Leeson, especially given William's use of the word *trespassing*. It would make sense that if he died at Inglewood the fees would be modest, especially when compared to what the Farringtons had paid a year before to bury one of their retired butlers. The removal of a body would have cost less than a burial proper.

If she's right about that, Jane thinks as she opens the door to the pub, then the undertaker's invoice puts Leeson's death at just over a month after N went missing. Which fit with the theory she was developing: that Leeson had come back here to Inglewood, hoping to find N.

24 George Farrington momentarily saw the dead man as he'd appeared that night not so long ago in the parlour at Inglewood: overly mannered, twitchy, halting in conversation. The shot had made an impossible red flower out of the white shirt he was wearing and parts of the body that should not be seen were gawping out of his wound.

'I've met this man before,' George said over his shoulder to Norvill. 'He's a patient at the convalescent hospital.'

The group assembled around the body was transfixed, the

situation so unreal that George could hardly believe it himself. One minute he'd been in the boat and the next the Chester girl was screaming and everyone on shore was racing around trying to find her. Celia's chest was still heaving, although she was now firmly in her mother's grip, Charlotte pressing the child's shoulders against her abdomen as if she were trying to will her back into the womb. Edmund was staring wide-eyed at his wife. The boys, meanwhile, were less shocked than curious—oblivious, George thought, to their mother's and sister's roles in this.

The housemaid was still on her knees beside the dead man, bloodstains on her hands and white cuffs. She was glaring up at Norvill, her face flushed in a way that George suddenly remembered having seen before.

'Edmund, would you please escort Miss Hayling to the lake to wash her hands? And might I suggest that the ladies be taken back to the house with the children?' George glanced at Sutton, who was pacing nervously, and looked around for Rai. Norvill would be useless—he had never shot a man in his life, had little experience of death at all. 'Mother, would you please fetch me a blanket?' George kept his voice even, but inside he was seething—such a waste, such stupidity, and over, in a tangential way, a woman. Norvill responding too dramatically to Charlotte's frenzy and stupidly picking up a shotgun.

Edmund made a cup with his palms and dipped his hands into the lake. The housemaid was beside him, water lapping at her knees. He washed her hands clean and then wiped at her stained cuffs with a handkerchief, wanting the bloodstain erased, all traces of what had happened gone. Behind him he heard the boys whispering and he turned toward them. 'Tom, Ned, come here.' He smiled weakly at the housemaid, trying to remember her name. She'd been very good with the children, though he wasn't quite clear as to why Celia had been allowed off on her own and why this girl hadn't stayed with her. He vaguely recalled some debate about the housemaid's shoes.

'Is that better?' he asked. The cuffs were still tinged pink.

'Yes, Mr. Chester, thank you.'

They stood up and the boys moved dutifully toward their father, a trace of excitement still palpable between them, and a hint of a smile on Thomas's face.

'Go and wait by the boat,' Edmund said, more sternly than he'd intended.

The boys looked over at the grey blanket covering the body, then turned to where the boat was sitting farther along the shore. They did not move until Edmund stood and took a step in their direction.

As he offered the maid his hand, Edmund noticed a fleck of blood on his own cuff. 'Why don't you go and wait with the boys? Mind them.'

The maid nodded but her lip twitched.

'What is it?'

She shook her head.

'It's all right, speak your mind.'

'It's just that he wasn't a bad man, sir, he wasn't going to cause any harm.'

'You said you knew him?'

'I did, sir.'

'In what capacity?'
'He was a friend.'

George stood a few feet away from the body, mulling over how the situation was going to play out. There was no question of fault: the man had been trespassing on private grounds and he was, or had been—though George hated to take advantage of the term—committable. It wasn't a question of reporting the matter to the authorities, but of how to handle it. Without care, word of the incident would spread and Norvill would be marked by the gossip, and so, too, would he and the rest of the party, the Chesters and Suttons included. Already it must have struck Edmund as odd that Norvill would charge forth with such authority to protect a child who wasn't his, strange that Charlotte's panic would cause him to act so quickly and aggressively.

'What must we do, George?' his mother asked, placing one hand under her son's arm. 'The poor fellow.'

'Do you remember him?'

'Of course, I do.'

'What was he doing here,' Sutton asked, 'skulking about like that?'

'Did he say anything?' Charlotte stepped forward shakily.

George looked to the boat where the housemaid and children were waiting. The maid had rushed to the man before anyone else had, would know if he'd spoken.

'His death was instantaneous,' George said, meeting Sutton's eye. 'Has anyone seen Rai?'

'I think he's scouting the area,' Norvill said, 'looking for others.'

'Rai!' George called.

The Hindu emerged from the bushes just as Leeson had done, the dog behind him.

'I need you to summon Wilson. Tell him only there's been an accident, say nothing else. Edmund will go with you to see the ladies and children safely back to the house.'

Rai bowed almost imperceptibly and turned to go.

Edmund recovered his hat from a nearby boulder. As he did so, he glanced at the blanket that was covering all but the dead man's tufted hair and dress shoes. When he'd first reached him, the man's mouth was open and hanging to one side as if he'd been stricken with palsy, when only a minute before, in the instant when he'd emerged from the woods, he had seemed jubilant, as if arriving late for the picnic and delighted at the day. He'd alarmed no one but Norvill. The shotguns Rai had lined up for the afternoon shoot were leaning against the rocks near where Norvill was sitting, ready enough to hand that Norvill had picked one up after Celia's first scream. Not a word had passed between Norvill and the man, Edmund reflected, none of the pomp that usually preceded engagement: no 'Halt,' no 'Declare yourself.' Still, the man's proximity to the women, his muddied appearance and wild look were enough to justify the assault. Any investigation would support the claim of self-defence and, for George's sake, the authorities would be careful to avoid incriminating language in their report. In the end George would be unmarked, but Norvill and, Edmund supposed, Charlotte would be much affected, whether word of what happened went beyond those assembled or not.

We believe that the shooting did not make the papers. What had happened took on the form of village gossip—stories that said more about the person telling them than they did about the Farringtons or the Chesters. In later years the events of that day were let slip here and there as a kind of confession—a line in a letter or a thought in a diary—declarations that now make sense to us, and to Jane, although it was hard to see them for what they were, to sense the reverberations of the day when the matter at its centre—Leeson himself—was absent from the account.

'The day of the exploring party was sunny,' the one with the soft voice says, as she watches Jane enter the pub. 'The photographer waited on the far side of the lake. He had on a greatcoat and when he stepped out of the boat with his tripod and boxes everyone applauded.'

'They were probably applauding the sun,' the poet said drily, 'because they'd forgotten what it looked like.'

'I think I was let go shortly after the picnic,' the theologian says, though he's roused from his daydream when a group of hikers straggle out of the pub door, slipping back into their jackets and donning their caps as they pass through us.

'Let go from what?' the idiot asks.

'From my post. Farrington hired me. It lasted . . .' He squinted up at the globe light that hung outside the pub and in his concentration we could see some semblance of a man with cropped grey hair, a trimmed beard and a prominent nose. 'It might have lasted a year.'

George Farrington would later admit that when Bernard Hibbitt presented himself at Inglewood estate with three trunks and a bamboo aviary containing, of all things, a *linnet*, he was taken aback. Not only was Hibbitt older than George had expected by almost a decade—a man in his fifties, not forties as he'd claimed—but he appeared incapable of uncurling his lip, as if everything he set his eyes on left him with a sense of distaste.

George could only blame himself. He had arranged Mr. Hibbitt's hiring solely through letters. On paper the man had a superior education, and the reference he had provided from his last post was excellent. More importantly, Hibbitt had written that he was willing to step in for the former village tutor immediately. Still, by the time Hibbitt had entered the parlour, George knew that if the agreement had not been hastily arranged because of his own impatience, it was likely that Hibbitt wouldn't have been hired. And if there had been other applicants, Hibbitt wouldn't have lasted the day.

Standing beside the sofa as stiffly as the stuffed pheasant under the nearby glass, Bernard Hibbitt listened while George Farrington outlined the terms of his employment. He inquired after the pupils and Farrington elaborated on the number and disposition of the boys who would be under his tutelage. Hibbitt conveyed his enthusiasm as best he could, restating his belief in the duty of the educator to ensure opportunities for advancement to all children, regardless of the conditions from which they'd risen.

Things did not go well from there. Within a week of that conversation a number of the parents in the village had complained about how sternly religious they found Hibbitt to be, citing his threats of damnation as a means of enforcing studiousness. It wasn't that a handful of them didn't employ similar tactics; it was Hibbitt's *enthusiasm* they objected to: how he wed his threats to corporal punishment. Which is why, a mere ten days after they'd first been introduced, Hibbitt found himself standing in Farrington's small parlour once again, casting his eyes nervously over the watercolour landscapes gracing the walls, the clocks *tick-tock*ing unevenly while he waited to see if he was going to be sent out.

Hibbitt prided himself on engaging with other men, especially those of ways and means, without duplicity, so when Farrington, having offered tea that Hibbitt refused due to a welling discomfort in his stomach, asked if he meant the boys harm, he replied stiffly from the sofa, 'Only when they deserve it.'

Farrington paused to consider his tutor's logic, and Hibbitt became conscious of the way he was sitting, each bone in his torso stacked in perfect alignment, his hands resting flatly on his knees.

'Did your own father strike you when you were a child?' Farrington asked at last.

'He did.'

'Well'—Farrington sighed, as if the difference ought to indicate his stand and instruction on the matter—'mine did not.'

The walk Farrington proposed out over the lawn and through the gardens was uncomfortable for Hibbitt. Although his anxiety was diminished, he was still conflicted as to what exactly had been decided, from which families the complaints had come, and how he was expected to maintain order without corporal means.

In the end he did all but ask if he could still *strike them a little*. The walk was made even more awkward by the fact that Hibbitt preferred to move with purpose whereas Farrington strolled like a woman. They were also under surveillance: the stable hand Dawes, who was the older brother of one of Hibbitt's more amiable pupils, watched them unabashedly as he filed the hooves of a carriage horse. Mrs. Farrington was similarly caught glaring down at the men from one of the upstairs rooms, turning away when Hibbitt looked up from his inspection of the alpine plots. He attempted a quick smile but she had released the curtain before it reached his lips.

Hibbitt checked, as he always did in these situations, that his coat and felt bowler were in order. It was, after all, vital that he take great pains not only in his presentation but also in his manner if he was to conceal his attraction to other men. He needed to appear innocuous, and believing himself to be so, he regarded those who watched him overlong as subjects requiring greater dissimulation on his part.

On their last turn at the end of the property Farrington gestured to the trellis he was putting in by the folly, and Hibbitt thought that he detected a similar quality in his companion, a looseness of the body and lightened manner that had become more evident the farther removed he was from his house—an animation that, although directed toward the progress of the magnolias and *Daphnes*, was most pleasant to behold.

As he opened the cottage door for Farrington two weeks later, the tutor tried to parse what he'd done wrong. The boys had been behaving better since he'd softened his approach, and all but one were memorizing their verses and handing their lessons in on time.

Farrington took his hat off and brushed his coat sleeves as if the fog had affixed itself there. He closed the door behind him and said, 'Bernard,' as if they were friends.

Still perplexed by what kind of business might necessitate a visit so late in the evening, Hibbitt suddenly realized that he had no wine or sherry to offer. He said stupidly, 'Mr. Farrington, I hope I haven't failed you in some way, to bring you out at this hour—' Though even as he said the words, he started to suspect by the man's expression that it was the other thing.

'No, Hibbitt, you have not.'

They were still standing, and Hibbitt was thinking he ought to manoeuvre the chairs nearer to the flagging fire when Farrington stepped in front of him. In all of his previous experience, it had never happened like this. Still, Hibbitt knew in an instant that he would be required to declare himself first, and that if he did not, nothing would happen. So slowly, and without stepping back, he went down on his knees, and George Farrington removed his coat.

Rules were quickly established. Hibbitt was not allowed to visit Inglewood House or the grounds and could only approach the property when messaged because George suspected his demeanour might give the recent nature of their acquaintance away. Norvill Farrington was a regular visitor and George knew his brother would relish having a suspicion to wield against him. The beauty of the message system was its simplicity: if one of the servants was cleaning George's best saddle on the wood frame by the stable this meant *wait inside the mouth of the first cave at the end of the trail.* A book sent to the school with a blue book-mark meant that Hibbitt would be expected in the pumphouse by the lake after supper. In each case he was to drop a handker-chief on the path if he was seen. Once, however, in daylight, the two men fell to walking the trail from the village within visual proximity of each other and George dared, unexpectedly, to turn up the trail toward the grotto, lifting a gloved hand to indicate that he should be followed. It was an absurdly easy business for them to meet in those spring months, and even in the rainy stretch of the summer, although once Hibbitt felt certain he'd been seen in the woods as he cut back from the caves. He was peeling a fig George had brought him, and looking up the trail from under the dome of his umbrella he thought he caught a glimpse of one of Prudence's maids.

What Hibbitt thought then, in his arrogance, was that the world was ordered in a way that served him: that the stable boy, or the footman, or the house girl who sometimes came to the schoolroom with a wrapped book he'd 'requested loan of' from George's library, were somehow his emissaries as well as Farrington's. It gave him a slow pleasure to have them stand on the threshold of the cottage or in the door jamb at the school and wait while he unwrapped his offerings and composed a receipt of thanks. And so, that autumn, when the books stopped coming and the saddle stopped receiving its extra care, he pushed the idea of what was really lost out of his head and tried to convince himself that he missed being waited on as much as he missed the object and acts that occurred beyond the purview of the waiting servant's patient stare.

Hibbitt was never sure if it was George or Prudence who suddenly called off the affair. What little he eventually gleaned came from the gossip of the house's low-ranking servants—gossip that habitually spread to the village and, if lascivious, to the older boys under his care. All he knew at the time was that shortly after one of his rendezvous with George in the cave, Norvill had arrived for a picnic, along with a number of other guests from London. George, thrusting himself angrily into Hibbitt on that last occasion, had seemed almost enraged, complaining afterwards about the stress of the arrangements, the suffocating details, the idea that he had to whore himself out for funding.

Talk of Norvill Farrington sleeping with a married woman had cropped up in the butcher shop the day after the picnic. According to a stable hand known to one of the boys under Hibbitt's care, a fearful row at the house had occurred, followed quickly by a set of early departures.

25 The waitress from last night, Katie, her hair in a high ponytail, smirks at Jane when she walks into the pub, so Jane sits in one of the booths in the dining area and a different girl in a short black skirt comes over to take her order.

We are starting to feel like locals here. It doesn't take much for us; we seize on the familiar, crave routine. We recognize the workbooted men at the bar, the rough cluster of boys Blake's age guzzling pints at the high table and the smell from the deep fryer that wafts to us when the kitchen door swings open.

Those of us who can read stand behind Jane and survey the specials on the chalkboard, play at making informed decisions; try words like *fennel* and *parsnip* in our mouths to see if a taste or texture appears.

Blake arrives well before eight, unaware that Jane has been here almost an hour. He slides into the booth, offers Jane his hand palm-up on the table, and says, 'I don't even know your last name. You could fuck off back to London and I'd never be able to find you again.'

Jane narrows her eyes. 'I don't know yours either.'

He laughs, retracts his hand. 'I think I've got it worked out that you wouldn't exactly be racing around the country trying to find me.' His eyes settle on the empty bowl of soup and the last scraps of lettuce on the plate she's pushed toward the wall. 'Heading out?'

'No.'

'Okay, back in a minute.' He stands up. As he passes her side of the booth he leans in and kisses her on the mouth.

Blake brings Jane a glass of wine and then clears her plate, taking it over to the barman and coming back with his pint. He's showing off, and she lets him. A petty part of her is thinking that he wouldn't know what fork to use in a good restaurant, that he probably doesn't own a suit, that she ought to be tolerant and let him have his little display. But then, when he's sitting across from her, when he takes her hand and rubs his thumb back and forth over her skin, she's buoyed despite herself; even though he's only nineteen, he's been sweet and tender and honest with her.

'So is now a good time to ask if you have a girlfriend?'

He raises his eyebrows. 'You applying?'

'What about the waitress over there? Or that girl from two nights ago, in the silver vest top?'

He smiles and lifts his shoulders.

'How many women have you slept with?' As soon as it comes out of her mouth she feels ridiculous.

'Seriously, *that's* where you're taking this?'

Jane imitates his noncommittal shrug.

Blake starts bouncing his knee under the table like a nervous kid. 'Five. Listen, Helen, it's not a thing, so stop thinking it is.'

'What?'

'Our ages.'

'I'm thirty-four.'

'And? Who gives a fuck? This doesn't have to be some huge all-or-nothing event.' He's annoyed, and for a second she thinks that he's getting up to leave but instead he comes around and plops himself down onto the bench beside her. 'What do you want me to say here? I would like to have sex with you again, but I'd also be happy sitting here with you and talking all night.'

'Right, well, I'm not exactly sure how to take that.'

He leans in and kisses her and then dunks his thumb into his pint and runs it lightly under her right eye and then under her left.

'What are you doing?!'

'War paint.'

Jane laughs. 'This is a war?'

'No. This is something else.'

By ten o'clock the waitress working the other end of the pub, and every other girl within five years of Blake's age, has walked past the table to have a look at Jane. It becomes a running joke; every time someone walks to the back of the pub where their booth is, Blake automatically says, 'Sorry about that.' It occurs to Jane more than once that she should tell him her real name, admit something more truthful about herself, but the banter is easy— 'If you could only listen to one piece of music for the rest of your life . . .' and 'Where would you like to travel to?'—and more honest than 'So, how long will you be in Inglewood?'

A tinny version of 'Anarchy in the U.K.' blares in Blake's coat pocket. He roots around for his mobile, says *hullo* and then excuses himself to speak to the caller. Jane watches him exit the pub; she assumes he's talking to his maybe-current girlfriend or a mate he's told about the thirty-four-year-old from London he's banging. While she waits for him to come back she slides her hand over the wood grain of the table, swirls her finger over the pool of condensation left by his last pint.

When she was fifteen, she, William and Lily had sat in the booth opposite the one where she is now. At the end of the lunch William had gone to pay but realized he'd forgotten his wallet in the glovebox. He explained the situation to the barman, asked if he could run up the road to get it, said that the girls would stay. The barman called them 'collateral' and laughed. Jane had forgotten that.

If *that* Jane was still here, if she still existed in some way—a self-conscious fifteen-year-old in hoop earrings and a new blue dress who wants, more than anything, to be seen—what would she make of Jane now? Would she be happy that grown-up Jane is looking over at her, at her nervousness and exaggerated pro-nouncements, at the spot of gravy Lily had splashed onto Jane's lap, at the shoes that gave her a blister within an hour of putting them on?

We watch Jane watching herself, watching the girl she was before we met her. Her finger circling the mark made by Blake's pint in this world, Lily spinning a key on a ribbon in the other.

Sitting in the pub and waiting for Blake to return it occurs to Jane that accountability is a complicated thing: trying to ferret out what you owe yourself and what you owe others.

Lewis made an offhand comment about this once to Jane at a Friday-night dinner at his house. He had tested the chicken curry he'd made to see if it was too spicy for the girls and was dumping in a can of coconut milk to compensate for the heat. He turned to Jane. 'You're lucky, you know, that you don't have anyone to be responsible for.' He saw the expression on her face and apologized, said that he was talking about the curry, that he liked it hot but the girls couldn't handle the chilies—adding that they hadn't had spicy curry in five years.

Both Lewis and Claire felt the burden of accountability in spades. Jane suspects Claire liked it that way. She and Lewis were the types who'd get everyone out of a burning building before the rafters fell, who'd go back for the stragglers. Even Claire's suicide was a way of refusing to push the inconvenience of her cancer onto anyone else. The fact that hanging herself was the wrong decision for Jane and Lewis doesn't negate the set of considerations that went into the decision. Jane knows that she is more like Henri. She and her father interpret: choose to be accountable when it works for them, when the wind is blowing a certain way or holidays line up or some poor girl from a

Victorian asylum goes missing and makes a hole in a page just big enough for all of Lily to fit into.

Sitting in the pub, Jane tries to line up her story the way we try to line up ours. There was a girl called N. There was a girl called Lily. One day Jane stood in a beautiful tract of woods and a five-year-old ran along a trail ahead of her and Jane became transfixed with the way the sun flickered over the leaves at her feet, a box of light framed by the trees. And so she stopped and played at stepping into it. Because of that moment, she has put a bar of light into every story she has ever read or told. That is not accountability. It's a way of trying to place one's self in the world; it's *conjecture*. Which is a way of saying, *It's a lie.*

Blake comes back to the booth and apologizes. He admits sheepishly that he was supposed to babysit his younger sister, but he's bailed, and has been trying to reach his brother to fill in. He looks embarrassed, and when he sits beside Jane again he slides his hand under the table, pushes the hem of her skirt above her knee, reasserts himself.

'My name isn't Helen.'

Blake shakes his head as if he has water in his ears. 'That's'— and he searches for the right word—'unexpected.' After a minute he says, 'Are you a murderer?'

Jane laughs, but it's not a normal laugh, it's the kind that could snag and become something else. No one has asked her that before and the question is both horrible and a release.

Blake starts to say her name and the *H* comes out before he stops, says, 'I don't exactly know what to do here.'

Jane can sense him backing away, can feel the space he's made on the bench between them.

'It's Jane.'

'Jane?'

'Yes, I promise.'

'And you're married? And some posh bastard is on his way up here right now to have a go at me?'

'I'm not married.'

Blake rubs his neck. Before he can say anything, the *ping* of a text goes off on his mobile, and maybe buying time to think, he checks it and then puts it back in his pocket.

It occurs to Jane that even though she's glad she has told Blake her secret, it's probably too much for him. She's twisted their narrative around and made it too strange, and to her surprise she feels immensely sad about that, not because she wanted to keep him but because he seems like a good person and because whatever it was that passed between them, it at least felt real.

'Do you want to talk about this now?' he asks.

Jane smiles at him. 'Not necessarily.'

The mobile *pings* again and Blake checks it, exhales. 'To be clear: I'll be twenty in three weeks, and even though I am obviously a *man*, I have to get home to babysit because my parents were supposed to be at their friends' place an hour ago.' He stands up and for a second Jane is unsure what, exactly, he intends to do. 'Come on.' He reaches his hand out. 'We'll set Gemma up in front of the telly and go hang out in my bedroom.'

—

Blake's sister Gemma is a pudgy twelve-year-old who squints up from under her fringe when she's introduced to Jane before promptly turning back to the telly. Blake's parents hover in their cluttered sitting room after Blake introduces Jane, and Martin narrows his eyes and mumbles, 'We met yesterday.' He scratches Sam's chest while Blake's mom drapes a brown paisley scarf over her shoulders and shoots her husband a look that says, *Why didn't you mention anything to me?*

Jane is close to saying, *I can see this is a bit awkward*, when Blake gestures to the door. 'Right, have a good time, me and *Jane* will just be doing "homework" up in my room.'

His mom swats him on the arm with her handbag and then turns to Jane, raising her eyes to the ceiling and shaking her head in a *kids today* kind of way before she realizes the accidental implication.

At ten Gemma clomps up the stairs to bed, and Jane and Blake settle on the sofa with a bowl of microwave popcorn. Blake flips through a binder of burnt DVDs and puts on a Swedish film that he says is his favourite.

'Are you trying to impress me?'

'Absolutely.'

To Jane's surprise it turns out that Blake knows the film so well he can talk about the director's other work and point out the gaffe in the background of the dinner party scene where a gauzy white curtain that has been mostly closed is suddenly gaping open. While Jane watches the film he occasionally nuzzles her neck or runs a hand over her thigh, and when she fends him off he gives up and drops his head onto her lap, says, 'I can't stop thinking of all the things I want to do to you.'

Jane shakes her head. 'That's not happening in your parents' house.'

'Fine. We have a garden, I know you like the outdoors.' He stands up. 'Let's go.'

Jane doesn't get up, so he plunks himself back down and leans into her, rubs the stubble on the side of his face lightly against her temple. 'You like me more than you know.'

When Blake's parents come back they are tipsy and more animated than when they left. They've obviously had a conversation about the woman sitting in their house with their son, and have arrived at a wait-and-see conclusion. Jane is rinsing teacups and Blake is sitting on the counter tossing the last of the popcorn into his mouth when Blake's father asks Jane if this is her first time in Inglewood.

'No, I've been here once before.'

'When?' Paula's voice is too chirpy, as if she's trying to gauge exactly how long Jane has known her son.

'I was fifteen.' Jane puts the garden-vegetables-themed dish-towel she's been using to dry the cups down on the counter and says gently, 'Which was in the early 1990s, because I am currently *thirty-four*.'

Martin clears his throat to cover the awkward silence that follows, his arms spanning the two counters in the kitchen as if he needs to prop himself up. 'Were you on holiday?'

Jane smiles thinly and thinks about how to reply to that, about the implications of the word *holiday* and how the warm familial image it conjures—of her and William and Lily pootling through the woods together—doesn't fit at all with what transpired in the end. 'No.'

'Family is it?'

Paula swats Martin's arm with the back of her hand. 'Oh, stop. Leave her alone. And you,' she points at Blake, 'off the bloody counter.'

'Well, it was sort of a holiday,' Jane says, and then she corrects herself, 'I mean, it was meant to be a kind of day out.' She looks at Blake who has hopped down from the counter and who is now leaning against it next to his parents; takes in the triangle they make—Martin a fair bit taller than Blake and Paula—a tidy arrangement of a dark-haired family with similar features, the easygoing and happy sort you'd see in the window of a village photo studio.

'Remember the girl who went missing on the Farrington trail? Lily Eliot? 1991. She was five? Her father was a botanist?' Jane can see from Martin and Paula's expressions that they do remember, but that Blake, obviously, doesn't know what she's talking about. He would have been—what—a newborn, or maybe a one-year-old? Martin and Paula would remember because they were new parents with a baby at home and it would have been the worst thing imaginable—the idea that a child could simply disappear. 'Anyway,' Jane says and takes a deep breath, 'I was the minder who was with her when she got lost. That was the last time I was here.'

What follows is easier than any of us expects. A pot of tea is put on and a plate of biscuits is set out and the four of them move to the round wooden kitchen table. Martin and Paula describe the search-and-rescue operations—the constables coming in from nearby districts, the teams of tracking dogs, how the two of them took turns going with the volunteer groups out into the woods. Through these simple descriptions, Jane glimpses something she's never been permitted to see before.

'We were shown a photograph of Lily and told what she was wearing,' Paula says, 'and there was a key on a ribbon we were told to look for. I swear I lived in terror of finding it.'

Blake doesn't say anything; he listens to his parents and watches Jane as if he's trying to gauge whether she's okay.

'They never caught him,' Paula says, and when she realizes that Jane doesn't know what she's talking about, she looks at her lap, explains, 'Everyone thought it was Michael Wilson. He and his wife owned the old hardware shop at the top of the village. But there was nothing to prove it and—' Paula stops and wraps her hands around her teacup.

'And they never found her body,' Jane says.

For a second no one says anything, and all of us in the room, all of us gathered around the four people at the table, feel as if a veil has been lifted. We have been so selfish in our own pursuits, have refused to see any truth that did not enrich our own.

We turn to find the girl but she is upstairs on Gemma's bed where we left her—nestled amongst a row of stuffed bears dressed in T-shirts and bow ties and tutus—watching as Gemma makes her way through a video game of moats and towers in which a princess in a beautiful dress waits to be rescued.

As Blake walks Jane to the inn, he doesn't say much. Jane is trying to remember what businesses are at the top of the street, trying to place where the hardware shop would have been before the Wilsons sold the property and moved out of the village. 'You know how it was back then,' Paula had replied, when Jane asked if Michael Wilson was ever brought in for questioning. 'People gossiped. If you were even a little bit different or kept to yourself. The constables went round the shop a few times but that was it. Still, his business plummeted because of it, so he and the Mrs. eventually left.'

When Jane was first in therapy Clive assured her that what he called *the information exchange* would work both ways: if she remembered a pertinent detail about the day Lily went missing he would relay it to the police, and if anything was discovered on their end they would relay it, through Clive and her grandparents, to her. When the weeks and months went by without anyone imparting the kinds of details Blake's parents had just provided her with, Jane stopped believing that this arrangement was true. Instead she started to believe that they were waiting for *her* to remember something first, that if she did they'd reward her with information of their own, a kind of exchange or barter. So for months Jane tried harder to see whatever it was that she hadn't seen that day: a man passing them on the footpath, or a flash of a jacket in the trees, Lily turning repeatedly in a specific direction. In the end she convinced herself that she wasn't being told anything because she hadn't earned it, because she didn't deserve the truth.

Despite their kindness, Blake's parents—the kind who know, but don't want to know, what their almost-twenty-year-old son is up to—had stood stiffly when he said it was late and that he was going to walk Jane back. Jane sensed that it isn't because they don't like her or feel some degree of sympathy for what she's been through, but because, despite all that, they still disapprove. When Jane and Blake reach the pool of light under the lamp of the inn Jane pulls out her key and Blake says, 'My cousin Max died last summer. That's why I'm not at uni.' He scuffs the toe of his boot. 'We'd taken ketamine with some girls at a rave and he was fucked up and stepped onto the road without looking. I'm not saying they do, but I feel like my parents blame me.'

Jane touches the thatch of hair that's fallen over his eye and moves it gently to the side. 'I'm sorry.'

'When do you have to go back to London?' Blake stuffs his hands into his jacket pockets and looks across the road, and Jane realizes that even though she's told him the truth about her name, about Lily, there's still the whole lie about her work at Inglewood between them.

'Probably in a day or two.'

He nods and turns his attention to the moth twitching around the globe light and then he takes a few steps toward the picnic table and kicks its struts with his boot. On his second kick he shouts, 'Fuck!' so loud Jane thinks it will wake the elderly couple whose window is on the front of the inn just below hers.

Without meaning to, Jane starts counting like she did after that last fight with Ben: *one thousand one, one thousand two, one thousand three.*

'Fuck. Sorry.' Blake comes close and butts his head lightly against her shoulder. 'Don't be angry.'

Because she isn't angry, and because she wants to, Jane takes Blake's hand and leads him upstairs to her room. Once there, she pulls his sweater up and over his head and pushes him gently down on the bed. She knows she shouldn't keep him, knows that there are other ways to find or feel tenderness and she knows, too, that Paula is probably sitting in the rust-coloured wingback near the door, waiting, like any parent would, for her child to come home.

26 Out of the kind of idleness common to her weekday afternoons, Charlotte Chester once began what she referred to in her diary as a 'catalogue of touch.' Jane read about it the summer she started compiling the Chester archives. It began, Charlotte had written, with a paper cut.

Charlotte and Celia were in the front parlour of the new house beside the museum making a collage for Edmund. Fumbling with the shears, Celia asked her mother to help her cut out the duck she'd found illustrated in a periodical. She wanted to affix a top hat to it on the paper they were using for pasting. Distractedly flopping the publication onto her lap, Charlotte had grazed the side of her finger. She made a small sound, inspected the incision and put the affected knuckle in her mouth. Celia, six at the time, promptly plopped down off her chair, approached her mother and, reaching for the wound, kissed it. The hours that day had passed dully, but suddenly, in that instant, Charlotte felt keenly aware, could parse two separate sensations: the sting of her finger and the wet press of her daughter's lips. It had been a long time since she'd been so acutely in her body. Edmund had been absent, travelling back and forth to the mill or up late at night tending to urgent matters with the museum—yesterday a theft, last week the delayed shipping of an expected exhibit of fossils. Hers had become a life of the mind: books as lived experience, ideas for charitable projects she did not begin, a tedium that wore a circle around her children, whose play she supervised without passion.

'Does it still hurt?' Celia stood at Charlotte's knee, a look of uncertainty clouding her face.

'No, darling, it just tickles.'

That night, the sheets from her husband's factory settled coolly in the place where Edmund ought to have been, Charlotte decided to consume herself for one whole day with the sense of touch. She would make it an experiment, would do as she had seen the members of Edmund's societies do: form through careful and sustained observation a hypothesis about the various modes and expressions of her subject. The effort would require a notebook, which she could easily steal from Edmund's study, and the kind of attenuation she knew she could not steal, the kind she had started to lack.

In the end, Charlotte wrote, the catalogue was a disappointment. She'd noted the unexpected warmth of the keys taken
from the maid, the cool brass of the library doorknob, the vis-
cous quality of the honey clumped by Thomas into his younger
brother's hair after a row at lunch. There was the constant swish
of her skirts against her stockings, the side of her hand inching
across a letter to her mother, the repeated smoothing of the raw
silk of her dress. And then, almost miraculously, the bell of a
purple foxglove lifted from where it had fallen to the carpet, her
finger slipping gently into the satin of its cup.

A year later, in Scarborough, when she joined Norvill for two
weeks on the pretense of visiting a distant cousin, she repeated
this practice with him. They would wake in his bed and she
would set to memory the rough pads of his fingers stroking her
cheek, his lips nibbling her chin, even the way the soft of her
stomach nestled against the taut plane of his. His house was
modest, perched halfway up a cliff that banistered the sea, let
to him by an acquaintance of George's who owned a fleet of
fishing vessels. On the days when Norvill had to slip into the
city to advise on the survey work he was overseeing, Charlotte
occupied herself with the brace of the coastal wind, the grit
of the sand she'd bring back in her skirts from the beach, the
slick ribbon of seaweed she once touched lightly to her tongue.
It was easy, from that distance, to see that her children were
cloying. To love them less for how they leaned into her, tugged
at her even from across the country. It was not the same with
Edmund, whom, on those aimless afternoons window-shop-
ping along winding village streets, she loved more. When the

clerk in the jewellery store on M– Street showed her an impossibly small ammonite fossil that had been set into a ring, she realized with a pang that it was Edmund she would like to receive it from, not Norvill.

It was not that Edmund had disappointed her or that his touch was not pleasurable. She knew any number of women in her circle who did not have things as well as she. Charlotte could see the strain in their faces, the flinch at the card table or on stairwells when their husbands leaned close or moved to guide them by the arm. Once, at an exhibition in London, Edmund dared to take Charlotte into the gallery where the painted nudes had been hung, even though none of the other women had gone. She admired him in his ease, playing subtly at being aroused, and wondered why exactly she felt so removed from him.

Afterwards, in the carriage, when he ran his hand over her bodice, pulled at the ribbon streaming down from her collar, she realized it was the children who were the cause— that giving birth to them had necessitated a transfer of love, and her body had become affiliated in new directions. In their house she was constantly pulled at, once slapped by Thomas when she refused him a sweet, exhausted by the demands and piddling violences, and even by the rare and precious hours of cradling that Celia still sometimes permitted. Norvill, as much as she had come to love him, represented an escape from such needling, although he was starting to create problems of his own. The two of them had become less careful than they were in the beginning; and once, even after she had asked him to remove himself, he had stayed inside, pushing deeper until he was finished.

On Charlotte's last day in the house on the cliff, Norvill asked her to come and live with him. He went down on his knees in the bedroom, his shirt half on; there was a sickle-shaped mark on his chest from where she'd accidentally scratched him.

'I couldn't possibly.' She continued packing.

'Leave Edmund.'

'Again,' she said, 'you're being ridiculous.'

He sat down on the bed with his back to her. In the quiet they could hear the housekeeper gathering cutlery in the next room— the Inglewood maid George had sent to take care of Norvill. There was a pocket of silence and Charlotte almost spoke, but waited until the clatter of the breakfast things being loaded onto a tray in the dining nook resumed.

'I do think of it,' she said.

'What?' He turned around. He was still handsome—though wind-burnt from the survey work. The strain of the shooting, of having to leave Inglewood, had aged him.

Charlotte set the dress she was struggling to fold onto the bed and felt the billows of silk exhaust themselves in her hands. 'I have, these past weeks, in your occasional absence, *imagined*— she said the last word sternly so that he would not mistake it for sentiment—'a possible life with you. And dared'—again a stern emphasis—'*once*, to picture us there, on the beach with some child of our own, living out our days . . .' She searched for the word and then settled on '. . . simply.'

Norvill grabbed her hand. 'And why not?'

'Because I love Edmund, too.'

Jane has read Charlotte's diaries and Edmund's letters, and in those months when she assembled the material for the Chester family display we read and reread them too. And we saw how time works—how it pulls some stones off the beach and casts others onto the sand—how Edmund became the kind of subject he'd once celebrated. A plaque was made in his name and hung beside the Chester family cabinet in the slant-roofed room that had been both storage and a servant's quarters in the Chester's first residence. We think of him and of the Chesters often—even here, so close to the Whitmore and Inglewood House—because the home they made became ours, and because time in the museum moved in a different way than it did outside, and we liked that. Whereas the tourists and school children, the locals on weekend excursions experienced the Chester over the course of two or three hours, curious but swept up by the demands of their everyday lives, we *lived* there, had the patience to study the details. The museum was a place where we'd come to feel at home, where the clocks had stopped ticking, where time had settled into its rusted hinge.

We are certain that Edmund knew about Norvill and Charlotte. The summer she went to Scarborough he dashed off business letters with uncharacteristic indifference, slashed a week of appointments from his diary, proposed a new configuration of the board that would eventually see Norvill expelled. A stain of ink the size of a fist appeared suddenly on his desk and he wrote to his sister that everyone was at a loss as to how to remove it. We know how things were done in that world, but Jane does not. We understand that a man can stand in the hall while his wife receives a letter from a distant cousin, and

intentionally not observe its arrival. We understand polite effi-
ciencies—how the maid might knock the ladle lightly against
the side of the tureen as Charlotte glances up from the flawless
weave of the table linen to find Edmund smiling thinly. How
Edmund might state that the morning paper has said that the
weather has taken a turn on the coast; that he's wondering if it's
still advisable for her to leave.

We are, all of us, observers. Even Herschel, who has lost his
tongue, who sits on the outside of our circle to *tweep* his yes and
whoot his no, sees what is happening—sees Jane and sees Blake,
his chin pressed against the top of her head, his arm under her
pillow while they are sleeping; sees the tidal pull one person
can effect upon another. So we stand around the room, stir the
curtains, watch the tap slowly dripping and wish we could feel
even one water drop on our palms. And in the dark, in drifts
of memory, we recall some of the people and things we have
happened upon, moments that aroused us from the stupor of
our lives—the plumes of a peacock unfolding under an elm, the
bright platter of a sky coroneted by trees, a list retrieved from
between an armoire and the wall of a house by the sea:

Flat of palm on abdomen
Shift of sheets
Hard shelf of his hips against the soft of mine
Curve of water glass against my lips—his hand trembling
Coarse planking of the wood floor
The hitch of a sliver

Blake's phone rings at half-nine and he stumbles out of bed to yank it from the pocket of his trousers. He listens for a second and then covers the bottom of the phone to relay that it's his father, asking why he isn't at work.

Later, while he is in the shower, Jane uses Blake's mobile to go online and check her new e-mail account for a message from William. After yesterday's phone call she'd run upstairs from the records office to use the computer terminals in the public library and set up a generic e-mail account in Helen Swindon's name. Before she lost her nerve she'd dashed off a note thanking him in advance for any assistance he could offer in relation to her search for connections between the Whitmore and Inglewood House in 1877.

William's name pops up in small bold letters in her otherwise empty inbox just as the taps in the shower squeal off and the pipes in the wall groan and thump.

> Ms. Swindon—
> In regards to your inquiry . . . unable to find any reference to
> the three visitors . . . relevant sections concerning Whitmore
> death at Inglewood attached. Let me know if I can be of
> further assistance.
> Regards, W.E.

Two minutes later, Blake stands naked in front of the window and announces that since he's already late, he's going to skive off work. He unwraps a ginger biscuit from the tea tray, shoves it in his mouth and asks Jane what she wants to get up to.

She throws his shirt at him. 'Some of us actually have work to do.' The stretchy grey jumper her sister-in-law had left in the boot is sitting on top of her overnight case; she loops it over her head and slides her arms into the woolly sleeves. 'I need to sort through some of the Farrington material at the records office.'

Blake rolls his eyes; then he whips his jeans up over his hips and slings his brown leather belt strap through its buckle, watching her watch him. 'You'll have to eat, right?'

'Ostensibly.'

'I'll come and fetch you at one.'

Blake slips out on his own and a few minutes later Jane and Sam head downstairs to see if Maureen is still in the kitchen. Jane wants to tell her that she had a guest stay over, pay any difference, apologize; maybe say he's a friend, the visit unexpected—though the village is so small that if Maureen saw Blake, she'd know him.

Last night, as Blake's thumb traced Jane's bottom lip, Charlotte Chester and her catalogue of touch had sprung to Jane's mind; now, thinking about the complexity of explaining her 'guest' to Maureen, about the social mores around relationships people don't approve of, she's reminded of Norvill and Charlotte, of the way they must have manoeuvred Victorian conventions—even in a seaside resort like Scarborough.

The breakfast room is already locked, but the door of the sitting room opposite it is ajar. Jane taps it lightly and it swings open. Inside, a man with brown hair and a bald spot as perfectly round as a drink coaster is sitting on a sofa in front of the television. The room smells of furniture polish and tea.

'Sorry, I'm looking for Maureen.'

The man turns around. He has a lean face and slack features, deep-set lines around his mouth, a stamp of exhaustion that Jane equates with manual labour.

'She's gone out. I'm Andy, her husband. Can I help?' He turns back to the television as if he's afraid he's missed something.

Over his shoulder Jane can see bleary black and white footage of a shirtless man lit up in a dome of light. The camera pans sideways and three more men peer out of the darkness. They are thin, shirtless and ragged, and for a second, Jane thinks they are ghosts.

'The footage has just come up,' Andy says, over his shoulder. 'They got a camera down through one of the boreholes and this is the first time—' His eyes well up and he turns back to the telly. 'My family were all miners, four generations, so . . .'

For the next twenty minutes Jane and Andy sit together and watch the video: the men blinking at the camera as they wave blurrily to their loved ones. The newsreader cuts to vigils occurring in countries all over the world—a horseshoe of candles in a village's main square, a group of men camped outside their own mine with a sign that says, *Bring them home*. It is early morning in the country where the miners live, and reporters have gathered at dawn around the camp the families have set up in the desert near the entrance to the shaft. The light in the film taken above ground is unexpectedly strange after the dusk of the men's world underground—the bright red of a woman's sweatshirt, the surprise of a yellow scarf, the intricate weave of a little girl's poncho.

A bar of light moves across the glass plate of the library's photocopier and Jane shakes her head. She forgot to put the pamphlet she's holding down on the glass. A sheet of blackened paper slides out the far end of the machine and the librarian at the nearby desk catches Jane's eye and tweaks her mouth up in a half-smile that means, *Please don't waste the toner.* Jane angles the pamphlet in place, lowers the lid, hits 'copy' again, and a page of names, telephone numbers and e-mail addresses spouts out the other end. Blake hasn't asked much about it, but Jane knows that everything she's said to him about the research she's doing reaffirms his belief that she's involved with the Trust and the work they're doing at the Farrington estate. She feels some discomfort over the lie but also a sense that—because N figures in the Farrington story—her affiliation with the estate and her investment in its history is based on a kind of truth.

At the computer bay between the New Arrivals shelves and the beanbag chairs of the Young Readers section Jane sends the attachment that William had included in his e-mail to the library printer, then pays the clerk. She hadn't wanted to open the document on Blake's phone, afraid that it would download and he'd find it later, see William's name. In total, William has sent typed excerpts from three letters, the first dated just a few weeks after the shooting party in 1877.

> Inglewood, September 25, 1877
> George Farrington to Mr. P. Eaton c/o Eaton, Roberts
> & Henley Ltd.

> . . . Norvill has gone to the coast in the wake of the
> regrettable incident—the Commissioners are, as of last
> week, satisfied. The brother of the deceased has been con-
> tacted and states he has no grievance. I have met with the
> Superintendent who is inclined to document the event
> economically—the situation appears thusly resolved.

Inglewood, October 21, 1877
George Farrington to Norvill Farrington

I trust you are settling at Harrison's. I understand the accommodations are modest. Grierson has extended your survey ~~nine~~ ten months and agreed to let use [sic] monies in the Granton account. Nora has sent two notes to Mother and indicates that your spirits are improving. I have had a last call from the magistrate Flynn and the regrettable incident is—I assure you—behind us. Mr. Leeson has been reburied at the Whitmore.

Yunnan Province, March 12, 1878
George Farrington to Mr. P. Eaton c/o Eaton, Roberts & Henley Ltd.

Please ensure the agreed-upon transfer of monies to the Whitmore on my behalf should I encounter further difficulties crossing the border, or in the event that I fail to return.

Walking back to the records office, Jane absorbs how clearly Norvill is implicated in the shooting. This would explain William's delicate aside at the lecture: he wanted to communicate that the Chesters and Farringtons were connected, needed to state that the shooting party had occurred, because it led directly to expedition funding from the Suttons for George's 1878 trip, and more crucially, from Edmund in 1881. But because William's focus was on Norvill Farrington's contributions to both the Chester Museum and the Geological Society, he'd demurred when it came to the tragic events of the day, stated that little was written about the gathering, that Prudence's diaries said almost nothing. Given William's focus, Jane realizes, nothing would have been gained by implicating the Farringtons and the Chesters in a long-dead scandal they'd successfully quashed. And, perhaps the site of the shooting party and the picnic at the lake was too close for him, too raw. Maybe this was why he'd skipped over Leeson's murder and enthused about *Primula* and *Rhodiola*, about Norvill's geologic maps and his hypothesis of 'faunal succession,' knowing crates of Norvill's brachiopods and mollusks were stored in the Chester's vaults below him as he spoke.

When Jane gets back to the reading room she pulls out a chair and sets her pencils and notebook on the table in front of her. Then she studies William's references more carefully. It is only on her second reading that she sees the name 'Nora': *Nora has sent two notes to Mother and indicates that your spirits are improving.* Jane's eyes flick back to the name and she shivers. It feels so strange to come across a woman's *N* name after years of searching, and even though there's only a remote possibility that the woman George has mentioned is the same one who walked to Inglewood House from the Whitmore, Jane can't help but follow up on the reference, so she opens the Farrington index and runs her finger down the list of the estate's archives again.

The Farrington index indicates that the records office holds two ledgers concerning Inglewood staff. One is an account book of taxes paid on servants and the other is the estate Register of Employment—a large red book she'd glanced through a few days ago. While Jane waits for the Register to be sent up from the stores, she sifts through the Farrington material she'd requested yesterday: a binder of mottling business letters in plastic sleeves, a box of invoices and receipts in ornate calligraphy. Most of it doesn't concern the household staff. The majority—deposited by George's executors—appears to relate to botanical work, expedition costs, investments and the daily—and diminishing—economies of the estate.

When Freddy returns to his desk after delivering a microfiche to the gentleman working at the table behind Jane's, she asks him about Prudence's diaries: Does the Trust that is borrowing the diaries keep them in London, or are they here?

Freddy frowns. Perhaps he assumed she'd know more about the work on the estate than she appears to. 'No,' he says, 'everything's local. The Trust has an archivist named Gwendolyn. She was based here for a bit but now she's working out of the Farrington House at Inglewood. The diaries are with her.'

Two weather systems are converging overhead. If we look up and to the right of the parking lot where we are standing, clouds net the sky; to the left there's a canopy of blue. Jane is waiting for Blake, who is already ten minutes late, and so we are waiting with her, the breeze lifting the ends of her hair as she looks down to check her watch. If she hadn't left her mobile in London she would text him to say not to come or ask him to hold off until the Employee Register comes up from the stacks.

While we wait for Blake, the idiot paces between the white

lines of a parking space furthering his thesis on the nature of our being. 'I've been thinking,' he says intently.

'Don't,' the theologian snaps.

'Go ahead,' the one with the soft voice says, 'I'm interested.'

The idiot begins to circle Jane, the way a lecturer might move around a classroom. 'First,' he says, 'we must discern causality, actuality, and then *interior* versus *exterior* work. That which the atoms of the body exert *upon* each other, from that which arises from foreign influences to which the body may be exposed.'

Cat groans and the musician makes a prattling noise that sounds like drums.

'What I mean,' he says, 'is a physical system that works on other such systems, a force acting across a distance.'

The theologian raises his head. 'Do you mean *vis viva*?' he asks. 'A living force?'

'Yes,' sighs the idiot, as if he's come home from a long trip away, 'I mean *life*. Our life, our living force.'

For the next few minutes, we debate, in our own terms, what the idiot means. We watch a chocolate wrapper cartwheel across the pavement and try to apply his theories to it.

'Do you mean fluttering?' Cat asks.

'Yes,' the idiot says, 'and no.'

'Time?' John offers.

'Yes.' The idiot nods enthusiastically. 'And no.'

The musician makes a tuba sound—'*Pom pom pom poooom, pom pom pom pom*'—and the idiot raises a hand in the air to signify that he's thinking.

'Good. Modulation. Energy as more than something contained or expelled. Energy as *potential*.'

The theologian proposes an experiment. He suggests we try to move an object at a distance—the brown bag that's fallen out of the rubbish bin at the edge of the parking lot or the bird's nest in the crook of the closest tree.

'But you said—' Cat states incredulously.

The theologian replies quietly, 'Things have changed.'

'If we *are* energy—' the idiot continues, but he stops because like the rest of us he can sense something shift, a ripple in the group.

We glance around. Everything we can see—the line of shrubs, the shop awning across the road, Jane's skirt hem, the ruff of Sam's fur, the early autumn leaves—is lifting or quivering.

'Storm?' asks John. But that isn't what's different; it's a presence like ours standing silently with us.

'Who's there?' the one with the soft voice asks, and we all crane our necks and peer around the parking lot the same way we did in the Chester when she asked when a bird was no longer a bird.

'*Whoot?*' asks Herschel.

And then, as if answering her own question, the one with the soft voice whispers, 'Leeson?'

The white Transit that turns into the parking lot has *Metcalfe's Garden Company* embossed in large green letters on its panels and the proclamation *Specialists in restoration and landscape work* in brown underneath. Blake pulls up two feet from where Jane is standing and then jumps out to open the passenger-side door. We clamber in the back with Sam to sit amongst the sagging bags of fertilizer and the empty planters. By the time Blake pulls out of the parking lot we sense we are back to our usual number. 'Attendance,' says the theologian, and one after another, starting with the girl, we all say, 'Here.'

There's a plastic bag of picnic supplies in the well between the front seats. Jane rummages through it: overwrapped corner-shop sandwiches with wilted lettuce stuck to the sides, a bottle of wine that a week ago she would never have consented to drink, crisps and two glossy lemon puddings with sprinkles on the top.

She drops the pudding back into the bag and asks, 'Where are we going?'

'It's a surprise.' Blake raises his eyebrows and smiles charmingly, as if he's done something wonderful—and crowded in the back of the van we think that maybe he has. Time has taught us to appreciate the gesture.

Blake parks on the side of the road across from the Whitmore's main gate. He turns to Jane and says, 'Shall we?'

Jane leans forward in her seat. Through the wrought iron she can make out the faded brown brick of the gatehouse and, beyond that, the east wing of what was once the main building's women's ward. 'What are we doing here?'

Blake shrugs. 'I saw all that stuff in your room. Thought it would be fun to break and enter.' He grabs the bag between the seats and then locks the van once Jane is out. 'A bunch of us used to come out here when we were younger to mess around. We have to go in through the woods.'

The brick of the Whitmore's main buildings is the same umber we remember, though some of it is covered in graffiti. The slate roof of the administration block has collapsed in one corner and the windows of the long galleries—a quarrelled stretch of clouded glass—have been replaced with pressboard. The grass is weed-licked and long.

Blake walks across the lawn, grinning at Jane, the plastic bag of picnic supplies swinging in his hand, Sam trotting happily beside him. At the greening fountain he drops his peacoat for Jane to sit on and then sprawls out on the grass; he is facing the ruin of the building, and she is facing the cleft in the woods they just came from.

If we try, we can remember the fountain working. How bright and charming it was, its marble the white of the Greek temples Professor Wick once described at an afternoon lecture series given by the patients. The cherub at the centre of the fountain holding a jug that spouted the purest water—though the poet once shook his head and said that it was a pity to live in a world where the fountains did not pour wine.

We lie on the grass with Jane and Blake, and drowsy tufts of cloud drift above us. We want to stay with Jane to see if she will talk about the Whitmore, but we feel a competing desire to explore the grounds, to wander through the emptied wards of the buildings. Pulses of lived experience are already lighting up the caverns of what we call memory, and for some of us, there is an easing, a sense of calm that comes in proximity to the idea of 'home.' We know that on the other side of the Whitmore's dim exterior, the galleries and day rooms, sickbeds and laundry, the rose-windowed chapel will have changed, that time and use will have altered them. Still we know that these rooms, even the shape and weight of them, can give us something Jane cannot: a folding-over of our lives, a direct way in.

'Stay with Jane,' Cat says to the girl, and all of us wait until the child sits in the grass beside Sam.

A hundred small fissures of time open as we walk toward the old wood door. One of us remembers a sickbed and being fed awkwardly with a spoon, the light tap of the metal on his front teeth. Another remembers feeling cold, as if all the blood had drained from his body, as if there couldn't be blankets enough. Some of us remember the ball, some of us the airing courts, some of us singing in rehearsals for the talent show, the warble of our breath in our throats. And one of us remembers Christmas, everyone working in the kitchen to make sweetmeats and preserves for gifts. The tang of jam in our mouths—in what we remember of our mouths. A burst of raspberries, their small, flecked seeds on our tongues.

27 After lunch, when she returns to the records office, Jane discovers that the servant ledger nestled in the back of the bowed leather *Register of Employment for Inglewood House* lists a Nora Hayling in service, starting the 22nd of August 1877. Some of the other staff entries have end dates inked in a different hand, and notes about termination or retirement, but Nora does not. The only entry that coincides closely with the date Nora was hired is a reference to a Mary Margaret Teems, who was let go on the 26th of July that same year for pilfering flour and sugar.

During her dissertation research years ago, when Jane first discovered N and the story of the trio's long walk to Inglewood, she'd leafed through the Whitmore patient casebooks looking for an *N* name, though she hadn't searched at that time for Eleanors or Honoras, names that could be shortened to Nora. So now she fills out a request slip for the Whitmore women's book from 1877, prepared to start again, even though she is feeling dubious about the possibility of Nora from Inglewood being connected to N from the Whitmore. While Jane knows that patients at convalescent hospitals like the Whitmore could be a mix of professionals and paupers, the educated and the working class, it was unlikely a patient like N—especially because she was a woman—would be able to transition so quickly into a maid's position. Though John Hopper, she suddenly remembers, was released that December and almost immediately went to work as an apprentice clockmaker.

When the Whitmore's women's casebook disappoints—turning up nothing but Marthas, Frannies, Alices and Emmas—Jane decides to clear her head by taking Sam, who has been waiting patiently in the car, for a walk up the high street of one of the nearby villages. Even in those childhood summer months when she and Lewis would go stay with Claire in the cottage at the Lakes she had never travelled far, and so she feels pleasure in the idea of an excursion, in driving for twenty minutes and arriving somewhere new.

At the top of the main square in one of the Dales' villages there is a cenotaph. It's surrounded by the requisite gaggle of fifteen-year-olds dressed in heavy black boots and duffel coats. Jane parks the car and wanders past them toward an old-fashioned sandwich and pastry shop. It's the sort meant to appeal to tourists, where the girls who work behind the counter are allowed to have nose rings and wear blue nail polish, but still have to tie their hair under white caps with lacy fringes and scoot around in long black dresses with floor-length aprons. There is an espresso machine in the window, the beautiful old-fashioned kind that makes great coffee, so Jane loops Sam's leash around the empty bike stand out front and goes in to wait in the queue of locals on breaks from work and tourists with time on their hands.

The girl who makes Jane's coffee has a thick brown fringe and a pretty face, the idiosyncratic kind high-street clothing shops use in their adverts—naturally beautiful but with one flaw, a gap tooth or wide-set eyes, but always young. She smiles at Jane and asks if that's her dog outside.

'Yes, is he okay there?'

'He's all right. I just wondered if he needed some water; we usually have a bowl out.'

'Sure, thanks.'

The girl slips into the narrow sink area at the end of the counter. Jane watches her, thinking that she's probably Blake's age. She wonders briefly if they know each other, have some sort of history he'd call up if Jane described meeting her. She studies the girl, not jealously but curiously: watches her reach up over the metal sink by the dishwasher, grab a plastic bucket off the shelf of pots overhead and fill it with tap water. The girl's dress is a mass-market version of what the female servants at Inglewood would have worn as they washed teacups and scrubbed pots in the deep sinks in the kitchen where she'd met Blake, girls who would have ascended the narrow stairwell that went up to the attic rooms at the end of very long days, who would have slept on the far side of a baize door that separated one world from another.

On the drive back to the records office Jane is thinking about N, about how little time she has left to find her, about what Blake will say when she tells him she's leaving, and about the girl in the servant's dress with the brown hair, who she now, for whatever reason, imagines as the type of girl Blake should be with. Her thoughts swim in circles, and the same phrase, the one that always comes with thoughts of N, rises again: *Patients C. Leeson, H. Morley, and girl N– missing.*

Jane taps the car's brakes without meaning to and her body jerks forward. Sam slides with a small thump into the back of her seat. She glances up at her rear-view mirror, thankful the woman in the VW wasn't following too close behind. *And girl N– missing.*

N wasn't a patient at the Whitmore; she *worked* there, was so expendable no one bothered to cite her full name. And she didn't 'escape' the women's ward; she saw Herschel and Leeson take off, and took it upon herself to follow them.

Freddy brings the Whitmore Hospital's *Servant Engagement and Discharge Book* back up from the basement and in its fusty pages Jane finds a Nora Hayling. She is fifteen years of age when she is hired in 1874 as a laundress. No previous engagements are cited, though unlike most servants of her class, she'd been educated at a local school. In 1876 she was promoted, with the strike of a pen, to assistant seamstress. Unlike the other women listed in the book—the assistant nurses, housemaids, and women's attendants—there is no discharge note, no *left to be married*, no *resigned* or *retired on pension*, no *died in hospital* or death date. There are also no references to her or her position in the Whitmore's logbooks, except ones that reference the seam-stress proper—a woman called Humphreys; notes such as *the seamstress requires* and then an order for twenty yards of cotton or a reel of lace. The *Engagement* book reveals that Humphreys would already have been in her fifties when Nora was hired, which means she might have wanted to find someone to foist fine work on, a young girl with sharp eyes and nimble fingers, one who was educated to a reasonable standard, easy to work with, willing to learn.

Jane draws a line down the centre of a clean page and writes Nora Hayling's details from the Whitmore on one side, and from the Inglewood servants' book on the other. She allows herself to imagine the possibility that Nora Hayling is N: that it is late August 1877, and N has been missing for more than a fortnight, and suddenly she is there at Inglewood, being hired as a house-maid. That she is working for the Farringtons at the time of the outing by the lake where Norvill and Charlotte are flirting and George is soliciting funds for his expedition, and Leeson is shot.

But even with all this, there is a gap: if she did not go up to the door that night of the escape from the Whitmore with Leeson and Herschel, as George's letter suggests, then where did she go? And why did she make her way back to the estate?

The number of cars parked around Inglewood House has increased since the Sunday four days ago when Jane climbed the stone wall and snuck into the house with Sam. The church parking lot is full, even though there's no service, and the two gardening company Transits that usually sit at the mouth of the old servant's tunnel are boxed in by a long moving truck stationed at the foot of the front lawn. Two movers in white coveralls heft a sideboard down its ramp.

Jane hasn't asked Blake anything about the Trust's work because she is supposed to be involved in it. He'd asked her how long they thought the first stage would take and she'd said, 'You know what these things are like . . .' fingering the dark fringe of his hair and ignoring his blank expression, the one that said, no, he didn't.

The movers toggle the sideboard back and forth, shifting the weight of its heavy pedestals between them, and Jane follows them up the walkway. Just before she reaches the front steps and the Doric columns that flank them, she hesitates, roots around in her bag for her notepad and pen, flipping the pages over until she comes to a sheet of writing with the word *Farrington* underlined at the top. If someone asks her what she's doing on the property she can always pretend to be a grad student doing research. The movers in front of her have stopped at the open door to finesse the angle of the sideboard.

'No, no. To your right,' the heavier-set of the two calls gruffly, and the sideboard shifts slightly.

'Got it,' the lankier one replies, and with the sideboard's tall back perched at a precarious angle they inch inside the door and disappear around the corner into the entry hall.

Jane hesitates to follow them. She can hear the shuffle of their boots over the track of carpet laid down over the hardwood, the older of the two saying, 'Easy, easy.' She can imagine the two of them tottering the sideboard past someone in the main hall whose job it is to check off all the chairs and desks and paintings; who would ensure that everything is deposited in the correct place. Someone who would know Jane has no right to be here. Her gaze drifts up to a heavy brass door knocker in the shape of a lion's head—the very same one that Leeson would have rapped when the trio arrived here. *This is where they stood*, Jane thinks, *this is the last place N was seen*.

Over the past few days the main floor of the house has been filled with twice the amount of furniture that was here when Jane last wandered through it. Enormous desks, high-backed chairs and tables of every size and composition peek out from under sheets, blankets and plastic wrap; a new row of boxes and crates lines the main hall. Jane peeks around the corner into the library and is almost run over by the two movers who, released of the burden of the sideboard, are heading out again, the lean one laughing at something the older one said. They stop when they see Jane, as if the joke is inappropriate.

'Miss,' the lanky one says. He nods courteously as they pass through the entry, and then picks up the conversation again.

The library is half assembled: the furniture still draped but put in place so that Jane can make out the arrangement of a long sofa, three high-backed chairs and a screen; the round reading table where the butler would have placed the morning paper near the window, a pianoforte in the corner along with a stool with leaf-scroll feet. One of the armchairs, a bird's-eye maple with brocaded yellow upholstery, is uncovered as if someone has just been sitting there, its fabric worn gently from use. There's a trace of perfume in the room, and although Jane knows it probably belongs to the archivist she's looking for, it's floral enough that she can imagine it belonging to Prudence or coming in gusts from the rose bushes outside.

Another set of movers, younger this time, comes into the library. Each of them is carrying a wood-frame box, the kind you move paintings in. They set the boxes down gently in the corner, nod at Jane and then traipse out again, their voices, the easy chitchat of 'Are you going to Jack's after?' echoing down the hall. When they leave, Jane can hear the sound of someone typing. She follows it around the corner and through an open door into the old dining room where she finds a woman with dark hair cut into a fashionable bob sitting at a two-hundred-year-old table and pecking away on a laptop. When she glances up and sees Jane she jumps a bit, puts her hand over her chest and says 'Mother of God, you scared me.'

It's almost four p.m., and even though she's finishing up for the day, Gwendolyn is friendly. The references that give Jane some semblance of authority—Miranda at the records office, and William Eliot in London, who Jane says 'is helping me with some research'—immediately put Gwendolyn at ease. She unwinds the woolly pink scarf she's been wearing to make up for the cold of the room and says, 'Miranda's a laugh, isn't she?' as if she assumes Jane has spent time with the woman socially. It turns out that Gwen and Jane did their postgraduate studies at UCL two years apart and had a number of professors in common, though the ones Jane didn't get on with Gwen liked, and one of those had recommended her for this job.

The request to look at Prudence Farrington's diaries is simple enough, and William Eliot's name seems to carry some weight.

Gwen says she'll have to check with her supervisor—'liability and all that,'—but that it ought to be fine so long as Jane has an LRO card and works with the material here, supervised. When Jane first mentioned the 'diaries' Gwen's gaze had drifted over to a locked filing cabinet on the wall, an ugly metal thing wedged against the cherry blossom wallpaper beside two modern steel shelves crammed with cardboard boxes. 'We're not very organized yet, we just got electricity on Monday.' She points to the photocopier and fax machine sitting against a wall where the sideboard the movers carried in probably once stood. 'I don't think those have been plugged in yet. And we're already two months behind. Anyway, do you want my mobile number or do you just want to stop in tomorrow to see if my supervisor at the Trust okays it?'

'Stopping in is fine.'

'Great, let's say nine.'

Undressing that night in her room at the inn, Blake watching from where he's flopped on the bed, Jane remarks that she hadn't seen him on the Inglewood grounds when she looked from the library window.

Blake laughs. 'I *did* go in. I was sent to the duck pond for fucking off, had to scrub my hands raw to get rid of the smell of Victorian goose shit.'

Jane pulls back the duvet and slips in beside him. He leans over and kisses her. After a minute he sits up and raises his hands, pretending he's filming her, mimicking the crank style of an old-fashioned camera, one eye squinched shut as if with the other he's looking through a lens.

'What are you doing?'

'I want to remember this.' He keeps filming.

'Remember what?'

'You, you idiot.' He drops the imaginary camera and kisses her eyelids, moves down her neck whispering into her skin, 'Record, record, record.'

In the morning, just after eight, Jane slips out of bed to get something for breakfast—takeaway coffees, pastries. This is to avoid going through explanations again with Maureen: *guests need to be booked in advance, paid for beforehand, their details taken so we know in an emergency who is staying in the rooms.* Sam raises his head a few inches when she opens the door but he doesn't get up, so she decides to leave him with Blake, who is snoring, slack-mouthed, into his pillow. She frames them there as she turns to go: Blake under the mountain of the duvet, Sam's head pressed between his front paws at the foot of the bed, his white tail fanning out behind him.

We rouse ourselves when Jane leaves the room but we don't follow her out, and the girl asks why we aren't going with her.

'It's just coffee,' the musician says, but we know he is lying. We have followed Jane out for coffee before, have followed her in restaurants from her table to the loo, moved in her flat from one side of the kitchen to the other in order to track her thinking.

'She'll be back,' Cat says chirpily, and the one with the soft voice bends down to the girl and says, 'We'll all go to Inglewood House with her later. It'll be fun.'

'Now then—' Cat says, as if there is some task we need to get up to, as if we haven't all been subdued in the wake of our decision to follow Jane back from the Whitmore. We'd had a row at the gate as to whether those of us who belonged at the Whitmore should stay, whether knowing who we'd been and what we'd done was enough of an ending. It was the theologian who'd convinced us to get back in the van.

'Not much doing here,' he said, slapping his hands together in a ghostly imitation of a clap. 'Pretty desolate. And work that needs to be done.'

'What work?' the musician asked quietly.

'Songs to sing, poems to write, lessons to be planned.' The theologian stepped gaily over the road in an approximation of a dance and we stood back and angled our heads, trying to decide what might have taken possession of the man we thought we knew. 'I suppose,' he continued drily—as if the fake show of enthusiasm had depleted him—'that the nature of said work has yet to be determined.' He ushered us into the van and as Blake closed the door he added, 'But let's not allow such trivialities to diminish our dedication to the task.'

When Jane gets back to the inn with a tray of coffee and a bag of croissants she had to drive to the next village to find, Blake is drying off from his shower and Sam is standing by the door because he hasn't been let out yet.

'The police were here for you.'

'Sorry?' Jane shakes her head.

'And the room charges were slipped under the door, which I suppose means you're leaving.' Blake picks a card up from the tea tray. 'A Constable Avison? I said you were out for the day because I didn't know what else to say. They hung around for half an hour and made a bunch of calls. You just missed them.' He is matter-of-fact and distant. 'I think I have this right.' He hands her the card. 'Please tell Ms. Standen that we *strongly encourage* her to call us.'

Jane doesn't say anything. She doesn't know where to start.

Blake pulls his jeans on. 'On the plus side it appears that your name really is Jane.'

'Did they say what they wanted?'

Blake laughs, but it's not a laugh that she knows. 'No. Probably because they could see how badly I wanted to know, standing there in my fucking boxers and everything.'

'I don't work for the Trust.'

He pulls his T-shirt on over his head. 'Yeah, I get that now. I'm not a *total* fucking idiot.'

Because she doesn't know how else to do it, Jane closes her eyes and blurts out: 'I slapped the father of the girl who went missing at a public event last week and then I took off from my job at a museum in London and didn't tell anyone where I was going. I'm sorry I lied.'

When she opens her eyes he is putting his boots on. Once they're laced he says, 'Sam needs to go outside,' and grabs his jacket off the chair and walks out, slamming the door behind him.

Jane puts the constable's card in her pocket and packs her things. Maureen stiffly takes the keys, deducts the deposit from the amount owing with quick jabs at her calculator and then pauses mid-stroke while she's writing out the receipt. Jane wonders if the constables gave away the fact that 'Helen' was not her real name.

'I'm sorry for any trouble,' Jane says.

Maureen glances over to her husband, who is leaning against the door jamb with his arms crossed. He looks angry, as if Jane has disappointed him too—as if she's made them both complicit in some kind of wrongdoing.

Sitting in the car, Jane cradles her head in her hands and tries not to cry. She opens the glovebox to have something to do, rustles through it. There's an old parking permit from Lewis's last lab, a yoga schedule, the Mercedes manual from 1970. She pulls the manual out and brings it to her nose, wishing it might still carry the scent of her grandparents, some trace of being a child.

28 Walking up the avenue that divides the great lawn of Inglewood house, Jane tries to compose herself. She can still feel the heat of her face, the knot in her stomach that won't go away. What could have been days or even weeks has suddenly turned into a day maybe, or into hours. She looks over her shoulder at the clipped green expanse of the lawn to see if anyone is following her but there's only the line of shrubs and bushes at the edge of the property, the sculpted heads of marble horses peeking through the gaps in the evergreen, a cluster of parked trucks and cars by the road.

To calm herself down Jane imagines Herschel Morley, Charles Leeson and the young woman who may or may not be Nora Hayling walking out of the Whitmore and across eleven miles of forest and fields to arrive here: a great lawn bordered by hedges and what would have been, at night, the eerily bright marble of rearing horses in the recesses between the hewn trees.

It's possible that a census will place Nora in time, locate where she lived before and after the Whitmore, identify family, suggest what happened. It's possible that when N left Herschel and Leeson on the steps, she did something as simple as head down into the village, knock on her parents' door and go home. Still, it's the other possibilities—infinite ones—that make Jane anxious to read Prudence's diaries, to find some note that might finalize the equation, draw an unbroken line between Inglewood House and the Whitmore, between Nora Hayling and N.

Prudence Farrington's diaries range from 1870 to 1910, although within that span entire years are missing or lost. As Gwen takes five volumes out of the file cabinet, Jane knows to expect gaps, missing weeks or months due to bouts of illness or travel. Gwen confesses that she has only read the diaries once so far, and not deeply, though she remembers being surprised that the two years after George's death were so scantly recorded. Jane has seen this before in her research at the Chester: the writer mourning or self-censoring or turning instead to black-edged letters. Sometimes, too, the executor intervenes: tearing out pages or burning whole books to expunge impassioned feelings, accidental indiscretions.

Gwen points to a tall-backed chair at the other end of the dining room table where a book support has been set up and tells Jane that she can work there. Then she pulls a pair of rubber gloves out of a box sitting on what must have been an original window seat—its cushion the same dusky pink as the cherry blossoms on the Oriental wallpaper. 'I've actually met William Eliot,' Gwen says, as if just remembering Jane's mention of him yesterday. 'His wife and daughter rented a cottage up here for a month last year when he was doing some research for his book. I have a daughter Mina's age and they played a few times. He seems like a lovely man.'

Jane is working her way through the spring of 1877 a few hours later when Gwendolyn gets up and apologizes. She has to fetch some lunch, and there isn't a fridge or microwave working in the house yet so she'll be walking down to the pub. She stands for a moment at the end of the table and Jane realizes this means she has to leave as well—the material can't be left unsupervised, and even though Jane is usually the one supervising, she doesn't properly belong here.

Gwendolyn puts the diaries back into the file cabinet and locks it, then locks the dining room door behind them with a skeleton key. 'I'll only be twenty minutes or so.' She offers Jane the option of waiting in the library, warning her to avoid the man supervising the movers as he's in a bit of a mood because one of the workmen dropped a Queen Anne side table. 'You're welcome to look at the books on the shelves. We're just in the process of cataloguing them.'

Because the movers are traipsing in and out of the library—once hauling a wood bench so large that it takes four of them to carry it—Jane stands in the corner out of the way, near the brocade curtains, and surveys the titles the Trust is placing back on the shelves. Most of the books concern botany, geography and history, their spines splitting or warped, though they would have been relatively new when George purchased them, probably to keep current with the scientific discoveries and political boundaries of the day. She likes this about George—that he must have been less concerned with having a gentleman's library than with the importance of the material in the books themselves. In a row of volumes that are mostly verse, Jane pulls out a tatty copy of Virgil, then a lightly worn blue calfskin Milton, then a book with a torn cover and no discernible title save for an illustrated embellishment of a hive of bees. She opens it up to the first leaf: *To my muse. I see what I see.*

'In the razed field, / in the cusp of its wealth,' says the poet, and Cat claps and Herschel *tweep*s. 'We lay on the rough skin of earth, / and loved with our mouths.' The poet leans over Jane's shoulder, reading as she is reading: 'To speak and name the field song, / to pluck wonder like a flower, / is to waver between worlds: / the gods and ours.'

Jane closes the book and turns it over in her hands, looking for the author or publication date, and the poet seems to deflate. He knows he has been in this room before with that very book placed in front of him. He had stopped here with the succubus after being released from the Whitmore. He remembers feeling anxiety—a combination of terror at being outside the hospital's gates and dread of being returned to what Dr. Thorpe had called 'your wife's *care*.' He had shredded his notebook in the carriage on the way over, and yet his wife had insisted they come, leading him straight into the house like a dog on a chain. All of it—the newness of the situation, the lightness of the air, the motes in front of his eyes—had induced in him a kind of panic. His hands scrabbling and near useless as his wife thrust his own book into them and demanded he sign it.

What the poet remembers most is how he wanted to knock her teeth out because she kept showing them to him, smiling widely, though her eyes were on George Farrington. Some sort of exchange was being made, an agreement he couldn't keep track of. He remembers a peal of laughter emitting from his wife's ugly mouth, then a '*Delightful!*' which led to the girl being called in.

It was the girl the poet knew from the other world, the world he had just been expelled from. She was the same one, he was certain of it, although she was healthier now—more substance to her, a rosy brightness to her skin. She curtseyed and smiled at him, left a tray of tea and biscuits, a pair of scissors nestled amongst the cups and saucers. For a brief instant he could breathe again, and so he closed his eyes to compose a line in his head about *knowing*.

The succubus beside him suddenly picked up the scissors, her hands touching so many surfaces—a desk, drawers, an envelope, a chair—until there was nowhere in the room where the poet could stand that was free of his wife's contamination. 'You take it,' she said to George Farrington, in a voice the poet had heard the first time he bedded her. She sat down and tilted her neck, and Farrington took the shears to the black snakes of her hair, clipping a tress from near her neckline. The Countess turned and levelled her eyes at the poet even as she spoke to Farrington. 'Now,' she said, 'let's take one from him.'

Jane returns the poet's book to the shelf and draws the curtains farther so she can look over the back lawn for Blake. The gardens have come a long way in the past week: the central mound has been turned over, a new row of rose bushes has been planted, and the trellises have been reset. There are so many changes that even as Jane cranes her neck to gaze over the grounds for the gardener whose body and gestures she knows, she's wondering what work is his, what parts of the garden he might have planted in the stretch of days they were together, and what he would say if he came up to the house and saw her now.

The Trust's plan, according to Gwen, is to open the grounds in the coming summer, to have the gardens trained and in full bloom by then, the alpine beds exactly as George had planted them. There will be teahouse seating just outside the library windows and a kitchen downstairs that will serve soups and sandwiches— the basics. The Farrington archives will be relocated to the old study and a small research library on Victorian plant hunting will be established. The main floor of the house will eventually be open to the public for admission. 'A kind of museum,' Gwen had said, 'mostly botanically themed,' and Jane had smiled politely, not wanting to say that these were difficult times for museums, that people seemed more content with looking at a jpeg of a glass-blown iris or a scarab bracelet, and less concerned with seeing the fragility and wear, the poignancy, of real things.

'We're planning on having a concert on the grounds on opening day,' Gwen had added. 'You know, get a big name to headline, make it a black tie and white gloves kind of do.' She smiled over at Jane warmly, as if they were friends. 'I'm sure the Eliots will drive up for it. You should come too.'

When Gwen returns, Jane resumes making her way through Prudence's narrative. In her diary entry on the 29th of August 1877, Prudence notes that the housekeeper has taken on *a new girl* who has come without references but is well educated. A few entries later, in blotchy ink that was probably the result of a change of pen, Prudence writes that Dr. Thorpe has paid a visit. *He arrived at three and took tea, after which the men retired to the library. Thorpe gifted George with a handwritten copy of one of Mr. Samuel Murray's unpublished verses—which I have yet to read. It was agreed that Nora would be allowed to stay on.*

Jane stares down at the open diary for a full minute. Unlike with Dr. Palmer's journals, where the writing was so tight, so nearly illegible that Jane was worried she was drawing a connection between the Whitmore and Inglewood House because it was something she *wanted* to see, Prudence's writing is Spencer-perfect. Dr. Thorpe's name isn't a question; his involvement in Nora's employment is clear.

Prudence's subsequent entries mention fittings for dresses, the modification of old bonnets, and the mending of night-wear and undergarments, as if Nora was the first seamstress Prudence had had in her regular employ. There are notes as to who should receive the embroidered workbags Nora is making for Christmas—a thrift that might explain Nora's value in a household whose finances were waning. As she reads through each entry, inching closer to the week of the picnic and the shooting, it dawns on Jane that William had either not read Prudence's diaries carefully, or he'd misrepresented their contents in his lecture, stating dismissively that they didn't have much to say about the Chester–Farrington picnic. That week, after the initial details of preparation—the airing of the rooms and the orders for lobster and exotic fruits to be sent up from London—there are a number of cryptic notes. On the day of the shooting, Prudence wrote: *The children have been confined to the nursery, C– did not come down for dinner, tincture brought up to my room.* This was followed by *Norvill returned to consult the men*, and *extra room arranged*—which could mean, Jane surmised, that Prudence had wondered if the constable they'd sent for might need to stay over.

The last note on the page is in looser writing, as if she'd woken up in the night or taken up her pen after a few glasses of sherry. It reads simply, *Poor George*.

Two weeks later, in a short entry, Prudence notes that Norvill is leaving for the coast. She carefully lists the departure time of his train and all of the stops along his way, as if tracking his journey from Inglewood to Scarborough, trying to imagine him arriving. A week after that she writes, *Thwaite's photographs have been delivered. They are of good composition though memories of the day itself are wrenching.*

'Gwendolyn?'

She raises her eyes but keeps typing. She's been transcribing a local history of the estate for almost an hour.

'Are there any photographs? Prudence is talking about a Thwaite? He came up and photographed the gardens.'

'There are, but they haven't been sorted yet. That's my assistant's job. She's actually a volunteer so it's slow-going.

They should be in the lower drawer over there—' Gwen points over her laptop at the file cabinet and then glances at the time on her computer screen. 'It's almost four, so can we say another hour? I have to head down to London tomorrow so there won't be anyone here to help you. You can come back on Monday if you'd like.'

Jane finds three squat boxes of photographs neatly stacked in the file drawer but when she opens them the mix of originals, copies and photocopies is disheartening. She's already anxious someone will find out she's here, that Maureen will have called the police, or that Blake will see her through the window and tell Gwen that she's been lying about her name, lying about her connection with William.

At first glance there's nothing that seems to distinguish one box from the other. Jane can't discern any system or rationale but surmises, once she's rummaged through a handful of photos on the top of each pile, that the boxes might be organized roughly by era. She starts with one where the clothes in the photos match the 1870s and '80s, and leafs through the images, waiting for something she recognizes to present itself.

George Farrington appears in about a third of the photographs Jane is working through. He strikes Jane as far more handsome in these candid shots than in his formal studio-based portraits, where he stands stiffly with a top hat in one hand and a book in the other. The studio portraits are the ones that crop up in the books Jane's been reading. One of them, a static image of Farrington in front of an urn, is familiar from William's last chapter in *The Lost Gardens of England*, and for a second Jane remembers how she felt when she arrived at the start of that chapter, how she read every word that William had written, looking for some trace, some thought of her.

Norvill is less expected. In one photo where he is in his early twenties, he is standing without a jacket in front of a scarp of rock, holding a length of rope. He has a gentle face, fair hair with sun-kissed streaks in it, and an athlete's body. His steady gaze makes him appear both arrogant and honest. It has always struck Jane as odd that he would have been a climber, in the footsteps of his famous brother; it occurs to her now, studying him, that maybe he had been the climber first, because he was studying geology, and it was George who followed.

The majority of the photographs are of the gardens, albumen prints from glass negatives that have browned over the century, the trees dark and shadowy behind the bright patches of light flowers, their pinwheel shapes, the closed fists of the roses, captured crisply. The close-ups of the gardens seem to have been copied multiple times, and as Jane sorts through the duplicates it occurs to her that the gardening company outside had probably used the images to ascertain what was planted where. These detailed images would fill in the blanks in the Farrington gardeners' notebooks, in George Farrington's own garden journals.

In a packet of *cartes de visite* and personal photos, there is an image of Charlotte Chester in a paisley dress. The image has been cut in a circle, as if placed in a small bedside frame or carried inside a pocket watch. It shocks Jane to see her in this context, to see her here at Inglewood, pared off from Edmund and the children.

The rest of the figures in the packet are strangers: a man in a hack, another in a hammock, an Indian who must be George's valet standing by the stables with a seed bag in his hand, surrounded by peacocks. Jane's gaze slides quickly over the theologian because she does not know him—although he, now standing at her shoulder, recognizes himself: a man invited to pose against a stone wall in order to establish scale, a trivial embellishment in an image intended to show off the first blooms of the spring garden, the lilting magnolias.

The photograph of the Farrington household is near the bottom of the second box. It is from a later period than interests Jane: the small day-hats and high collars on the female servants suggest the mid-1880s. It was taken on the front lawn between two spheres of ornamental shrubbery, and the group is arranged around Prudence, who stands solemnly beside Norvill in her black mourning dress. She is plump and soft-chinned, her arm looped under her son's. Cato—the lurcher who'd featured in almost every image of George—is gone, replaced by a terrier curled up next to a Doric column, a young boy's hand on the dog's head.

We watch Jane study each face the way she first studied the hummingbirds: one after the other, equal weight and consideration given to every person. *There is the stable boy, the under butler, a man in a wide-brimmed straw hat who must be the head gardener; here is an aging footman with a side part.* Jane moves her eyes over their features and at the end of the second row she sees the smiling face of a young woman in a housemaid's uniform, a simple black dress with lace cuffs. She is in her mid-twenties here, her expression less wistful than when Jane first saw her photo in the records office, but Jane remembers her exactly—the gloss of dark hair, the narrow shoulders and bright complexion of the girl with the sewing basket sitting on the lawn of the Whitmore.

Jane asks Gwen if she might borrow a piece of unlined white paper from the photocopier. Gwen says, 'Go ahead,' and watches as Jane draws circles on it that correspond to the positions of the staff in the household photograph. She writes Prudence Farrington's name in the middle circle and Norvill Farrington's beside it, and in the place of the housemaid in the second row she writes: *Nora Hayling*.

And because Gwen is an archivist, and knows that every scrap of information can carry within it tremendous value, she smiles at Jane over her laptop and says, 'Well done, you.'

29

As she looks at the photograph of herself on the lawn at Inglewood House, the one with the soft voice feels the doubling that comes with the bowed gift of time; it is a doubling that she feels again as she looks at Jane packing up her notebook and pencils to walk out with Gwen.

I have to do something, she had thought once, when she had a body, when she had a name, when Herschel and Leeson trudged across the lawn and no one, not even the Matron, saw them. Nora had slipped out through the kitchen to go after them, thinking that she might be able to convince them to return, that if they came back quickly no one would know they'd left the picnic. But the day was beautiful and the trees were fluttering their leaves at the sun, and the ground was drying beneath her. After a while, she stopped plotting her arguments. By the time she caught up with Herschel and Leeson in a clearing, the distance between her and the Whitmore felt good.

For two weeks she'd been keeping her head down, organizing her workday in ways that would allow her to avoid Bream. After he cornered her in the storeroom and forced her up against the shelves, she told the Superintendent that she had a fever and Thorpe allowed her to take the hospital mending up to her room. For three days she barricaded the door with her wobbly dresser, listening for the sound of footsteps in the hall. It wasn't that Thorpe wouldn't believe her, if she told. It was just that he was a man, and not wanting to think that it had happened as she said, he might try to find some fault in her.

In the middle of the whisking woods, Herschel and Leeson ahead of her, Nora lifted her head and thought, *This is what my life could be.* It didn't bother her that the idea came without a corresponding image or a clear notion. It was enough that it suggested something else, a different way of relating to the world, another mode of being.

When they arrived at the foot of the Inglewood estate lawn, Nora thought about all the turns they'd made in the woods, the seemingly endless circles, the three times they'd realized they'd doubled back on themselves, and she laughed. How comical it was that they would arrive here—at the house of the botanist she had danced a quadrille with at the ball, the one whose face she'd studied while Samuel recited his poem, who'd turned his fleeting attention on her later, taking the exotic flower from his lapel and placing it gently behind her ear. *It seems that you are one of the only ladies at the ball without a flower.*

The footman who went to fetch George Farrington barely glanced at her—and she realized she had no desire to be seen, or to be caught up in the extradition that would likely follow. She saw that Herschel and Leeson would be fine, that the footman would indeed bring the congenial Farrington to meet them.

She stepped off the gravel path and disappeared into the trees.

The police station in Moorgate is the same one where Jane had waited all those hours during the search for Lily. It is remarkably unchanged—grey-green walls, chipped paint, a stack of thumbed-through nature magazines strewn over a square table, institutional waiting-room chairs. She walks over to the woman at the intake desk and she asks for Constable Avison, handing her the card he left with Blake.

The woman, her hair in a tight ponytail, her uniform perfectly pressed, leads Jane to the back of the station, and as Jane walks beside her she notices a butterfly tattoo peeking out from under the cuff of her sleeve. The interview room where she leads Jane is just like the one from twenty years before, a concrete square with one-way glass, though the formerly grey walls have been repainted a baby blue.

Avison plods in, wipes his hand across his face and sits down heavily. He thumbs open a file and slides a piece of paper across the table between them. It is a pixilated version of Jane's own face, from a photo Lewis had taken at one of the girls' birthday parties. The word *Missing* is in capital letters above it. Jane touches the page carefully with the tip of her finger, positions it on the desk so that it's sitting straight in front of her, so that she can read the bare essentials of who she is: height, weight, hair colour, eye colour, no distinguishing features. She begins to make an awkward apology, tries to explain that there was some confusion about where she was going, that she'd forgotten her mobile.

Avison isn't listening; he's riffling through the forms he's brought, and a few of them slide off the table onto the floor. Coming up for air, he finds the one he wants and fills out the top few lines in scraggly masculine writing.

'Am I in trouble?' Jane asks, not sure if this is just about disappearing, or if William has pressed charges.

'I suppose that depends.' Avison turns the form to Jane with an X marked next to the line that reads 'under his/her own volition.' 'But if I were you I would call your brother before you leave here.'

Jane signs her name and Avison takes the paper back. He indicates that Jane should follow him out. He drops the form onto a plastic tray at an empty desk and then makes a *shoo* gesture with his hand.

'Does a Constable Holmes still work here?' Jane asks. She points to where a trolley loaded with AV equipment is sitting. 'He had a desk in that corner.'

'*Chief* Holmes?' Avison crosses his arms, looking at Jane differently. 'You know him? He's in his office.'

Jane shakes her head and pulls her bag over her shoulder. She just wants to know that someone here might remember what it was like *then*, that if she needed to talk about that time in her life, what she felt and went through, she could.

When she calls Lewis from the station, he is livid. But his voice also wavers with relief. 'You didn't answer your mobile and didn't show up at the lake, so we called the police. Dad's flown in and he's up at the cottage, Gareth is calling every twelve hours, we had people handing out posters . . . What in Christ's name were you thinking?'

'Did Gareth tell you what happened?'

'Of course. Why do you think we were so bloody worried?'

Jane clears her throat. 'Is William going to press charges?'

Lewis doesn't say anything at first, and Jane closes her eyes, thinking that whatever happens she deserves it.

'He's called twice to see if we've found you. He didn't recognize you, Jane.'

What we remember, as Jane walks back to the car thinking about William, are those stretches of time when we believed we could no longer bear watching her. How during those weeks and months when Jane's thoughts had little to do with us, we felt like we were dying all over again. The hardest part, of course, was feeling that the world was moving on without us—the shift of Jane's arm as she opened a cabinet, the wind lifting the long grass in the park, Sam nosing his empty bowl across the floor— agency in every corner. Our glimpsed memories were tactile then: a body in bed with the weight of a book, a child's breath against the side of one's neck, the cool circle of a pearl button under one's fingers. One of us remembered a parcel of plum taken between teeth, another waking to a lover's face, Herschel remembered waking to birdcall, to the sheen of a winter sun shawled by clouds—experiences that we would never be able to replicate. In our grief the memory of touch was everywhere: common touch, accidental touch, unexpected touch—a man dipping a woman's cuffs into water to rinse them clean.

But now we have, we suppose, what Jane has as she drives back into Inglewood: a mix of joys and misgivings, a sense that maybe the narratives we have been trying to build our lives on are less fixed than we ever imagined, or peripheral to something else. In a way it's like remembering the exact weight of the weather in the instant you knew yourself loved, even as you feel that weather changing.

What the one with the soft voice, what Nora remembers, is how, in the aftermath of the shooting, her hands raw from scrubbing the blood from her cuffs, Norvill came into the house and shouted her name. She remembers being shocked that he knew it. He had burst in through the garden, startling Mrs. Sutton, who had stepped out to get some air, and was standing in the library when Nora reached him, his clothes speckled with blood, his chest heaving.

'George wants you there when the authorities arrive, to tes-tify to the man's—' And he paused, subduing his expression. 'To testify,' he repeated more evenly, meeting Nora's gaze, 'to the poor man's condition.' He cleared his throat and steadied himself by gripping the back of a nearby chair. 'You won't have to discredit him. We simply need you to testify to the fact that he is a patient at the Whitmore.'

When Norvill and Nora returned to the lake they found George sitting on a rock some distance from the blanketed body. What was left of the picnic—the roast, cheeses and fruitcake—had been carefully packed away as if in the absence of help George wanted to busy himself with some task, to be useful.

As soon as Norvill was within earshot, George said, 'You'll have to go away, find some excuse, take a commission.' His voice was gruff but there was also a streak of satisfaction under it.

'Why?'

'Why!' George was beyond angry; he slid off the rock and approached Norvill, not caring that Nora was there. 'Where do I begin? The dead man? Or the married woman? Or Mother? Imagine her having to make idle chatter with you across the breakfast table after *this*!'

Norvill picked up a stone and tossed it sideways into the lake. 'I see.'

George gasped. 'Do you?' He stepped forward as if to strike his brother, but then stopped short. 'And,' George huffed, his eyes settling on Nora as if to ascertain what she might or might not already know, 'you must end things with Charlotte. You both appeared ridiculous.'

We know from Jane's work on the Chester archives, and from Charlotte's later admissions to Nora, that Norvill did not end things. That even though he let the strings of the relationship go while preparing for his removal to the coast, Charlotte was more reluctant. It wasn't just that she thought she could love him;

it was that he had become entangled in a tragedy borne of his feelings *for her*. That afternoon of the picnic, sketching and lingering on the rock, she'd felt as if some sort of palpable organism, some natural order, was humming and expanding, encompassing everyone in the party but her. She imagined that if she looked around the lake or dared to step even a little distance into the woods she'd see the world pulsing, like a giant bed of moss or the great banyan Edmund had told her about—something the others felt connected to, but that she could never be.

Once, later, standing on a chair in Scarborough while Nora stitched a hem, she confessed that it was Norvill who had changed this, who had brought something inside her back to life.

Jane parks the Mercedes in the church parking lot and lets Sam out. Since she left the station she has been trying to imagine what sort of shape her wrongness might have taken; she has been playing at it as if it is a puzzle, removing one piece—William's indifference—and replacing it with another—William's possible concern—even as she knows that his concern isn't, or ought not to be, the central part of the equation. This has led her to thoughts of Charlotte and Norvill, to what it is people are looking for in each other, and what, by extension, Jane is looking for in N. Prudence's diaries—her disdain for Charlotte, for the headmaster George befriended, for the East, or for anything that might take her sons away from her—are making Jane rethink the contents of Charlotte's diaries; though really it's the gaps that interest her now. There were, after all, two hiatuses in Charlotte's diaries that Jane hadn't paid much attention to. These, she now understands, correspond to the trips Charlotte made to be with Norvill at the coast, trips that Edmund, in his defeat, likely permitted so long as his wife was discreet—although Jane imagines his compliance would have come without formal declaration.

It's not improbable that he wanted his wife's happiness after all. Not impossible that both times, she'd come back flushed and rejuvenated and, perversely, more in love with him. Perhaps, although the cost was high, seeing Charlotte's spirit returned to her was a relief to Edmund—especially if she shared her renewal with him.

Jane hasn't realized until now that those years of struggle for Charlotte and Edmund correspond to the years when the Chester museum was fully realized—when the collections that had been idling pleasantly alongside Edmund's factories and family concerns were given almost everything he could offer in terms of money, attention and time. The clocks cleaned and working perfectly, the whale knit to the ceiling, the hummingbirds purchased, and the Vlasak plant specimens procured: each glassy piece a true correspondent to the animate thing it was modelled on, a marvel of petals, stems and leaves, the strawberry plant weighted with a glaze of frost—captured exactly as it might have been in the last brisk days of autumn.

The day of the picnic, Nora shifted from one foot to the other; she had yet to purchase a second pair of shoes and the sole of the left one had lost some of its stitching and was flapping annoyingly near the toe. She'd confided this to Charlotte, who had reluctantly allowed her to station herself at the slip between the alders where the Chester children had shouldered their way through, the shrub's green leaves silvering while she waited. The conversations of the men, when they stood close enough for her to listen, were wonderful. Mr. Chester was telling Mr. and Mrs. Sutton about his museum, the rarities of nature he'd collected and seen. 'The world is a large place,' Chester said, and he ran his hand over his vest, lightly fingering his pocket watch. 'Though I suppose you know that.' He was speaking to the Suttons, but sensed Nora's eyes on him and nodded in her direction. He said this last phrase looking at her face, as if he could discern a worldliness at work there.

When Leeson burst through the bushes, Nora was feeding Cato a bump of bread. The dog spun and Norvill appeared with a shotgun, and Nora did not have time to reach him. Leeson halted when he saw Norvill and the shot that stopped him again was loud and strangely flat, a burst that arced and tattered. Leeson's arms swinging in a circle as he sought to right himself.

Nora's face was above Leeson's before George reached them, her hands cradling his head. And she was there when Norvill bent down and saw what he'd done. A flicker of understanding crossed Norvill's countenance: he saw that Nora knew the man.

This is why it came as a surprise a month later when Prudence, taking her tea in the gazebo, announced that Norvill needed a maid for the house in Scarborough and that she had been requested. 'The footman has no skills, he can barely mail a letter, and Norvill needs someone who can clean *and cook*, and take dictations related to his work; his hands are sore from the constant chiselling.' Prudence stood up and smoothed her skirt, her eyes welling because she preferred Nora to the others and because now that George had gone back to the Himalayas, the house was too quiet. That night, taking her tinctures, she confessed that Nora's leaving would be difficult, that she was beginning to feel that she was alone in the whole of the world.

Norvill came to Inglewood a week later to visit his mother and to collect Nora. The day before their departure he put on a tweed jacket and announced that he was heading out to the main cave to make stratigraphical sketches; it would consume most of the afternoon should anyone—meaning Prudence—need him. In a moment of compassion, or perhaps with sudden awareness that he would need someone to assist him, he'd stopped and turned just before the French doors to ask Nora if she'd like to join him.

The entrance to the cave was a narrow slit at the base of a limestone cliff. Step into its darkness and you were suddenly in its throat: damp and dripping and hollow. There was *almost* an entry hall, Nora could sense it: a high sand-coloured vault framed by jagged columns that hung from the ceiling and rough balusters that sprung up from the ground. Nora lifted her hem and stepped over the puddle in the walkway. As she squeezed between two large mounds that looked like petrified mush-rooms, Norvill chided her for not removing her bustle, held the lamp in each hand higher so that she could see where her skirt had caught. There were pools of water in the depressed regions of the warped floor and Norvill took her hand to guide her along the slippery wall. At the first intersection, dripping sounds came from three directions, a *plik plonk plik* that reminded her of the clocks in the small parlour. The world smelled of an *absence* of grass, an absence of green things.

In the cavern Norvill called 'the Inverted Forest' he took his sketch pad out of his satchel, gave Nora one of the lamps and asked her to hold it against the wall she would find some twenty paces past where she was standing.

'Go slowly,' he cautioned, and just as he said so a large glinting tooth—what she could only conceive of as a giant incisor—appeared hanging from the roof of the cavern inches above her head. She lifted up the lamp and saw dozens, no, hundreds more.

Norvill stayed where he was, even though he could see she was frightened. He said, 'It's as if the trees stripped by winter have been strung upside down. That's why we call it the Inverted Forest.'

'No,' she replied, even though she knew it was not her station, 'it's as if we are inside the mouth of that bear you have stuffed in your entry, and are about to be swallowed.'

What Nora didn't tell Norvill, even as the years progressed and they fell into an easy affinity—he always treating her as help, though he gave her secretarial tasks and praised her liberally— was that she'd had a strange sensation in the cave in that hour when she was asked to hold the lamp up toward the lined and glittering wall behind her. She did not believe in spirits or ghosts, and she was not deceived by the mesmerizing theatrics she'd once seen Samuel Murray perform in a comedy for the Superintendent—the poet with black around his eyes and a gypsy scarf over his head, predicting everyone's future in return for coins made of paper. No, what she felt instead was a kind of tenor—like on those rare days when a shift in the weather or a word dropped by a stranger recalls you to some other time, to how you felt or where you once stood or what work you were doing; recalls you to the person you were then.

The tenor of the cave reminded her of Leeson. Of how she had been cold in the woods that day they left the Whitmore, and how, in one of the clearings, he'd seen that and had suggested she move to a spot of sun. Herschel had come back then, conveying urgency, so their movement had resumed; and Leeson had plucked her hand and tucked it into his when they reached the fallen tree, escorting her over it.

In the cave the memory of Leeson had been there—so vitally present it was as if he had left his body by the lake and remained with her, watching.

'Higher,' Norvill said, a second pencil in his mouth.

Nora lifted the lamp and debated asking him if he felt something similar.

But then he spat the pencil onto his lap. 'Come now, Miss Hayling, lift it back up to where it was. Or is your arm getting tired?'

The late-afternoon air carries the first fusty smell of autumn, and even though the trees are still green, the leaves, here and there, are letting go. Overhead a crow on the ridge of the church roof caws, then flaps up and over the bell tower.

'*Accck*,' replies Herschel, and he lifts his arms up and down.

A group of hikers with walking sticks and stuffed packs walk past Jane as she heads across the road and into the field that sits between the woods and the trail. One of the women lags behind to pet Sam, looking around for his person until she spots Jane standing along the grassy verge. Jane waves as if to say, *He's with me.*

It's here that we briefly lose the girl—though she *is* a child and prone to do this: run headlong out of our orbit on the promise of some great adventure.

'I'll go,' Cat sighs, moving off toward the trail.

But then the one who has been circling us for days says, in a gentle voice, 'I'll find her'—because he is good at that, and there are four slats on the gate, and two low branches bolstering the oak, and six hikers coming off the trail, and the world, today, is evens.

A hundred years ago, Jane reasons, Nora Hayling was a flesh-and-blood human being who probably walked across the road she herself has crossed almost daily this week, coming out of the servant tunnel and passing between the church and George's waterfall as she strode smartly into the village on errands for Prudence or on her half-days off, her body ghosting the same places Jane's body has been. In one of Jane's imaginings, the sun is on Nora's face and she is closing her eyes under it, breathing in deeply through her nose; in another version, it's that hour before rain when the air feels like dew. Or maybe it's winter, the first lilt of snowfall, and Nora stops to lift her glove to see if she can catch a crystal of snow, study it before it disappears. And in that wondrous, short span of time, when the perfect sphere of it is there on her palm, maybe Nora sees Herschel, standing in the woods with his hand out to the field the day they took their long walk. Or maybe she sees Leeson sitting in the net of sun on the stump beside her, saying that the countryside was theirs to wander over as they saw fit, his face lit up and his eyes accidentally meeting hers, and Nora thinking, *How lovely, how lovely it is to be seen.*

We see Jane. See her as she walks Sam along the stone wall, as she stops under the oak, tugs a leaf off its lowest branch and slips it into her pocket. Leaning against the wall by the stables she writes a note to Blake and at the bottom she adds *call me* and includes her number in London. Then she does what he'd done in his note to her, and underlines *please.*

Jane stretches out the kink in her neck and looks back to the woods, to the place where Lily went missing, and some of us feel the shape our hearts once took hang like pendulums in the hourless clocks of our chests.

Sam barks at Jane and wags his tail and she picks up a stick and tosses it, says, 'Go on!' And we watch as Sam runs nose-down through the waving grass, and we are as happy as she is to watch him run, to witness his unfettered pleasure.

Some nights when there were only a few of us in her room, and it was still early and we were not yet tired from watching, we would ask each other to name the first thing we could remember.

'Sand,' one of us said, 'the good kind, not like the pebbled bits by the sea, but the fine grain you'd find in an hourglass.'

And then we would try to puzzle if this sand was a memory from life or from a story—or something we glimpsed in the in-between we think of as 'now.'

'Was it in your hand or under your feet?' we asked. 'Was, it warm or cold?' 'Was there water nearby?' 'Did you swim?' 'Who were you with—a man or a woman, a boy or a girl?'

'I remember a park,' another said, 'with gas lamps and a bench near the water.'

The boy remembered a terrier bouncing up to catch a stick, and a carousel with brightly painted horses. The girl remembered her mother's face appearing over hers so that they could rub noses.

'Mwah!' said Cat at this, and she went around blowing kisses at everyone.

'What we saw first is less vital than what we saw last,' the theologian droned, though the idiot corrected him, waved his hand at all the talk of Ceasing, said, 'It is what things *become*, sir. The world is congregated by force, and no force is lost, it can only be converted.'

So how do we begin? We begin with Jane—and not because she is here for us, but because we are also here for her, even though she does the work of conjuring us.

Jane opens her notebook and smooths a new page. She sees the trio tromping through the spool of the woods, and Herschel *caw*ing, and Leeson stepping over a thatch of sunlight. Together we watch as Jane imagines a small kindness in a clearing— Leeson taking Nora's hand—and we laugh because one of us knows that she has it wrong, that his palm was rough and his arm unsteady.

On the first blank page she writes: *The Whitmore Hospital for Convalescent Lunatics sat along a carriage track most people travelled only once* . . . and then she pauses under the oak tree to consider the fact of it.

After an hour, Sam trots over and nuzzles her face. Looking up, she can see that it's getting late, that they ought to get on the road because she is expected at the cottage where Henri is waiting for her and because Lewis is driving up.

'Onward!' we say, because we, too, have been daydreaming. So we try to pick up where we think we last left off—though memory being what it is, we are not always sure what is yet to come and what has already happened.

'Attendance,' sighs the theologian.

'Here!' we say. 'Here,' and 'Here,' and 'Here.'

And across the road the clock tower strikes six o'clock—a strong brass chord—and a chorus of bells follows.

ACKNOWLEDGEMENTS

On October 20, 1877, a patient (or patients) at a hospital for convalescent lunatics wandered for eleven or so miles through the woods to make their way to a great man's door. The great man, in real life, was the poet Alfred Lord Tennyson, and his letter to the Governor of Witley Hospital inspired the opening narrative of this novel. I would like to thank David Lord Tennyson for permission to use the contents of Lord Tennyson's original letter (with the necessary fictional substitutions of name and place) as well as the current keepers of the letter itself: The Lilly Library at Indiana University, Bloomington, Indiana. I would also like to thank Colin Gale at Bethlem Royal Hospital's Archives and Museum in London. Not only was I allowed generous access to the hospital's rare and wholly compelling Victorian archives, but that access allowed me to put together Tennyson's letter (which did not mention his visitors by name) with Robert Cowtan, whose casebook I happened upon during my research. Cowtan was a patient at the real-life Witley Hospital—a man known for a belief in his great powers of walking—and it was he who made the real-life epic trek to Tennyson's house.

I am grateful for the support and funding provided by the following organizations, and grateful for the work of those people within them: The Canada Council for the Arts, The British Columbia Arts Council and The Office of Research and Scholarship at Kwantlen Polytechnic University. The University of Edinburgh provided me with a studentship to pursue a PhD involving resonant objects in Victorian writers' museums and that work has bolstered much of this novel.

Thanks also to The University of Lancaster (UK), Maquarie University (Australia) and Memorial University (Canada) for writer-in-residence positions that contributed directly to the development of this book.

At a point early in the writing of this novel I was invited in to the back rooms of the Natural History Museum in London. I remember a lovely woman from the botany department opening an unmarked drawer and announcing very casually that I was looking at a pinecone brought back by Darwin on *The Beagle*. Thank you, Natural History Museum, for that.

Thanks to Mary Jo Anderson, first reader and first enthusiast.

To Claudia Casper, Joel Thomas Hynes and Helen Humphreys for conversations about books and writing, and for their own fine examples.

To Jack Hodgins, Robert Finley, Anosh Irani, Jeanette Lynes and Harry Tournemille for reading bits, pieces or the whole, and for giving advice that mattered.

To Jane Messer for reminding me after a month of studying ferns in the Botanical Gardens in Sydney that a writer of fiction can make a species of fern up.

Thank you, Aisslinn Nosky, for your music. *Merci*, Lindsey Syred.

Thanks to my family, and especially to my mother.

To Kerry Ohana for sustaining me.

To Glenn Hunter, who discovered Robert Cowtan's life outside of the asylum. Thank you for knowing the names of things, and how those things work, for making me laugh and for twenty-plus years of unflagging belief in the writing process.

Cooper and Juniper exhibited more patience in the years it took to write this book than anyone would have thought two young Border collies could. *Woof*, puppies.

To everyone at Doubleday Canada/Random House of Canada for believing in this book and for ushering it along, especially Kristin Cochrane, Suzanne Brandreth and Ron Eckel,

Samantha North, Ashley Dunn and Kelly Hill.

I am grateful to Anna Kelly at Hamish Hamilton in the UK, and Alexis Washam at Hogarth/Crown in the US, for taking the book on with such enthusiasm and for their excellent notes.

Finally, thanks to my editor, Lynn Henry, who made this a better book. I thank her for the depth of her engagement, the breadth of her intelligence, for years of friendship and for her very, very fine heart.

The following resources (textual and historical) should also be acknowledged here: *The Victorian Asylum* by Sarah Rutherford, Oxford: Shire Publications, 2008.

Presumed Curable: An illustrated casebook of Victorian psychiatric patients in Bethlem Hospital, by Colin Gale and Robert Howard, Petersfield: Wrightson Biomedical Publishing Ltd., 2003.

'A Lunatic Ball' (Chapter V of *Mystic London*) by Maurice Davies, London: Saville, Edwards and Co., 1875.

Rambles by the Ribble by William Dobson, London: Simpkin, Marshall and Co., 1864.

The glasswork of Leopold and Rudolf Blaschka inspired the Vlasak cabinet. The poetry of Hölderlin inspired Samuel Murray's poems. The writings and estate of the late-Victorian plant hunter Reginald Farrer contributed to my understanding of what George Farrington and Inglewood might have been like.

Ultimately, this book is a work of fiction. For that reason I encourage anyone interested in the real lives and histories of those staying in, or working in, mental hospitals in the Victorian era to visit the Bethlem Royal Hospital Archives and Museum website http://www.bethlemheritage.org.uk or the Museum itself. The Wellcome Trust http://www.wellcome.ac.uk is also an excellent resource.

One last influence deserves mention here. In 2003, Harper Perennial Canada published a series of interviews by Eleanor Wachtel. One of them was with the eminent thinker George Steiner. In his interview, Steiner mentioned the role of the remembrancer. He said, 'A remembrancer is a human being who knows that to be a human being is to carry within yourself a responsibility, not only to your own present but to the past from which you have come. A remembrancer is a kind of witness through memory.' He ended his talk by suggesting that everyone choose ten names from a memorial wall and that they learn them by heart so that they could recite them to themselves or to others. He suggested we do this 'so that someone on this earth remembers.' This idea of remembrance and of saying the names—whether of family, friends or strangers—had a profound effect on me and it has shaped much of my creative and academic work.

The epigraph by John Berger is from *here is where we meet*, London: Bloomsbury, 2005.

The epigraph by George Eliot is from her novel *Adam Bede*, Oxford: OUP, 2008.

The epigraph by Anna Robertson Brown is from the published version of her lecture *What Is Worthwhile?* New York: Thomas Y. Crowell and Company, 1893.

The epigraph by TS Eliot is from "Four Quartets" in his *Collected Poems 1909-1962*, London: Faber and Faber: 1963.

NAMES TO REMEMBER

....

....

....

....

....

....

....

....

....